**Praise for *New York Times* bestselling author
Lori Foster**

"A sexy, heartwarming, down-home tale that features
two captivating love stories… A funny and engaging
addition to the series that skillfully walks the line
between romance and women's fiction."
—*Library Journal* on *Sisters of Summer's End*

"Count on Lori Foster for sexy, edgy romance."
—*New York Times* bestselling author Jayne Ann Krentz
on *No Limits*

"Foster's fans will be glad to revisit favorite
characters. This earnest romance nicely rounds out
the series."
—*Publishers Weekly* on *All Fired Up*

**Praise for *USA TODAY* bestselling author
Delores Fossen**

"The perfect blend of sexy cowboys, humor and
romance will rein you in from the first line."
—*New York Times* bestselling author B.J. Daniels
on *Blame It on the Cowboy*

"Clear off space on your keeper shelf, Fossen has
arrived."
—*New York Times* bestselling author Lori Wilde

Since her first book was published in January 1996, **Lori Foster** has become a *New York Times*, *USA TODAY* and *Publishers Weekly* bestselling author. She lives in Central Ohio, where coffee helps her keep up with her cats and grandkids between writing books. For more about Lori, visit her website at www.lorifoster.com, like her on Facebook or find her on Twitter, @lorilfoster.

Delores Fossen, a *USA TODAY* bestselling author, has sold over seventy-five novels, with millions of copies of her books in print worldwide. She's received a Booksellers' Best Award and an RT Reviewers' Choice Best Book Award. She was also a finalist for a prestigious RITA® Award. You can contact the author through her website at www.deloresfossen.com.

New York Times Bestselling Author

LORI FOSTER

SAWYER

**HARLEQUIN
BESTSELLING
AUTHOR
COLLECTION**

**HARLEQUIN®
BESTSELLING
AUTHOR
COLLECTION**

Recycling programs
for this product may
not exist in your area.

ISBN-13: 978-1-335-20991-7

Sawyer
First published in 2000. This edition published in 2021.
Copyright © 2000 by Lori Foster

Cowboy Above the Law
First published in 2018. This edition published in 2021.
Copyright © 2018 by Delores Fossen

This edition published by arrangement with Harlequin Books S.A.

For questions and comments about the quality of this book, please contact us at CustomerService@Harlequin.com.

Harlequin Enterprises ULC
22 Adelaide St. West, 40th Floor
Toronto, Ontario M5H 4E3, Canada
www.Harlequin.com

Printed in U.S.A.

CONTENTS

SAWYER

Lori Foster

To my son, Aaron.
Every step of the way, even as a small child, you've been one of the most unique, independent people I know. And one of the finest. I wish I could claim responsibility for that, but the truth is, all I've done is love you—and that has always been so easy to do. To say I'm proud would be an unbelievable understatement. But hey, what the heck! I *am* so proud, and I love you very much.

CHAPTER ONE

ONE MINUTE HE'D been reveling in the late afternoon sun, feeling the sweat dry on his shoulders and neck before he could wipe it away.

In the next instant, she was there.

He'd just glanced over at his son, Casey, only fifteen, but working as hard as any man, tall and strong and determined. His smile was filled with incredible pride.

The last two weekends he'd been caught up with patients, and he'd missed working outside with Casey, enjoying the fresh air, using his hands and body until the physical strain tired him.

Summer scents were heavy in the air, drifting to him as he layered another replacement board on the fence and hammered it in. A warm, humid breeze stirred his hair, bringing with it the promise of a harsh evening storm. He'd inhaled deeply, thinking how perfect his life was.

Then his son shouted, "Holy sh—ah, heck!" catching Sawyer's attention.

Not knowing what to expect, Sawyer turned in the direction Casey pointed his hammer and disbelief filled him as a rusted sedan, moving at breakneck speed, came barreling down the gravel road bordering their property. The turn at the bottom, hugging the Kentucky hills, was sharp; the car would never make it.

Sawyer got a mere glimpse of a pale, wide-eyed female face behind the wheel before, tires squealing, gravel flying, the car came right through the fence he'd just repaired, splintering wood and scattering nails, forcing him to leap for cover. Sheer momentum sent the car airborne for a few feet before it hit the grassy ground with a loud thump and was propelled forward several more feet to slide hood first into a narrow cove of the lake. The front end was submerged, hissing and bubbling, while the trunk and back wheels still rested on solid land, leaving the car at a crazy tilt.

Both Sawyer and Casey stood frozen for several seconds, stunned by what had happened, before ungluing their feet and rushing to the edge of the small cove. Without hesitation, Casey waded waist-deep into the water and peered in the driver's window. "It's a girl!"

Sawyer pushed him aside and leaned down.

His breath caught and held. "Girl" wasn't exactly an apt description of the unconscious woman inside. In a heartbeat, he took in all her features, scanning her from head to toes. As a doctor, he looked for signs of injury, but as a man, he appreciated how incredibly, utterly feminine she was. He guessed her to be in her mid-twenties. Young, a tiny woman, but definitely full grown.

The window was thankfully open, giving him easy access to her, but water rapidly washed into the car, almost covering her shins. Silently cursing himself and his masculine, knee-jerk reaction to her, he told Casey, "Go to the truck and call Gabe at the house. Tell him to meet us out front."

Casey hurried off while Sawyer considered the situation. The woman was out cold, her head slumped over the steering wheel, her body limp. The back seat of the car was filled with taped cardboard boxes and luggage, some of which had tumbled forward, landing awkwardly against her. A few open crates had dumped, and items—bric-a-brac, books and framed photos— were strewn about. It was obvious she'd been packed up for a long trip—or a permanent one.

Sawyer reached for her delicate wrist and was rewarded to feel a strong pulse. Her skin was velvety smooth, warm to the touch. He carefully placed her hand back in her lap, keeping it away from the icy cold water.

It took some doing, but he got the driver's door wedged open. If the car had surged a little deeper into the lake, he never would have managed it. More water flooded in. The woman moaned and turned her head, pushing away from the steering wheel, then dropping forward again. Her easy, unconscious movements assured Sawyer she had no spinal or neck injuries. After moving the fallen objects away from her, he carefully checked her slender arms, slipping his fingers over her warm flesh, gently flexing each elbow, wrist and shoulder. He drew his hands over her jeans-clad legs beneath the water, but again found no injuries. Her lips parted and she groaned, a rasping, almost breathless sound of pain. Frowning, Sawyer examined the swelling bump on her head. He didn't like it that she was still out, and her skin felt a little too warm, almost feverish.

Casey came to a skidding, sloshing halt beside him, sending waves to lap at Sawyer's waist. His gaze was narrowed with concern on the woman's face. "Gabe offered to bring you your bag, but I told him I'd call him back if you needed it." He spoke in a whisper, as if afraid of disturbing her. "We're taking her to the house with us, aren't we?"

"Looks like." If she didn't come to on the way to the house, he'd get her over to the hospital. But that was a good hour away, and most people in Buckhorn chose him over the hospital anyway, unless the situation was truly severe. And even then, it was generally his call.

He'd decide what to do after he determined the extent of her injuries. But first things first; he needed to get her out of the car and away from the debilitating effects of the cold water and hot sun.

Luckily, they weren't that far away from the house. He owned fifty acres, thick with trees and scrub bushes and wildflowers. The lake, long and narrow like a river, bordered the back of his property for a long stretch of shore. The ten acres surrounding the house and abutting the lake were kept mowed, and though it couldn't be called an actual road, there was a worn dirt path where they often brought the truck to the cove to fish or swim. Today they'd driven down to make repairs to a worn fence.

A crooked smile tipped up one side of his mouth. Thanks to the lady, the repairs to the fence were now more necessary than ever.

Sawyer carefully slid one arm beneath her legs, the other behind the small of her back. Her head tipped toward him, landing softly on his bare, sweaty shoulder. Her hair was a deep honey blond with lighter sun streaks framing her face. It smelled of sunshine and woman, and he instinctively breathed in the scent, letting it fill his lungs. Her hair was long enough to drag across the car seat as he lifted her out. "Grab her keys and purse, then get the shirt I left by the fence." He needed to cover her, and not only to counter the chill of the lake water.

He was almost ashamed to admit it, even to himself, but he'd noticed right off that her white T-shirt was all but transparent with the dousing she'd taken. And she wasn't wearing a bra.

He easily shook that observation from his mind.

Even with her clothes soaked, the woman weighed next to nothing, but still it was an effort to climb the small embankment out of the lake without jarring her further. She'd lost one thin sandal in the wreck, and now the other fell off with a small splash. The mud squished beneath Sawyer's boots, making for unsure footing. Casey scrambled out ahead, then caught at Sawyer's elbow, helping to steady him. Once they were all on the grassy embankment, Casey ran off to follow the rest of his instructions, but was back in a flash with the shirt, which he helped Sawyer arrange around her shoulders. Sawyer kept her pressed close to his chest, preserving her privacy and saving his son from major embarrassment.

"You want me to drive?" Walking backward, Casey managed to keep his gaze on the woman and avoid tripping.

"Yeah, but slowly. No unnecessary bumps, okay?" Casey was still learning the rudiments of changing gears, and he used any excuse to get behind the wheel.

"No problem, I'll just…" His voice trailed off as the woman stirred, lifting one limp hand to her forehead.

Sawyer stopped, holding her securely in his arms. He stared down at her face, waiting for her to regain complete awareness, strangely anticipating her reaction. "Easy now."

Her lashes were thick and dark brown tipped with gold and they fluttered for a moment before her eyes slowly opened—and locked on his. Deep, deep blue, staring into him, only inches away.

Sawyer became aware of several things at once: her soft, accelerated breath on his throat, the firmness of her slim thighs on his bare arm, her breasts pressing through the damp cotton of her shirt against his ribs. He could feel the steady drumming of her heartbeat, and the way her body now stiffened the tiniest bit. He felt a wave of tingling awareness shudder through his body, from his chest all the way to his thighs. His reaction to her was out of proportion, considering the circumstances and his usual demeanor. He was a physician, for God's sake, and didn't, in the normal course of things, even notice a woman as a woman when medical treatment was required.

Right now, he couldn't help but notice. Holding this particular woman was somehow altogether different. So often, he put aside his tendencies as a man in deference to those of a doctor; being a doctor was such an enormous part of him. But now he found it difficult to separate the two. The doctor was present, concerned for her health and determined to give her the best of his care. But the man was also there, acutely aware of her femininity and unaccountably responding to it in a very basic way. He'd never faced such a pickle before, and he felt equal parts confusion, curiosity and something entirely too close to embarrassment. For a moment while they stared at each other, it was so silent, he imagined he could hear her thoughts.

Then she slugged him.

Though she had no strength at all and her awkward blow barely grazed him, he was so taken by surprise he nearly dropped her. While Casey stood there gawking, making no effort to help, Sawyer struggled to maintain his hold and his balance with a squirming woman in his arms.

Out of sheer self-preservation, he lowered her bare feet to the ground—then had to catch her again as she swayed and almost crumpled. She would have fallen if both he and Casey hadn't grabbed hold of some part of her, but she still made the feeble effort to shrug them both away.

"No!" she said in a rough, whispering croak, as if her panicked voice could do no better.

"Hey, now," Sawyer crooned, trying the tone he'd often heard his brother Jordan use when talking to a sick or frightened animal. "You're okay."

She tried to swing at him again, he ducked back, and she whirled in a clumsy circle, stopping when her small fist made contact with Casey's shoulder. Casey jumped a good foot, unhurt but startled, then rubbed his arm.

Enough was enough.

Sawyer wrapped his arms around her from behind, both supporting and restraining her. "Shh. It's okay," he said, over and over again. She appeared somewhat disoriented, possibly from the blow to her head. "Settle down now before you hurt yourself."

His words only prompted more struggles, but her movements were ineffectual.

"Lady," he whispered very softly, "you're terrorizing my son."

With a gasp, she glanced up at Casey, who looked

young and very strong, maybe bursting with curiosity, but in no way terrorized.

Sawyer smiled, then continued in calm, even tones. "Listen to me now, okay? Your car landed in our lake and we fished you out. You were unconscious. It's probable you have a concussion, on top of whatever else ails you."

"Let me go."

Her body shook from head to toe, a mixture of shock and illness, Sawyer decided, feeling that her skin was definitely too hot. "If I let you go you'll fall flat on your face. That or try to hit my boy again."

If anything, she panicked more, shaking her head wildly. "No…"

After glaring at Sawyer, Casey held both arms out to his sides. "Hey, lady, I'm not hurt. I'm fine." His neck turned red, but his voice was as calm and soothing as his father's. "Really. Dad just wants to help you."

"Who are you?"

She wasn't talking to Casey now. All her attention seemed to be on staying upright. Even with Sawyer's help, she was wobbly. He gently tightened his hold, keeping her close and hindering her futile movements. "Sawyer Hudson, ma'am. I'm the man who owns this property. Me and my brothers. As I said, you landed in my lake. But I'm also a doctor and I'm going to help you." He waited for a name, for a reciprocal introduction, but none was forthcoming.

"Just…just let me go."

Slowly, still maintaining his careful hold on her, he turned them both until they faced the lake. "You see your car? It's not going anywhere, honey. Not without a tow truck and some major repairs."

She gasped, and her entire body went rigid. "You know my name."

He didn't understand her, but he understood shock. "Not yet, but I will soon. Now…" He paused as her face washed clean of color and she pressed one hand to her mouth. Sawyer quickly lowered her to her knees, still supporting her from behind. "You going to be sick?"

"Oh, God."

"Now just take a few deep breaths. That's it." To Casey, he said, "Go get the water," and his son took off at a sprint, his long legs eating up the ground.

Sawyer turned back to the woman and continued in his soft, soothing tone. "You feel sick because of the blow to your head. It's all right." At least, he thought that was the cause. She also felt feverish, and that couldn't be attributed to a concussion. After a moment of watching her gulp down deep breaths, he asked, "Any better?"

She nodded. Her long fair hair hung nearly to the ground, hiding her face like a silky, tangled curtain. He wrapped it around his hand and pulled it away so he could see her clearly. Her eyes were closed, her mouth pinched. Casey rushed up with the water bottle, and Sawyer held it to her lips. "Take a few sips. There you go. Real slow, now." He watched her struggling for control and wished for some way to lessen the nausea for her. "Let's get you out of this hot sun, okay? I can get you more comfortable in a jiffy."

"I need my car."

Didn't she remember crashing into the water? Sawyer frowned. "Let me take you to my house, get you dried off and give your belly a chance to settle. I'll have one of my brothers pull your car out and see about having it towed to the garage to be cleaned..."

"No!"

Getting somewhat exasperated, Sawyer leaned around until he could meet her gaze. Her lush bottom lip trembled, something he couldn't help but make note of. He chided himself. "No, what?"

She wouldn't look at him, still doing her best to shy away. "No, don't have it towed."

"Okay." She appeared ready to drop, her face now flushed, her lips pale. He didn't want to push her, to add to her confusion. His first priority was determining how badly she might be hurt.

He tried a different tack. "How about coming to my house and getting dry? You can use the phone, call someone to give you a hand."

He watched her nostrils flare as she sucked in a slow, labored breath—then started coughing. Sawyer loosened his hold to lift her arms above her head, supporting her and making it easier for her to breathe. Once she'd calmed, he wrapped her close again, giving her his warmth as she continued to shiver.

She swallowed hard and asked, "Why? Why would you want to help me? I don't believe you."

Leaning back on his heels, he realized she was truly terrified. Not just of the situation, of being with total strangers and being hurt and sick, but of him specifically. It floored him, and doubled his curiosity. He was a doctor, respected throughout the community, known for his calm and understanding demeanor. Women never feared him, they came to him for help.

Looking over her head to Casey, seeing the mirrored confusion on his son's face, Sawyer tried to decide what to do next. She helped to make up his mind.

"If...if you let me go, I'll give you money."

He hesitated only two seconds before saying, "Casey, go start the truck." Whatever else ailed her, she was terrified and alone and hurt. The mystery of her fear could be solved later.

She stiffened again and her eyes squeezed tight. He heard her whisper, *"No."*

Determined now, he lifted her to her feet and started her forward, moving at a slow, easy pace so she wouldn't stumble. "'Fraid so. You're in no condition to be on your own."

"What are you going to do?"

A better question was what did she *think* he was going to do. But he didn't ask it, choosing instead to give her an option. "My house or the hospital, take your pick. But I'm not leaving you here alone."

She took two more dragging steps, then held her head. Her body slumped against his in defeat. "Your... your house."

Surprised, but also unaccountably pleased, he again lifted her in his arms. "So you're going to trust me just a bit after all?"

Her head bumped his chin as she shook it. "Never."

He couldn't help but chuckle. "Lesser of two evils, huh? Now you know I gotta wonder why the hospital is off-limits." She winced with each step he took, so he talked very softly just to distract her. "Did you rob a bank? Are you a wanted felon?"

"No."

"If I take you in, will someone recognize you?"

"No."

The shirt he'd draped around her was now tangled at her waist. He tried not to look, but after all, he was human, a male human, and his gaze went to her breasts.

She noticed.

Warm color flooded her cheeks, and he rushed to reassure her. "It's all right. Why don't we readjust the shirt I gave you just a bit?"

She didn't fight him when he loosened his hold enough to let her legs slip to the ground. She leaned against him while he pulled the shirt up around her, slipping her arms through the sleeves. It was an old faded blue chambray shirt, the sleeves cut short, the top button missing. He'd often used it for work because it was soft and ragged. She should have looked ridiculous in it, wearing it like a robe. Instead, she looked adorable, the shirt in stark contrast to her fragile femininity. The hem hung down to her knees, and it almost wrapped around her twice. Sawyer shook his head, getting his thoughts back on track once again.

"Better?"

"Yes." She hesitated, clutching the shirt, then whispered, "Thank you."

He watched her face for signs of discomfort as they took the last few steps to the truck. "I'm sorry," he said softly. "You're in pain, aren't you?"

"No, I'm just—"

He interrupted her lie. "Well, lucky for you, I really am a doctor, and for the moment you can keep your name, and why you're so frightened, to yourself. All I want to do right now is help."

Her gaze flicked to his, then away. Sawyer opened the door of the idling truck and helped her inside. He slid in next to her, then laid his palm against her forehead in a gentle touch. "You're running a fever. How long have you been sick?"

Casey put the truck in gear with a rough start that made her wince. He mumbled an apology, then kept the gears smooth after that.

With one hand covering her eyes, she said, "It's... just a cold."

He snorted. Her voice was so raspy, he could barely understand her. "What are your symptoms?"

She shook her head.

"Dizzy?"

"A little."

"Headache? A tightness in your chest?"

"Yes."

Sawyer touched her throat, checking for swollen glands and finding them. "Does this hurt?"

She tried to shrug, but it didn't have the negligent effect she'd probably hoped for. "Some. My throat is sore."

"Trouble breathing?"

She gave a choked half laugh at his persistence. "A little."

"So of course you decided to go for a drive." She opened her mouth to protest, but he said, "Look at me," then gently lifted each eyelid, continuing his examination. She needed to be in bed getting some care. On top of a likely concussion, he suspected an upper respiratory infection, if not pneumonia. Almost on cue, she gave another hoarse, raw cough. "How long have you had that?"

She turned bleary, suspicious eyes his way. "You're a real doctor?"

"Wanna see my bag? All docs have one, you know."

Casey piped up with, "He really is. In fact, he's the only doctor Buckhorn has. Some of the women around here pretend to be sick just to see him." He smiled at her. "You don't need to be afraid."

"Casey, watch the road." The last thing he needed was his son filling her ears with nonsense, even if the nonsense was true. He had a feeling she wouldn't appreciate the local women's antics nearly as much as his brothers or son did. Sawyer treated it all as a lark, because he had no intention of getting involved with any of the women, and they knew it.

He had a respected position in the community and refused to take advantage of their offers. Driving out of the area was always difficult, not to mention time-consuming. He'd had a few long-distance, purely sexual relationships when the fever of lust got to him and he had to have relief. He was a healthy man in every way, and he didn't begrudge himself the occasional weakness due to his sex. But those encounters were never very satisfying, and he sometimes felt it was more trouble than it was worth.

She turned to him, her blue eyes huge again, and worried. She nervously licked at her dry lips. Sawyer felt that damn lick clear down to his gut, and it made him furious, made him wonder if another out-of-town trip wasn't in order. She was a woman, nothing more, nothing less. And at the moment, she looked pale, on the verge of throwing up, and her mood was more surly than not.

So why was he playing at being a primitive, reacting solely on male instincts he hadn't even known he had?

Her worried frown prompted one of his own. "You had a lot of stuff stowed in your back seat. Moving?"

She bit her lip, and her fingers toyed with the tattered edge of the shirt he'd given her, telling him she didn't want to answer his questions. After another bout of coughing where she pressed a fist to her chest and he waited patiently, she whispered, "How do you know my name?"

He lifted one brow. "I don't."

"But…" It was her turn to narrow her eyes, and the blue seemed even more intense in her annoyance, shaded by her thick lashes, accompanied by her flushed cheeks. Then the annoyance turned to pain and she winced, rubbing at her temples.

Compassion filled him. Finding out the truth could wait. For now, she needed his control. There was no faking a fever, or that croupy cough. "You're confused. And no wonder, given how sick you are and that knock on the head you got when your car dove into the lake."

"I'm sorry," she mumbled. "I'll pay for the damage to your fence."

Sawyer didn't reply to that. For some reason, it made him angry. Even the little talking they'd done had weakened her; she was now leaning on him, her eyes closed. But she was concerned for his damn fence? She should have been concerned about her soft hide.

Casey successfully pulled the truck into the yard beneath a huge elm. Gabe sprinted off the porch where he'd been impatiently waiting, and even before Casey killed the engine, Gabe had the truck door open. "What the hell's going on?" Then his eyes widened on the woman, and he whistled.

Sawyer leaned down to her ear. "My baby brother, Gabe," he said by way of introduction. She nodded, but kept silent.

To Gabe, he answered, "A little accident with the lady's car and the lake."

"Casey told me the lake got in her way." Gabe looked her over slowly, his expression inscrutable. "What's wrong with her? And why aren't you taking her to the hospital?"

"Because she doesn't want to go." Sawyer looked down at the woman's bent head. She was shying away from Gabe, which was a phenomenon all in itself. Gabe was the most popular bachelor in Buckhorn. He smiled, and the women went all mushy and adoring, a fact Sawyer and his brothers taunted him with daily and an accolade Gabe accepted with masculine grace.

Of course Gabe wasn't exactly smiling now, too concerned to do so. And the woman wasn't even looking his way. She'd taken one peek at him, then scooted closer to Sawyer, touching him from shoulder to hip.

In almost one movement he lifted her into his lap and stepped out of the truck. He didn't question his motives; he was a doctor and his first instinct was always to care for the injured or sick. She didn't fight him. Instead, she tucked her face close to his throat and held on. Sawyer swallowed hard, moved by some insidious emotion he couldn't name, but knew damn good and well he'd rather not be feeling. Gruffly, he ordered, "Casey, get a bed ready and fetch my bag."

Casey hurried off, but Gabe kept stride beside him. "This is damn strange, Sawyer."

"I know."

"At least tell me if she's hurt bad."

"Mostly sick, I think, but likely a concussion, too." He looked at his youngest brother. "If I can't handle it here, we'll move her to the hospital. But for now, if you're done with the interrogation, I could use your help."

One of Gabe's fair brows shot up, and he crossed his arms over his chest. "Doing what, exactly?"

"The lady had a lot of stuff in the back seat of her car. Can you go get it before it floats away in the lake or gets completely ruined? And get hold of Morgan to have her car towed out." She lifted her head and one small hand fisted on his chest. Sawyer continued before she could protest, meeting her frantic gaze and silencing her with a look. "Don't take it to the garage. Bring it here. We can put it in the shed."

Gabe considered that a moment, then shook his head. "I hope you know what the hell you're doing."

Slowly, the woman looked away, hiding her face against him again. Sawyer went up the porch steps to the house. To himself, because he didn't want to alarm anyone else, he muttered, "I hope so, too. But I have my doubts."

CHAPTER TWO

IF SHE HAD her choice, Honey Malone would have stayed buried next to the warm, musky male throat and hidden for as long as possible. For the first time in over a week, she felt marginally safe, and she was in no hurry to face reality again, not when reality meant villains and threats, along with an aching head and a weakness that seemed to have invaded every muscle in her body. In varying degrees, she felt dizzy and her head throbbed. Every other minute, her stomach roiled. She couldn't even think of food without having to suppress the urge to vomit. And she was so terribly cold, from the inside out.

At the moment, she wanted nothing more than to close her eyes and sleep for a good long time.

But of course, she couldn't.

It was beyond unfair that she'd get sick now, but she couldn't lie to herself any longer. She *was* sick, and it was sheer dumb luck that she hadn't killed herself, or someone else, in the wreck.

She still didn't know if she could trust him. At first, he'd called her honey, and she thought he knew her name, thought he might be one of them. But he denied it so convincingly, it was possible she'd misunderstood. He'd certainly made no overt threat to her so far. All she knew for sure was that he was strong and warm and he said he only wanted to help her. While he held her, she couldn't find the wit to object.

But then his strong arms flexed, and she found herself lowered to a soft bed. Her eyes flew open wide and she stared upward at him—until her head began to spin again. "Oh, God." She dropped back, trying to still the spinning of the room.

"Just rest a second."

More cautiously now, she peeked her eyes open. The man—Sawyer, he said his name was—picked up a white T-shirt thrown over the footboard and pulled it on. It fit him snugly, molding to his shoulders and chest. He wasn't muscle-bound, but rather leanly cut, like an athlete. His wide solid shoulders tapered into a narrow waist. Faded jeans hugged his thighs and molded to his...

Face flaming, she looked down at the soft mattress he'd put her on. Her drenched, muddy jeans were making a mess of things. "The quilt—"

"Is an old one. Don't worry about it. A little lake water isn't going to hurt anything." So saying, he pulled another quilt from the bottom of the bed and folded it around her chest, helping to warm her. She gratefully snuggled into it.

That taken care of, he looked over his broad shoulder to the door, and as if he'd commanded it, his son appeared, carrying a medical bag. Casey looked nonplussed to see where his father had put her. "Ah, Dad, I already got a bed ready for her, the one in the front room."

Sawyer took the medical bag from Casey, then said, "This one will do."

"But where will you sleep?"

On alert, Honey listened to the byplay between father and son. Casey was earnest, she could see that
much in his young, handsome face, but Sawyer had his
back to her so she could only guess at his expression.

"Casey, you can go help Gabe, now."

"But—"

"Go on."

Casey reluctantly nodded, casting a few quick
glances at Honey. "All right. But if you need anything
else—"

"If I do, I'll holler."

The boy went out and shut the door behind him.
Nervously, Honey took in her surroundings. The room
was gorgeous, like something out of a *Home Show*
magazine. She'd never seen anything like it, and for
the moment, she was distracted. Pine boards polished
to a golden glow covered the floor, three walls and the
ceiling. The furnishings were all rustic, but obviously
high quality. Black-and-white checked gingham curtains were at the windows that took up one entire wall,
accompanied by French doors leading out the back to a
small patio. The wall of glass gave an incredible view
of the lake well beyond.

There was a tall pine armoir, a dresser with a huge,
curving mirror, and two padded, natural wicker chairs.
In one corner rested a pair of snow skis and a tennis
racket, in the other, several fishing poles. Assorted
pieces of clothing—a dress shirt and tie, a suit jacket,
a pair of jeans—were draped over bedposts and chair
backs. The polished dresser top was laden with a few
bills and change, a small bottle of aftershave, some
crumpled receipts and other papers, including an open

book. It was a tidy room, but not immaculate by any measure.

And it was most definitely inhabited by a man. *Sawyer.* She gulped.

Summoning up some logic in what appeared a totally illogical situation, she asked, "What will your wife—"

"I don't have a wife."

"Oh." She didn't quite know what to think about that, considering he had a teenage son, but it wasn't her place to ask, and she was too frazzled to worry about it, anyway.

"Your clothes are going to have to come off, you know."

Stunned by his unreserved statement, she thought about laughing at the absurdity of it; that, or she could try to hide.

She was unable to work up enough strength for either. Her gaze met his. He stared back, and what she saw made her too warm, and entirely too aware of him as a man, even given the fact she was likely in *his* bedroom and at his mercy. She should have been afraid; she'd gotten well used to that emotion. But strangely, she wasn't. "I—"

The door opened and a man stepped in. This one looked different than both Sawyer and the younger man, Gabe. Sawyer had dark, coal black hair, with piercing eyes almost the same color. His lashes were sinfully long and thick and, she couldn't help noticing, he had a lot of body hair. Not too much, but enough that she'd taken notice. Of course, she'd spent several minutes pressed to that wide chest, so it would have been pretty difficult *not* to notice. And he'd smelled too good for description, a unique, heady scent of clean, male sweat and sun-warmed flesh and something more, something that had pervaded her muscles as surely as the weakness had.

Gabe, the one now fetching items from her car, was blond-haired and incredibly handsome. In his cutoffs, bare feet and bare chest, he'd reminded her of a beach bum.

His eyes, a pale blue, should have looked cool, but instead had seemed heated from within, and she'd naturally drawn back from him. His overwhelming masculinity made her uneasy, whereas Sawyer's calm, controlled brand of machismo offered comfort and patience and rock steady security, which she couldn't help but respond to as a woman. Accepting his help felt right, but the very idea alarmed her, too. She couldn't involve anyone else in her problems.

Now this man, with his light brown hair and warm green eyes, exuded gentle curiosity and tempered strength. Every bit as handsome as the blond one, but in a more understated way, he seemed less of a threat. He looked at her, then to Sawyer. "Casey says we have a guest?"

"She ran her car into the lake. Gabe and Casey are off taking care of that now, getting as much of her stuff out of it as they can."

"Her stuff?"

"Seems she was packed up and moving." He flicked a glance at Honey, one brow raised. She ignored his silent question.

"Care to introduce me?"

Sawyer shrugged. He gestured toward her after he

took a stethoscope out of his bag. "Honey, this is my brother Jordan."

Jordan smiled at her. And he waited. Sawyer, too, watched her, and Honey was caught. He'd called her by name again, so why did he now look as if he was waiting for her to introduce herself? She firmed her mouth. After a second, Jordan frowned, then skirted a worried look at his brother. "Is she…?"

Sawyer sighed. "She can talk, but she's not feeling well. Let's give her a little time."

Jordan nodded briskly, all understanding and sympathy. Then he looked down at the floor and smiled. "Well, hello there, honey. You shouldn't be in here."

Honey jumped, hearing her name again, but Jordan wasn't speaking to her. He lifted a small calico cat into his arms, and she saw the animal had a bandaged tail. As Jordan stroked the pet, crooning to her in a soothing tone, the cat began a loud, ecstatic purring. Jordan's voice was rough velvet, sexy and low, and Honey felt almost mesmerized by it. It was the voice of a seducer.

Good grief, she thought, still staring. Was every man in this family overflowing with raw sexuality?

"A new addition," Jordan explained. "I found the poor thing on my office doorstep this morning."

Rolling his eyes, Sawyer said to Honey, "My brother is a vet—and a sucker for every stray or injured animal that crosses his path."

Jordan merely slanted a very pointed look at Honey and then said to Sawyer, "And you're any different, I suppose?"

They both smiled—while Honey bristled. She didn't exactly take to the idea of being likened to a stray cat.

"Jordan, why don't you put the cat in the other room

and fetch some tea for our guest? She's still chilled, and from the sounds of her cough, her throat is sore."

"Sure, no problem."

But before he could go, another man entered, and Honey could do no more than stare. This man was the biggest of the lot, a little taller than even Sawyer and definitely more muscle-bound. He had bulging shoulders and a massive chest and thick thighs. Like Sawyer, he had black hair, though his was quite a bit longer and somewhat unruly. And his eyes were blue, not the pale blue of Gabe's, but dark blue, almost like her own but more piercing, more intent. She saw no softness, no giving in his gaze, only ruthlessness.

He had a noticeable five o'clock shadow, and a stern expression that made her shiver and sink a little deeper into the bed.

Sawyer immediately stepped over to her and placed his hand on her shoulder, letting her know it was okay, offering that silent comfort again. But she still felt floored when he said, "My brother Morgan, the town sheriff."

Oh, God. A *sheriff?* How many damn brothers did this man have?

"Ignore his glare, honey. We pulled him from some unfinished business, no doubt, and he's a tad…disgruntled."

Jordan laughed. "Unfinished business? That wouldn't be female business, would it?"

"Go to hell, Jordan." Then Morgan's gaze landed heavily on Honey, though he spoke to Sawyer. "Gabe called me. You mind telling me what's going on?"

Honey was getting tired of hearing Sawyer explain. She looked up at him and asked in her rough, almost unrecognizable voice, "Just how many brothers do you have?"

Jordan smiled. "So she does have a voice."

Morgan frowned. "Why would you think she didn't?"

And Sawyer laughed. "She's been quiet, Morgan, that's all. She's sick, a little disoriented and naturally wary of all of you overgrown louts tromping in and out."

Then to Honey, he said, "There's five of us, including my son, Casey. We all live here, and as it seems you're going to stay put for a spell, too, it's fortunate you've already met them all."

His statement was received with varying reactions. She was appalled, because she had no intention at all of staying anywhere. It simply wasn't safe.

Jordan looked concerned. Morgan looked suspicious.

And in walked Gabe, toting a box. "Nearly everything was wet by the time I got there, except this box of photos she had stashed in the back window. I figured it'd be safer in the house. Casey is helping to unload everything else from the truck, but it's all a mess so we're stowing it in the barn for now. And it looks like it might rain soon. It clouded up real quick. I think we're in for a doozy."

Honey glanced toward the wall of windows. Sure enough, the sky was rapidly turning dark and thick, purplish storm clouds drifted into view. Just what she needed.

Sawyer nodded. "Thanks, Gabe. If it starts to lightning, have Casey come in."

"I already told him."

"Morgan, can you get the county towing truck in

the morning and pull her car out of the lake? I want to put it in the shed."

Morgan rubbed his rough jaw with a large hand. "The shed? Why not Smitty's garage so it can be fixed? Or do I even want to know?"

"It's a long story, better explained *after* I find out what ails her. Which I can't do until you all get the hell out of here."

The brothers took the hint and reluctantly began inching out. Before they could all go, though, Sawyer asked, "Any dry clothes in her things, Gabe?"

"Nope, no clothes that I saw. Mostly it's books, hair stuff…junk like that." He dropped the box of framed photos on the floor in front of the closet.

"I don't suppose any of you have a housecoat?"

Three snorts supplied his answer.

If Honey hadn't been feeling so wretched, she would have smiled. And she definitely would have explained to Sawyer that the clothes she wore would have to do, because she wasn't about to strip out of them.

"Any type of pajamas?"

He got replies of, "You've got to be kidding," and, "Never use the things," while Morgan merely laughed.

Squeezing her eyes shut, Honey thought, *No, no, they're not all telling me they sleep in the nude!* She did her best not to form any mental images, but she was surrounded by masculine perfection in varying sizes and styles, and a picture of Sawyer resting in this very bed, naked as a Greek statue, popped into her brain. Additional heat swept over her, making her dizzy again. She could almost feel the imprint of his large body, and she trembled in reaction. She decided it was her illness making her muddled; she'd certainly never been so focused on her sexuality before. Now, she was acutely aware of it.

She opened her eyes and would have shaken her head to clear it, but she was afraid the motion would make her unsettled stomach pitch again.

Casey stuck his head into the room. "I have an old baseball jersey that'd fit her."

"No, thank you—"

Sawyer easily overrode her. "Good. Bring it here."

The brothers all looked at each other, grinning, then filed out. Sawyer leaned down close, hands on his hips, and gave her a pointed frown. "Now."

"Now what?" All her worries, all the fears, were starting to swamp back in on her. She coughed, her chest hurting, her head hurting worse. She felt weak and shaky and vulnerable, which automatically made her defensive. "I'll be fine. If…if Morgan would pull my car out, I'd be appreciative. I'll pay you for your trouble…."

Sawyer interrupted, shaking his head and sitting on the side of the bed. "You're not paying me, dammit, and you aren't going anywhere."

"But…"

"Honey, even if he gets your car out in the morning—and there's no guarantee, figuring how it's stuck in the mud and it looks like a storm's on the way—but even if he did, the car will need repairs."

"Then I'll walk."

"Now why would you wanna do that? Especially considering you can barely stand." His tone turned gentle, cajoling. He produced a thermometer and slipped it under her tongue, making it impossible for her to reply.

"We have plenty of room here, and you need someone to look after you until you're well."

She pulled out the thermometer. "It's…it's not safe."

"For you?"

Honey debated for a long moment, considering all her options. But he was trying to help, and with every second that passed, she grew more tired. The bed was so soft, the quilt warm, if she was going to move, it had to be now before she got settled and no longer wanted to. She started to sit up, but Sawyer's large, competent hands on her shoulders gently pressed her back on the bed.

Not bothering to hide his exasperation, he said, "Okay, this is how it's going to be. You're either going to tell me what's going on, or I'm going to take you to the hospital. Which'll it be?"

She searched his face, but the stubbornness was there, along with too much determination. She simply wasn't up to fighting him. Not right now.

"It's not safe because…" She licked her lips, considered her words, then whispered, "Someone is trying to hurt me."

Sawyer stared at her, for the moment too stunned to speak.

"Is this something I should know about, Sawyer?" Morgan asked.

He almost groaned. Wishing he could remove the fear from her eyes, he gave her a wink, then turned to face his most difficult brother. "Eavesdropping, Morgan?"

"Actually, I was doing tea duty." He lifted a cup and saucer for verification. "Hearing the girl's confession was just a bonus."

"It wasn't a confession. She's confused from—"

"No." Trembling, she scooted upward on the bed, clutching the quilt to her chest. She chewed her lower lip, not looking at Morgan, but keeping her gaze trained on Sawyer. After a rough bout of coughing, she whispered, "I'm not confused, or making it up."

Sawyer narrowed his eyes, perturbed by the sincerity in her tone and the way she shivered. If anything, she sounded more hoarse, looked more depleted. He needed to get the questions over with so he could medicate her, get her completely dry and let her rest. "Okay, so who would want to hurt you?"

"I don't know."

Morgan set the tea on the bedside table. "*Why* would anyone want to hurt you?"

Tears glistened in her eyes and she blinked furiously. One shoulder lifted, and she made a helpless gesture with her hand. "I…" Her voice broke, and she cleared her throat roughly. Sawyer could tell how much she hated showing her vulnerability. "I don't know."

Agitated, Sawyer shoved Morgan away from where he loomed over her, then took up his own position sitting next to her on the bed. "Honey—"

The sky seemed to open up with a grand deluge of rain. It washed against the windows with incredible force. Within seconds the sky grew so dark it looked like midnight rather than early evening. Lightning exploded in a blinding flash, followed by a loud crack of thunder that made the house tremble and startled the woman so badly she jumped.

By reflex, Sawyer reached out to her, closing his hand over her shoulder, caressing her, soothing her. "Shh. Everything's okay."

A nervous, embarrassed laugh escaped her. "I'm sorry. I'm not normally so skittish."

"You're sick and you're hurt." Sawyer leveled a look on his brother. "And you aren't going anywhere tonight, so put the thought from your head."

Morgan promptly agreed, but the curling of his lips showed how amused he was by Sawyer's possessive declaration. "Sure thing. We can sort everything out in the morning after you're rested." He slapped Sawyer on the shoulder. "Let the doc here fix you up. You'll feel better in no time."

Casey came in with the baseball jersey. "Sorry, it took me a little while to find it."

Sawyer accepted the shirt. "Good. Now we can get you out of these wet clothes."

Jordan lounged in the doorway, a small half-smile on his mouth. "Need any help?"

And once again, Sawyer had to shove them all out the door. You'd think they'd never seen an attractive woman before, the way they were carrying on, when in fact they all had more than their fair share of female adoration. But as Sawyer closed the door and turned back to her, seeing her lounged in *his* bed, her long hair spread out over *his* pillow, her wide, watchful gaze, he knew he was acting as out of sorts as the rest of them. Maybe more so. He'd just never been so damn *aware* of a woman, yet with this woman, he felt he could already read her gaze. And he strongly reacted to it.

That just wouldn't do, not if he was going to be her doctor.

He laid the shirt on the foot of the bed, resolute. "Come on." After pulling the damp quilt aside, he hooked his hands beneath her arms, lifted her, then proceeded to unbutton the shirt he'd loaned her as if he did such things every day. She was silent for about half a second before suddenly coming to life. With a gasp, she began batting at his hands.

"I can do it!" she rasped in her rough, crackly voice.

He cradled her face in his palms. "Are you sure?"

For long seconds they stared at each other, and just as his heartbeat began to grow heavy, she nodded.

Pulling himself together, Sawyer sighed. "All right." He suffered equal parts relief and disappointment. "Get those wet jeans off, and your panties, too. You're soaked through to the skin and you need to be dry and warm. Leave your clothes there on the floor and I'll run them through the wash." He slid open a dresser drawer and retrieved his own dry jeans and shorts, then as he was reaching for the door to leave, he added, "I'll wait right out here. Call me when you're done or if you need help with anything."

He stepped into the hallway and ran right into every single one of his brothers. Even his son was there, grinning like a magpie. He glared at them all while he unsnapped and unzipped his wet jeans. They smiled back. "Don't you guys have something to do?"

"Yeah," Gabe said with a wide grin. "We're doing it."

"At times you're entertaining as hell, Sawyer," Jordan added with a chuckle.

Sawyer shucked off his clothes, content to change in the middle of the hallway since they pretty much had him boxed in. He was annoyed as hell, but unwilling to let them all see it. As he stripped down to his skin, Gabe automatically gathered up the discarded clothes, helping without being asked. Then he handed them to Jordan who handed them to Morgan who looked around, saw no one else to give them to and tucked them under his arm.

After he was dressed again, Sawyer crossed his arms over his chest, returning their insolent looks. "And what's that supposed to mean, exactly?"

Morgan snorted. "Only that you're acting like a buck in mating season. You're looming over that poor woman like you think she might disappear at any minute. You're so obvious, you might as well put your brand on her forehead." Morgan pushed away from the wall and ran his hand through his hair. "The problem is, Sawyer, we don't know who she is or what she's hiding."

Sawyer disregarded his brothers' teasing remarks and frowned over their concerns. He didn't need Morgan to tell him there were going to be complications with the woman. His own concern was heavy. "So what do you want me to do? Take her back to her car? Do you want to lock her up for the night until you fit all the pieces together? The woman is sick and needs care before her situation becomes critical."

Casey frowned. "Is she really that bad off, Dad?"

Rubbing his neck, trying to relieve some of the mounting tension, Sawyer said, "I think she has bronchitis, possibly pneumonia. But I haven't exactly had a chance to check her over yet."

Just then every window in the house rattled with a powerful boom of thunder, and in the next second, the lights blinked out. It was dark in the hallway, and all the men started to grumble profanities—until they heard a thump and a short, startled female yelp of pain in the bedroom.

Sawyer reacted first, immediately reaching for the

doorknob, then halting when he realized all his brothers intended to follow him in. One by one they plowed into him, crushing him against the door, muttering curses. Over his shoulder, Sawyer barked, "Wait here, dammit!" then hurried in, slamming the door in their curious faces.

The wall of windows in his room offered some light from the almost constant strobe of lightning, but not enough. He searched through the shadows until he located her, sitting on the floor by the bed. Her wide eyes glimmered in the darkness, appearing stunned.

But it was nothing compared to how Sawyer felt when he realized her damp jeans and silky panties were around her ankles—and her upper body was completely bare.

The breath froze in his lungs for a heartbeat, every muscle in his body clenching in masculine appreciation of the sweet, utterly vulnerable female sight she presented. Lightning flickered, illuminating her smooth, straight shoulders, her full round breasts. Her taut nipples. Her fair hair left silky trails down her body, flowing sensuously over and around her breasts. He felt the stirrings of a desire so deep it was nearly painful, and struggled to suppress his groan of instant need.

Then, with a small sound, she dropped her head forward in defeat and covered her face with her hands. That was all it took to shake him out of his sensual stupor. Determined, he started forward, dredging up full doctor mode while burying his instinctive, basic urges.

But one fact rang loud and clear in his head.

Damn, he was in deep—and he didn't even know her name.

CHAPTER THREE

SHE WANTED TO DIE. To just curl up and give up and not have to worry about another thing. She felt beyond wretched, more embarrassed than she'd ever been in her life, getting more so with every second that passed, and she was so tired of worrying, of finding herself in impossible situations, giving up seemed the best option. She was just so damn weak, she couldn't do anything.

So instead, she got obnoxious. Without raising her head, she asked, "Are you done gawking?" Her voice was a hideous thin croak, a mixture of illness, embarrassment and pain. It was all she could do to keep herself sitting upright.

"I'm sorry." He crouched down and lifted her as if she weighed no more than the damn cat Jordan had been petting. Very gently, he placed her on the edge of the bed, then matter-of-factly skimmed her jeans and underwear the rest of the way off, leaving her totally bare. In the next instant, he tugged the jersey over her head. He treated her with all the attention and familiarity he might have given a small child, even smoothing down her hair. "There. That's got to be more comfortable."

His voice sounded almost as harsh as her own; she couldn't quite return his smile.

After pulling back the covers, he raised her legs onto the mattress, pressed her back against the headboard with a pillow behind her, then said, "Wait right here while I get some light."

He was gone only a moment, but from the time he stepped out into the hallway until he returned, she heard the drone of masculine voices, some amused, some concerned, some insistent.

God, what must they think of her? She was an intruder, a pathetic charity case, and she hated it.

Sawyer returned with an old-fashioned glass and brass lantern, a flashlight and a small plastic tote of medicine bottles. He closed the door behind him, shutting out the brothers' curious gazes. For that, at least, she was thankful.

"Now, back to business." He unloaded his arms next to the bed on the nightstand, turning up the lantern so that the soft glow of light spread out, leaving heavy shadows in all the corners of the room. "The town is so small, we lose electricity with nearly every storm. It's not something we get too excited over. By morning the lights will be on."

Morning?

He shook the thermometer, and again stuck it in her mouth. "Leave it there this time."

Oh, boy. He was done with stalling, now operating in total efficiency status. Well, fine. She didn't want to talk to him away. Talking took energy, which she didn't have, and hurt her raw throat and made her stomach jumpier than it already was. She honestly didn't know how much longer she could stay awake. Lethargy pulled at her, making her numb.

He approached again, sitting beside her on the bed.

He was so warm, heat seemed to pour off him. He gave her a stern look. "I'm going to listen to your lungs. Just breathe normally through your nose, okay?"

She nodded, and he opened the neckline of the jersey and slipped his hand beneath. He didn't look at her, staring at the far wall instead as if in deep concentration. But his wrist was hot, a burning touch against her sensitive skin, contrasting sharply with the icy coldness of the stethoscope.

She forgot to breathe, forgot everything but looking at his profile, at his too long, too thick lashes, his straight nose, his dark hair falling over his brow in appealing disarray. The lantern light lent a halo to that dark hair and turned his skin into burnished bronze. His jaw was firm, his mouth sexy—

"Normal breaths, honey."

Oh, yeah. She sucked in a lungful of air, accidentally filling her head with his delicious scent. She immediately suffered a coughing fit. Sawyer quickly retrieved the thermometer and looked at it with the flashlight. "Almost a hundred and two." He frowned. "Can you sit forward just a second?"

Without waiting for her reply, he leaned her forward, propping her with his body, practically holding her in an embrace against that wide, strong chest. His arms were long and muscled, his body hard and so wonderfully warm. She wanted to snuggle into him but forced herself to hold perfectly still.

Again, he seemed oblivious to the intimacy of the situation.

She was far, far from oblivious.

He lifted the jersey to listen to her lungs through her back. Honey merely closed her eyes, too mortified to do much else. After a long moment, he made a sound of satisfaction.

He carefully leaned her back and recovered her with the quilt. "You've definitely got bronchitis, and if you'd gone on another day or two, you'd have likely ended up with pneumonia. On top of that, I'd be willing to bet you have a concussion." He gently touched a bruised spot on her forehead with one finger. "You hit the steering wheel hard when the car dove into the lake. I suppose I can only be grateful you were wearing your seat belt."

He sounded a bit censuring, but she nodded, so exhausted she no longer cared.

"Are you allergic to any medications?"

"No."

"Can you swallow a pill okay?"

Again she nodded, words too difficult.

He started to say something else, then looked at her face and hesitated. He sighed. "Honey, I know this is hard for you. Being in a strange house with all these strange men wandering about, but—"

"Your brothers are a bit overwhelming," she rasped in her thick voice, "but I wouldn't exactly call them strange."

He smiled. "Well, I would." He raised his voice and shouted toward the door, "I'd call them strange and obnoxious and overbearing and *rude!*"

Honey heard one of the brothers—she thought it was Gabe—shout back, "I know a lot of women who'd object to the obnoxious part!" and a hum of low masculine laughter followed.

Sawyer chuckled. "They mean well. But like me, they're concerned."

He patted her knee beneath the quilt, then handed her the tea. "You can swallow your pills with this. It's barely warm now."

Honey frowned at the palm full of pills he produced. After all, she didn't really know him, and yet she was supposed to trust him. Even knowing she had no choice, she still hesitated.

Patiently, he explained, "Antibiotics and something for the pain. You'll also need to swallow some cough medicine."

"Wonderful." She threw all the pills down in one gulp, then swallowed almost the entire cup of tea, leaving just enough to chase away the nasty taste of the cough liquid he insisted she take next. Whoever had made the tea went heavy on the sugar—which suited her just fine.

Sawyer took the cup from her and set it aside, then eyed her closely. "The door next to the closet is a half bath. Do you need to go?"

Why didn't she simply expire of embarrassment? She was certainly due. "No," she croaked, then thought to add, "thank you."

He didn't look as if he quite believed her, but was reluctant to force the issue. "Well, if you do, just let me know so I can help you. I don't want you to get up and fall again."

Yeah, right. Not in this lifetime. That was definitely a chore she would handle on her own—or die trying. "I'm fine, really. I'm just so tired."

Sawyer stood and began pulling the quilts off her. They were damp, so she didn't protest, but almost immediately she began to shiver. Seconds later he recovered her with fresh blankets from the closet. He laid two of them over her, tucking her in until she felt so cozy her body nearly shut down.

"Go on to sleep. I'll come back in a couple of hours to check on you—because of the concussion," he added, when she blinked up at him. "I'm sorry, honey, but I'll have to wake you every hour or two just to make certain you're okay. All you'll have to do is open those big blue eyes and say hi, all right?"

"All right." She didn't really like the idea, because she knew she wouldn't be able to sleep a wink now, worrying about when he'd come in, if she'd be snoring, if she'd even make sense. Usually she slept like the dead, and very little could disturb her, but since this had started she'd been so worried, and she'd had to be on her guard at all times.

At least now she could rest in peace and quiet for a while, and that was more than she'd had recently.

Sawyer tucked a curl of hair behind her ear and smoothed his big thumb over her cheek. The spontaneous, casual touches disconcerted her. They weren't what she was used to and she didn't quite know what to think of them. He acted as if it were the most natural thing in the world for him to pet her, which probably meant it was merely his way and had no intimate connotations attached. He was, after all, a doctor.

Still, his touch felt very intimate to Honey. Like a lover's caress.

"Holler if you need anything," he said gently. "The family room is close enough so one of us will hear you."

He moved the lantern to the dresser top and turned it down very low, leaving just enough light so she wouldn't wake disoriented in the strange room. Outside, the storm still raged with brilliant bursts of light and loud rumbling thunder.

He picked up the flashlight and damp quilts and went out, leaving the door open a crack. Honey rolled slowly to her side and stacked her hands beneath her cheek. His bed was so comfortable, the blankets so soft and cozy. And it smelled like him, all masculine and rich and sexy. Her eyes drifted shut, and she sighed. Sleep would be wonderful, but she really didn't dare. As soon as the storm let up, she had to think about what to do.

Sawyer was a nice man. His whole family was nice; she couldn't put them at risk, couldn't take advantage of their generosity and their trusting nature. She supposed she could call a cab to take her into town and buy another used car there. The one she'd been driving didn't have much value anyway, hardly worth repairing.

But her stuff. They'd unloaded everything into the barn, Gabe said. She hadn't even noticed a barn, and if she found it, could she retrieve everything without alerting them to her intentions? She had no doubt they'd feel honor bound to detain her, thanks to her illness.

She just didn't know what to do. Since she knew she wouldn't be able to sleep, she figured she had plenty of time to come up with a plan.

TWENTY MINUTES LATER Sawyer peeked in on her— again. He couldn't quite seem to pull his gaze away for more than a few minutes, and his thoughts wouldn't budge from her at all. She was in his bed—and he knew it, on every level imaginable.

It had taken her less than two minutes to fall deeply asleep, and since then, he'd been checking her every few minutes, drawn by the sight of her cuddled so naturally, so trustingly in his bed. He leaned in the door frame, watching her sleep, enthralled by the way the gentle lantern light played over the curves and hollows of her body.

"She doin' okay?"

Sawyer quickly pulled the door shut as he turned to face Jordan. "She's asleep, and her breathing sounds just a little easier. But she's still really sick. I think she needs some rest more than anything else. She's plain wore out."

"If you want, we can all spell you a turn on waking her up through the night."

"No."

Jordan's eyes narrowed. "Sawyer, it's dumb for you to do it alone. We could—"

"I'm the doctor, Jordan, so I'll do it." He was determined to get his brother's mind off altruistic motives and away from the room. "The rest of you don't need to worry. It's under control."

Jordan studied him a long minute before finally shrugging. "Suit yourself. But I swear, you're acting damn strange."

Sawyer didn't refute that. His behavior did seem odd, considering his brother didn't know why he was so insistent. But when Jordan walked away, Sawyer again opened the door where she slept. Nope, he didn't want his brothers seeing her like this.

The little lady slept on her stomach, and she kept kicking her covers off; the jersey had ridden to her waist.

Damn, but she had a nice backside. Soft, white, perfectly rounded. The kind of backside that would fit a man's hands just right. His palms tingled at the thought, and his fingers flexed the tiniest bit.

With a small appreciative smile, Sawyer once again covered her. At least her fever must be lower, or she'd still be chilled deep inside. The fact she felt comfortable enough not to need the blankets proved the medicine was doing its job. Still, he touched her forehead, smoothed her hair away, then forced himself to leave the room.

When he walked out this time he ran into Morgan.

"We need to talk."

Sawyer eyed his brother's dark countenance. He'd have been worried, except Morgan pretty much always looked that way. "If you're going to offer your help, don't bother. I'm more than able to—"

"Nope. I figure if you want to hover all night over the little darling, that's your business. But I want to show you something."

For the first time, Sawyer noticed Morgan was gripping a woman's purse in his fist. "Our guest's?"

"Yep. I decided I didn't like all this secretive business, and being she's staying here, I was fully justified—"

"You snooped, didn't you?"

Morgan tried to look affronted and failed. "Just took a peek at her wallet for I.D. I'm a sheriff, and I had just cause with all this talk of someone hunting her and such."

"And?" Sawyer had to admit to his own overwhelming curiosity. He wondered if the name would match the woman. "Don't keep me in suspense."

"You won't believe this, but it's *Honey Malone.*"

Morgan chuckled. "Damn, she sounds just like a female mobster, doesn't she?"

It took Sawyer two seconds before he burst out laughing. *Honey.* No wonder she thought he knew her name. He was still grinning when Morgan poked him.

"It's not that funny."

"Ah, but it is! Especially when you know the joke."

"But you're not going to share it?"

Sawyer shook his head. "Nope. At least, not until I've shared it with Miss Malone."

Since he had the arrogant habit of refusing ever to let anyone rile him, Morgan merely shrugged. "Suit yourself. But you should also know I braved this hellish rain to run out to the car radio and run a check on her. Nothing, from either side of the law. No priors, no complaints, no signed statements. If someone is trying to hurt her, the police don't know a damn thing about it."

Sawyer worked that thought over in his mind, then shook his head. "That could mean several things."

"Yeah, like she's making it all up." Morgan hesitated, but as he turned to walk away, he added, "Or she's more rattled than you first thought and is delusional. But either way, Sawyer, be on your guard, okay?"

"I'm not an idiot."

"No." Morgan pointed at him and chuckled. "But you are acting like a man out to stake a claim. Don't let your gonads overrule your common sense."

Sawyer glared, but Morgan hadn't waited around to see it. Ridiculous. So he was attracted to her, so what? He was human, and he'd been attracted to plenty of women in his day. Not quite this attracted, not quite this...*consumed.* But it didn't matter. He had no in-

tentions of getting involved any more than necessary
to get her well. She was a patient, and he'd treat her
as such. Period.

But even as he thought it, he opened the door again,
drawn by some inexplicable need to be near her.

Damn, but she looked sweet resting there in his bed.
Incredibly sweet and vulnerable.

And once again, she'd kicked the blanket away.

HONEY WOKE slowly and struggled to orient herself to
the sensation of being in strange surroundings. Carefully, she queried her senses, aware of birds chirping
in near rapture, the steady drone of water dripping outside and a soft snore. Yet she was awake.

Her throat felt terrible, and she swallowed with dif-
ficulty, then managed to get her heavy eyes to open
a tiny bit. As soon as she did, she closed them again
against a sharp pain in her head. She held her breath
until the pain ebbed, easing away in small degrees.

Her body felt weighted down, warm and leaden,
and a buzzing filled her head. It took a lot of effort
to gather her wits and recall where she was and why.

She was on her stomach, a normal position for her,
and this time she opened her eyes more carefully, only
a slit, and let them adjust to the dim light filtering into
the room. As her eyes focused on the edge of a blanket,
pulled to her chin, she shifted, but her legs didn't want
to move. Confused, she peered cautiously around the
room. The rain, only a light drizzle now, left glittering
tracks along the wall of windows, blurring the image
of the lake beyond and the fog rising from it. The gutters must have been overloaded because they dripped
steadily, the sound offering a lulling, soporific effect.

The day was gray, but it was definitely morning, and the birds seemed to be wallowing in the freshness of it, singing their little hearts out.

Frowning, she looked away from the windows, and her gaze passed over Sawyer, then snapped back. She almost gasped at the numbing pain that quick eye movement caused.

Then she did moan as the sight of him registered.

Wearing nothing more than unsnapped jeans, he lounged in a padded wicker chair pulled close at an angle to the foot of the bed. His long legs were stretched out, his bare feet propped on the edge of the mattress near her waist pinning her blankets in place. No wonder her legs didn't want to move. They couldn't, not with his big feet keeping her blankets taut.

She remembered him waking her several times throughout the night, his touch gentle, his voice low and husky as he insistently coaxed her to respond to him, to answer his questions. Her skin warmed with the memory of his large hands on her body, smoothing over her, resetting her blankets, lifting her so she could take a drink or swallow another pill.

She warmed even more as she allowed her eyes to drink in the sight of him. Oh, she was awake now. Wide awake. Sawyer had that effect on her, especially when he was more naked than not, available to her scrutiny. He was a strong man, confident, even arrogant in his abilities. But there was an innate gentleness in his touch, and an unwavering serenity in his dark eyes.

The muscles of his chest and shoulders were exaggerated by the long shadows. She felt cool in the rainy, predawn morning, yet he looked warm and comfortable in nothing more than his jeans. His abdomen, hard and flat, had a very enticing line of downy black hair bisecting it, dipping into those low-fitting jeans. Her heart rate accelerated, her fingers instinctively curling into the sheets as she thought about touching him there, feeling how soft that hair might be and how hard the muscles beneath it were.

One of his elbows was propped on the arm of the chair, offering a fist as a headrest. His other arm dangled off the side of the chair, his hand open, his fingers slack. He was deeply asleep, and even in his relaxed state his body looked hard and lean and too virile for a sane woman to ignore. He appeared exhausted, and no wonder after caring for her all night. She studied his whisker-roughened face a moment, then gave in to temptation and visually explored his body again. A soft sigh escaped her.

She needed a drink. She needed the bathroom. But she could be happy just lying there looking at him for a long, long time.

"G'mornin'."

With a guilty start, her attention darted back to his face. His eyes were heavy-lidded, his thick black lashes at half-mast, his dark gaze glittering at her. Honey closed her own eyes for a moment, trying to get her bearings. His voice had been low, sleepy, *sexy.*

Ahem. "Good morning." The words, which she'd meant to be crisp, sounded like a faint, rusty impersonation.

Sawyer tilted his head. "Throat still sore?"

She nodded, peeking a glance at him and quickly looking away again. "You're, ah, pinning my blankets down."

She heard the amusement in his tone when he murmured, "Yeah, I know."

Then he dragged his feet off the bed and stood and stretched—right there in front of her, putting on an impressive display of flexing muscle and sinew and masculine perfection. Without even thinking about it, she rolled to her back to watch him, keeping her blankets high.

With one arm over his head, she saw the dark silky hair beneath his arm, the way his biceps bulged, and she heard his growled rumble of pleasure. As he stretched, his abdomen pulled tighter and the waistband of his jeans curled away from his body. Her vision blurred. He ran both hands through his hair and over his face, then he smiled.

She tried to smile back, she really did. But then he scratched his belly, drawing her gaze there, and she saw that his jeans rode even lower on his slim hips and that his masculine perfection had changed just a tad. Okay, more than a tad. A whole lot more.

He had an erection.

She didn't exactly mean to stare, but since he was standing only a foot away from the bed and she was lying down and he was so close, it was rather hard to ignore. Heat bloomed in her belly, making her toes curl.

He reached out and placed a warm palm on her forehead. "Your fever seems to be down. Luckily, the electricity came on in the middle of the night, otherwise, without the air-conditioning, the house would have been muggy as hell. If this rain ever stops, they're predicting a real scorcher, and with you being sick I'd hate for you to suffer through the heat, too." He smoothed her hair away from her set face, looking at her closely. "You want to use the john?"

She was so flustered by his good-natured chatter in light of her lascivious thoughts, she couldn't answer, even though her situation was beginning to get critical.

He solved the problem for her. Whisking the covers aside, he hooked one arm behind her and levered her upright. She scrambled to get the jersey shirt pulled down over her hips, covering her decently. He didn't seem to notice her predicament.

"Come on. I'll help you in, then wait out here."

She didn't want him waiting anywhere, but he hustled her out of the bed and toward the bathroom, holding her closely, not really giving her time to think about it. He walked her right up to the toilet, then cautiously let her go. "If you need anything, don't be too squeamish to call out, okay?"

Never, not in a million years. She stared at him, blinked twice, then nodded, just to get him out of the room. With a smile and a touch to her cheek, he backed out and pulled the door shut.

Even in her dazed state, Honey was able to appreciate the incredibly beautiful design of the bathroom. Done in the same polished pine but edged with black ceramic tile, it looked warm and masculine and cozy. The countertops were white with black trim, and there was a shower stall but no tub, a black sink, and a small blocked window with the same black-checked gingham curtains. Amazing that a household of men would have such a nice, clean, well-designed home.

After she'd taken care of business, Honey washed her hands, splashed her face and took a long drink of water. She looked at herself in the round etched mirror over the sink and nearly screamed. She looked horrid. Her hair was tangled, her face pale, the bruise on her forehead providing her only color, and that in shades of gray and purple and green. God, she looked as sickly as she felt, and that was saying a lot!

She glanced longingly at the shower, but then she heard Sawyer ask impatiently, "Everything okay?"

It would take more time and effort than she could muster to make herself look any better. With a sigh, she edged her way to the door, holding on to the sink for support. She barely had the door open and he was there, tall, shirtless, overwhelmingly potent. Without a word he wrapped his arm around her and practically carried her back to the bed.

He tucked her in, then asked, "Would you like some tea or coffee?"

Her mouth watered. Now that she wasn't so tired, she noticed other needs, and hot coffee sounded like just the thing to clear out the cobwebs and relieve her sore throat. "I'd kill for coffee."

"When you don't have the strength to swat a fly? Never mind. Nothing so drastic is necessary. The coffee is already on. Morgan and Gabe are both early risers, so one of them has already seen to it because I smell it. Cream and sugar?"

"Please."

He started to turn away, and she said, "Sawyer?"

He looked at her over his shoulder. "Hmm?"

"My things…"

"They're safe. Gabe and Casey got everything stored in the barn before the worst of the storm hit, but if you like, I'll check on them after I've dressed."

After he'd dressed. The fact of his partial nudity

flustered her again, and she felt herself blush. She'd
simply never been treated to the likes of a man like him
before. Her experiences were with more…subtle men.
Sawyer without his shirt was more enticing, more overpowering, than most men would have been buck naked.

She cleared her sore throat. "I'd really like my toothbrush. And…and I'd dearly love to shower and get the
lake water off—"

"I dunno." He gave her a skeptical look and frowned.
"Let's see how you do after eating a little, okay? I don't
want you to push it. You still sound like a bullfrog,
and I'm willing to bet you have a bit of a fever yet. But
first things first. Let me get the coffee. It'll make your
throat feel better."

His peremptory manner set her on edge. Straight-
ening her shoulders as much as she could while lying
huddled beneath a layer of blankets, she groused, "It's
not up to you to decide what I can or can't do."

He halted in mid stride and slowly turned to face
her. The intensity of his dark gaze almost made her
squirm, but after a good night's rest, she felt emotionally stronger, if not physically, and she couldn't continue to let him baby her or dictate to her. Now was as
good a time as any to assert herself.

Tilting his head, he said, "Actually—I can."

"No—"

He stalked forward, startling her with the sudden-
ness of it. His bare feet didn't make a sound on the polished flooring, but he might have been stomping for
the expression on his face. Bracing one hand on the
headboard and the other on the pillow by her cheek,
he leaned down until their noses almost touched. Her

head pressed into the pillow, but there was no place to retreat to, no way to pull back.

His breath touched her as he studied her face. "You're seriously ill, and I didn't stay up all night checking on you just so you could turn stubborn this morning and set yourself on a decline."

She mustered her courage and frowned up at him. "I know I'm not a hundred percent well, but—"

He made a rude sound to that statement. "It's a wonder you even made it to the bathroom on your own. I can tell just looking at your flushed cheeks and lips that you still have a fever. What you need is plenty of rest and medicine and liquids."

She hated to sound vain, so the words came out in a rough, embarrassed whisper. "I smell like the lake."

At first his brows lowered and he stared at her. Then, almost against his will it seemed, he leaned closer and his nose nearly touched her throat beneath her ear. She sucked in a startled breath, frozen by his nearness, his heat, the sound of his breathing. He nuzzled gently for just a moment, then slowly leaned away again, and his gaze traveled down her throat to her chest and beyond, then came back to her face, and there was a new alertness to his expression, a sensual hardness to his features.

She swallowed roughly and croaked, "Well?" trying to hide the effect he'd had on her, trying, and failing, to be as cavalier.

His lips twitched, though his eyes still looked hot and far too intent. He touched her cheek, then let his hand fall away. "Not a single scent of lake, I promise. Quit worrying about it."

She couldn't quit worrying, not when he stayed so

close. And she knew a shower would revive her spirits, which she needed so she could think clearly. She tried a different tack. "I'm not used to going all day without a shower. I'll feel better after I clean up."

He continued to loom over her, watching her face, then finally he sighed. "Somehow I doubt that, but then, what do I know? I'm just the doctor." When she started to object, he added, "If you feel such a strong need to get bathed, fine. I'll help you, and no, don't start shaking your head at me. I'm not leaving you alone to drown yourself."

"You're also not watching me bathe!"

He started to grin, but rubbed his chin quickly instead. "No, of course not. The shower is out because I doubt you could stand that long. And as wobbly as you seem when you're on your feet, I'm not taking the chance. But this afternoon, after I've seen a few patients, I'll take you to the hall bath. We have a big tub you can soak in. By then I'll have your clothes run through the washer, and you can wear your own things. We'll manage, I think."

Worse and worse. "Sawyer, I don't want you doing my laundry."

"There's no one else, Honey. Morgan has to go into the office today, and Jordan is making a few housecalls. Casey has never quite learned the knack of doing laundry, though I'm working on him, and if I know Gabe, he'll be off running around somewhere."

She stared at him, dumbfounded, then shook her head. "Let me clarify. I don't want *any* of you doing my laundry."

"The clothes you came in are wet and muddy. By now, they probably do smell like the lake. Unless you want to continue living in Casey's shirt, someone needs to do it, and you're certainly not up to it." She started to speak, and he held up a hand. "Give over, will you? I doubt doing a little laundry will kill me. If it did, I'd have been dead a long time ago."

She seemed to have no options at all. With a sigh, she said, "Thank you."

"You're welcome."

His continued good humor made her feel like a nag. Trying to get back to a more neutral subject, she asked, "Do you see patients every day?"

He straightened from the bed. "Don't most doctors?"

"I really don't know."

"Well, they do. You can take my word on it. Illness has no respect for weekends or vacations. And since I'm the only doctor around for miles, I've gotten used to it."

Nervously pleating the edge of the blanket, she wondered if this might be her best chance to slip away. It was for certain if he didn't want her up to shower, he wouldn't want her up to leave on her own. "Do you have an office close by?"

He crossed his arms over his chest. "Very close."

"Oh?" She tried to sound only mildly interested.

"You're not going anywhere, Honey."

Her tongue stuck to the roof of her mouth.

"Don't look so shocked. I could see you plotting and planning."

"But…how?" She'd kept her expression carefully hidden. At least, she thought she had.

"I can read you."

"You don't even know me!"

He looked disgruntled by that fact. "Yeah, well, for

whatever reason, I know you well enough already to see how your mind works. What'd you think to do? Hitchhike into town when we were all away from the house?"

She hadn't, simply because she hadn't thought that far ahead yet. But it might not have been a bad idea. She'd be able to tell by the license plates if the driver was local or not, ridding the risk of being picked up by the people who were after her.

When she remained quiet, he shook his head and muttered, "Women." He went out the door without another word, and Honey let him. She had a lot to think about. This might be her only chance to save Sawyer and his family from getting involved. She'd left in the first place to protect her sister. The last thing she wanted to do was get someone else in trouble.

Especially such an incredible man as Sawyer.

CHAPTER FOUR

SAWYER TAPPED on the door and then walked in. Honey was in the bed, her head turned to the window. She seemed very pensive, but she glanced at him as he entered. He saw her face perk up at the sight of the tray he carried.

Grinning, he asked, "So you're hungry?"

She slid higher in the bed. "Actually...yes. What have you got there?"

He set the tray holding the coffee and other dishes on the dresser and carried another to her, opening the small legs on the tray so it fit over her lap. "Gabe had just pulled some cinnamon rolls from the oven, so they're still hot. I thought you might like some."

"Gabe cooks?"

Sawyer handed her the coffee, then watched to make sure it was to her liking. Judging by the look of rapture on her face as she sipped, it was just right. "We all cook. As my mom is fond of saying, she didn't raise no dummies. If a man can't cook, especially in a household devoid of women, he goes hungry."

She'd finished half the cup of coffee right off so he refilled her cup, adding more sugar and cream, then gave her a plate with a roll on it. The icing had oozed over the side of the roll, and she quickly scooped up a fingerful, then moaned in pleasure as she licked her finger clean.

Sawyer stilled, watching her and suffering erotic images that leaped into his tired, overtaxed brain. His reactions to her were getting way out of hand. Of course, they'd been out of hand since he'd first seen her. And last night, when she kept kicking the covers away, he'd almost gone nuts. Pinning them down with his feet had been a form of desperate self-preservation.

He hadn't had such a volatile reaction to a woman in too many years to count. No, he'd never been entirely celibate, but he had always been detached. Now, with this woman who remained more a stranger than otherwise, he already felt far too involved.

He cleared his throat, enthralled by the appreciative way she savored the roll. "Good?"

"Mmm. Very. Give my regards to the chef."

She sounded so sincere, he almost laughed. "It's just a package that you bake. But Gabe really can do some great cooking when he's in the mood. Usually everyone around here grabs a snack first thing in the morning, then around eight they hit Ceily's diner and get breakfast."

"If they can cook, why not eat here?"

He liked it that she was more talkative today, and apparently more at ease. "Well, let's see. Gabe goes to town because that's what he always does. He sort of just hangs out."

Her brows raised. "All the time?"

With a shrug, he admitted, "That's Gabe. He's a handyman extraordinaire—his title, not mine—so he's never without cash. Someone's always calling on him to fix something, and there's really nothing he can't fix." Including her car, though Sawyer hadn't asked him to fix it. Not yet. "He keeps busy when he wants. And when he doesn't, he's at the lake, lolling in the sun like a big fish."

Gabe stuck his head in the door to say, "I resent that. I bask, I do not loll. That makes me sound lazy."

Sawyer saw Honey gulp the bite in her mouth and almost choke as she glanced up at his brother. As a concession to their guest, Gabe had pulled on frayed jean shorts rather than walking around in his underwear. He hoped Jordan and Morgan remembered to do the same. They each had more than enough female companionship, but never overnight at the house, so they were unused to waking with a woman in residence.

Gabe hadn't shaved yet, and though he had on a shirt, it wasn't buttoned so his chest was mostly bare. Sawyer shook his head at his disreputable appearance. "You are lazy, Gabe."

Gabe smiled at Honey. "He's just jealous because he has so much responsibility." Then to Sawyer, "Now, if I was truly lazy, would I plan on fixing the leak in your office sink this morning?"

Sawyer hesitated, pleased, then took a sip of coffee before nodding. "Yeah, you would, considering you can't go to the lake because it's raining."

"Not true. The best fishing is done in the rain."

He couldn't debate that. "Are you really going to fix the sink?"

"Sure. You said it's leaking under the cabinet?"

Sawyer started to explain the exact location of the leak, but Honey interrupted, asking, "Where is his office?"

Gabe hitched his head toward the end of the hallway. "At the back of the house. He and my dad built it on there after he got his degree and opened up his own practice. 'Course, I helped because Sawyer is downright pathetic with a hammer. He can put in tiny stitches, but he has a hell of a time hitting a nail or cutting a board straight."

Honey carefully set down her last bite of roll. "Your dad?"

"Yep. He's not a military man, like Sawyer's dad was, but he is a pretty good handyman, just not as good as me."

Standing, Sawyer headed toward Gabe, forcing him to back out of the doorway. He could see the questions and the confusion on Honey's face, but it was far too early for him to go into long explanations on his family history. "Go on and let her drink her coffee in peace."

Gabe put on an innocent face, but laughter shone in his eyes. "I wasn't bothering her!"

"You were flirting."

"Not that she noticed." He grinned shamefully. "She was too busy watching you."

That sounded intriguing—not that he intended to dwell on it or to do anything about it. Likely she watched him because he was the one most responsible for her. "I'll be at the office after I've showered and gotten dressed."

"All right. I'll go get my tools together."

Sawyer stepped back into the room and shut the door, then leaned against it. Just as Gabe had mentioned, Honey watched him, her blue eyes wide and wary. He nodded at her unfinished roll. "You done?"

"Oh." She glanced down at the plate as if just remembering it was there. "Yes." She wiped her fingers on the napkin he'd provided and patted her mouth. "Thank you. That was delicious. I hadn't realized I was so hungry."

Eating less than one cinnamon roll qualified as hungry? He grunted. "More coffee?"

"Yes, please."

Her continued formality and good manners tickled him. Here she was, bundled up in his bed, naked except for his son's jersey, and with every other word she said *please.* She still sounded like a rusty nail on concrete, but she didn't look as tense as she had last night. Probably the need for sleep had been more dire than anything else. As he refilled her cup, emptying the carafe, he said, "I have spare toothbrushes in my office. If you'd like, I can give you one. I'd go get yours, but I'm not sure which box it's in."

"I'm not sure, either."

"Okay, then. I'll fetch you one in a bit." He finished his own coffee while leaning on the dresser, looking at her. "Before I start getting ready for my day, you want to tell me who you are?"

She went so still, it alarmed him. He set down his empty cup and folded his arms over his chest. "Well?"

"I think," she muttered, not quite meeting his gaze, "that it'll be simpler all around if I don't involve you."

"You don't trust me?"

"Trust a man I've known one day?"

"Why not? I haven't done anything to hurt you, have I?"

"No. It's not that. It's just… Sawyer, I can't stay here. I don't want to endanger you or your son or your brothers."

That was so ludicrous he laughed. And her lack of

trust, regardless of the time limits, unreasonably annoyed him. "So you think one little scrawny woman is better able to defend herself than four men and a strapping fifteen-year-old?"

Her mouth firmed at his sarcasm. "I don't intend to get into a physical battle."

"No? You're going to just keep running from whatever the hell it is you're running from?"

"That's none of your business," she insisted.

His jaw clenched. "Maybe not, but it would sure simplify the hell out of things if you stopped being so secretive."

She pinched the bridge of her nose and squeezed her eyes shut. Sawyer felt like a bully. Just because she'd sat up and eaten a little didn't mean she was up to much more than that. He sighed in disgust—at himself and her—then pushed away from the dresser to remove the tray from her lap.

She glanced at him nervously. "I... I don't mean to make this more difficult."

He kept his back to her, not wanting her to see his frown. "I realize that. But you're going to have to tell me something sooner or later."

A heavy hesitation filled the air. Then he heard her draw in her breath. "No, I don't. My plans don't concern you."

Everything in him fought against the truth of her words. "You landed in my lake."

"And I offered to pay for the damages."

He turned to face her, his muscles tense. "Forget the damn damages. I'm not worried about that."

She looked sad and resolute. "But payment for the

damages is all I owe you. I didn't ask to be brought here. I didn't ask for your help."

"You got it anyway." He stalked close again, unable to keep the distance between them. "No respectable man would leave a sick, frightened woman alone in a rainstorm. Especially a woman who was panicked and damn near delusional."

"I wasn't—"

"You slugged my son. You were afraid of me."

She winced again, then worried her bottom lip between her teeth. His heart nearly melted, and that angered him more than anything else. He sat on the edge of the bed and took her hands in his. "Honey, you can trust me. You can trust us." She didn't quite meet his gaze, staring instead at his throat. "The best thing now is to tell me what's going on so I know what to expect."

She looked haunted as her gaze met his, but she also looked strong, and he wasn't surprised when she whispered, "Or I can leave."

They stared at each other, a struggle of wills, and with a soft oath Sawyer stood and paced away. Maybe he was pushing too fast. She needed time to reason things through. He'd wear her down, little by little. And if that didn't work, he'd have Morgan start an investigation—whether she liked it or not.

One thing was certain. He wasn't letting her out of his sight until he knew it was safe.

With his back to her, his hands braced on the dresser, he said, "Not yet."

"You can't keep me here against my will."

"Wanna bet?" He felt like a bastard, but his gut instincts urged him to keep her close regardless of her insistence. "Morgan is the town sheriff, and he heard everything you said. If nothing else, he'd want to keep you around for questioning. I'm willing to give you some time. But until you're ready to explain, you're not going anywhere."

He could feel her staring at his back, feel the heat of her anger. She wasn't nearly so frail as he'd first thought, and she had more gumption than the damn old mule Jordan kept out in the pasture.

Despite the raspiness of her voice, he heard her disdain when she muttered, "And you wanted me to trust you."

His hand fisted on the dresser, but he refused to take the bait. He pulled open a drawer and got out a pair of shorts, saying over his shoulder, "I need to shower and get dressed before patients start showing up. Why don't you just go on back to sleep for a spell? Maybe things'll look a little different this afternoon."

He saw her reflection in the mirror, the way her eyes were already closing, shutting him out. He wanted to say something more, but he couldn't. So instead he walked away, and he closed the door behind him very softly.

SHE SLEPT the better part of the day. After taking more medicine and cleaning up as much as she could using the toothbrush he provided and the masculine-scented soap in the bathroom, she simply konked out. One minute she'd been disgruntled because he was rushing her back to bed, and the next she was sound asleep. Sawyer roused her once to take more ibuprofen and sip more water, but she barely stirred enough to follow his directions. He held her head up with one hand, aware of the silkiness of her heavy hair and the dreamy look in her sleepy eyes. She smiled at him, too groggy to remember her anger.

Fortunately for him, since he couldn't stay by her side, she hadn't kicked off her blankets again. He'd worried about it, and gone back and forth from his office to her room several times during the day, unable to stay away. After Casey had finished up his chores, he promised to stay close in case she called out.

She hadn't had any lunch, and it was now nearing dinnertime. When Sawyer entered the room, he saw his son sitting on the patio through the French doors. He had the small cat with him that Jordan had brought home. Using a string, he enticed the cat to pounce and jump and roll.

This time Honey was on her back, both arms flung over her head. He could see her legs were open beneath the covers. She was sprawled out, taking up as much room as her small body could in the full-size bed. In his experience, most women slept curled up, like a cat, but not Honey. A man would need a king-size bed to accommodate her.

He was still smiling when he stepped outside with Casey. "She been sleeping okay?"

"Like the dead." Casey glanced up at him, then yelped when the cat attacked his ankle. "She looks like someone knocked her out, doesn't she? I've never seen anyone sleep so hard. The cat got loose and jumped up on the bed and before I could catch her, she'd been up one side and down the other, but the woman never so much as moved."

"She's a sound sleeper, and I think she was pretty exhausted, besides. Thanks for keeping a watch on her."

Sawyer saw a movement out of the corner of his eye and turned. Honey was propped up on one elbow, her hair hanging forward around her face, her eyes squinted at the late afternoon sunshine. Most of the day it had continued to drizzle, and now that the sun was out, the day was so humid you could barely draw a deep breath.

Honey looked vaguely confused, so he went in to her. Casey followed with the cat trailing behind.

"Hello, sleepyhead."

She looked around as if reorienting herself. The small cat made an agile leap onto the bed, then settled herself in a semicircle at the end of Honey's feet, tucking her bandaged tail in tight to sleep. Honey stared at the cat as if she'd never seen one before. "What time is it?"

"Five o'clock. You missed lunch, but dinner will be ready soon."

Casey stepped forward to retrieve the new pet, but Honey shook her head. "She's okay there. I don't mind sharing the bed."

Casey smiled at her. They all loved and accepted animals, thanks to Jordan, and it pleased his son that their guest appeared to be of a similar mind. "You want something to drink?"

She thought about that for a moment, then finally nodded. "Yes, please."

Sawyer was amused by her sluggish responses and said, "Make it orange juice, Case."

"Sure thing."

Once Casey was gone, Sawyer studied her. She yawned hugely behind her hand, then apologized.

"I can't believe I slept so long."

He resisted the urge to say, *I told you so,* and stuck to the facts instead. "You've got bronchitis, which can take a lot out of you, not to mention you're just getting over a concussion. Sleep is the best thing for you."

She sat back and tucked the covers around her waist. After a second, she said, "I'm sorry about arguing with you earlier. I know you mean well."

"But you don't trust me?"

She shrugged. "Trust is a hard thing. I'm not generally the best judge of character."

This sounded interesting, so he pulled up a chair and made himself comfortable. "How so?"

She gave him a wary look, but was saved from answering when Casey came back in. He handed her the glass of iced orange juice and a napkin.

"Thank you."

"No problem." He turned to Sawyer. "I'm going to go down and do some more work on the fence."

"Only for about an hour. Dinner will be ready by then."

"All right."

As Casey started out, Honey quickly set her glass aside and lifted a hand. "Casey!"

He turned, his look questioning.

"I noticed your shoulders are getting a little red. Have you been out in the sun much lately?"

"Uh…" He glanced at his father, then back to Honey. "Yeah, I mean, I've been outside, but there's hasn't really been much sun till just a bit ago."

"I know it's none of my business, but you should really put on a shirt or something. Or at least some sunscreen. You don't want to burn."

Sawyer frowned at her, then looked at Casey. Sure enough, there was too much color on his son's wide shoulders and back. Casey looked, too, then grimaced. "I guess it was so cloudy today, I didn't think about it."

She looked prim as she lectured. "You can burn even through the clouds. I guess because I'm so fair, I'm especially conscious of the sun. But I'd hate to see you damage your skin."

Casey stared at her, looking totally dumbfounded. Too much sunshine was probably the last thing the average fifteen-year-old would have on his mind. "I'll, uh... I'll put some sunscreen on. Thanks."

Sawyer added, "And a shirt, Case."

"Yeah, okay." He hurried out before he drew any more attention.

Sawyer looked at Honey. She was smiling, and she looked so sweet, she took his breath away. He didn't like her interference with his son, but since she was right this time, he couldn't very well lecture her on it.

"You have a wonderful son."

He certainly thought so. "Thank you."

"He doesn't really look like you. Does he take after his mother?"

"No."

She looked startled by his abrupt answer, and Sawyer wished he could reach his own ass to kick it. He didn't want her starting in on questions he didn't want to answer, but his attitude, if he didn't temper it, would prompt her to do just that.

"I got your clothes washed. If you're feeling up to a bath, we can get that taken care of before dinner, then you can change." Not that he wanted her trussed up in lots of clothes when she looked so enticing wearing what she had on. But he knew it'd be safer for his peace of mind if she at least had panties on.

Except that he'd already seen the tiny scrap of peach silk she considered underwear, and knowing she wore that might be worse than knowing she was bare, sort of like very sweet icing on a luscious cake.

Luckily he'd done the laundry while no one else was around. He didn't want his brothers envisioning her in the feminine, sexy underwear. But he knew they would have if they'd seen it. He could barely get the thought out of his mind.

"I'm definitely up for a bath. I feel downright grungy."

She looked far from grungy, but he kept that opinion to himself. "We'll use the hall bath. Morgan's room opens into it, but he isn't home yet. I think he's on a date. And Gabe only uses the shower in the basement."

Her eyes widened. "Good grief. How many bathrooms do you have?"

She looked confused again, and he grinned. "As many as I have brothers, I guess. Little by little we added on as everyone grew up and needed more room."

"It's amazing you all still live together."

He lifted one shoulder in a lazy shrug. "My father left us the house, and my mom moved to Florida after Gabe graduated. Morgan stays here in the main house with me and Case, but he's building his own place on the south end of the property. It should be done by the end of the summer."

"How much property do you have?"

"Around fifty acres. Most of it's unused and heavily treed, just there for privacy, or if any other family decides to build on it. Morgan'll have his own acreage, but still be close enough, which is the way we all like it. Jordan's settled into the garage. He converted it to an apartment when he was around twenty because he's something of a loner, more so than the rest of us, but with his college bills, he couldn't really afford to move completely out on his own. Now he could, of course, since there's even more call for a vet in these parts than there is for a doctor, but he's already settled. And Gabe has the basement, which runs the entire length of the house. He's got it fixed up down there real nice, with his own kitchen and bath and living room, and his own entrance, though he usually just comes through the house unless he's sneaking a girl in."

"He's not allowed to have women over?"

"Not for the night, but that's not really a rule or anything now, just something my mother started back when Gabe was younger and kept trying it." Sawyer grinned, remembering how often he and his brothers used to get in trouble. "Gabe has always attracted women, and sometimes I think he doesn't quite know what to do with them. Dragging one home for my mother to get rid of seemed to be a favorite plan of his."

Honey chuckled, and he could tell by her expression she didn't know he was serious. He grinned, too. She'd get to know Gabe better, then she'd realize the truth.

"Keeping women out is just something that we've all stuck to. Especially with Casey around. He's old enough now not to be influenced, but he was always a nosy kid, so you couldn't do much without him knowing. He has a healthy understanding of sex, but I didn't want him to be cavalier about it."

She pulled her knees up and rested her crossed arms on them. Smiling, she said, "I guess your wife wouldn't have liked it much, either, if a lot of women had been in and out of the house."

Annoyance brought him to his feet, and he paced to the French doors. The topic shouldn't be a touchy one, and usually wasn't. But Honey didn't know all the circumstances, all the background. He said simply, "My wife never lived in this house."

She didn't reply to that, but he knew she now felt awkward when that hadn't been his intention. He glanced over his shoulder, saw her worried gaze and grimaced at his own idiocy. He'd opened a can of worms with that confession, and he didn't know why. He never discussed his ex-wife with anyone except his family, and then only rarely.

"I got divorced while I was still in medical school. In fact, just a month after Casey was born. She was still pretty young and foolish and she wasn't quite up to being a mother. So I took complete custody. My mother and Gabe's father really helped me out with him until I could get through medical school. Actually, everybody helped. Morgan was around nineteen, Jordan fifteen and Gabe twelve. In a lot of ways, Gabe and Casey are like brothers."

She looked fascinated, almost hungry for more information. He walked over to her and sat again. "What about you? You have much family?"

"No." She looked away, then made a face. "There's only my father and my sister. My mother passed away when I was young."

"I'm sorry." He couldn't imagine how he'd have gotten through life without his mother. She was the backbone of the family, the strongest person he knew and the most loving.

Honey shrugged. "It was a long time ago. I'm not very close with my father, but my sister and I are."

"How old's your sister?"

"Twenty-four."

"How old are you?"

She looked at him suspiciously, as if he'd asked for her Social Security number. After a long hesitation, she admitted, "I'm twenty-five."

He whistled. "Must have been rough for your father, two kids so close in age and your mother gone."

She waved that away. "He hired in a lot of help."

"What kind of help?"

"You know, nannies, cooks, tutors, pretty much everything. My father spent a lot of time at work."

"Didn't he do anything with you himself?"

She laughed, but there wasn't much humor in the sound. "Not a lot. Dad wasn't exactly thrilled to have daughters. I think that's what he hated most about Mother dying—she hadn't given him a son yet. He thought about remarrying a lot, but he was so busy with his business, and he worried that someone would divorce him and get part of it. He was a little paranoid that way."

Sawyer looked her over, searching her face, seeing the signs of strain. She'd put up a brave front, but he could see the hurt in her blue eyes and knew there was a lot about her life that hadn't always been satisfactory. "Sounds like a hell of a childhood you had."

Color washed over her cheeks, and she ducked her face. "I didn't mean to complain. We had a lot more than most kids ever do, so it wasn't bad."

Except it didn't sound like she'd had a lot of love or affection or even attention. Sawyer had always appreciated his family, their support, the closeness, but now he realized just how special those things were. They came without strings, without restriction or embarrassment, and were unconditional.

She was still looking bashful over the whole subject, so he decided to let it drop. At least for now. "I guess if you're going to take that bath, we should get on with it or you'll miss dinner. And Jordan really outdid himself tonight for you."

"Now Jordan's cooking?"

He shrugged. "We take turns. Nothing fancy. I told him to make it light since I wasn't sure what you'd feel up to. He's got chicken and noodles in the Crock-Pot, and fresh bread out of the bread machine."

She shook her head. "Amazing. Men who cook."

Laughing, Sawyer reached for her and helped her out of the bed. She clutched at the top blanket, dragging it off the mattress and disturbing the cat, who looked very put out over the whole thing. Honey apologized to the animal, who gave her a dismissive look and re-curled herself to sleep.

"You'll have cat hair in the bed."

"I don't mind if you don't. It's your bed."

"You're sleeping in it."

They stared at each other for a taut, electric moment, then Honey looked away. Her hands shook as she busied herself by wrapping the blanket over and around her shoulders. It dragged the ground, even hiding her feet.

He supposed that was best; even though the jersey covered her from shoulders to knees, he didn't want his brothers ogling her—and they would. They were every bit as aware of an attractive woman as Sawyer, and Honey, in his opinion, was certainly more attractive than most. His brothers might not comment on the sexy picture she made with her hair disheveled, her feet bare and her slender body draped in an overlarge male shirt, but they'd notice.

She seemed steadier now, but he kept his right arm around her and held her elbow with his left hand, just in case. She was firmly in his embrace, and he liked it.

To get his mind off lusty thoughts and back on the subject at hand, he asked, "Don't you know any men who cook?"

She sent him an incredulous look. "My father's never even made his own coffee. I doubt he'd know how. And my fiancé took it for granted that cooking was a woman's job."

They'd almost reached the door, and Sawyer stopped dead in his tracks. His heart punched against his ribs; his thighs tightened. Without even realizing it, his hands gripped her hard as he turned her to face him. "You have a fiancé?"

Her eyes widened. The way he held her, practically on her tiptoes, pulled her off balance, and she braced her palms flat against his chest. He saw her pupils dilate as awareness of their positions sank in. "Sawyer…"

Her voice was a whisper, and he barely heard her over the roaring in his ears. He pulled her a little closer still, until her body was flush against his and her heartbeat mingled with his own. "Answer me, dammit. Are you engaged?"

She didn't look frightened by his barbaric manner, which was a good thing since he couldn't seem to get himself in hand. That word *fiancé* was bouncing off his brain with all the subtlety of a bass drum. If she was going to be married soon…

"Not…not anymore."

"What?" He was so rattled, he wasn't at all sure he understood.

"I'm not engaged, not anymore."

Something turbulent and dangerous inside him settled, but in its place was a sudden blast of violent heat, an awareness of how much her answer had mattered to him.

He looked down at her mouth, saw her parted lips tremble, and he went right over the edge. He leaned down until he could feel her warm breath on his mouth, fast and low, and the vibrancy of her expectation, her own awareness.

And then he kissed her.

CHAPTER FIVE

HONEY CLUTCHED at him, straining to make the contact more complete. Her blanket fell to the floor in a puddle around her feet. She barely noticed.

She didn't think about what was happening, and she didn't think about pulling away. Overwhelmed by pure sensation, by heat and need she'd never experienced before, she wanted only to get closer. She'd thought the attraction was one-sided, but now, feeling the faint trembling in Sawyer's hard body, she knew he was affected, too.

Sawyer's mouth was warm and firm, and he teased, barely touching her, giving her time to change her mind, to pull back. Until she groaned.

There was an aching stillness for half a heartbeat, then his mouth opened on hers, voraciously hungry, and his hands slid around to her back, holding her so tightly she could barely breathe. She felt the hot slide of his tongue and the more brazen press of his swollen sex against her belly. A delicious sensation of yearning unfurled inside her, making her thighs tingle and her toes curl. Her fever was back, hotter than ever.

A knock sounded on the door.

They both jumped apart, Sawyer with a short vicious curse, Honey with a strained gasp. She almost fell as her feet tangled in the forgotten blanket, and would have if Sawyer hadn't reached out and snagged her close again. He stared down into her face, his expression hard, his gaze like glittering ice, then called out, "What?"

The door opened and Jordan stuck his head in. He took one look at them, made a sheepish face and started to pull it shut again.

Sawyer caught the doorknob, keeping the door open. "What is it?"

Honey fumbled for the blanket, wishing she could pull it completely over her head and hide. It was so obvious Jordan knew exactly what he'd interrupted. Yet she'd only known Sawyer a day and a half, less if you counted how much she'd slept.

It didn't matter to her body, and not really to her heart.

"Dinner'll be ready in about ten minutes." Jordan glanced at her, gave a small smile at her fumbling efforts to cover herself and again tried to sidle out.

"Can you make it twenty?" Sawyer asked, apparently not the least uncomfortable, or else hiding it very well. "She was just about to bathe."

Jordan slanted her an appraising look, and Honey wanted to kick Sawyer. She was off balance, both emotionally and physically. That kiss…wow. She'd never known anything like it. How the hell could he stand there and converse so easily when she could barely get the words to register in her fogged brain? And how could he manage to embarrass her like that?

Firmly, but with a distinct edge to her croaking voice, she said, "I don't want you to hold up dinner on my account." She made a shooing motion with her free hand, trying to be nonchalant. "Just go on and eat. Really."

Jordan caught her fluttering hand and grinned. "Nonsense. We can wait. Morgan is running a little late, anyway. He had some trouble in town."

She felt Sawyer shift and tighten his arm around her. "What kind of trouble?"

"Nothing serious. A cow got loose from the Morrises' property and wandered into the churchyard. Traffic was backed up for a mile."

Honey tilted her head, thrilled for a change of topic. "The cow was blocking traffic?"

"No. Everyone just stopped to gawk. Around here, a cow on the loose is big news." Then, with a totally straight face and a deadpan voice, Jordan added, "Luckily, the cow wasn't spooked too badly by all the attention."

Honey bit back her smile.

At that moment, the cat leaped off the bed to twine around Jordan's ankles. Without even looking down, he scooped up the small pet and cuddled her close, encouraging the melodic, rumbling purr. To Honey, he said, "Go on and take your bath. There's no rush."

They stepped into the hallway en masse, two powerful men, an ecstatic cat and a woman wrapped head to toes in a blanket. They nearly collided with Casey, who was liberally caked in mud. He'd removed his shoes so he wasn't tracking anything in, but mud was on his legs clear to his knees. The shirt he'd worn, thanks to her interference—she still didn't know what had come over her—was dirt and sweat stained. He looked more like a man than ever.

Holding up both hands, Casey said, "Don't come too

close. The fields are drenched and muddy as hell…uh, heck. And half that mud is on me."

Jordan clapped him on the back. "Well, you'll have to use Gabe's shower, because the little lady wants a bath."

Casey stared at her.

Honey deduced that the phenomenon of having a female bathing in the all-male household warranted nearly as much attention as a cow on the loose.

Her face was getting redder by the second. If she didn't have a fever, she soon would. Never in her life had bathing been such an ordeal, or been noted and discussed by so many males.

The front door slammed, and not long after, Morgan rounded the hall, already stripping his shirt off with frustrated, jerky movements. Powerful, bulky muscles rippled across his broad shoulders and heavy chest as he stamped around the corner of the hall. He had his hands on the button to his tan uniform slacks when he realized he had an audience.

He didn't look the least discomforted at being caught undressing in the middle of the day, in the middle of the house, in front of a crowd.

"Sorry," he grumbled without an ounce of sincerity, and yanked his belt free. "I'm just heading for the shower. It must be ninety out there, and the damn humidity makes it feel like a sauna." He pointed an accusing finger at Jordan. "It was only the thought of a cool shower that kept me from kicking that damn ornery heifer, who no matter what I tried, refused to budge her big spotted butt."

Jordan laughed out loud, gleefully explaining, "Your shower will have to wait because—"

Honey, knowing good and well he intended to an-
nounce her bath once again, pulled loose from Sawyer
and stomped on Jordan's toe. Since he had on shoes
and she didn't, he looked more surprised than hurt. He
stared down at his foot, but then so did the rest of the
men. They all looked as if they expected to see a bug
to account for her attack. When no bug was found, all
those masculine gazes transferred to her face, and she
lifted her chin. Just because they were men didn't mean
they had to wallow in insensitivity.

Jordan blinked at her, one brow raised high, and she
quickly stepped back to Sawyer's side.

Her bravado wilted under Jordan's questioning gaze.
Oh, God, she'd assaulted him! In his own home and in
front of his family. Sawyer chuckled and put his arm
around her.

Morgan stared at her with bad-tempered amusement. "Wanting a long soak, huh? I suppose I can use
Gabe's shower…"

Casey stepped forward. "After me. I claimed it first."

"I'm older, brat."

"Doesn't matter!" And then Casey took off, racing
for the shower. With a curse, Morgan started after him.

Honey wanted to slink back to bed and hide. The
bath, which had sounded so heavenly moments before, now just seemed like a form of public humilia-
tion. She was tired and her throat hurt and her head
was beginning to ache. She turned to Sawyer, stam-
mering, "I can wait."

Sawyer stared at her mouth.

Jordan stepped up and steered them both down
the hall as if they were nitwits who needed direction.
"Nonsense. Go take your soak. You'll feel better af-

terward." He limped pathetically as he walked, and Honey had the sneaking suspicion he did it on purpose, just to rattle her, not because she'd actually hurt him.

They were a strange lot—but she liked them anyway.

WARM WATER COVERED her to her chin, and she sighed in bliss. Finally, she felt clean again.

Where Sawyer had found the bubble bath, she didn't know, but she seriously doubted any of his brothers would lay claim to it. She smiled, wondering what they all thought of her. From the little bit she'd seen of them, they had a lot of similarities, yet they were each so different, too.

Of course, that might make sense considering their mother was evidently remarried. Honey couldn't imagine marrying once, much less twice. After the way her fiancé had used her, she wanted nothing to do with matrimony.

"You all right in there?"

"I'm fine. Go away."

"Just checking."

She smiled again. Sawyer had been hovering outside her door for the entire five minutes she'd been in the tub. He was something of a mother hen, which probably accounted for his chosen profession. He was meant to be a doctor. Everything about him spoke of a natural tendency to nurture. She liked it; she liked him. Too much.

The ultra-hot kiss… Well, she just didn't know what to think of it. Her lips still tingled and she licked them, savoring the memory of his taste. She'd almost married Alden, yet *he'd* never kissed her like that. And she'd certainly never thought about him the way she thought about Sawyer.

She'd known Alden two years and yet had never really wanted him. Not the way she wanted Sawyer after less than two days.

What would have happened if Jordan hadn't interrupted? Anything, nothing? She simply wasn't familiar enough with men to know. Not that familiarity would have helped, because she knew, even in her feverish state and even without a wealth of experience, Sawyer was different from most men. He was unique, a wonderful mix of pure rugged masculinity and incredible sensitivity.

He'd run the bathwater for her, placed a mat on the floor and fresh towels at hand and stacked her cleaned jeans and T-shirt on the toilet seat. All without mentioning the kiss and without getting too close to her. After he'd gotten everything ready, he'd looked at her, shook his head, then left with the admonition she should take as long as she liked, but not so long she got dizzy or overtired herself.

She intended to linger just a few minutes more. In all likelihood, the brothers would hold dinner for her. From all indications they enjoyed the novelty of having a woman underfoot and wouldn't pass up this opportunity to make her the center of attention again, as if she alone was the sole entertainment. She wasn't used to it, but she supposed she'd manage. For now, they were probably still organizing their own bath schedule, but how long would that take? Alden had always taken very short showers, his bathing a business, not a pleasure, whereas she'd always loved lingering in the water, sometimes soaking for hours.

She drained the tub and stepped out onto the mat. The steamy bath had relieved her throat some, and her muscles felt less achy after the soak. The towel Sawyer had provided was large and soft, and she wrapped herself in it, wishing she could just go back to bed and sleep for hours but knowing she wouldn't. She wanted to learn more about the brothers, she wanted to see the rest of the house and she needed to decide what to do.

She saw the edge of her peach panties showing from under the shirt, and she blushed. Somehow, the fact that Sawyer was now familiar with her underwear made their entire situation even more intimate, which meant more dangerous if she was honest with herself. How long would it take someone to figure out she was here? In a town this small, surely news traveled fast. Any strangers in town would have no problem finding her.

If she were smart, she'd forget her attraction to Sawyer, which weakened her resolve, and hightail it away as soon as possible.

"You about done in there?"

There was a slightly wary command to Sawyer's tone now. She grinned and called out, "Be right there. I'm getting dressed."

Silence vibrated between them, and Honey could just imagine where his thoughts had gone. She bit her bottom lip. Sawyer was too virile for his own good.

She heard him clear his throat. "Do you need any help?"

She almost choked, but ended up coughing as she finished smoothing her T-shirt into place. She pulled the door open and said to his face, "Nope."

His gaze moved over her slowly, from the top of her head, where she had braided her long hair and then knotted it to keep it dry, to her T-shirt and down her jeans to her bare feet.

She bit her lip. "I don't know what happened to my sandals."

"Gone."

"Gone?"

He shook himself, then met her steady gaze. "Yeah. One fell off in the lake and sank. The other might still be in your car—I dunno. At the time, I wasn't overly worried about it, not with an unconscious woman in my arms."

"Ah."

"You're not wearing a bra."

"You can tell?" She quickly crossed her arms over her chest and started to go back into the bathroom to look for herself in the mirror. Sawyer caught her.

He slowly pulled her arms away and held them to her sides. She didn't stop him. Everything she'd just told herself about staying detached faded into oblivion under his hot, probing gaze.

There they stood in the middle of the hallway, only a foot apart, and somehow fear, sickness and worry didn't exist. All she could think of was whether or not he'd kiss her again, and if he found her satisfactory. She'd always been pleased with her body, but then, she wasn't a man.

In a hoarse tone, he noted, "You have goose bumps." Gently, his big, rough hands chaffed up and down her bare arms.

"The…the house is cold."

He lifted one broad shoulder. "We keep the air-conditioning pretty low this time of year. Men are naturally warmer than women. Especially when the woman is so slight. I'll get one of my shirts for you to put on."

Excitement at the way he watched her made it impossible to speak. She nodded instead.

"You two going to stand there all day gawking? I'm starved."

Sawyer swiveled his head to look at Gabe. He still held Honey's arms. "How can you be starving when you didn't do anything all day?"

"I cooked rolls this morning, fixed your leak, then visited three women. That's a busy day in anyone's book." He grinned, then asked, "Should I just drag the table in here so we can all gather in the hallway? Is that what we're doing?"

Sawyer narrowed his gaze at his brother, but there was no menace in the look. "I have an appointment with Darlene tomorrow so she can get her flu shot. Maybe I'll mention your fondness for Mississippi mud pie. I hear Darlene's quite a cook."

Gabe took a step back, his grin replaced with a look of pure horror. "You fight dirty, Sawyer, you know that?"

Honey was amazed at the amount of grudging respect in Gabe's tone, as if fighting dirty impressed him. And then he stomped away. Sawyer laughed.

She wondered if she would ever understand this unique clan of men. She looked up at Sawyer. "What in the world was that all about?"

A half smile tilted his mouth. "Darlene has the hots for Gabe and she's looking to get married. She's been chasing him pretty hard for a while. Gabe has this old-fashioned sense of gallantry toward women, so he can't quite bring himself to come right out and tell her to leave him alone. He remains cautiously polite, and she remains determined."

"So if you mentioned a pie…"

"She'd be here every day with one." He grinned again and gently started her on her way. He moved slowly to accommodate her. The bath had tired her more than she wanted to admit, even to herself. Being sick or weak wasn't an easy concept to accept. Not for Honey.

"Why doesn't Gabe like her?"

"He likes her fine. She's a very attractive woman, beautiful even. Gabe went through school with her. I sometimes think that's the problem for him. He knows all the women around here so well. Gabe doesn't want to get serious about anyone, so he tries to avoid the women who are too obvious."

"Darlene's obvious?"

Sawyer shrugged. "Where Gabe's concerned, they all are. Darlene was just the first name to come to mind."

"Then she won't really be here tomorrow?"

"Nope." He put his arm around her waist and offered his support. "Come on, let's get that shirt and get to dinner so the savages can eat. If I leave them hungry too long, they're liable to turn on each other."

SAWYER WATCHED HER nibble delicately on her meal. And he watched his brothers watch her, amused that they were all so distracted by her. She looked uncomfortable with all the notice, but she didn't stomp on any more toes.

He doubted she had the energy for that. Her face was pale, her eyes dark with fatigue. Yet she refused to admit it. She had a lot of backbone, he'd give her that. As soon as she finished eating, he planned to tuck her back up in bed where she belonged.

He sat across from her—a deliberate choice so he *could* watch her. Gabe sat beside him, Casey sat beside her, with Morgan and Jordan at the head and foot of the table.

She'd been all round eyes and female amazement as she'd looked at the house on the way to the kitchen. Her appreciation warmed him. Most women who got through the front door were bemused with the styling of the house, all exposed pine and high ceilings and masculine functionality. The house wasn't overly excessive, but it was certainly comfortable for a family of large men. It had been his father's dream home, and his mother had readily agreed to it. At least, that's how she liked to tell it.

Sawyer grinned, because in truth, he knew there were few things his mother ever did readily. She was a procrastinator and liked to think things over thoroughly. Unlike his guest, who'd barreled through his fence and landed in his lake and then proceeded to try to slug him.

Sawyer noticed Morgan staring at him, and he wiped the grin off his face.

He returned his gaze to Honey and saw her look around the large kitchen. They never used the dining room, not for daily meals. But the kitchen was immense, one of the largest rooms in the house, and the place where they all seemed to congregate most often. For that reason they had a long pine table that could comfortably seat eight, as well as a short bar with three stools that divided the eating area from the cooking area. Pots hung on hooks, accessible, and along the out-side wall there was a row of pegs that held everything from hats and jackets to car and truck keys. The en-tire house had black checked curtains at the windows, but the ones in the kitchen were never closed. With the kitchen on the same side of the house as his bedroom, there was always a view of the lake. His mother had planned it that way because, she claimed, looking at the lake made the chore of doing dishes more agree-able. After they'd gotten older and all had to take their turn, they'd agreed. Then they'd gotten a dishwasher, but still there were times when one or more of them would be caught there, drinking a glass of milk or snacking and staring at the placid surface of the lake.

Honey shifted, peeking up through her lashes to find a lot of appreciative eyes gazing at her. She glanced back down with a blush. She was an enticing mix of bravado and shyness, making demands one minute, pink-cheeked the next.

He liked seeing his shirt on her, this one a soft, worn flannel in shades of blue that did sexy things for her eyes. And he liked the way her heavy hair half tumbled down her nape, escaping the loose knot and braid, with silky strands draping her shoulders.

She didn't look as chilled, and he wondered if her nipples were still pebbled, if they pressed against his shirt.

His hand shook and he dropped his fork, taking the attention away from Honey. To keep his brothers from embarrassing him with lurid comments on his state of preoccupation, he asked Honey, "How come your car was filled with stuff, but no clothes?"

She swallowed a tiny bite of chicken and shrugged.

She'd drunk nearly a full glass of tea but only picked at her food. "I left in a hurry. And that stuff was already in my car."

Sawyer glanced around and saw the same level of confusion on his brothers' faces that he felt.

Morgan pushed his empty plate away and folded his arms on the edge of the table. "*Why* was the stuff already in your car?"

She coughed, drank some tea, rubbed her forehead. Finally she looked at Morgan dead on. "Because I hadn't unloaded it yet." She aligned her fork carefully beside her plate and asked in her low, rough voice, "Why did you decide to become a sheriff?"

He looked bemused for just a moment, the customary scowl gone from his face. "It suited me." His eyes narrowed and he asked, "What do you mean you hadn't unloaded it? Unloaded it from where?"

"I'd just left my fiancé that very week. All I'd unloaded out of the car were my clothes and the things I needed right away. Before I could get the rest of the boxes out, I had to leave again. So the stuff was still in there. What do you mean, being a sheriff suits you? In what way?"

Her question was momentarily ignored while a silence as loud as a thunderclap hovered over the table. No one moved. No one spoke. All the brothers were watching Sawyer.

He drew a low breath. "She's not engaged anymore."

Gabe looked surprised. "She's not?"

"No."

"Why not?" Morgan demanded. "What happened?"

Before Sawyer could form an answer, Honey turned

very businesslike. "What do you mean, being a sheriff suits you?"

A small, ruthless smile touched Morgan's mouth as he caught on to her game. He leaned forward. "I get to call the shots since I'm the sheriff. People have to do what I say, and I like it. Why did you leave your fiancé?"

"I found out he didn't love me. And what makes you think people have to obey you? Do you mean you lord your position over them? You take advantage?"

"On occasion. Did *you* love your fiancé?"

"As it turns out…no. What occasions?"

Morgan didn't miss a beat. "Like the time I knew Fred Barker was knocking his wife around, but she wouldn't complain. I found him drunk in town and locked him up. Every time I catch him drinking, I run him through the whole gambit of sobriety tests. And I find a reason to heavily fine him when I can't stick him in jail. He found out drinking was too expensive, and sober, he doesn't abuse his wife." He tilted his head. "If you didn't love the guy, why the hell were you engaged to him in the first place?"

"For reasons of my own. If you—"

"Uh-uh. Not good enough, honey. What reasons?"

"None of your business."

His voice became silky and menacing. "You're afraid to tell me?"

"No." She stared down her nose at him. Even with dark circles under her red-rimmed eyes and her hair more down than up, the look was effectively condescending. "I just don't like being provoked. And you're doing it deliberately."

Morgan burst out laughing—a very rare occurrence—and dropped back in his chair. The way Jordan and Gabe stared at him, amazed, only made him laugh harder.

Sawyer appreciated the quick way she turned the tables on his dominating brother. It didn't happen often, and almost never with women. Evidently, Morgan had been amused by her, too, because he could be the most ruthless bastard around when it suited him. Sawyer was glad he hadn't had to intervene. He wouldn't have let Morgan badger her, but he had been hoping Morgan could get some answers.

He found Honey could be very closemouthed when it suited her. It amazed him that she could look almost pathetically frail and weak one moment, then mean as a junkyard dog the next.

Gabe waved his fork. "Morgan does everything deliberately. It's annoying, but it does make him a good sheriff. He doesn't react off the cuff, if you know what I mean."

Jordan looked at Sawyer. "Not to change the subject—"

Morgan snorted. "As if you could."

"—but do we have anything for dessert?"

"Yeah." Sawyer watched Honey as he answered, aware of her new tension. She wasn't crazy about discussing her personal life, but he had no idea how much of it had to do with her claimed threats or the possibility of a lingering affection for her ex. His jaw tightened, and he practically growled, "Frosted brownies."

Jordan sat back. "They're no good?"

"They're fine. And in case none of you noticed, there's a new pig in the barnyard."

Honey started, the tension leaving her as confusion took its place. "A pig?"

"Yeah." Casey finished off a glass of milk, then poured another. He was a bottomless pit, and growing more so each day. "Some of the families can't afford to pay cash, so they pay Dad in other ways. It keeps us Adam's apple high in desserts, which is good, but sometimes we end up with more farm animals than we can take care of. We have horses, and they're no problem, but the goats and pigs and stuff, they can be a nuisance."

Jordan looked at Sawyer. "The Mensons could use a pig. They had to sell off a lot of stock lately to build a new barn after theirs almost collapsed from age."

Sawyer continued to watch Honey, concerned that she was pushing herself too hard. At the moment, she didn't look ill so much as astonished. He grinned. Buckhorn was a step back in time, a close community that worked together, which he liked, but it would take some getting used to for anyone out of the area. "Feel free, Jordan. Hell, the last thing I want is another animal to take care of."

"They'll insist on paying something, but I'll make it real cheap."

"Trade for some of Mrs. Menson's homemade rock candy. Tell her I give it away to the kids when they come, and I'm nearly out."

"Good idea."

Honey looked around the table at all of them as Casey went to the counter to get the brownies. Her face was so expressive, even before she spoke, he knew she was worried. "You know everyone around here?"

With a short nod, Sawyer confirmed her suspicions.

"We know them, and most people in the surrounding areas. Buckhorn only boasts seven hundred people, give or take a couple dozen or so."

Suddenly she blurted out, "Have you told anyone about me?" and Sawyer knew she was talking to everyone, not just him. What the hell was she so afraid of?

Casey dropped a brownie on the side of her plate, but she barely seemed to notice. Her hands were clenched together on the edge of the table while she waited for an answer.

"Dad told me not to say anything to anyone," Casey offered, when no one else spoke up. "So far, I'd say no one knows about you."

"Why do you care?" Sawyer waited, but he knew she wouldn't tell him a damn thing. "Is it because you think these people you claim want to hurt you might follow you here?"

Morgan, still lounging back in his chair, rubbed his chin. "I could run a check on you, you know."

She snorted over that. "If you can, then you already have. But you didn't find anything, did you?"

He shrugged, disgruntled by her response to what had amounted to a threat. She didn't threaten easily.

Jordan leaned forward. "You say someone is after you. Could it be this fiancé of yours?"

"Ex-fiancé," Sawyer clarified, then suffered through the resultant snorts and snickers from his demented brothers.

"I thought so at first. He…well, he wasn't happy that I broke things off. He was actually pretty nasty about it, if you want the truth."

"Truth would be nice."

She glared at Sawyer so ferociously, he almost smiled. But not quite.

"I think it wounded his pride or something," she explained. "But regardless of how he carried on, my father is certain it couldn't be him."

"Why?"

"If you'd ever met Alden, you'd know he doesn't have a physically aggressive bone in his body. He'd hardly indulge in a dangerous chase. He's ambitious, intelligent, one of my father's top men. And my father pointed out how concerned Alden is with appearances and that he'd hardly be the type to cause a scene or run the risk of making the news." She shrugged. "That's what my father likes most about him."

Sawyer curled his lip, more angered at her father's lack of support than anything else. "Alden? He sounds like a preppy."

"He *is* a preppy. Very into the corporate image and climbing the higher social ladder, though I didn't always know that. My father scoffed at the idea that Alden would chase me because regardless of his temper, I wouldn't be that important to him in his grand scheme of things."

He watched her face and knew she was holding something back, but what? Sawyer pushed her, hoping to find answers. "Even though you walked out on him?"

"I left, I didn't walk out."

"What the hell's the difference?"

She sighed wearily. "You make it sound like I staged a dramatic exit. It wasn't like that at all. I found out he didn't care about me, I packed up my stuff, wrote him a polite note and left."

Her body was tense, her expression carefully neutral. Sawyer narrowed his gaze. "Why did he ask you to marry him in the first place if he didn't care about you?"

She closed up on him, her face going blank, and Sawyer knew she still didn't trust him, didn't trust any of them. It made him so angry his hands curled into fists. He wasn't the violent type, but right now, he would relish one of Morgan's barroom brawls.

Sawyer surged to his feet to pace. He wanted to shake her; he wanted to pull her up against his body, feel her softness and kiss her silly again until she stopped resisting him, until she stopped fighting. He tightened his thighs, trying for an ounce of logic. "How in hell are we supposed to figure this out if you won't even answer a few simple questions?"

Morgan leaned back and stacked his hands behind his head. Jordan propped his chin on a fist. Gabe lifted one brow.

"You're not supposed to figure anything out." Honey drew a deep breath, watching him steadily. "You're just supposed to let me go."

CHAPTER SIX

SAWYER'S DARK EYES glittered with menace, and his powerful body tensed.

Watching him with an arrested expression, Morgan murmured, "Fascinating."

Jordan, also watching, said, "Shh."

Honey turned to Gabe, ignoring the other brothers, and especially Sawyer's astounding reaction to her refusal of help. She couldn't look at him without hurting, without wishing things could be different. She'd known him almost no time at all, yet she felt as if she'd known him forever. He'd managed, without much effort, to forge a permanent place in her memory. After she was gone, she'd miss him horribly.

Gabe grinned at her. It seemed they all loved to be provoking, but she wasn't up to another round. All the questions on Alden had shaken her. She'd tried to answer without telling too much, juggling her replies so that Sawyer might be appeased but at the same time wouldn't learn too much. Alden had been so vicious about her refusal to come back to him, to continue on with the marriage, she didn't dare involve anyone else in her troubles, especially not Sawyer, until she better understood the full risk, and why it existed in the first place.

She'd been looking blankly at Gabe for some time

now, and she cleared her throat. "Does your handyman expertise extend to cars?"

"Sure."

Jordan kicked him under the table. Honey knew it, but in light of everything else they'd done, it didn't seem that strange or important.

While Gabe rubbed his shin and glared daggers at Jordan, Sawyer stalked over to her side of the table. With every pump of her heart, she was aware of him standing so close. She could feel his heat, breathe his scent, unique above and beyond the other brothers, who each pulsed with raw vitality. But her awareness, her female sensitivity, was attuned to Sawyer alone. Her skin flushed as if he'd stroked those large, rough hands down her body, when in fact he'd done no more than stand there, gazing down at her.

When she refused to meet his gaze, he propped both hands on his hips and loomed over her. "Gabe can fix your car, but you're not going anywhere until I'm satisfied that it's safe, which means you're going to have to quit stalling and explain some things."

Honey sighed again and tilted her head back to see him. Sawyer was so tall, even when standing she was barely even with his collarbone. Since she was sitting, he seemed as tall as a mountain. She really was tired of getting the third degree by overpowering men. "Sawyer, how can I explain what I don't understand myself?"

"Maybe if you'd just tell us what you do understand, we could come up with something that makes sense."

Leave it to a man to think he could understand what a woman couldn't. Her father had always been the same, so condescending, ready to discount her input on everything. And Alden. She shuddered at her own stupidity in ever agreeing to marry the pompous ass. Now that she'd met Sawyer and seen how caring a man could be…

With a groan she leaned forward, elbows on the table, and covered her face with her hands.

She was getting in too deep, making comparisons she shouldn't make. Morgan was right, he could start tracking her down. And since she didn't know what the threat was, only that it was serious, it was entirely possible he'd accidentally lead the threat to her—and to this family. She couldn't have that.

Car keys hung accessible on the wall by the back door. Sawyer wouldn't be sleeping in the same room with her tonight; there was no need. She'd have to take advantage of the opportunity. She'd borrow one of their vehicles, go into town and then get a bus ticket. She could leave a note telling Sawyer where to find his car.

Just the thought of leaving distressed her on so many levels, she knew she had to go as soon as possible, whether she felt up to it physically or not.

Sawyer evidently wanted her for a fling; he'd made his interest very obvious with that last kiss. He'd also indicated he found her to be a royal pain in the backside, and no wonder, considering she'd wrecked his fence and left a rusted car in his lake, along with taking his bed and keeping him up at night. When he wasn't watching her with sexual heat in his dark eyes, he was frowning at her with unadulterated frustration.

She felt the same incredible chemistry between them, but she also felt so much more. He had the family life she'd always wondered about, the closeness and camaraderie, the sharing and support that she'd always believed to be a mere fairy tale. So often she'd longed for the life-style he possessed. And he was that special kind of man who not only accepted that life-style, but also contributed to it, a driving force in making it work for everyone.

She found Sawyer very sexually appealing, but he also felt safe and comforting. Security was a natural part of him, something built into his genetic makeup. And after the way her engagement had ended, she would never settle for half measures again, not when there was so much more out there.

She heard the shifting of masculine feet, a few rumbling questions, then Sawyer leaned down, his hand gently cradling the back of her head. "Honey?"

With new resolution she pushed her chair back, forcing Sawyer to move. "You're not going to let up on this, are you?"

Morgan snorted. Sawyer shook his head.

"All right." With an exaggerated sigh, she looked down, trying to feign weary defeat when inside she teemed with determination. "I'll tell you anything I can. But it's a long, complicated story. Couldn't it wait until the morning?"

She peeked up and caught Sawyer's suspicious frown. With a forced cough that quickly turned real, she said, "My throat is already sore. And I'm so tired."

Just that easily, Sawyer was swayed. He took her arm and helped her away from the table. "The morning will be fine. You've overdone it today."

By morning, she'd be long gone. And once she got to the next town, she'd contact her sister and let her know she was all right, then she could go with her original plan. She'd hire a private detective and pay him to figure out what was going on while she stayed tucked away, and those she cared about would stay safely un-involved. She'd never forget this incredible family of men…but they would quickly forget her.

"Sawyer…" Morgan said in clear warning, obviously not pleased with the plan. Honey knew that particular brother couldn't care less if she was sick. Even though she wasn't really *that* sick, not anymore. But he didn't know it.

"It's under control, Morgan." Sawyer's tone brooked no arguments.

Morgan did hesitate, but then he forged on. "I know Honey's still getting over whatever ails her, but we really do need—"

With a loud gasp, she froze, then stiffened as his words sank in. Slowly, she turned to face Morgan. "You know my name."

There was no look of guilt on his hard, handsome face, just an enigmatic frown.

Sawyer shook his head in irritation while glaring at Morgan. "Around here, everything female is called honey."

Casey nodded. "We've got an old mule out in the field that Jordan named Honey because that's all she'd answer to."

She almost laughed at the sincerity on Casey's face, but instead she pulled free of Sawyer's hold and blazed an accusation. "He wasn't using an endearment. He was using *my name*."

Morgan shrugged. "Honey Malone. Yeah, I went through your purse."

Her eyes widened. "You admit it? Just like that?" She nearly choked on resentment and coughed instead.

While Sawyer patted her on the back and Casey hurried to hand her a drink, Morgan said, "Why not?" He rolled his massive shoulders, not the least concerned with her ire. "You show up here under the most suspicious circumstances and you claim someone is trying to hurt you. Of course I wanted some facts. And how could I run that check on you if I didn't have your name? I thought you'd already figured that out."

Her mouth opened twice, but nothing came out. She should have realized he'd already gone through her things, only she'd been so busy trying to hold her own against him, and she'd taken his words as an idle threat, not a fait accompli. She was making a lot of stupid mistakes, trusting them all when she shouldn't.

Tonight. She had to leave tonight.

Then she remembered her bare feet and wanted to groan. She couldn't very well get on a bus without shoes. Maybe she could swipe a pair from Casey. She glanced at his feet and saw they were as large as Sawyer's. Good grief, she was in a house of giants.

Sawyer tipped up her chin. "He only looked in your wallet to find your name. He didn't go through every pocket or anything. Your privacy wasn't invaded any more than necessary. Your purse is in the closet in my room, if you want to check and make sure nothing is missing."

She ground her teeth together. "It isn't that." The last thing she was worried about was them stealing from her. She had little enough with her that was worth anything.

"Then what is it?"

She thought quickly, but trying to rationalize her behavior while the touch of Sawyer's hand still lin-

gered on her face was nearly impossible. Everything
about him set her off, but especially his touch. No matter where his fingers lingered, she felt it everywhere.
"I... I don't have any shoes."

He frowned down at her bare feet for a long moment. "Are your feet cold?"

She wanted to hit him, but instead she turned away.
Her brain was far too muddled to keep this up. If she
didn't get away from him, she'd end up begging him
to let her stay. "I'm going to bed now. Jordan, thank
you for dinner."

He answered in his low, mesmerizing voice, no less
effective for the shortness of his reply. "My pleasure."

She glanced at him. "I'd offer to help with the
dishes, but I have the feeling—"

"Your offer would definitely be turned down." Sawyer released her, but added, "I'll be in to check on you
in a few minutes."

The last thing she needed was to be tempted by him
again. "No, thank you."

He stared at her hard, his gaze unrelenting. "In a
few minutes, Honey, so do whatever it is you feel you
have to do before going to bed. I left the antibiotics and
the ibuprofen on the bathroom counter so you wouldn't
forget to take them. After you're settled, I want to listen to your chest again."

There was a lot of ribald macho humor over that
remark. Jordan choked down a laugh, and this time
Gabe kicked him.

With a glare that encompassed them all, Honey
stalked off. She was truly weary and wondering where
in the world she was going to find shoes for her feet
so she could steal a car and make her getaway from a

group of large, overprotective, domineering men whom she didn't really want to leave at all.

Gads, life had gotten complicated.

HE KNOCKED ON the door, but she didn't answer. Sawyer assumed she was mad and ignoring him, not that he'd let her get away with it. He opened the door just a crack—and saw the bed was empty. She was gone. His first reaction was pure rage, tinged with panic, totally out of proportion, totally unexpected. He shoved the door wide and stalked inside, and then halted abruptly when he saw her. His gut tightened and his heart gave a small thump at the picture she presented.

Honey sat on the small patio outside his room. She had her feet curled up on a chair, her head resting to the side, and she was looking at the lake. Or maybe she wasn't looking at anything at all. He couldn't see her entire face, only a small part of her profile. She looked limp, totally wrung out, and it angered him again when he thought of her stubbornness, her refusal to let him help her.

No one had ever refused his help. He was the oldest, and his brothers relied on him for anything they might need, including advice. Casey got everything from him that he had to give. Members of the community sought him out when they needed help either with a medical problem or any number of others things. He was a figurehead in the town, on the town council and ready and willing to assist. He gave freely, whatever the need might be, considering it his right, part and parcel with who and what he was. But now, this one small woman wanted to shut him out. *Like hell*.

Her physical impact on his senses was staggering.

But it was nothing compared to the damn emotional impact, because the emotions were the hardest to fight and to understand. If it was only sex he wanted, he'd drive over the county limits and take care of the need. But he wanted *her* specifically, and it was making him nuts.

Being summer, it was still light out at eight o'clock, but the sun was starting to sink in the sky, slowly dipping behind a tree-topped hill across the lake. The last rays of sunshine sent fiery ribbons of color over the smooth surface of the water. A few ducks swam by, and far out a fish jumped.

Sawyer went back and closed the bedroom door silently, drawn to her though he knew he should just walk away. As he passed the bathroom, he noticed her toothbrush, still wet, on the side of the sink, along with a damp washcloth over the spigot, and his comb that he'd lent her. Those things looked strangely natural in his private domain, as if they belonged. She'd evidently prepared for bed, then was lured—as he often was—by the incredible serenity of the lake.

Though the house had a very comfortable covered deck across the entire front and along one side by the kitchen, he'd still insisted on adding the small patio off his bedroom. In the evening, he often sat outside and just watched the night, waiting for the stars or the clouds to appear, enjoying the way mist rose from the lake to leave lingering dew on everything. The peacefulness of it would sink into his bones, driving away any restlessness. Many times his son or one of his brothers would join him. They didn't talk, they just sat in peace together, enjoying the closeness.

He'd never shared a moment like this with a woman, not even his wife.

He approached Honey on silent feet. She looked melancholy and withdrawn, and for a long time he simply took in the sight of her. He'd seen her looking fatigued with illness and worry, and he'd seen her eyes snapping with anger or panic. He'd watched her cheeks warm with a blush, her brow pucker with worry over his son. He'd even seen her muster up her courage to embrace a verbal duel with Morgan. Sawyer had known her such a short time, but in that time, he had truly related to her. Whereas hours might be spent on a date, her health had dictated they bypass the cordial niceties of that convention, and their relationship had been intimate from the first. The effects were devastating. He'd already spent more time in her company than most men would through weeks of dating.

Every facet of her personality enthralled him more than it should have. He wanted to see her totally relaxed, without a worry, finally trusting him to take care of her and make things right.

And most of all, he wanted to see her face taut with fierce pleasure as he made love to her, long and slow and deep.

He slid the French door open, and she looked at him.

There were two outdoor chairs on his private patio, and he pulled one close to her. He spoke softly in deference to the quiet of the night and the quiet in her blue eyes. "You look pensive."

"Hmm." She turned to stare back out at the lake, tilting her head at the sound of the crickets singing in the distance. "I was…uneasy. But this is so calming, like having your problems washed away. It's hard to maintain any energy out here, even for irritation."

"You shouldn't be irritated just because we want to help."

Her golden brown lashes lowered over her eyes. "Dinner with your family was...interesting. Around our house, there was only my sister and me. It was always quiet, and if we talked, it was in whispers because the house was so silent. Dinner wasn't a boisterous event."

"We can take a little getting used to."

She smiled. "No, I enjoyed myself. The contrast was wonderful, if that makes any sense."

That amused him, because meals at home were always a time to laugh and grouse and share. She'd probably find a lot of contrasts, and he hoped she enjoyed them all. But it also made him sad, thinking of how lonely her life must have been. "It makes perfect sense," he assured her.

"Good."

Because it had surprised him, he added, "You held your own with my brothers."

She laughed, closing her eyes lazily. "Yes. Morgan is a bully, but I have the feeling he's fair."

Sawyer considered her words and the way she'd spoken them. "Honorable might be a better word. Morgan can be very unfair when he's convinced it's for the best. He's a no-holds-barred kind of man when he's got a mission."

Her long blond hair trailed over her shoulder all the way to her thigh, catching the glow of the setting sun as surely as the lake did. She tilted her chin up to a faint warm breeze, and his blood rushed at the instinctively feminine gesture and the look of bliss on her face. "It was so cold inside," she whispered, "I wanted to feel the sunshine. I came out here to warm up, then couldn't seem to make myself go back in."

They did keep the air low, but not so much that she should be uncomfortable. He reached over and placed his palm on her forehead, then frowned. "You could be a little feverish again. Did you take the ibuprofen I left in the bathroom?"

"Yes, I did. And the antibiotic." She blinked her eyes open and sighed. "Did I thank you for taking such good care of me, Sawyer?"

A low thrumming started in his veins, making his body throb. He could feel his own heartbeat, the acceleration of his pulse—just because she'd said his name. "I don't know, but it isn't necessary."

"To me it is. Thank you."

He swallowed down a groan. He wanted to lift her onto his lap and hold her for hours, just touching her, breathing in her spicy scent, which kept drifting to him in subtle, teasing whiffs. Right now, she smelled of sunshine and warmth and the musky scent of woman, along with a fragrance all her own, one that seemed to be seeping into his bones. It drove him closer to the edge and made him want to bury himself in the unique scent.

But beyond that, he wanted to strip her naked and settle her into his bed. He wanted to look his fill, to feel her slender thighs wrap tight around his hips, her belly pressed to his abdomen, her body open and accepting as he pushed inside for a nice long slow ride, taking his time to get her out of his blood.

He wanted to comfort her and he wanted to claim

her, conflicting emotions that left him angry at his own weakness.

He was aware of her watching him, and then she said, "Can I ask you a few questions?"

He laughed, and the sound was a bit rusty with his growing arousal. "I'd have to be a real bastard to say no, considered how my brothers and I have questioned you tonight."

She sent him an impish smile. "True enough." She curled her legs up a little higher then rested her cheek on her bent knees. "Why did Morgan really become a sheriff?"

That wasn't at all what he'd been expecting, and her interest in his brother brought on a surge of annoyance. "You think there's a secret reason?"

"I think there's a very personal reason." She shooed a mosquito away from her face, then resettled herself. "And I'm curious about him."

Sawyer felt himself tense, though he tried to hide it. "Curious, as in he's a man and you're a woman?"

She looked at his mouth. "No. Curious as in he's your brother, and therefore a part of you."

Satisfied, his twinge of unreasonable jealousy put to rest, Sawyer turned to look at the lake. "There's no denying our relationship, is there? Morgan and I share a lot of the same features, even though he is a bit of an overgrown hulk. Except I have my father's eyes, and he has my mother's."

"You look alike more so than the other two."

"We had a different father. Our father died when Morgan was just a baby."

"Oh." She shifted, unfolding her long legs and sitting upright. She reached over and touched his arm, just a gentle touch with the tips of her fingers, lightly stroking, but the effect on his body was startling. He felt that damn stroke in incredible places.

"I'm sorry," she whispered. "I had thought your mother just divorced."

He covered her hand with his own to still the tantalizing movement. "She was that, too."

"But…"

To keep the emotions she evoked at bay, he launched into a dispassionate explanation. "She married Jordan's father when I was five, and divorced him shortly after Jordan was born. I barely remember him, but he lost his job after the marriage and he started drinking. It became a problem. At first my mother tried to help him through it, but she would only tolerate so much in front of her children, and he couldn't seem to help himself, or so she's said. So she left him. Or rather, she divorced him and he took off and we never hear from him. My mother never requested child support, and he never stayed around long enough to offer it."

"Oh, God. Poor Jordan."

"Yeah. He wasn't much more than an infant when they divorced, so he didn't know his father at all. He's never mentioned him much. He was always a quiet kid. Morgan loved to beat up the boys who gave Jordan any grief. We both used to try to protect him. We sort of understood that he was different, quiet but really intense."

"He's not so quiet now." She made a face, wrinkling her nose, probably remembering the way Jordan had teased her about her bath. "He's not as demanding as Morgan, but I wouldn't exactly call him shy."

"No. He's not shy." Sawyer smiled, thinking of how

she'd stomped on Jordan's foot. "None of my brothers are. But Jordan isn't as outgoing as the others, either."

"When did he change?" An impish light twinkled in her eyes. "After his first girlfriend?"

She was teasing, and Sawyer liked that side of her, too. "Actually, it happened when he was only ten. He found some kids tormenting a dog. He told them to leave the dog alone, and instead, one boy threw a rock at it. The dog, a really pitiful old hound, let out a yelp, and Jordan went nuts on the boys." Sawyer chuckled, remembering that awesome day. "He was like a berserker—impressed the hell out of everyone who watched."

Honey shook her head. "Males are so impressed by the weirdest things."

Sawyer glanced at her. "This wasn't weird! It was life-altering stuff. Sort of a coming-of-age kinda thing. My mother had always taught us to be good to animals, and Jordan couldn't bear to see the old dog harassed. The boys were two years older than Jordan, and there were three of them. Morgan and I were on the sidelines, waiting to jump in if we needed to, but being so much older, we couldn't very well start brawling with twelve-year-olds."

"Too bad they weren't older."

He heard her impudent wit, but pretended she was serious. "Yeah. Neither of us is fond of idiots who abuse animals. We wouldn't have minded a little retribution of our own. But Jordan held his ground and did a good job of making his point. He ended up with a black eye, a couple dozen bruises, and he needed stitches in his knee. My mother liked to have a fit when she saw him. And Morgan and I got lectured for hours for not stopping the fight. But no one messed with Jordan again after that. And anytime an animal was hurt or sick, someone would tell Jordan. I swear, that man can whisper an animal out of an illness."

"So that started him on the road to being a vet. What made Morgan decide to be a sheriff?"

Sawyer turned her hand over and laced his fingers with hers. Her hands were small, slender, warm. Along the shore of the lake, a few ducks waddled by then glided effortlessly into the water, barely leaving a ripple. Peonies growing on the other side of the house lent a sweet fragrance to the air, mixing with her own enticing scent.

He was horny as hell, and she wanted to talk about his brothers.

"Morgan is a control freak," he managed to say around the restriction in his throat.

"I noticed."

Since she'd been a recipient of his controlling ways, he supposed she had. "He used to get into a lot of scrapes, sort of a natural-born brawler. Give him a reason to tussle and he'd jump on it. He got in trouble a few times at school, and my mother was ready to ground him permanently. Gabe's dad was a good influence on him."

Honey started. "Your mother was married three times?"

Sawyer didn't take offense at her surprise. No one had been more surprised by that third marriage than his mother herself. "Yeah." He smiled, dredging up fond memories. "I was eight years old when Brett Kasper started hanging around. My mother wanted nothing to do with him, and I'd ask her why, since he was so obviously trying to get in good with her and he was a nice guy and *we* all liked him—even Morgan. Brett would offer to clean out her gutters, play baseball with us, run to open doors for her. But he was always honest about why he did it. He'd tell us he was wooing our mother and ask for our help." Sawyer laughed. "We'd all talk about him to her until finally she'd threaten to withhold dessert if we mentioned his name again. I now understand how burned she felt, losing her first husband in the military, divorcing her second husband as a mistake."

"Because you went through a divorce, too?"

He wouldn't get into that with her. The divorce hadn't bothered him that much, unfortunately. It was all the deceit that had changed his life.

Sawyer shrugged. "My mother worked damn hard to keep everything going, raising four sons, working, keeping up the house. My father's pension helped, even paid for a lot of my college. And we all pitched in, but it wasn't easy for her."

"She must be incredible."

"Brett used to say she was as stubborn as an aged mule and twice as ornery."

"What a romantic."

Sawyer laughed. "He didn't cut her any slack, which is good because my mother is strong and she wouldn't want a man who couldn't go toe to toe with her. Brett wanted her and he went after her, even though she was gun-shy and didn't want to take another chance. Sometimes she was rude as hell to him. But Brett was pushy and he kept hanging around until he finally wore her down."

Honey gave him a dreamy smile. "A real happy ending."

"Yeah. They've been married twenty-eight years

now. Brett's great. I love him. He's always treated us the same, as if he'd fathered the lot of us. Even Morgan, who can be so damn difficult."

"You said he helped Morgan?"

"He helped redirect Morgan's more physical tendencies by signing him up for boxing. And he set up a gym of sorts in the basement, which we all used until Gabe moved down there. Now there's just a weight room in what is supposed to be a den. My mother frets every time she sees it."

Honey laughed again, a low, husky sound that vibrated along his nerve endings and made him acutely aware of how closely they sat together, their isolation from the others, the heaviness of the humid summer air. He reacted to it all and kissed her knuckles before he could stop himself.

Just that brief touch made him want so much more.

Trying to regroup, he said, "Morgan chose to be a sheriff because he likes control, and for him, that's the ultimate control. But regardless of what he says, it isn't control over other people, it's control of himself. He knows he's more wild than not, that he'll always be more aggressive than most people. Choosing to run for sheriff was his way of forcing himself to be in control at all times."

She gave a very unladylike snort. "I think he's a big fraud."

Her misperceptions prompted Sawyer to grin. He could just tell she and Morgan would butt heads again and again if they spent much time around each other.

Of course, that was iffy, with her planning to leave and him planning to eventually let her.

"The hell of it is, Morgan never starts fights, he just

finishes them. With that scowl of his, he can bring on a lot of attitude that men, especially bullies, generally object to. And to be fair, he always gives the other guy a chance to back off, but there's that gleam in his eyes that taunts. Morgan's always had an excess of energy and he gets edgy real quick. So to burn up energy, he either fights or he…" Appalled at what he'd almost said, Sawyer stemmed his ridiculous outpouring of personal confidences, wondering if he'd already stepped over the line. He was so comfortable with her, a fact he'd only realized, and she was so damn easy to talk to, he'd completely forgotten himself.

She tilted her head, her eyes alight with curiosity. "Or what?"

"Never mind."

"Oh, no, you don't!" She shook her head even as she fought off a yawn. "No way. You can't just tease me like that and then not tell me."

She looked sleepy and warm and piqued, all at once. Again he felt that unfamiliar rush of lust and tenderness and knew he was reacting to her when he shouldn't. But he just couldn't help himself. She drew him in without even trying.

Caught by her gaze, he admitted in a hoarse tone, "Morgan either fights…or he makes love. Either way, he burns off energy."

Her cheeks immediately colored and her eyes widened. "Oh. Yeah, I guess… I guess that could work."

Having caught her uncertainty, Sawyer leaned forward to see her averted face. "You don't sound certain."

She cleared her throat. "Well, it's not like…that is…" She peeked at him, her brow furrowed in thought. "Is it?"

Sawyer stared at her, blank-brained for just a mo-

ment, then he surged to his feet. Damn, if she was asking him if sex was really all that vigorous, he didn't
think he could suffice with a mere verbal answer.
Surely a woman as sexy, as attractive as she would
already know! Damn her, she plagued his brain with
her contradictions, her looks earthy and sensual, her
behavior so modest. Bold one minute, timid the next.

He stared down at the lake for long moments, trying to get himself together and fight off the surge of
lust that swamped him. He heard her stand behind him.

"Sawyer?"

"What?" He didn't mean to sound so brusque, but it
felt as if she were killing him and his resolve by small
degrees. Torturous, but also extremely erotic.

"Can I ask you something?"

Her tone was hesitant and shy, and he prayed her
question wouldn't be about sex. He was only human,
and she was too much temptation.

He looked at her over his shoulder and tried to
dampen his frustration. "What is it with all these questions? I thought your throat was sore."

"It is. But your family is so different, so special. It's
the way I always thought families should be. I've enjoyed hearing about them. And I have had a few things
vexing my mind."

A grin took him by surprise; she sounded so worried. "Vexing you, huh?"

"Yes."

"All right." Turning, he gave her his full attention.
The setting sun did amazing things to her fair hair
and her blue eyes while making her skin appear even
smoother. It was still hot and humid outside, even
though it was evening, and she'd removed his shirt.

He could visually trace the outline of her breasts beneath the T-shirt, the full shape of them, the roundness,
even the delicate jut of her nipples. His abdomen pulled
tight in an effort to fight off the inevitable reaction in
his body, but he still felt himself harden. He could see
the narrowness of her midriff, the dip of her waist. She
hadn't tucked the T-shirt in, and still the flare of her
hips was obvious and suggestive.

She shaded her eyes with a small hand and blurted,
"Why did you kiss me?"

Taken completely off guard, he blinked at her. After
a moment, he said, "Come again?"

"Earlier." She bit the side of her mouth and shifted
nervously. "When you kissed me. Why'd you do it?"

She had to ask? He was thirty-six years old, had
been kissing females since he was twelve, and yet none
of them had ever asked him such a thing. Trying to figure out what she was thinking, he countered her question with one of his own. "Why do you think I did it?"

She looked so young when she turned bashful. He
wondered at the man who'd given her up, who hadn't
really loved her, as she'd put it. Sawyer had already decided he was a damn fool. Now, seeing her like this, he
was glad. She deserved better than a fool, better than
a man who'd be stupid enough to let her go.

He stepped closer, so tempted to kiss her again, to
show her instead of tell her about her appeal. But he
knew it wasn't right, that he was taking advantage of
her situation and confusion. She stared down at her
bare feet. "My sister always told me I was pretty."

He wanted to see her eyes, but no matter how he
willed it, she wouldn't look up. "You're very pretty.
But I hardly kiss every pretty woman I see." And in

truth, he'd known women much more beautiful. They simply hadn't interested him; they didn't draw him as she did. "Besides," he added, trying for some humor, "your face is bruised, and your lips are chapped, and there's dark circles under your eyes."

"Oh." She touched her cheeks, then let her hands drop away with a frown.

He waited while she thought about that. "Alden used to tell me I was shaped...okay."

"Okay?"

She gave a grave nod. "Men can be...enticed, by physical stuff, I know."

She was attempting to sound blasé, and he barely held back his laugh. Alden must have been a complete and total putz. She was much better off without him. "Honey, you're sexy as hell, and sure, to some men that's all that matters, but again—" He gave a philosophical shrug.

"You don't kiss every sexy woman you see?"

"Exactly."

She licked her lips, and her expression was earnest, if reserved. "So then why did you?"

Very softly, he admitted, "I shouldn't have."

"That doesn't answer my question."

Her cheek was sun-warmed beneath his palm as he tilted up her face, determined to see her eyes, to read her. Besides, he couldn't seem to *not* touch her. "What's your real question, sweetheart?"

Her eyes darkened, and the pulse in her throat raced, but she didn't look away this time. She fidgeted, shifting from one foot to the next. "Did...did you think since I was available, but determined not to be here too long, you could just...you know. Have a quick fling?"

He couldn't remember the last time he'd smiled so much. But she amused and delighted him with her every word—when she wasn't provoking him and pricking his temper. She was both the most open, honest woman he'd ever met, sharing her feelings and emotions without reserve or caution, and the most stubbornly elusive, refusing to tell him any necessary truths. "Anyone who knows me could tell you I'm hardly the type for a quick indiscreet fling, or any kind of fling. But certainly not with someone who didn't want the same."

She looked startled. "You think I don't want—"

Interrupting that thought seemed his safest bet. "I don't think you know what you want right now. But it surely isn't to be used."

Her eyes narrowed in suspicion. "Meaning?"

"Meaning I'm human, and I get restless like any other man. But I have a reputation here, and a lot of people look up to me. I have to be very circumspect."

She stared at him, her expression almost awed that such sanctimonious words had escaped his mouth. He felt like an idiot. "Honey, I'm sorry, but I just can't—"

She took an appalled step back. "I wasn't asking you to!"

His mouth quirked again, but he ruthlessly controlled it. "When I get too restless, there are women I know *outside* of town who feel just as turned off by commitment as I do. They're content with physical release and no strings."

Her mouth formed an O.

Feeling aggrieved, he explained, "They're *nice* women, who are content with their lives, but they get lonely. The world being what it is, it's not easy to find someone respectable who isn't looking for marriage. We suit, and it's simple and convenient and—"

Her face was bright red. He couldn't believe he'd gotten into this.

"I see. So you…indulge yourself with these women you don't really care about. But I don't fall in that category?"

His teeth clicked together. He wanted to shake her. He wanted to haul her up close and nestle his painful erection against her soft belly. He shook his head, as much for himself as for her. "You most definitely don't fall into that category. You're young and confused and scared. You're not from around here and you don't know me well enough to know I have no desire to remarry. And that's why I said I shouldn't have kissed you." He shoved his hands into his pockets and took a determined step away. "It won't happen again, so you don't have to worry about it."

She drew a long, considering breath. "I wasn't worried. Not really. I just wasn't sure…" She bit her lip and then blurted, "Most of the time you don't seem to like me very much. You feel responsible for some dumb reason, and you're kind enough, but… I just wasn't sure what to think about the kiss."

She obviously had no experience with aroused men, to mistake his personal struggles for dislike. And no sooner did he have that thought than he tried to squelch it. It was dangerous territory and would lead him into more erotic thoughts of what he'd like to show her, and just how much he liked her. Instead of explaining, he said, "I'd like you a whole lot more if you'd stop keeping secrets."

She got her back up real quick, turning all prickly on him. "We agreed we'd talk in the morning."

"So we did." He was more than ready to let it drop before he dug himself in too deep. "Why don't you head on in." If she stood there looking at him even a minute more, he was liable to forget his resolve and gather her close and kiss her senseless—despite all the damn assurances he'd just given her. These uncontrollable tendencies had never bothered him before; now he felt on the ragged edge, like a marauder about to break under the restraint. The things he wanted to do to her didn't bear close scrutiny. "You look ready to drop," he quickly added, hoping she wouldn't argue.

Sighing, she turned to go in. "I feel ready to drop."

Sawyer followed her through the door. The cold air-conditioning was a welcome relief as it washed against his heated skin. It may be evening, but summer in Kentucky meant thick humidity and temperatures in the nineties, sometimes even through the night.

Honey came to an abrupt halt beside the bed and stared at the fresh linens. "Someone changed the bed."

"I did. I figured you'd want clean sheets."

She gave him a querulous frown for reasons he couldn't begin to fathom, then sat on the edge of the mattress and reached for the cat. Until she did so, Sawyer hadn't realized the cat was back. Her calico coloring made her blend perfectly with the patchwork quilt.

Honey lifted the cat onto her lap and stroked her, being especially careful with her bandaged tail. "So I know you won't kiss me again, but I still don't know why you did in the first place."

Watching her pet the cat mesmerized him—until she spoke, breaking the spell with her unsettling question. He didn't want to answer her because he knew it would somehow complicate things further. But she had that stubborn, set look again, and he figured she wouldn't go to bed until he satisfied her curiosity. He crossed his arms over his chest and studied her while searching for the right words. "I kissed you because I couldn't seem to stop myself."

"But why?"

He growled, "Because you're quick-witted and sweet and you have more courage than's good for you. And you're stubborn and you make me nuts with your secrets." Almost reluctantly, he admitted, "And you smell damn good."

She stared up at him, bemused. "You kissed me because I annoy you with my stubbornness and...and my *courage?*"

He gave a sharp nod. "And as I said, you're smart and you smell good. Incredibly good."

"But I thought—"

"I know what you thought." She'd complained about smelling like the lake when to him, she'd smelled like herself, a woman he wanted.

He started to ask her why she'd kissed him back, because she had. She'd nearly singed his eyebrows with the way she'd clung to him, how her mouth had moved under his, the way she'd greedily accepted his tongue, curling her own around it.

He shuddered, then headed for the door, escape his only option. Somehow he knew he'd be better off not knowing what had motivated her. "I won't sleep in here tonight, but if you need anything just let me know. I'm using the front bedroom."

She rushed to her feet. "I hadn't thought… I didn't mean to chase you out of your own room!"

There was so much guilt in her face, he slowed for just a heartbeat. "You didn't chase me out. I just figured since you were already settled…"

"I'll switch rooms." She took an anxious step toward him. "You shouldn't have to be inconvenienced on my account."

He hesitated a moment more, caught between wanting to reassure her and knowing he had to put distance between them. "It's not a problem. Good night."

She started to say something else, but he pulled the door shut. Truth was, he liked knowing she was in his bed. He didn't know if he'd ever be able to sleep there again without thinking of her—and dreaming.

CHAPTER SEVEN

THE HOUSE WAS eerily quiet as she slipped the bedroom door open, using only the moonlight filtering in through the French doors to guide her way. Though she hadn't lied about being exhausted, she hadn't slept. The clean sheets no longer smelled of Sawyer's crisp, masculine scent. She'd resented the loss.

She listened with her ear at the crack in the door, but there was nothing. Everyone was in bed, as she'd suspected, probably long asleep. She pictured Sawyer, on his back, his long body stretched out, hard, hot. Her heart gave an excited lurch.

He'd kissed her because she was smart.

And sweet and stubborn and… She'd wanted to cry when he'd given those casual compliments. She'd almost married a man who'd never even noticed those things about her, and if he had, he wouldn't have found them attractive. For him, her appeal had been based on more logical assets, what she could bring him in marriage, her suitability as a partner, the image she'd project as his wife.

Occasionally he'd told her she was lovely, and he'd had no problem using her body. But nothing he'd ever done, not even full intimacy, had been as hot, as exciting, as Sawyer's kiss. God, she'd been a fool to almost marry Alden.

Her father had once claimed she could have any husband she wanted based on her looks and his financial influence, neither of which she'd ever considered very important. Sawyer couldn't be interested in her father's influence, because he didn't know about it and didn't need it, in any case. And from what he'd said, he didn't find her all that attractive. She smiled and touched her cheek. She was a wreck, and she didn't even care. He'd kissed her, and he'd told her she smelled good, and he liked her wit and stubbornness and courage. Such simple compliments that meant so much. Without even realizing it, he'd given her a new perspective on life, a new confidence. She'd no longer doubt her own worth or appeal, thanks to his grudging admission.

She knew she had to leave before she threw herself at him and begged him to pretend she was one of the women from outside of town. Every time she was around him, she wanted him more.

She'd left a note on the bed, made out to Sawyer and sealed in a bank deposit envelope she'd found on his dresser. It was a confession of sorts, explaining how she felt and part of the reasons she had to leave. It was embarrassing, but she felt she owed him that much, at least. She knew he wouldn't be happy with her furtive defection, but from what he'd said, he'd be even less happy if she lured him into an intimacy he was bound and determined to resist.

Her purse had been in the closet, as the brothers had claimed, and all her credit cards and I.D. were still inside. She was ready to go.

The door was barely open when the small cat leaped off the bed to follow her out. When Honey reached for the cat, meaning to close her back in the bedroom so she wouldn't make any noise, the cat bounded out of reach. Honey wasn't sure what to do, but it was certain she couldn't waste time hunting for the animal in the dark. She'd been through the house, but she wasn't familiar enough with the setup to launch a search; odds were she'd knock something over.

She was halfway down the hallway, moving slowly and silently though the blackness, when the cat meowed. Every hair on her body stood on end while she waited, frozen, for some sign she'd been discovered. Nothing. The brothers slept on.

Honey glared behind her, but could only see two glowing green eyes in the darkness. Again she reached for the cat; again it avoided her. She felt the brush of soft fur as the cat moved past, then back again, always just out of reach. Honey cursed silently and prayed the cat would be quiet, and that she wouldn't trip on it and knock anything over.

The house was so large, it took her some time to make her way to the kitchen, especially with the cat winding around her ankles every few steps. She'd always liked cats, but now she was thinking of becoming a dog woman.

A tiny, dim light on the stove gave scant illumination across the tiled kitchen floor. She could barely see, but she knew the keys were hanging on a peg on the outside wall, close to the door, so she used the stove light as a compass of sorts, helping her to orient herself to the dark room. Shuffling her feet to avoid tripping on unseen objects, including felines, she made her way over to the door, trying to avoid the heavier shadows of what she assumed to be the table and counter. Once her searching hand located the keys, she had another dilemma. There were too many of them!

Her heart pounded so hard it was almost deafening. Her palms were sweaty, her stomach in a tense knot. The damn cat kept twining around her bare feet, meowing, making her jumpy. She had no idea where the pet food was kept and had no intention of trying to find out.

Finally, knowing she had to do something or she'd definitely faint, she ignored the cat and decided to take all the keys. When she found one that operated the closest vehicle, she'd drop the rest in the grass, leaving them behind.

She tucked her purse under her arm and wiped her sweaty palms on her jeans. Carefully, shuddering at every clink and rattle, she lifted the various key rings. There were five sets. She swallowed hard and, clutching the keys in one hand, her purse in the other, she reached for the kitchen door. The cat looked up and past her, meowed, then sprinted away. Honey turned to see where the cat was headed and barely caught sight of a large, looming figure before a growling voice took her completely off guard.

"You were actually going to steal my car!"

She jerked so hard, it felt like someone had snapped her spine. At first, no sound escaped her open mouth as she struggled to suck in air, then her heartbeat resumed in a furious trot, and she shrieked involuntarily. Shrill. Loud. The cat took exception to her noise, and with a hiss, darted out of the room. Honey seriously thought her heart might punch right through her chest, it was racing so frantically. It didn't matter that the voice was familiar; she'd been sure she was all alone, being incredibly sneaky, and then he was there. The sets of keys fell from her limp hand in a clatter on the tile floor. Her purse dropped, scattering the contents everywhere.

Sawyer was there in an instant, his hands clasping her shoulders and jerking her around to face him, hauling her up close on her tiptoes again. Her body flattened against his, and she could feel his hot angry breath on her face, feel the steel hardness of his muscles, tensed for battle.

"You were going to steal my goddamn car!"

"No…" The denial was only a whisper. She still couldn't quite catch her breath, not after emptying her lungs on that screech.

He took one step forward, and her back came up against the door while his body came up against her front. "If I hadn't been sitting there in the shadows, you'd be sneaking out right now." He shook her slightly. "Admit it."

She swallowed, trying to find her tongue. Instead, the damn tears started. He'd been there all along? She'd never stood a chance? She sniffed, fighting off the urge to weep while trying to decide what to say, how to defuse his rage.

She trembled all over, and she couldn't find the willpower to explain. She felt Sawyer practically heaving, he was so angry, and in the next instant he groaned harsh and low and his hands were on her face, his thumbs brushing away the tears, his mouth hungrily searching for hers. The relief was overwhelming.

She cried out and wrapped her arms around him. He'd said it wouldn't happen again, that not only didn't he want her for a fling, he didn't want her for anything.

She'd told herself that was for the best. She'd told herself she hadn't cared. But inside, she'd crumbled.

Now he wanted her, and she was so weak with fear and excitement, all she could do was hold on to him.

One of his hands slid frantically down her side, then up under her shirt. He bit her bottom lip gently and when she opened her mouth, his tongue thrust inside, just as his long, hot fingers closed over her breast.

She jerked her mouth away to moan at the acute pleasure of it—and the kitchen light flashed on.

Blinded, Honey shaded her eyes while Sawyer jerked her behind him and turned to face the intruder.

"Just what the hell is going on?" There was two seconds of silence, then, "Ah. Never mind. Stupid question. But why the hell is she screaming about it?"

Morgan's voice. *Oh, my God, oh my God, oh, my God.* Honey peeked around Sawyer, then yelped. Good grief, the man was buck naked and toting a gun!

Sawyer shoved her back behind him again with a curse. "Damn it, Morgan, put the gun away."

"Since it's just you, I will. That is, I would if I had any place to put it." Honey could hear his amusement, and she moaned again.

Sawyer muttered a low complaint. "You could have at least put some shorts on."

"If I'd known you were only romping in the kitchen I would have! But how the hell was I supposed to know? She *screamed,* Sawyer. I mean, I know you're rusty and all, but damn. You must have completely lost your touch."

Honey clutched at Sawyer's back, her hot face pressed to his bare shoulder. This couldn't be happening.

Sawyer crossed his arms over his chest. "She screamed because I caught her trying to steal the car keys." He kicked a set toward Morgan. The sound of them skidding over the floor was almost obscene. Honey didn't bother to look to see if Morgan picked them up. The man was blatantly, magnificently naked, and didn't seem to care. She shuddered in embarrassment and burrowed closer against Sawyer, pressing her face into his hot back, trying to blot the vision from her mind.

Morgan gave a rude grunt. "I see. She was stealing one of our cars. And so you kissed her to stop her?"

"Don't be a smart ass."

Suddenly she heard Casey say, "What's going on? I heard someone scream."

Honey thought if there was any luck to be had for her, she would faint after all. She waited, praying for oblivion, and waited some more, but no, she remained upright, fully cognizant of the entire, appalling predicament she'd gotten herself into.

Sawyer's body shifted as he gave a heavy sigh. "It's all right, Casey. Honey was just trying to sneak off in the night. She was going to steal a car."

"I was not!" Honey couldn't bear the thought of Sawyer's son believing such a thing about her. She cautiously peeked around Sawyer and saw Jordan and Gabe amble into the room. *Just what she needed.* Morgan, bless his modest soul, had sat down behind the bar. All she could now see of him was his chest. But that was still more than enough, especially since the gun remained in his hand, idly resting on the bar counter.

Gabe held up a hand. "I already heard the explanations. Damn, but she has a shrill scream. I had to scrape myself off the ceiling, it startled me so bad."

Jordan held the cat in the crook of one arm, gently soothing it. "I even heard her all the way out in the garage. When I got here, the poor cat was nearly hysterical."

Ha! Honey eyed them all, especially that damn traitor feline, and tried to muster up a little of that courage Sawyer claimed she had. At least they weren't *all* naked, she told herself, then shuddered with relief. Casey had pulled on jeans, and Gabe had on boxers. Jordan had a sheet wrapped around himself, held tight at his hip with a fist.

She felt remarkably like that damn cow in town who'd drawn too much attention.

"I wasn't stealing the car." They all stared at her, and the accusing look on Casey's face made her want to die. She wiped away tears and cleared her throat. "I left a note on the bed, explaining. I just wanted to get to town and I thought it'd probably be too far to walk. I would have left the car there for you to pick up."

Jordan frowned. "What'd you want in town that one of us couldn't get for you?"

"No, you don't understand. I was going to take the bus."

Morgan shook his head in a pitying way. "We don't have bus service in Buckhorn," he explained with little patience. "You'd have gotten to town and found it all closed up. Around here, they roll the sidewalks up at eight."

Her heart sank. "No bus service?"

Gabe pulled open the refrigerator and pulled out the milk. He drank straight from the carton. "The only bus service is in the neighboring county, a good forty miles away."

Honey watched him with a frown. "You shouldn't do that. It's not healthy."

Sawyer turned to glare down at her, his face filled with incredulous disbelief. She shrugged, feeling very small next to him. In a squeak, she said, "Well, it isn't."

Gabe finished the carton. "I knew it was almost empty."

"Oh."

Sawyer flexed his jaw. "What about your car? Your stuff? You don't even have any shoes, remember?"

He was still so furious, she took a step back. And even though Casey had looked wounded by what she'd attempted to do, he came to her side. He didn't say anything, just offered his silent support by standing close. She sent him a grateful smile, which he didn't return.

She shifted. "After I got things taken care of, I'd have sent for my stuff."

"Taken care of how?"

She'd known Sawyer was large, but now he seemed even bigger, his anger exaggerating everything about him. There was no warmth in his dark eyes, no softness to his tone. She wasn't afraid of him, because she knew intuitively that he'd never hurt her. None of the brothers would hurt a woman; that type of contemptible behavior just wasn't in their genetic makeup. But she was terribly upset.

She opened her mouth, hoping to put him off until she wasn't quite so rattled, and he roared, *"No, God dammit, it will not wait until the morning!"*

She flinched. Silence filled the kitchen while she tried to decide how to react to his anger. Jordan stepped over to her, flanking her other side. "For God's sake, Sawyer, let her sit down. You're terrorizing her."

Sawyer's eyes narrowed and his jaw locked. With a vicious oath he turned away, then ran a hand through his dark hair. Just then Honey noticed Sawyer wore only boxers himself. Tight boxers. That hugged his muscled behind like a second skin.

Her lips parted. Her skin flushed. Blinking was an impossibility.

She stood there spellbound until Jordan set the cat down and started to lead her away. He held her arm with one hand and his sheet with the other and tried to take her to the table. Belatedly she realized his intent and held back because that would put her alongside Morgan, and she knew no one had thrown him any pants yet.

"I'm all right," she whispered, wishing Sawyer would look at her instead of staring out the window at the pitch black night.

Jordan released her with a worried frown. She went back to the door and began picking up the keys and the contents of her purse. No one said anything, and when she was done, she carefully replaced the keys where they belonged. With her back to all of them, she said, "I wanted to get to the next town. I have a credit card, and I could charge a room, then call my sister to let her know I'm okay."

Jordan, Gabe and Morgan all asked, "You have a sister?" and, "Does she look like you?" and, "How old is she?"

Honey rolled her eyes. She couldn't believe they could be interested in that right now. "She's way prettier than me, but dark instead of fair, and she's a year younger. But the point is, she'll be worried. I told her I'd call her when I got settled somewhere. Then I'm going to hire a private detective to find out who's after me."

Casey frowned at her. "Why couldn't you do that from here?"

How could she tell him she was already starting to care too much about them all? Especially Sawyer? She tempered the truth and admitted, "I want to make things as simple as possible. I don't want to involve anyone else in my private problems."

Sawyer still hadn't turned or said a word, and it bothered her.

Gabe rooted through the cabinets for a cookie. "Why not just go to the police?"

She really hated to bare her soul, but it looked as if her time had run out. She clutched her purse tightly and stared at Sawyer's back. "My father is an influential man. Recently he decided to run for city council. He's been campaigning, and things have looked promising so far. When I broke off my engagement, he was really angry because he'd planned to use the wedding as a means to campaign, inviting a lot of important, connected people to the normal round of celebrations that go with an engagement. Our relationship was already strained, and we'd barely spoken all week. He... well, he hit the roof when I told him I thought someone was after me. He thinks I'm just overreacting, letting my imagination run away because I'm distraught over the broken engagement. When I said I was going to the police, he threatened to cut me off because he says I'm causing him too much bad publicity, and he's certain I'll only make a fool of myself and draw a lot of unnecessary negative speculation that will damage his campaign."

Morgan started to stand, but when she squealed and covered her eyes, he sat back down again. "Casey, go get me something to wear, will you?"

"Why me? I don't wanna miss what's going on."

Morgan frowned at him. "I'm not dressed, that's why. And she's acting all squeamish about it, so she'd probably rather I didn't get up and parade around right now. Course, if you don't care how she feels…"

Put that way, Casey had little choice. He looked thoroughly disgruntled, and agreed with a lot of reluctance. "All right. But you owe me." He sauntered off, and the cat, apparently enjoying all the middle-of-the-night excitement, bounded after him.

Morgan folded his arms on the bar, looking like he'd made the most magnanimous gesture of all by offering to put on clothes. "So since your daddy threatened to cut the purse strings, you ran off instead?"

Now, that did it! It was almost one o'clock in the morning; she was tired, frazzled, embarrassed and worried. The last thing she intended to put up with was sarcasm.

Honey slammed her purse down on the counter and stalked over to face Morgan from the other side of the bar. Hands flat on the bar top, she leaned over until she was practically nose to nose with him. "Actually," she growled, forcing the words through her teeth, "I told him to stick his damn money where the sun doesn't shine."

Morgan pulled back, and astonishment flickered briefly in his cobalt eyes, mixed with a comical wariness. "Uh, you said that, did you?"

"Yes, I did. My father and I have never gotten along, and money won't change that."

Jordan applauded. "Good for you!"

She whipped about and pointed a commanding finger at Jordan. "You be quiet! All of you have done your best to bulldoze me, and I'm getting sick and tired of it. I don't take well to threats, and I couldn't care less about my father's money."

Jordan chuckled, not at all put off by her vehemence. "So what happened?"

Deflated by their eternal good humor, Honey sighed. Men in general were hard enough to understand, but these men were absolutely impossible. "He threatened to cut off my sister, instead, and though she reacted about the same as I did, I can't be responsible for that. I had no choice except to leave."

Sawyer spoke quietly from behind her. "Except that you got sick, so you didn't make it very far. At least, not far enough to feel safe."

She didn't turn to face him. Her gaze locked onto Gabe's, and he smiled in encouragement. As long as she didn't see the disappointment and resentment in Sawyer's eyes, she thought she'd be all right.

"Someone had been following me for two days. I wasn't imagining it. I know I wasn't." She spoke in the flatest monotone she could manage. She didn't want them to hear her fear, her worry. It left her feeling too exposed. "The first day I managed to dodge them."

"You say 'them.' Was there more than one person?"

She glanced at Morgan. "It's just a figure of speech. I never saw inside the car. It was a black Mustang, and the windows were darkened. I noticed it the day after I ended things with Alden. When I left the bank where I worked, the car was in the parking lot, and it followed me. I'd promised my sister to stop at the grocery, so I did, and it was there when I came out. It spooked me, so I drove around a little and managed to lose it by jumping on the expressway into the heavy traffic, then taking an exit that I never take."

Morgan rubbed his chin. "Must not have been a professional if you lost 'em that easy."

"I don't know if they're professional or not. I don't know anything about them."

Gabe leaned against the countertop, ankles crossed, eating cookies. "You know, I hate to say this, but you could have just been spooked. If that's all that happened—"

"That's not all! I'm not an idiot."

He held up both hands, one with a cookie in it, and mumbled, "I wasn't suggesting you are."

Totally ruffled, she glared at him a moment longer, then continued. "The car was there again the next day. And that's too much of a coincidence for me."

They each made various gestures of agreement, all but Sawyer, who merely continued to watch her through dark, narrowed eyes.

"This time it followed me right up until I pulled into my sister's house. The car slowed, waited, and I practically ran to get inside. Then it just drove away."

"I still think it's your ex," Jordan said. "If you left him, he probably wanted to know where you'd gone. I would have."

"Me, too," Gabe concurred.

"I thought it might be Alden at first. But it just doesn't fit." Honey watched Casey come back in with jeans and toss them to Morgan. Casual as you please,

Morgan stood to put them on, and she quickly turned her back, but she could already feel the heat climbing up her neck to her cheeks. The man could improve with just an ounce of true modesty!

"So what changed your mind?"

Sawyer didn't look so angry now. Or rather, he didn't look so angry at *her*. He still seemed furious over the circumstances.

"I talked to Alden. He kicked up a fuss about me breaking things off, yelling about how humiliated he'd be since so many of his associates knew we were engaged. And he even threatened me some."

With cold fury, Sawyer whispered, "He threatened you?"

A chill went up her spine as she remembered again the lengths Alden had gone to just to punish her for breaking things off. And worst of all, she knew he wasn't motivated by love, but obviously by something much darker. "He used the same type of threats as my father. Alden told me he'd get me fired from my job, and he did. The bank claimed they were just scaling down employees, but Alden has a relative in a management position at the bank."

"You could sue," Jordan pointed out, and she saw he was now as angry as Sawyer. It was an unusual sight to see, since Jordan had always looked so serene. Now his green eyes were glittering with anger, his lean jaw locked.

"I... I might have," she admitted, dumbfounded by their support, "but that night when I was at my sister's house, someone broke in. She was out on a late date, so I was alone. I could hear them going through the drawers, the cabinets. I *know* it was the same peo-

ple who'd been following me. They saw where I was
staying and then they came back. They went through
everything. I just don't know why, or what they were
looking for. I'm ashamed to admit it, but I don't think
I've ever been so afraid in my life. For the longest time
I couldn't move. I just laid in the bed, frozen, listening.
When I realized they'd eventually search the bedroom,
I forced myself to get up. I didn't bother getting clothes,
I just grabbed up my purse, slipped out the bedroom
window and snuck to my car. I saw the curtain open
in the front room as I started the engine, then I just
concentrated on getting away. I was nearly hysterical
by the time I got to my father's."

She lowered her face, embarrassed and shaken all
over again. Masculine hands touched her, patting her
back, stroking her head, and gruff words of comfort
were murmured. She was caught between wanting to
laugh and wanting to cry.

She pulled herself together and lifted her chin. After
a deep breath, she continued, and the men all subsided
back to their original lounging posts.

"My father took me seriously this time, at least for
a while. He sent some men over to check out the apartment, but they said nothing seemed to be out of place.
The only thing open was the window I'd gone through,
and there was no one there when they arrived. Again,
my father thought I was just overreacting. He wanted
to call Alden, thinking I'd feel better when we got
back together."

Sawyer never said a word, but Morgan grunted.
"Did you tell him the bastard had cost you your job?"

She shrugged. "My father said he was just acting
out of wounded male pride."

"Hogwash." Gabe tossed the rest of the cookies aside to pace around the kitchen. Though he wore only his underwear, he made an awesome sight. "Men don't threaten women, period."

"That's what my sister said. My father had sent men to get her, also, before he decided there wasn't a problem, that I'd made it all up. Luckily she believed me. She promised not to go back to the house until after a security alarm was put in—a concession from my father, which my sister refused, saying she'd get her own."

Jordan grinned. "Your sister sounds a lot like you."

Why that amused him, she couldn't guess. "In some ways."

Gabe looked thoroughly disgusted. "Someone is following you around town, looting through your house with you in it, and the best your father could do was offer an alarm system?"

Honey held up her hands. She couldn't very well explain her father's detachment when the very idea would be alien to such protective men. Why, even now, they'd gathered in the kitchen, in the middle of the night, pulled from their beds, and no one was complaining. They just wanted to help.

Those damn tears welled in her eyes again.

Morgan flexed his knuckles, and the look on his face was terrifying. Even though she felt disturbed rehashing the whole story, Honey smiled. They were all so overprotective, so wonderful. She couldn't drag them into her mess. She had no idea how much danger she might actually be in. "When I left my father's that afternoon, the car was there again, following me, and I *did* panic. I took off. But it followed, and even tried to run me off the road."

Jordan stared at her. "Good God."

"It kept coming alongside me, and when I wouldn't pull over, it…it hit the back of my car. The first time, I managed to keep control, but then it happened again, and the third time I went into a spin. The Mustang had to hit his brakes, too, to keep from barreling into me, and there was an oncoming car and the Mustang lost control. He went off the side of the road and crashed into a guardrail. The other car stopped to see if he was hurt, but I just kept going."

"And you've been going ever since?"

She nodded. "I left Alden a week ago. It seems like a year. I stopped once and traded in my car, which was a nice little cherry-red Chevy Malibu, not worth much with the recent damage in the back. I bought that old rusted Buick instead. But I've been so on edge. I stopped to get gas once, and saw the Mustang again. I have no doubt I'm being followed, I just don't know why. Alden didn't really care about me, so it seems insane he'd go to this much trouble to harass me. And harassing me certainly wouldn't make me reconsider marrying him."

Sawyer pulled out a kitchen chair then forced her to sit in it. He said to Jordan, "Why don't you put on some coffee or something? Casey, you should go on back to bed."

Casey, who'd been sitting at the table, his head in his hand, looking weary, said, "No way."

"Chores still have to be done tomorrow."

"I'll manage."

Honey, relieved to be off her feet, smiled at him.

"Really, Casey. You should get some sleep. There's not anything else to hear tonight, anyway."

Sawyer crouched down beside her, his expression intent, his nearness overpowering. She couldn't be this close to him without wanting to touch him, to get closer still. And right now, he had all that warm, male skin exposed. She turned her face away, but he brought it back with a touch on her chin. "Now there's where you're wrong, sweetheart. You're going to tell me why you agreed to marry this bastard in the first place, and why he wanted to marry you. Then you're going to tell me what made you change your mind. And if we have to sit here all night to get the full truth, then that's what we'll do."

She knew she'd get no rest until he had his way, and she was limp from the nerve-racking experience of trying to steal away and getting caught in the act. She folded her hands primly in her lap and nodded. "Very well. But at least get dressed." She looked over her shoulder at the others. "*All* of you. If I'm to be forced through the inquisition, I demand at least that much respect."

Sawyer stared at her hard, and she couldn't tell if it was amusement, annoyance or sexual awareness that brought on that hardness to his features. His gaze skimmed over her, then lit on her face. "Fair enough. But Casey will stay here to keep an eye on you. Don't even think about running off again."

He walked away, and she admitted she'd been wrong on all accounts. It was distrust that had been so evident on his face. And she had to admit she'd deserved it.

CHAPTER EIGHT

WHEN SAWYER STALKED into his room to grab some pants, still angry and doubly frustrated, the first thing he saw was the rumpled bed where she'd lain. Heat drifted over him in waves, making his vision hazy. He wanted her so badly he shook with it, and he knew the wanting wouldn't go away. He hadn't even known that kind of lust existed, because it never had for him before. Unlike Morgan, and even Gabe, he'd always had a handle on his sexuality. He was, more often than not, cool and remote, and *always* in control.

And after the way his wife had played him, used him, after suffering such a huge disappointment, he'd made a pact never to get involved again. Yet he'd been involved with Honey from the second he'd seen her in the car. He'd lifted her out, and awareness had sizzled along his nerve endings. He wanted to rail against the truth of that, but knew it wouldn't do him any good. When he'd caught her stealing keys from the kitchen, his only thought was that she was leaving, not about the damn car, not about the danger she'd be in.

He hadn't wanted her to go.

He needed to get her out of his system so he could function normally again, instead of teetering between one extreme reaction and another. He didn't like it. He wanted his calm reserve back. But how?

And then he saw the note and remembered. She'd written a note to explain why she felt it necessary to sneak away from him. His fists clenched, and every muscle pulled taut as he struggled with his fierce temper—a temper he hadn't even known he had until he'd met Miss Honey Malone. Damn, but it filled him with rage. She didn't trust him at all, on any level. Curiosity and resentment exploded inside him, and he took two long strides to the mattress and snatched up the sealed envelope. His name was written across the front in a very feminine scrawl. He started to tear it open, but caught himself in time and carefully loosened the seal instead.

She'd written on a cash receipt, probably the only paper she could find on his dresser. All stationery was kept in his office. He drew a deep breath, ready to witness her lame excuses for trying to sneak out— and what he read instead made his knees buckle. He dropped heavily to the side of the bed as his heart raced.

Sawyer,

I know you won't be happy that I'm leaving this way, but it's for the best. I'm finding I want you too much to stay. Since you made it clear you'd rather not get involved, and I know it wouldn't be wise anyway, I have to leave. I can't trust myself around you.

His eyes widened as he read the words, amazed that she'd written them and even more so that she'd had the audacity to put a smiley face there, as well, as if poking fun at herself and her lack of restraint around him. The little drawing looked teasing and playful and made him hard as a stone. She wanted him? And she thought he should be amused by that?

He swallowed hard and finished the note.

To be honest, you're just too tempting. Shameful of me to admit, but it's true. And I'm afraid I'm not sure how to deal with it, since I've never had to before. I hope you understand.

Please forgive me for taking your car. I'll leave it at the bus station with the keys inside, so bring a spare set to open it. When I get things resolved, I swear I'll send you a check to pay for the damage to your fence, and your incredible hospitality. I won't ever forget you,

Honey

He wanted to go grab her and put her over his knee, not only because she would have risked herself in what he now realized was very real danger, but because she'd have been leaving for all the wrong reasons. And she'd offered him a check. He wanted to howl. He didn't want her money and he never had. How many times did he have to tell her that?

Morgan tapped on the door and stuck his head inside. "You found the note?"

Sawyer quickly folded it. Since he hadn't put pants on yet he had nowhere to put it. "Yeah. It, uh, it said she'd leave the car at the bus station with the keys locked inside, just like she told us."

Morgan crossed his arms and leaned against the

door frame. He still wore only jeans, but he had at least put the gun away. "I don't suppose you'd let me see the note?"

"Why?"

"Idle curiosity?"

Sawyer grunted. "Yeah, right. More like plain old nosiness." Sawyer kept his back to his brother, more than a little aware of how obvious his erection was at this point.

His gaze met Morgan's in the mirror over the dresser, and he saw Morgan was struggling to contain his grin. "I gather you got something to hide there?"

Opening a drawer and pulling out a casual pair of khakis, Sawyer mumbled negligently, "Don't know why you'd think that."

"The way you're clutching that note? And acting so secretive and protective?" He laughed. "Don't worry. I won't say a word. Take your time getting dressed. I think I'll just go round up something to eat."

"Morgan?"

"Yeah?"

"Don't mention to her that I have the note."

"Whatever you say, Sawyer." Then he laughed again and walked away.

After carefully easing his zipper up and buttoning his slacks, Sawyer smoothed out the note, removing the wrinkles caused by his fist. He neatly folded it and slid it into his back pocket, making certain it was tucked completely out of sight. He'd talk to her about the note—hell, yes, he had a lot to say about it—but that could be taken care of after everything else was straightened out.

He didn't bother with a shirt or shoes, and when

he entered the kitchen, he saw the rest of the men had felt the same. Gabe had on shorts; Morgan and Jordan wore jeans.

Honey was at the stove cooking.

His every instinct sharpened at the sight of her. She, too, was barefoot, her hair now pulled back in a long, sleek ponytail that swished right above her pert behind—a smooth, very soft behind he'd stroked with his palms. As he drank in the sight of her with new admiration, he felt like a predator, ready to close in. With that tell-all note, she'd sealed her own fate. He wanted her, and now that he knew she wanted him, too, he'd have her; he wasn't noble enough to do otherwise. After the other issues were resolved, he'd explain to her one more time how he felt about commitment, and then they'd deal with the personal issue of lust.

He glanced at his brothers who sat around the table like a platoon waiting to be fed, and he frowned. They shrugged back, each wearing a comical face of helplessness. Sawyer growled a curse and stepped up to Honey. "What the hell are you doing?"

Without raising her head, she barked back, "Cooking."

His brows lifted. He heard one of the brothers snicker. Crossing his arms over his naked chest, he said, "You wanna tell me why?"

She whirled, a hot spatula in her hand, which she pointed at his chest, forcing him to take a hasty step back. "Because I'm hungry. And because they're hungry!" The spatula swung wildly to encompass the men, who quickly nodded in agreement to her fierce look. "And I'm tired of being coddled and treated like I'm helpless. You want me to stay, fine. I'll stay. But I'll be damned if I'm going to lay around and be waited on and feel like I owe the lot of you."

Sawyer leaned away from the blast of her anger, totally bowled over by this new temperament. Cautiously, he took another step back. "No one wants you to feel beholden."

"Well, I *do!*"

"Okay, okay." He tried to soothe her and got a dirty look for his efforts. "You want to cook, fine," he added with a calm he didn't feel.

"Ha! I wasn't asking your permission. And don't try that placating tone on me because Jordan already did. And he's much better at it than you are."

He glanced at his brother, only to see Jordan's ears turn red. She was intimidating his brothers! Sawyer crowded close again and opened his mouth, only to meet that spatula once more.

"And don't try bullying me, because Morgan has been at it since I met him, and I'm not putting up with it anymore. Do you know he told me I wasn't allowed to cook because I was sick? He tried to force me to sit down. Well, I'll sit down when I'm good and ready. Not before."

Sawyer had no idea what had set her off this time, but he almost grinned, anxious to find out. Now that he'd decided against denying himself, he wanted to absorb her every nuance instead of fighting against her allure.

"Am I allowed to ask what you're cooking, or will you threaten me with that spatula again?"

She tilted her head, saw he wasn't going to argue with her and nodded. "Grilled ham and cheese. Do you know Gabe was about to give that box of cookies to Casey? Or at least, the ones he hadn't already eaten. If we're going to do this interrogation, we might as well eat properly rather than shoving sugar down our throats."

Sawyer looked at Gabe in time to see him sneak a cookie from his lap and pop it into his mouth. He laughed out loud.

"You think that's funny? And here you are a doctor. You should be telling them about healthy diets and all that."

"Honey, have you looked at my brothers? They're all pretty damn physically fit."

She tucked her chin in, and a delicate flush rose on her cheeks. "Yeah, well, I noticed, but Casey is still a growing boy. He should eat better." She put another sandwich on a plate, and it was only then Sawyer noticed there were six plates, meaning she'd made one for him, too. The sandwiches were neatly cut, and there were pickle slices and carrot curls beside them. He honestly didn't think any of his brothers had ever in their lives eaten carrot curls.

She'd turned the coffeepot off and poured glasses of milk instead. Sawyer started carrying plates to the table, since his brothers had evidently been ordered to sit, given that none of them were moving much. They all looked uncomfortable, but then, they weren't used to getting waited on. Their mother hadn't been the type to mollycoddle once they'd all gotten taller than her, which had happened at the tail end of grade school.

"Casey gets more physical exercise than most grown men. And he gets a good variety of things to eat. My mother harped on that plenty when he was first born."

Casey grinned. "And they're all still at it. I get measured almost daily to make sure I'm still growing like I should be, and because Grandma calls and checks. She says the good part is, they all eat more vegetables and fruits because they keep the stuff around for me."

Honey looked slightly mollified by their explanations. Sawyer held her chair out for her, and as she sat, he smoothed his palm down the tail of her hair, letting his fingers trail all the way to the base of her spine, where they lingered for a heartbeat. He imagined her incredible hair, so silky and cool, loose over his naked body as she rode him, his hands clamped on her hips to hold her firm against him. A rush of primal recognition made his breath catch. He wanted to pick her up from the table and carry her off to his room.

Of course he wouldn't do that, so he ignored the startled look she gave him and forced himself to step away.

Everyone waited until she'd taken her first bite, then they dug in with heartfelt groans of savory appreciation. It *was* good, Sawyer had to admit, even the damn carrot curls.

Sitting directly across from her, he couldn't help but watch as Honey took a small bite of her own sandwich. His thoughts wandered again to the note. *She wanted him.* He forgot to chew as he watched her slender fingers pick up a sliver of carrot, watched her soft lips close around it. He saw her lashes lower, saw soft wisps of blond hair fall over her temple.

Gabe nudged him, and he choked.

"I don't mean to drag you from whatever ruminations you were mired in, but don't you want to ask her some questions? I mean, that is why we're all up at two in the morning, gathered around the table eating instead of sleeping, right?"

Sawyer drank half his milk to wash down the bite of sandwich and nodded. "Come on, Honey. 'Fess up."

She sent him a fractious glare, but she did pat her mouth with her napkin, then folded her hands primly as if preparing to be a sacrifice. She didn't look at anyone in particular, but neither did she lower her face. She stared between him and Gabe, her chin lifted, her shoulders squared.

"I found out my fiancé had only asked to marry me to inherit my father's assets. All his stock, his company, the family home, is willed to my future husband, whoever the man might be."

There was a shock of silence as they all tried to comprehend such a mercenary act, but Sawyer was more tuned to her features. This was such a blow to her pride; he saw that now. He shouldn't have forced this confrontation, certainly not in front of everyone.

"Honey…"

"It doesn't matter." She still hadn't looked at him. Her fingers nervously pleated her napkin, but her chin stayed high. "My father and I never got along. I love him, but I don't like him much. I think he feels the same way about me. He's always resented having daughters instead of sons." Her gaze touched on each of them, and she gave a small smile. "He'd love the lot of you, a household full of big, capable men. But my sister and I never quite measured up."

"I have to tell you, I don't like your father much."

She laughed at Jordan. "Yeah, well, he's had hell putting up with me. We've butted heads since I was sixteen. When I refused to get involved in the business, which is basically electronics, new computer hardware and very state-of-the-art sort of things, he cut me out of his will. I knew it, but I didn't care. What I didn't know is that he'd changed the will to benefit the man I'd someday marry." Her mouth tightened and her eyes flickered away. Then in a whisper, she finished. "When Alden started pursuing me, I thought it was because he cared. Not because he had discovered my father's intentions."

There was, of course, the natural barrage of questions. Sawyer got up and moved to sit beside her but remained silent, letting his brothers do the interrogating. He no longer had the heart for it. He picked up her cold hand from her lap and cradled it between his own. She clutched at him, squeezing his fingers tight, but otherwise made no sign of even noticing his touch.

Gently, Gabe asked, "Why didn't you want to be in your father's business?"

She answered without hesitation. "It's a cutthroat environment. Company spies, takeovers, social climbers. It kept my father away from home the entire time my sister and I were growing up. I hate the business. I'd never involve myself in it. I wasn't even keen on marrying a man who worked for my father. But Alden led me to believe he was content with the position of regional manager, that he didn't aspire to anything more. It seemed...like a good idea."

She blushed making that admission, and Sawyer rubbed his thumb over her knuckles to comfort her. "Because your father approved of Alden?"

"Yes." She looked shamed, and he almost pulled her into his lap, then her shoulders stiffened and he saw her gather herself. In many ways, he was as drawn by her spirit and pride as he was by the sexual chemistry that shimmered between them.

She sighed. "I hadn't realized I was still trying to gain my father's approval. But then I went to see Alden at the office, to discuss some of the wedding plans, and his secretary was out to lunch. I heard him talking on the phone about his new status once the marriage was final. I listened just long enough to find out he was making grand plans, all because marrying me would put him in a better social and professional position. It hit me that I was angry and embarrassed over being so stupid, but I wasn't... I wasn't lovesick over learning the truth. In fact, I was sort of relieved to have a good reason to break things off, strange as that may sound. So I went back to his house, packed and left him the note."

Morgan rubbed his chin. "Company status seems like a pretty good reason for him to want you back, to possibly be following you."

She shrugged. "But why try to hurt me? Why try to run me off the road? Without me, there'd be no marriage and then he'd gain nothing. And when my sister's house was broken into, what were they looking for? That's what doesn't make sense. Alden is already in a good financial position. And as my father's regional manager, he's on his way to the top of the company. It's not like he *needed* to marry me to get anywhere. All that would accomplish was to speed things along."

"Maybe." Morgan finished his last carrot curl, then got up to fetch a pencil and paper. "I want you to write down your father's name, the company name, addresses for both and for this Alden ass, and anything else you can think of. I'll check on some things in the morning."

He hushed her before she could speak. "Discreetly. I promise. No one will follow you here from anything I say or do."

She tugged on Sawyer's hand, and he released her so she could write. Gabe stood up with a yawn. "I'll start work on your car tomorrow, as long as you promise you won't go anywhere without telling one of us first."

Absently, she nodded, her attention on making her list for Morgan.

"Good. Then I'm off to bed. Come on, Casey. You look like you're ready to collapse under the table."

Casey grinned tiredly, but rather than leave, he walked around the table and gave Honey a brief kiss on the forehead. She looked up, appearing both startled and pleased by the gesture.

Casey smiled down at her. "Thanks for the sandwich. It was way better than cookies."

Morgan gently clasped the back of her neck when he took the note from her. "I can see why you've been cautious, but that's over now, right?"

When she didn't agree quickly enough, he wobbled her head. "Right?"

She gave him a disgruntled frown. "Yes."

"Good girl. I'll see you in the morning. Saywer, you should hit the sack, too. You got almost no sleep the night before, and you're starting to look like a zombie."

Sawyer waved him off. He was anxious for everyone to get the hell out of the room. He had a few things he wanted to say to Honey that would be better said in private.

Jordan pulled her out of her chair for a hug. "Sleep tight, Honey. And no more worrying. Everything will be okay now. Sawyer will take good care of you."

She glanced at Sawyer, then quickly away. He wondered if his intentions showed on his face, given the timid way she avoided looking right at him. He didn't doubt it was possible. He felt like a sexual powder keg with a very short fuse.

Finally they were alone in the kitchen. Honey gathered up the plates and carried them to the dishwasher, her movements unnaturally jerky and nervous. Sawyer watched her through hot eyes, tracking her as she came back to the table for the glasses.

"You're feeling better?"

"Yes." She deftly loaded the dishwasher, as much to keep from looking at him as anything else. He could feel her reservations, her uncertainty. He stepped close enough to inhale her spicy scent, leaning down so his nose almost touched her nape, exposed by the way she'd tied her hair back. She stilled, resting her hands on the edge of the counter. She kept her back to him, and when she spoke, her voice was breathy. "My…my throat is still a little sore, but I don't feel so wrung out. I think all the sleep helped."

He crowded closer still and placed his hands beside hers, caging her in. Deliberately he allowed his chest to press against her shoulder blades. "I have patients in the morning, but in the afternoon I'll take you into town to get a few things."

"Things?"

"Whatever you might need." He nuzzled the soft skin beneath her ear. "More clothes, definitely shoes." His mouth touched her earlobe. "Anything you want."

"I'll pay for it myself."

"Not unless you have cash. Your credit cards can be traced." He kissed her skin softly, then added, "We

can call it a brief loan if that'll make you feel better."
He had no intention of letting her pay him back, but
she didn't need to know that now. Fighting with her
was the absolute last thing on his mind.

Her head fell forward. "All right."

He pulled his hands slowly from the counter, letting them trail up her arms to her sides, then down and
around to her belly. He heard her suck in a quick, startled breath. His body throbbed; he nestled his erection
against her soft behind, finding some comfort from the
razor edge of arousal and intensifying the ache at the
same time. His fingers kneaded her soft, flat belly, and
when she moaned, he trailed one hand higher to her
breast, free beneath the smooth cotton of the T-shirt.

Just as she'd done the last time he'd touched her
there, she jerked violently, as if the mere press of his
fingers was both an acute pleasure and an electrifying
pain. His heart thundered at the feel of her soft weight
in his hand. Her nipple was already peaked, burning
against his palm. She'd instinctively pulled backward
from the touch of his hand, and now she was pressed
hard against him.

He adjusted his hold, one hand clamping on her
breast, the other opened wide over her abdomen. In a
growled whisper, he said, "I read your note."

As he'd expected, she exploded into motion, trying
to get away. He held her secure with his firm hold and
said, "Shh. Shh, it's all right."

She sounded panicked. "I… I'd forgotten!"

"I know." He didn't release her, adjusting his hold to
keep her still, to keep her right where he wanted her.
"I should let you sleep. I should give you time to think
about this. But I want you too much. Now."

He could feel her trembling, the rapid hammering of her heart. He turned his hand slightly until his thumb could drag over her sensitive nipple, flicking once, twice. Her hands gripped the countertop hard, and she panted.

Opening his mouth on her throat, he sucked the delicate skin against his teeth. He wanted to mark her; he wanted to devour her. The primitive urges were new to him, but he no longer fought against them. She was his now, and there was no going back.

He caught her nipple between his rough fingertips and plucked gently. She moaned, then gave a soft sob, and all the resistance left her until she stood limp and trembling against him.

"You want me, Honey."

Her head moved on his shoulder, and her voice was faint with excitement. "Yes. That's why I had to leave. It's…too soon, but I was so disappointed when you said you didn't want me. I knew I couldn't trust myself…."

He pressed his erection hard against her and wondered what it would be like to take her this way, from behind, her plump breasts filling his hands, her legs quivering….

"It's only sex, sweetheart. That's all I can give you." The words emerged as a rough growl because he didn't want to say them, didn't want to take the chance she'd turn him away. But from somewhere deep inside himself, his honor had forced him to admit the truth to her.

To his surprise, she merely nodded, then repeated, "Only sex. That's probably for the best."

A surprising wash of indignation hit him, even as he admitted to himself the reaction was totally unfair. She'd only agreed with him, yet he'd thought she felt more. *He did.* Whether or not he admitted it, he knew it was true, and he hated it. He couldn't get involved. Never again.

He turned her around, then lifted her in his arms. "So be it. At least we're agreed."

She clutched at his shoulders and stared up at him with wide eyes. "What are you doing?"

He was burning up with urgent need, making his pace too rushed. He wanted to take his time with her, but as he looked down at her, seeing the same shimmering heat in her gaze, he wondered if he'd even make it to his room. It seemed much too far away.

"Sawyer?"

Her voice shook, and he bent to place a hard, quick kiss to her soft mouth. "I'm taking you to bed. Then I'm going to strip you naked and make love to you."

That sexy mouth of hers parted and she gasped. "But… It's late."

The bedroom door was already open and he walked in, then quietly shoved it closed with his heel. "If you think I'm going to wait one second more, especially after reading that note, you're dead wrong." He lowered her to the mattress, but followed her down, unwilling to have any space between them at all. In one movement he used his knee to open her slender thighs and settled between her legs. He wanted to groan aloud at the exquisite contact, at the feel of her soft body cushioning his. Damn, if he wasn't careful, he'd come before he ever got inside her.

He cupped her face to make certain he had her attention. "If you'd gotten away today, I'd have come after you." Her eyes turned dark, her pupils expanding with awareness. "There's something between us, and damned if I can fight it anymore. I don't think I could stand going the rest of my life without knowing what it'd be like to have you under me, naked, mine."

She stared up at him, her breathing fast and low, then with a moan she lifted while at the same time pulling him down. Their mouths met, open, hot, and Sawyer gave up any hopes of slowing down. He'd only known her a few short days, but he felt like he'd been waiting on her for a lifetime.

CHAPTER NINE

SHE WAS ALIVE with sensation, aware of Sawyer on every possible level, the hardness of his body, his heat, the way his kiss had turned commanding, his tongue thrusting deep into her mouth, stroking. She breathed in his hot, musky, male scent, felt the rasp of a slight beard stubble, and she moaned hungrily. Every touch, every movement, drove her closer to the brink. She'd never experienced this flash fire of desire before and probably would have argued over its existence. But now she was held on the very threshold of exploding, and all he'd done was kiss her.

Her hands moved over his bare back, loving the feel of hot flesh and hard muscle. She'd seen more male perfection in the past two days than most women experienced in a lifetime, but nothing and no one could compare to the man now making love to her. Desperately, she pulled her mouth free and groaned out a plea. *"Sawyer..."*

It seemed to be happening too fast. Her body was taut, her breasts swollen and acutely sensitive. And where his pelvis pushed against her, she ached unbearably.

"It's all right," he whispered against her mouth, the words rushed and low. "Let me get this shirt off you."

Before he'd finished speaking, the T-shirt was

tugged above her breasts. He paused, staring down at her with black eyes, and one large hand covered her right breast. His fingertips were caloused, and they rasped over her puckered nipple, around it, pinching lightly. She cried out, her body arching hard. The pleasure was piercing, sharp, pulling her deeper. He soothed her with mumbled words, then bent, and his mouth replaced his hand.

With a gasp, her eyes opened wide. She couldn't bear it. His mouth was so hot, his tongue rough, and then he started sucking. Hard. All the while his hips moved in that tantalizing rhythm against her in a parody of what was to come. She lost her fragile grasp on control, unaware of everything but the implosion of heat, the wave of sensation that made her muscles ripple and her skin burn, the link between her breasts and her groin and the way he touched her, how he moved against her...

Without thought, she dug her nails into his bare shoulders and she tightened her thighs around his hard hips, sinking her teeth into her bottom lip and groaning long and low with the intensity of her orgasm.

After a moment the feelings began to subside, leaving her shaken and confused. Sawyer raised his head, his lips wet, his eyes blazing. He stared at her and whispered, "Damn."

She shared his sentiments. Shock mingled with sated desire. She hadn't even known such a thing was possible, much less that it would ever happen to her. She wasn't, in the normal course of things, an overly sexual woman, and gaining her own pleasure had always been an elusive thing, not a bombarding rush.

He kissed her gently, and all she could do was struggle for breath, unable to even pucker for his kiss. His hand trembled as he smoothed hair away from her face, now pulled loose from the string she'd tied it back with. "I didn't expect that," he admitted, still softly, with awe.

She swallowed hard, trying to gain her bearings. A pleasurable throb reverberated through her limp muscles. She could barely think. "Wh...what?"

He touched her cheek and a gentle smile lit up his face. Without a word, he sat up astride her thighs and pulled the T-shirt the rest of the way off, lifting each arm as if she were a child. "You are so damn sweet."

She covered her aching breasts with her hands, shyness over what had just happened engulfing her. Sawyer ignored the gesture as he looked at her body with an absorption that left her squirming. His hands smoothed over her shoulders, down her sides. He touched her navel with his baby finger, dipping lightly, then flicking open the snap to her jeans.

"I want you naked. I want to look my fill."

What he said and the heat in his words made her entire body blush. He smiled, then moved to the side of her to wrest her jeans down her legs. "Lift your hips."

She swallowed her embarrassment and did as he asked, anxious to see what would come next. So far, nothing had been as she'd anticipated, or what she'd come to expect between men and women. Then he took her panties with her jeans, and as he looked at the curls between her legs, she squeezed her eyes shut.

They snapped open again when the bed dipped and she felt his mouth gently brush over the top of one thigh. "Sawyer!"

He reversed the position of his upper body so that

he faced the foot of the bed; his arms caged her hips and again he kissed her, this time flicking his tongue out and tasting her skin. "Open your legs for me," he growled low.

She released her breasts to clutch at the sheet, trying to ground herself against the unbearable eroticism of his command. He didn't hurry her, didn't repeat his order. He merely waited and finally, after two deep breaths, she found the courage to do as he asked. She felt stiff with expectation and nervousness and excitement as she felt herself slowly exposed.

He made a low rasping sound of appreciation, then whispered, "Wider."

Shaking from head to toe, she bent one knee, and with a raw groan, he took swift advantage. She felt his hot moist breath, the touch of his lips on the inside of her thigh, then higher, until he was there, kissing her, nuzzling into her femininity. With a jolt of red hot lust, she lifted her hips, the movement involuntary and instinctive, offering herself to him completely.

"Easy, sweetheart." His hands slid under her, locking around her thighs, keeping her still. Keeping her wide open.

She felt the bold stroke of his tongue, then the seeking press of his lips before he found what he wanted and treated her to another, more gentle but twice as devastating suckle.

She was sensitive and swollen from her recent climax, and the feel of his mouth there was both a relief and a wild torment. She had a single moment of cognizance and pulled a pillow over her head to muffle her raw cries, and then she was climaxing again. And again. Sawyer reveled in her reactions, and she found he could be totally ruthless when he chose to be. He used his fingers, gently manipulating her. He used his tongue to make her beg, his teeth to make her gasp. And she gladly obeyed.

When he stood by the side of the bed, she no longer tried to cover herself. She doubted she could move. Her legs were still sprawled, her breasts trembling with her low, shallow breaths, but she didn't care. She felt replete and wrung out and willingly pliant.

Sawyer shucked off his jeans, his face dark with desire, his breathing labored. Honey let her head fall to the side so she could see him better, and through narrowed, slumberous eyes, she took in the gorgeous sight of his naked body. Though she didn't move, her heart gave a heavy thump at the sight he presented.

His shoulders and chest were wide, his stomach hard, his thighs long and muscled. The hair around his groin was darker, and his erection was long and thick, pulsing in impatience. She shuddered at the sight of it, wondering if she could bear taking him inside when everything else he'd done had already shattered her. She felt emotionally raw, unable to cope with the depth of what she'd experienced, of what he could so easily make her feel.

She watched as he opened the nightstand drawer and pulled out a slim pack of condoms. He tore one open and deftly slid it on, then turned to stare down at her.

She whispered, "I didn't know, didn't think…" but she couldn't put into words the way he'd made her feel, how it both thrilled and alarmed her. She could tell by the grim set of his features he understood, and to some degree, felt the same. They both resented the strength of the desire between them. Mere sex shouldn't be so consuming, so uncontrollable.

"I can feel you everywhere," she added in the same low tone, almost fearfully because she'd never suspected sex could be so wild and forceful, to the point she was helpless against it. Her skin still tingled, her senses alive though her body was sated.

Remaining at the side of the bed, his eyes hot on her face, Sawyer reached down and cupped his hand over her sex. His fingers moved gently between her slick folds until they opened; he pressed his middle finger inside her, and his eyes closed on a groan. "Damn, you're wet and tight."

Honey bit her lip and tears seeped from the corners of her eyes as she struggled to accept this new onslaught of sensation. "It's...it's too much, Sawyer."

"And not enough," he rasped, then came into the bed over her.

She opened herself to him without reserve, lifting her face for his kiss. Though the hunger was still tightly etched in his features, his kiss was gently controlling. He took his time, making love to her mouth, bringing her desire back into full swing.

"Please."

Sawyer cupped her face and stared into her eyes. "Wrap your legs high around my waist. That's it. Now hold me tight."

His voice was so low and gruff she could barely understand him. She felt him probing, his erection pressing just inside, burning and appeasing, and her heart swelled. She gave a shuddering sob and closed her eyes, but he kissed her and said, "Look at me, Honey."

It was so wonderful, it hurt. She cried while she

stared at him, not out of sadness, but from inexplicable pleasure. She knew she'd probably fallen in love within the first hour of meeting him. She drew her palms down his chest to his small brown nipples and smoothed over them, determined to take everything she could. His expression hardened and he locked his jaw, rocking against her, entering her by excruciatingly slow degrees. She lifted her hips to hurry him along and was rewarded with his harsh groan. His muscles rippled and tightened, and then he thrust hard with a curse.

Honey held on to him, stunned by the shock of pleasure as he filled her. He tangled his fingers in her hair and locked his mouth onto hers and rode her hard. His chest rubbed against her stiffened nipples, his hips grinding into her with an incredible friction, his scent invading her.

She screamed as she climaxed, and Sawyer, still kissing her, swallowed the sound. He held her so close she felt a part of him. He held her and kissed her until she'd relaxed and then continued doing so even as he found his own release, his hold almost crushing it became so tight.

The kiss dwindled, turning light and soft and lazy as Sawyer sank onto her. His heartbeat rocked them both, and still he kept kissing her, easily, consuming her, soft lazy kisses that went on and on.

A noise in the hallway made him lift his head. He stared toward the closed door, and Honey couldn't remember if he'd locked it or not. After a second of squeaking floorboards, she heard Morgan call softly, "Sawyer?"

Sawyer dropped his forehead onto hers with a muffled curse. He swallowed, took two deep breaths and said with feigned calm, "Yeah?"

"Ah, I heard a scream. Again. But I'll assume you're…kissing her again." There was a slight chuckle. "Carry on." Then the sound of retreating footsteps.

Honey wanted to cover her face; she even wanted to blush. She couldn't manage either one. She closed her eyes and started to drift off to sleep. Sawyer kissed her slack mouth, smoothed his rough hand over her cheek, then rolled to her side. He was silent for a few minutes, and she felt the weight of lethargy settle into her bones. Right before she dozed off, she heard him murmur, "God knows I got more than I bargained for, but I intend to keep taking it while you're here."

And how long would that be, she wondered? Two days, maybe three? With Gabe fixing her car and Morgan checking into things, she wouldn't have much time at all. But like Sawyer, she intended to make every minute count.

In the next instant, she was sound asleep.

SAWYER WATCHED HONEY with a brooding intensity. She'd been here two weeks now, and he'd made love to her at least twice a day. Yet it wasn't enough, and he'd begun to doubt there could ever be enough. She wasn't out of his system—far from it. It seemed the more he had her, the more he wanted her, to the point he could think of little else.

She'd integrated herself completely into their lives. She now took turns cooking and cleaning, regardless of how they all complained. Unlike the other women who on rare occasions had visited the house, Honey didn't suggest they should sit and let her do it all. She didn't excuse them from duty just because they were male. No, she willingly allowed them their fair share. But she wanted to do her own part, too.

Seeing her in his kitchen cooking made him want her.

Seeing her pulling weeds from the flower beds around the house made him want her.

And listening to her argue with his brothers or coddle his son really made him burn with lust. Dammit. This wasn't the way it was supposed to be.

It was late in the day, and a barrage of patients had kept him busy for several solid hours. He hadn't had a chance to visit with her as he usually did. Twice she had poked her head into his office to offer him lunch or a quick snack. Even seeing her for those brief moments had brightened his day, as if he'd grown accustomed to her and had been suffering withdrawal from her absence.

He didn't like the feeling. Never before had he felt annoyed by having so many patients, or having to deal with the occasional imaginary illness. He was known for his patience and kindness, not his lust.

But lust today had ruled him, just as it had since he'd first laid eyes on her.

Right now, Honey was hanging over Gabe's shoulder while he looked at her car engine. Gabe had done a fair job of taking his time on the car. He'd ordered unnecessary parts, replaced things that didn't need replacing and generally stalled as long as he could. But Honey was getting antsy. There'd been no sign of the men after her, and Morgan hadn't been able to turn up a damn thing, though he'd alerted several people in town to let him know of any strangers passing through. Now all they could do was wait, but Honey was done waiting. She'd gotten it into her head that she was taking advantage of them and therefore should get out from underfoot.

Sawyer grunted to himself as he leaned on the shed door, watching her and Gabe together. His hair was still wet from his recent shower, but the heat pounding down on his head and radiating from the lush ground would quickly dry it. Already his T-shirt was starting to stick to his back, and his temper felt precarious at best, in sync with the sweltering summer weather and his disturbing thoughts of a woman he shouldn't want, but did.

Honey had no way of knowing her presence here had been carefully staged. His brothers had manipulated things so that she had no reason, and no way, to leave. Between Gabe toying with her car and Jordan supplying her everything she could possibly need from town, she'd had no reason to step foot off his property, which was how his brothers had planned it.

He appreciated their efforts, but they couldn't know what it was costing him.

Honey suddenly straightened and put her hands on her shapely hips. She glared at Gabe suspiciously while a sunbeam slanting through a high window in the large shed got caught in her fair hair, forming a halo. "Are you sure you know what you're doing?"

Gabe grinned and touched the tip of her nose with a grease-covered finger, leaving a smudge behind. "Of course I know what I'm doing, sweetie. Relax."

They'd all taken to calling her *sweetie* since they insisted on using an endearment, and her name was just that—her name. Honey had laughed and said that at least this way she could be distinguished from the mule and the cat and the various other assorted animals wandering the land.

Today she had on shorts Jordan had brought her. He'd made the purchases to keep Sawyer from taking her to town, afraid that once she was there, she'd find a way to sneak off. And none of them wanted her to do that.

But to Sawyer's mind, Jordan's fashion sense left a lot to be desired. The shorts were *too* short, displaying the long length of her slim legs and emphasizing the roundness of her pert little butt. But when he'd suggested as much, he'd gotten jeered by his brothers, who seemed to take maniacal delight in commenting on his every thought these days.

He still thought the shorts were too short, but he now suffered in silence. Just as he did when she wore the new skimpy cotton tank tops, or the flirty sundresses, or the lightweight summer nightgowns and robe. Then again, he didn't completely approve of any of the things she now wore. Jordan and Gabe had gotten together and figured out a list of everything she'd need, including some very basic female items he'd never have considered in his lust-induced fog. They'd also shown her where to add neccessities to the list kept posted on the front of the fridge. So now, among the items of aftershave and car oil, face cream and fingernail files had been added.

Every day it seemed she became a bigger part of their lives, and he didn't know what he was going to do when she eventually left. Which she would. Because once she was safe, he wouldn't ask her to stay.

Honey, tired of watching Gabe fumble under the

hood of her car, turned to flounce out of the shed. When she caught sight of him, her face lit up with a warmth that filled him to overflowing. "Sawyer! I didn't know you were here."

As usual, her eyes ate him up and sexual tension immediately vibrated between them. But she never touched him in front of anyone, too concerned with trying to keep their intimate involvement private. He didn't have the heart to point out his brothers were far from idiots and had already deduced more than he'd ever admitted even to himself. Besides, the fact she touched everyone *but* him was pretty telling, like the drunk who overenunciated to hide his state of inebriation. Honey was what Gabe called a touchy-feely woman, always hugging and patting people she cared about. And she cared about all of them, that was painfully obvious.

It was one of the main reasons his brothers insisted on prolonging her stay. Not that he'd let her leave anyway until the issue of her safety was resolved.

And that was the topic he brought up now. As she neared, he braced himself and said, "I think you should call your fiancé."

Just like that, the light died in her eyes and her welcome became wary, twisting at his heart. She stalled, her new sandals kicking up dust on the shed floor as she came to a standstill. She tried a sickly smile that made him ache. "My fiancé?"

"Ex-fiancé. This Alden idiot."

Gabe quickly wiped off his hands and strode over to them. "What the hell are you talking about, Sawyer?"

Sawyer rubbed his neck, trying to ease his growing tension. He didn't like the idea much himself. If he had his way, he'd never let her get within shouting distance of the bastard. But he couldn't take the pressure anymore, waiting for something to happen so they could act and put an end to it. And he couldn't seem to keep his hands off her.

To get things settled, they had to force the issue, and calling her ex was the only way he could think of to do it.

He stared down at her and resisted the urge to hold her close. "Morgan and I discussed it. We both still think Alden is involved somehow. You said yourself that his behavior was strange. The only problem is finding the link. If you call him, we can listen in and maybe we'll catch something you missed."

Her expression turned mulish, so he quickly clarified. "I'm not suggesting we're any better at this than you are. But at the time you left, you were upset. Now you're calm, and we're totally detached." Only he wasn't. He was in so far, he didn't know if he'd ever see daylight again. He cleared his throat and forged on. "Between us we might pick up a small detail that will make sense. I know the waiting is hard on you."

She nodded slowly, her eyes never leaving his face. "I was just telling Gabe that I think I should stop imposing on you all."

His stomach knotted. "And no doubt Gabe told you that was nonsense."

"Well, yes."

Gabe put his arm around her shoulders. "Damn right I did. She's not going anywhere until we know it's safe."

"And this is the best way to find out if it is or not," Sawyer replied, trying to ignore the way Gabe held her and the hot jealousy he couldn't deny. The only male who could touch her without setting off his possessive alarms was his son. And it was a good thing, since Casey seemed even more inclined than the rest to dote on her. Sawyer was almost certain Casey had his own agenda in mind, but unlike the others, Casey wasn't as easy to figure out. He'd always been a mature kid, proud and too smart for his own good, but he'd never been overly demonstrative with anyone but the family. In fact, he was usually more closed off, keeping his thoughts and feelings private. The way he'd so openly accepted Honey was enough to raise a few brows.

"You plan to set some bait?" Gabe asked, pulling Honey even closer as if to shield her. From Sawyer.

He scowled and nudged Gabe away, looping his own arm around Honey and hauling her up possessively against him, regardless of her chagrined struggle. "Not exactly bait. You know I wouldn't endanger her. But I want her to come right out and tell the bastard that she's been followed, that she's in hiding, that she damn well might go to the police despite her father's absurd edict if she doesn't get some answers. There's a good chance Alden will slip up and give something away."

Gabe gave a thoughtful nod. "It's not a bad plan. If he's innocent, we should be able to tell, don't you think?"

"I would hope."

Honey stepped away from both men. "Do I have any say-so in this?"

Sawyer looked at her warily. In the past two weeks he'd come to learn her moods well. Right now she was plenty peeved, and when Honey wasn't happy, she had no qualms about letting them all know it. The fact that she was one small woman in a household of five large men didn't appear to intimidate her one bit. "Uh...sure."

"Then *no*. I'm not doing it. What if Alden is at the heart of it all? What if he traces the call? He's certainly capable of doing that. Then the trouble could land right here at your own front door."

"And you still don't trust us to take care of you?" His temper started a slow boil; this was a constant bone of contention between them. "You think we're all so helpless we'd let someone hurt you? That *I'd* let anyone hurt you?"

In a sudden burst of temper, she went on tiptoes and jutted her chin at Sawyer. "I'm not thinking of me, dammit! *I'm thinking of you and your family!*"

Gabe glanced at Sawyer, a comical look of disbelief on his face. "She's trying to protect us?"

Sawyer crossed his arms over his chest and nodded, thoroughly bemused and annoyed. "Looks that way."

Throwing her hands into the air, Honey shouted, "You're not invincible!"

Sawyer rolled his eyes to the heavens. He wanted to shake her, and he wanted to take her back into the shed, slam the door on the world and make love to her again. Just that morning, right before dawn, he'd slipped into her bed and attempted to rouse her with gentle kisses and touches. But things always turned wild with Honey, no matter his resolve. When he'd left the room for his office shortly after seven o'clock, he'd been totally spent, and his legs had been shaking from the vigorous lovemaking they'd indulged in. Honey had gone soundly back to sleep. He'd never known a person who could sleep as hard and sound as she did. She'd be awake one moment, gone the next, especially after sex. A marching band could go through the room, and she wouldn't stir so much as an eyelash.

Now, it felt like months since he'd touched her. He turned away. "We're not dealing with organized crime, sweetheart. Buckhorn is a small county without a lot of need for reinforcements. It's natural for us to rely on ourselves to take care of problems whenever possible. But until we figure out exactly who is after you, we're helpless. Getting more information is the only sensible thing to do."

She looked ready to kick dirt at him, then she turned on her heel and stomped back to the shed. Gabe stared after her. She went to the back of the car and opened the trunk.

"I can't keep messing with her car much longer. She's starting to get suspicious. If I don't fix it soon, she'll figure it out, or else she'll decide I'm an inept idiot. I don't relish either prospect."

Sawyer's smile was grim. "Yeah, you must've changed everything that can be changed by now."

"Just about. Changing a few parts that had to be ordered was a stroke of genius, if I say so myself." Gabe shrugged. "I don't think she knows it's in better running order now than ever, but to be on the safe side, I took a few wires off in case she decides to give it a try. I'm still not willing to trust her to stay put."

"We can't keep her here forever."

Gabe rubbed some grease off his thumb, trying to look indifferent. But Sawyer heard the calculating tone to his words. "I don't see why not."

Sawyer sighed. "Because this isn't her home. She has a sister who's dying to see her again, despite the reassurances Honey gave her over the phone." Honey had called her sister, Misty, the morning she'd accepted the fact they wouldn't let her leave while there was danger. Misty had been relieved that her sister was safe, and very curious about the men she was staying with. Sawyer had spoken a few words with her, trying to allay her concerns. Misty had a husky voice and a lot of loyalty. Sawyer had liked her instantly.

"She can call her sister again. That's not a problem. Or better yet, her sister could visit her here."

All the brothers were curious about Misty Malone, much to Honey's amusement. Sawyer sighed. "She also has some issues she needs to resolve with her father."

"Ha! I personally think she'd be better off never laying eyes on the man again."

"If everything she's told us is accurate, then I'd agree. But I've never met the man and I have no idea what motivates him."

"You're defending him?"

Sawyer understood Gabe's disbelief. From what she'd said, Honey's father wasn't an easy man to like. "You've met Honey. You've gotten to know her in the last few weeks. Do you honestly believe any male could be so immune to her, but especially her father?"

Gabe seemed to chew that over. "I see what you mean. She's such a sweetheart, she's hard to resist. No, I can't imagine a man, any man, not loving her on sight."

Sawyer felt those words like a sucker punch in the solar plexis. It took his breath away. "I wasn't talking about love, dammit."

With a pitying look, Gabe shook his head. "Be glad you staked a claim first, Sawyer, because just about anyone else would be more than glad to talk about love. Maybe you should remember that while you're being so pigheaded."

It took two steps for Sawyer to be chest to chest with his youngest brother. Through his teeth, he growled, "Just what the hell is that supposed to mean?"

Gabe didn't back down, but then Sawyer would have been surprised if he had. Instead, he took a step closer so they almost touched, and his eyes narrowed. "It means, you stubborn ass, that she's—"

Honey suddenly shoved herself between them. She had a large box in her hands, and her scowl was hotter than the blazing sunshine. "Don't you two start! I've got enough to worry about right now without having to listen to you bicker!"

Flustered, Sawyer glared one more time at Gabe then forcefully took the box from Honey. "Men don't bicker."

"Ha! You were both muttering low and growling and acting like bulldogs facing off over a meaty bone. It's absurd for brothers to carry on that way."

Gabe blinked at her. "We were just…uh, discussing things."

"Uh-huh. Like what?"

Sawyer stared at her, stymied for just a moment, then he hefted the box. "What the hell have you got in here?"

Sidetracked, she said, "My stereo stuff. It's been in the trunk. Thank goodness nothing got wet when I went in the lake. Since I've had no reason to listen to music lately, I'd almost forgotten about it—until Casey and I decided to dance."

Gabe muffled a startled laugh. "You're going to *what?*"

She sniffed in disdain at his attitude. "Dance. To *my* music. What you men listen to is appalling."

Gabe trotted along beside them as Sawyer started toward the house with the box. "It's called country and it's damn good."

She made a face. "Yes, well, I prefer rock and roll."

"This oughta be good."

Her gaze turned to Gabe. "You plan to watch?"

"Hell, yes."

"If you do," she warned, as if she could make him reconsider, "you'll have to dance, too."

"Wouldn't miss it."

Sawyer marched through the back door, through the kitchen, down the hall and into the family room. The stereo was on a built-in shelf beside the huge stone fireplace centered on the outside wall. The speakers hung from the pine walls in four locations beneath the cathedral ceiling. This room wasn't carpeted, but instead had a large area rug in a Native American motif that covered the middle of the polished wood floor. Facing the front of the house, it had a wall of windows reaching to the ceiling, shaded by the enormous elms out front. Two comfortable couches, a variety of padded armchairs and some eclectic tables handmade from area denizens filled the room.

The first time they'd all gotten together and played music and chess and arm wrestled, in general goofing off and relaxing, Honey had looked agog at all the noise. Their boisterous arguments over the chess match, more intense than those over the wrestling, almost drowned out the country songs, and she had winced as if in pain. After half an hour she'd claimed a headache and said she was going down by the lake to sit on the dock and enjoy the evening air and quiet.

Sawyer had promptly followed her, ignoring the gibes of his brothers and Casey's ear-to-ear grin. Knowing he wouldn't be interrupted, not when they all worked so hard at conniving just such a situation for him, he'd made love to her under the stars. Dew from the lake had dampened their heated bodies, and Honey's soft moans were enhanced by the sounds of gentle waves lapping at the shore. Now, looking at her face, he could tell she was remembering, too.

He dropped the box and took a step toward her. Her eyes suddenly looked heavy, the pulse in her throat raced, her skin flushed. Damn, he was getting hard.

Casey hit him in the back. "Snap out of it, Dad. I'm too young to see this, and Uncle Gabe is about to fall down laughing."

Sawyer scowled at Gabe, who lifted his hands innocently even though his shoulders were shaking with mirth, then he turned to Casey and couldn't help but chuckle. "Where did you come from?"

"Well, according to you and that talk we had when I was seven—"

Sawyer put him a headlock and mussed his hair. "Smart ass. You know that wasn't what I meant."

The second Casey twisted free, laughing, Honey stepped forward and smoothed his hair back down. And he let her, grinning the whole time. Casey was a good head and a half taller than Honey, with shoulders almost twice as wide. Yet he let her mother on him. And every damn time she did, something inside Sawyer softened to the point of pain. He loved Casey so much, had loved him from the first second he'd held him as a squalling, red-faced infant, regardless of all the issues present, that anyone else who loved him automatically earned a place in his heart.

She finished with Casey's hair and gave him a hug of greeting. Sawyer felt ridiculously charmed once again—and he hated it.

"I brought in my music," she told Casey, as if any reprieve from country music was the equivalent of being spared the gallows. Casey hadn't yet told her he actually liked country. "You want to take a look, see if anything interests you?"

"That'd be great. I'll check them out as soon as I've washed up."

Gabe stood to stretch. "You get everything taken care of, Case?"

He nodded, then turned to Sawyer. "When Mrs. Hartley left here today, I saw she was limping."

Sawyer pulled his thoughts away from Honey with an effort. "She twisted her ankle the other day rushing in from her car when it was raining."

"She told me. So I followed her over there to help her out. I got her grass cut and did some weeding, then went to the grocery for her." To Honey, he said, "Mrs. Hartley is close to seventy, and she's real sweet. She's the librarian in town, and she orders in the books I like."

Honey laced her fingers together at her waist and beamed at Casey. "What a thoughtful thing to do! I'm so proud of you."

Casey actually blushed. "Uh, it was no big deal. Anyone would have done the same."

"That's not true." Honey's smile was gentle, warm.

"The world is filled with selfish people who never think of others."

The men exchanged glances. They really didn't think too much of helping out, since it was second nature to them. But Sawyer supposed to Honey it did seem generous, given the men she'd known.

Gabe saved Casey from further embarrassment by throwing an arm around him and hustling him along. "Go get washed so we can put the music on. I'm getting anxious." He winked at Honey, and then they were gone.

The family room had open archways rather than doors that could be closed, so they weren't afforded any real privacy, but already Sawyer felt the strain of being alone with her. He looked at her with hot eyes and saw she was studying some of the framed photos on the wall. There were pictures of all of them, but the majority were of Casey at every age.

Sawyer came up behind her and kissed her nape. He felt desperate to hold her, to stave off time, and he looped his arms around her. "Mmm. You smell good."

He could feel her smile, hear it in her response. "You always say that."

"Because you always smell so damn good." He nipped her ear. "It makes me crazy."

She leaned against him, and her tone turned solemn. "You've done an excellent job with Casey. I don't think I've ever known a more giving, understanding or mature kid. He's serious, but still fun-loving, sort of a mix of all of you. He's incredible." She leaned her head back to smile up at Sawyer. "But then, he inherited some pretty incredible genes, being your son."

Sawyer's arms tightened for the briefest moment,

making her gasp, then he released her. He shoved his hands into his back pockets and paced away. Maybe, considering he had insisted she call her fiancé tonight, he should at least explain a few things.

Honey touched his arm. "What is it?"

"Casey's not really mine." He no sooner said it than he shook his head. "That is, he's mine in every way that counts. But I didn't father him. I don't know who his father is—and neither did his mother."

CHAPTER TEN

"What did you say?"

Sawyer laughed at himself. He made no sense, so her confusion was expected. "My wife cheated. A lot. She didn't like my long hours studying, or my distraction with school in general. By the time Casey was born, I'd already filed for a divorce. It wasn't easy for her. She had no family, and she wasn't happy about the divorce. In fact, she was crushed by it. She pleaded with me not to leave her, but she…well, once I knew she'd been with other men, I couldn't forgive her. I understood it, but I couldn't forgive."

Honey wrapped her arms around him from behind, leaning her head on his back. She didn't say anything, just held onto him.

"I'd been sort of taking care of her for a long time, since high school even. Her parents died when she was seventeen, and an aunt took her in, but then she died, too, when Ashley was nineteen. She never had a job, and the idea of getting one horrified her. I just… I dunno. It seemed logical to marry her, to take care of her. We'd been dating forever, and I felt sorry for her, and there was no one else I wanted."

Honey kissed his back, showing her understanding. "Why did she cheat?"

Sawyer shrugged. "Hell, I don't know. She seemed plenty satisfied with…" He stalled, casting her a quick look.

"She seemed satisfied with you sexually? Of course she did. You're an incredible man, Sawyer." Her small hands were flat on his abdomen, making him catch his breath as she idly stroked him, meaning to offer comfort, but arousing him instead. All she had to do was breathe to turn him on; her touch made him nearly incoherent with lust.

"You're also an incredible lover," she added huskily, making his muscles twitch. "No woman would have complaints."

He looked away again. When she said things like that, it made him want to toss her on the couch and strip her clothes off. He reacted like an uncivilized barbarian, ready to conquer. Feeling a tad uncomfortable with that analogy, he rushed through the rest of his explanation. "She told me she felt neglected, so she cheated. And then she couldn't understand why I wouldn't forgive her, because in her mind, it was my fault. I filed for divorce, but then I found out she was several months pregnant. She was angry and taunted me with the fact it wasn't mine. But by then, I hardly cared. It was an embarrassment, but little else."

"Did everyone know?"

"Not at first. She got over being mad and just started pleading with me to take her back. She fought the damn divorce tooth and nail. I tried to be considerate with her, but I was also in the middle of med school and I had my hands full. When she went into labor, she begged me to go the hospital with her." He got quiet as he remembered that awful day, his guilt, his feelings of helplessness. His family had wanted to be support-ive, but no one knew what to do. The entire town had watched the drama unfold, and it was painful.

"There was no one else," he murmured, "and I couldn't leave her there alone. So I went. And after they handed me Casey, Ashley told me she was put-ting him up for adoption."

He shook his head, once again feeling the utter dis-belief. After holding Casey for just a few short hours, he knew he wouldn't let him go. It wasn't the baby's fault his mother had been discontent in her marriage, and while wonderful adoptions existed, he wouldn't put it to the chance.

He pulled away from Honey and went to stare blindly at a photo of Casey as a toddler. In a hoarse tone, he admitted, "I signed the birth certificate, claim-ing him as my own, and dared her to fight me on it." His throat felt tight, and he swallowed hard. "We're not without influence here. My family has been a force since my father's days, and Ashley knew in a battle she didn't stand a chance. She hadn't wanted Casey, and I damn sure did, so she reluctantly agreed. For a while, she was bitter about it. I don't know who all she com-plained to, but everyone around here knew the whole private story within days. They knew, but they didn't dare say anything."

Honey didn't approach him this time. She kept her distance and spoke in a whisper. "Where's his mother now?"

"I'm not sure. She got ostracized by the town, not because of me, because I swear I tried to make it easy on her. But she was bitter and that bitterness set ev-eryone against her. She moved away, and last I heard, she'd remarried and moved to England. That was years ago. Casey knows the truth, and I've tried to help him understand her and her decisions. And my own."

"You feel responsible."

He turned to face her. "I can't excuse myself from it, Honey. I played a big part in her actions. She resented my sense of obligation to others, and I resented her interference in my life. I *like* taking care of people, and I like being a doctor, yet that's what drove her away. She wanted more of my time, and I didn't want to give it to her, not if it meant taking away from my family and the community."

"And you don't ever want a wife to...interfere that way again?"

"I don't want to run the risk of another scandal. I haven't changed."

Her smile was gentle as she crossed the floor and hugged herself up against him. "There's no reason you should. You accept the influence of your name, but also the responsibility of it, like a liege lord, and you handle that responsibility well. If Ashley didn't understand, it's not your fault."

"She was my wife."

"She was also a grown woman who made her own terrible decisions. I can only imagine how you felt, with everyone knowing the truth, but I'm sure no one blames you."

"I blame myself."

She burrowed against him, her small body pressed tight to his own. Damn, but he wanted her.

All his life he'd been surrounded by family and neighbors and friends. That wouldn't change, but he knew when Honey left, he'd feel alone. And for the first time in his life he felt vulnerable, a feeling he instinctively fought against.

He wrapped his fist in her hair and turned her face up for his kiss. She tried to dodge his mouth, wanting to talk, to instruct him on his sense of obligation, but he wouldn't allow it. With a low growl, he held her closer and roughly took her mouth, pushing his tongue inside, stemming any protest she might make.

Just as she always did, Honey kissed him back with equal enthusiasm. Her hands clutched his shirt, and she went on her tiptoes to seal the space between them.

Sawyer groaned. He pulled his mouth free and kissed her throat, her chin. "I hate feeling like this," he said, meaning the way his need for her consumed him beyond reason. There were so many other things to consider right now, and all he wanted to do was get inside her.

Honey pressed her fingers to his mouth, and though she smiled, her eyes looked damp. "You feel responsible for me, and you're trying to do the right thing, because that's who you are. You help people by giving. You take in strays, both people and animals."

"The animals are Jordan's."

"But they're accepted by you. By all of you. Your wife was a stray. I'm a stray."

He grasped her arms and shook her slightly. "Dammit, Honey, I care about you."

She gave a soft, sad chuckle. "You care about everyone, Sawyer. But I don't want or need anyone to take care of me. This time, you aren't responsible."

"I wasn't making comparisons, dammit." His frustration level shot through the roof as he tried to find a balance for the feelings.

"I know." Her hand cupped his jaw, her eyes filled with emotion. "I won't lie and tell you I don't want a family. I was willing to marry a despicable creep like Alden for it, and he couldn't offer half what you do with your nosy, domineering brothers and your incredible son and your unshakable honor. But I have no intentions of clinging to a loveless relationship. I tried that with Alden, and look where it got me." She smiled, then shook her head. "I've been thinking about it, and I decided I deserve to be loved. I deserve a family of my own, and a happily ever after. I would never settle for anything less now."

Her words left him empty, made him want to protect her, to ask her to stay forever. But the one time he'd tried marriage it had been for all the wrong reasons. Now, he wanted Honey horribly, but he just didn't know about love, not a romantic, everlasting love. All he knew for certain was the uncontrollable lust that drove him wild.

She looked up into his face, her eyes soft, her expression softer, then she sighed. "Don't look so stern, Sawyer. You haven't done anything wrong. You didn't make me any false promises, and you didn't take advantage of me." Her teeth sank into her bottom lip to stop it from trembling. "All you did was show me how men can and should be. And for that, more than anything, I thank you."

She stepped away and drew a deep breath. "So, now that we've cleared that up, what do you say I make that phone call?"

He wanted to say to hell with it; he wanted to shake her for being so nonchalant about her own feelings.

Trying for a detachment he didn't possess, he

glanced at his watch. "Morgan should be home soon. Then we'll call."

From the open doorway, Morgan growled, "I'm home now."

Sawyer looked up and saw his brother lounging there, arms crossed belligerently over his chest, his eyes narrowed and his jaw set. He looked like a thundercloud. How much had he heard? Obviously enough, given his extra-ferocious scowl.

First Gabe, and now Morgan. They didn't approve of his methods, his urgency in getting the issue resolved. Despite what he'd told Gabe and Honey, Morgan had argued with him over the idea of contacting Alden. Morgan had called him an ass for denying that he cared. Sawyer had countered that he'd only known her for a little over two weeks, which had made Morgan snort in derision. *You knew Ashley for a short lifetime, but that didn't make the relationship any better.* Truthful words that had been gnawing at him all day.

Sawyer abruptly headed for the doorway to call Gabe and Jordan in, determined to blot Morgan's warning from his mind. Once the brothers were all collected, Sawyer noticed Honey wouldn't quite meet his gaze. It was as if she'd shut him out, already removing herself from him. He hated it, but told himself it was for the best.

The brothers were setting up the extra phones in the room so they'd all be able to listen in the hopes of catching a clue. Casey had Honey's collection of music pulled toward him, idly thumbing through CDs and tapes. Sawyer doubted there'd be any dancing tonight, but he understood Casey's need for a distraction.

Then Casey nudged Honey. "What's this?"

Absently, she glanced down, frowning at a plain tape with the word *Insurance* written on it. "I don't know."

Sawyer, hoping to ease her tension, said, "We'll be a few minutes yet if you want to check it out."

Casey carried the tape to the stereo and put it in. With the very first words spoken on the tape, a crushing stillness settled over the room. Murmured conversations and quiet preparations ceased, as slowly, everyone stopped what they were doing to listen.

Her gaze glued to the stereo as if transfixed, Honey whispered, "Sawyer," and he was by her side in an instant, taking her hand, as appalled as she.

The voices were unrecognizable to Sawyer, other than being male. But what they were discussing was painfully obvious: murder. And the fact that Honey knew the voices was easy to see by her horrified expression.

So you'll do it?

It won't be a problem. But we'll need some good-faith money upfront.

I can give you half now, the rest after she marries me and her father is gone. But remember, you have to wait for my instructions. If you kill the old man before the legalities are taken care of, I won't get a damn thing. Which means you won't get a thing.

How long are we talking?

A week or two. It's already in his will, but I want to make sure there won't be any mix-ups.

Honey turned wounded eyes to Sawyer. "That's Alden."

Sawyer pulled her closer, but her face remained blank, white with hurt and disbelief. One by one, his brothers and Casey gathered around her until she was listening to the tape from behind a wall of protective men.

You just make sure the wedding goes off without a hitch. I don't want to be wasting my time here.

I can handle the bride. Don't worry about that.

What if she objects to her daddy being snuffed? Will the conditions of the will alter if she divorces you?

No, she's completely clueless to my plans, so don't worry about her. She won't have any idea that I was behind it all. If anything, she'll want me to comfort her.

There was some masculine chuckling over that, and one of the men mumbled, *An added bonus, huh?*

Sawyer shot to his feet, his fists clenched, the corners of his vision clouded by rage. "I'll kill him."

Morgan grabbed Sawyer's shoulder. "Don't be stupid."

"Or so human," Gabe added, staring at him in fascination. "It shocks me. You're usually such a damn saint."

Honey slowly stood and faced them all. "I… I have to call the police."

Sawyer squeezed his eyes shut and tried to find his control. Gabe was right—he was acting out of character. He was the pacifist in the family, yet all he wanted to do was get Alden close enough to beat him to a pulp.

Morgan stepped around Sawyer. "Honey, I think you should still make that call."

She blinked owlishly, as if coming out of a daze. Feeling grim, Sawyer nodded. "We need to find out who the hell he hired."

Casey stood beside Honey, one arm around her waist. "He made the tape for insurance, just as it says, didn't he? He couldn't take the chance that the men he'd hired would go against him. Or maybe he planned to blackmail them later with it."

Morgan shrugged. "Who the hell knows. The man's obviously an idiot as well as a bastard."

"But why were they after me?"

She looked so lost, everyone was quiet for a moment, trying to find a gentle way to explain it to her.

Sawyer cleared his throat, taking on the duty. "Honey, when you left Alden, you fouled up all the plans. Not only did you make it impossible for him to recoup the money through the marriage, but when you packed up, you evidently took his tape by mistake."

"It…it was with my things. I just sort of shoved everything into a box. I was angry and not really paying attention."

"Exactly. I don't know why he would have hidden the tape among your things, but—"

"Oh, God, he didn't." She clutched at Sawyer, eyes wide. "When I pulled the stereo out, there was a tape shoved up against the wall behind it. Alden only has CDs so I assumed it wasn't his, and I just threw it in with the others."

"But now you have it, and it's evidence not only against the men after you, but against Alden, too. I imagine he had to tell them about it, knowing you'd find it sooner or later and they'd all go to jail. They have to get you, to get the tape."

Honey covered her mouth with a hand, then turned for the phone. "I need to call my father to make sure he's okay. And my sister—"

She looked so panicked, Sawyer gently folded her close, despite her struggles, and held her. "Baby, listen to me. You spoke with Misty yesterday, remember? If anything had been wrong, she'd have told you."

He felt her relax slightly, the rigidity seeping out of her spine. "Yes, of course you're right."

She drew a deep breath, and slowly, right before his eyes, Sawyer watched her pull herself together. She'd been given a terrible blow, but already her shoulders were squared, her expression settling into lines of determination. She stepped away from him. "Let's get this over with. I want to talk to Alden, to find out what I can, and then we can have the police pick him up. The tape will be enough evidence, don't you think?"

Morgan gave one hard nod. "Damn right, especially with the break-in at your sister's and the way you've been chased. But with any luck, he'll incriminate himself further on the phone, and we'll all be witnesses. Don't worry, Honey. It's almost over with. I have friends with the state police who can handle everything."

Sawyer didn't want to let her go, didn't want her to so much as speak to Alden, much less carry on a deceptive conversation, but she was adamant. When she turned her back and walked away from him, it was all he could do not to haul her back up to his side and tote her out of the room.

Honey took a seat by the phone, looking like a queen surrounded by her subjects, and she dialed Alden's number. It took several rings for him to answer, and when he finally did, Honey closed her eyes. "Hello, Alden."

There was a heavy pause. "Honey? Is that you?"

"Yes."

Another pause, then, *"Where the hell have you been?"*

Honey started, but in the next instant she scowled and tightened her hand on the phone. Sawyer felt a swell of pride for her courage.

"Have you been looking for me?"

"You're goddamned right, I've been looking for you. For God's sake, Honey, *I thought you were dead.*"

HONEY STARED AT the phone, her entire body trembling with rage. "Why would you think that, Alden? I left because I didn't want to marry you. Didn't you read my note?"

Her calm tone seemed to sink in to him. She heard him breathing heavily in an effort to control himself. "Yes, I read it. Where are you, Honey?"

She stared at her hands on the desk, not at the men who watched her so closely. "I'm afraid, Alden. Someone has been chasing after me."

He muttered low, then said in sugary tones, "Have you spoken with anyone?"

"About what? Our breakup?"

"About... Dammit, never mind that. Where are you living now? I'll come get you."

"I'm not living anywhere." In a calculated lie, she said, "I've been so afraid, just running from whoever is after me. I haven't had a chance to unpack. My clothes were all left at my sister's, but everything else is still in boxes in my trunk. I shouldn't have left, Alden. My father doesn't believe someone is after me, so I can't go to him."

"I know," he answered in soothing tones. "He's never been overly concerned for you. But I am, sweetheart. You know that. I wanted to marry you long before I learned about his will. If you want, we'll make him change it. He can leave everything to your sister. I don't care about the money, I just want you back with me, safe and sound. Tell me where you are so I can come get you."

"I don't know...." She tried to put just the right amount of hesitation into her tone.

"Listen to me, damn you!" He made a sound of pain and cursed. "People *are* after you, and they're dangerous. I know because they already put me in the hospital once. I spent almost a week there and I can tell you it wasn't pleasant!"

Honey glanced at Sawyer and saw his dark eyes glint with satisfaction. She held no sympathy for Alden, either, but knowing they'd hurt him scared her spitless. She didn't want the men anywhere near Sawyer or his family. "Why would anyone hurt you, Alden?"

"I don't know. I think it might have something to do with a shady deal your father made to buy some inside corporate information."

Honey raised her brows. That was an excellent lie, because it was one she would have believed. She made sounds of understanding, and Alden continued. "They won't hesitate to do the same to you, Honey. Let me bring you home where I can protect you while we sort this all out."

Sawyer covered the mouthpiece. "Tell him to meet you here tomorrow." He handed her a piece of paper that Morgan had slipped to him. Honey stared down at the address, recognizing that the location was an area on the outskirts of Buckhorn. Numbly, she shook her head, knowing he planned to put himself in danger. "No."

"No what?" Alden tried cajoling. "Listen to me,

Honey. I know you feel betrayed. And I'm sorry. I really do care for you—"

"Let me think, Alden!"

Sawyer walked over to her and gripped her shoulder. He shoved the paper toward her again, then whispered low, "Trust us, Honey. Tell him."

They were all looking at her, waiting. How in the world could she do this to them? She loved each of them. Then Morgan gave her the most furious face she'd ever seen on a human. He reached into his pocket and pulled out his sheriff's badge, flashing it at her as if to remind her this was his job, as if her hesitation had insulted him mightily.

Jordan shrugged at her, and he, too, spoke in a faint whisper. "Either you have him come here, on our own home ground where Morgan has some legal leverage, or we go after him. It's your decision."

She narrowed her eyes at the lot of them. Bullies every one. They had the nasty habit of ganging up on her whenever it suited them.

Alden suddenly asked, "Who's with you?" and suspicion laced his tone.

Knowing she had no choice and hating Alden for it, she did as the brothers asked. "I'm in a diner in a small town in southern Kentucky." She glanced at the note again, then said, "You can meet me in Buckhorn at the town landfill at nine o'clock tomorrow morning. It's… it's deserted. There won't be anyone around."

Sawyer nodded and whispered, "Good girl," and she elbowed him hard. He rubbed his stomach and scowled at her.

"Can you give me directions, sweetheart?" Alden

sounded anxious, and Honey's stomach knotted with dread even as she did as he asked.

"Just hang on until tomorrow morning, darling. You'll feel safer as soon as I get you home."

Though she nearly choked on it, she said, "Thank you," and after she hung up the phone, she glared at all the men, but concentrated most of her ire on Sawyer. "I hope you're happy," she meant to growl, but what emerged was a pathetic wail quickly followed by tears. The brothers looked appalled, and Sawyer, his face softening with sympathy, reached for her. Honey knew if he so much as touched her she'd completely fall apart, so she ran from the room.

She didn't want him to confront Alden. She didn't want him in danger. At the moment, she wished she'd never laid eyes on him. At least then she'd know he would stay safe, and because she loved him so damn much, even though he didn't feel the same, his safety was the only thing that seemed to matter.

She wanted to pretend sleep when Sawyer crept into the dark bedroom hours later, but she was shaking so bad, he knew right away she was awake. He sat on the side of the bed and smoothed his hand over her cheek.

"Are you all right, sweetheart?"

"Yes. Did you make all your plans?"

His hesitation was like an alarm, making her sit up. "Tell me, Sawyer."

"You'll stay here with Casey and Gabe."

"No. If you insist on doing this…"

"I do. Morgan has alerted the state police, and once Alden shows up, we'll grab him. There's no reason to worry."

"Like you wouldn't if you were left behind!"

"Honey…"

She hated acting like a desperate ninny, but she was choking on her helplessness, and she didn't like it. "If Morgan and the police have it in hand, why do you need to go?"

"Because he hurt you."

His quiet words nearly crumbled her heart. She launched herself at him and knocked him backward on the bed. "Sawyer."

He couldn't answer because she was kissing him, his face, his throat, his ear. Sawyer chuckled softly and tried to hold her still, but she reared back and tugged on the fastening to his pants. Surprised, but more than willing, Sawyer lifted his hips and helped her to get his pants off, removing his underwear at the same time. Honey stretched out over him, relishing the feel of his hot, hard flesh. She loved him so much, she wanted to absorb him, his caring, his strength and honor.

Sawyer groaned as she pressed against his pelvis, rocking gently. She felt the immediate rise of his erection along with his accelerated breaths. "Honey, slow down."

She had no intention of listening to him. Moving quickly to the side, she caressed him from shoulders to hip. His hands fell to the mattress, and his body stiffened. Honey bent and kissed his chest. "I love how you feel, Sawyer, how you smell, and how you…taste."

He caught his breath, then let it out in a whoosh when her mouth began trailing kisses down his chest to his abdomen. Both of his hands cupped her head, his fingers tangling gently in her long hair.

Her hand wrapped tightly around his erection, holding him secure, giving him fair warning of her intent. She heard a low growl and knew it was Sawyer.

Rubbing her face over his muscled abdomen, she whispered, "You know how you've done this to me?"

"This?" The word was a strangled gasp.

"Mmm, *this*," she clarified, and lightly ran her tongue down the length of his penis.

"Damn." His entire body jerked and strained, his hands tightening in her hair.

"And…this." She gently raked her teeth over him, down and then back up again.

"Honey."

"And this." His body lurched as her mouth closed hotly around him. She'd had no idea that pleasuring him would pleasure her, as well, but her heart raced with the incredible scent and taste of him and the muttered roughness of his curses. He slowly guided her head, his entire body drawn taut, his heels digging hard into the mattress.

She had no real idea how to proceed—she'd never done this before—but it seemed he enjoyed everything, so she supposed her inexperience didn't matter. But before long he was pulling her away despite her protests.

"You're a witch," he growled, then tucked her beneath him after hastily donning a condom. He entered her with one solid thrust, and she bit back a loud moan of acute sensation. As he moved over, his rhythm smooth and deep, he watched her face. "You liked doing that, didn't you?"

The room was dark, but moonlight spilled over the bed through the French doors, and she could see the intent expression on his face, how his eyes seemed to glow.

She licked her lips and felt his thrusts deepen. "Very

much." Smoothing a hand over his back, she asked, "Do you like doing it to me?"

He froze for a heartbeat, struggling for control, then with a vicious curse he wrapped her up tight, holding her as close as he could get her. "Hell, yes, I like it," he growled. His thrusts were suddenly hard and fast and frantic, and when she cried out, her entire body flooding with sensation, he joined her.

And through it all, his arms were around her, and she heard him whisper again. "I like it too much."

JORDAN STUCK his head in the door but kept his gaze judiciously on the ceiling. He spoke in a near silent murmur. "I hate to interrupt all this extracurricular activity, but you didn't hear my knock and we have visitors."

Sawyer immediately lifted away from Honey, and answered in the same quiet hush. "Who?"

"I don't know for sure. I was in my room about to bed down when I heard a noise. I looked out and saw someone in the shed. If I don't miss my guess, good old Alden called in the muscle. His bully boys are probably looking for the tape in her car."

"Goddammit," Sawyer hissed, angry at himself, "we should have thought of that." Sawyer was out of the bed in an instant and pulling on his pants.

Honey threw herself against his back, wrapping her arms tight around him. "No, Sawyer, just stay inside!"

"Shh." He took a moment to gently pry her hands loose and kiss her forehead. "It's all right, sweetheart."

Since she was barely covered by the sheet and evidently didn't care, it was a good thing Jordan had averted his face. He said without looking at her, "Morgan has called in the troops, sweetie, so don't get all frantic on me."

Sawyer had assumed as much, but he saw it didn't ease Honey at all. He glanced sharply at Jordan. "Casey?"

"I sent him to the basement. Gabe is with him, and they're waiting on her."

He nodded. "Come on, Honey. You need to get your robe."

"Don't do this, Sawyer."

Her pleading tone unnerved him, but he hardened himself against it. He'd do what he had to to protect her. "There's no time for this, babe. Come on, have a little trust, okay?"

She moved reluctantly, but she did scoot off the bed and put her arms into the robe he held for her. Wearing only his slacks, Sawyer followed Jordan out, keeping Honey safely at his back. "How did they know she was here?"

"Maybe Alden had the phone call traced, or maybe someone in town knows and spilled the beans. She's been here a couple of weeks now, and you've had a line of patients every day. And Honey, once you've seen her, isn't exactly a woman to forget."

Sawyer grunted at that. She was so damn sexy she made his muscles go into spasms. Jordan was right; no one would forget her, and her description would be easy enough to peg.

When they neared the basement steps, Gabe was there waiting. "You owe me for this one, Sawyer. You know how I hate missing all the action."

"Keep her safe, and you can name your price."

Gabe grinned at that. "If you get a chance, punch the bastards once for me."

He handed Honey over to his brother. She hadn't said another word, and she wouldn't look at him. Gabe gently put his arm around her. "Come on, sweetie. Casey is looking forward to the company."

"Gabe?" Sawyer waited until his brother met his gaze. "Don't come out, no matter what, until I come for you."

"We'll be fine, Sawyer. Go, but be careful."

Sawyer watched Honey disappear down the steps. She was far too passive to suit him at the moment, but he brushed it off. Morgan was already outside and no doubt could use their help. He closed the basement door, heard Gabe turn the lock, and he and Jordan rushed silently out the back door and across the damp grass. They kept low and in the shadows and they found Morgan just where Sawyer knew he would be, peering around the barn, the closest outbuilding to the shed, keeping the intruders in sight.

"You two sleuths sounded like a herd of elephants."

Morgan's sibilant mutter was filled with disgust, but Sawyer didn't take exception. "Did you see anything?"

"Two men, both big bastards. From the sounds of it, they're getting into Honey's car."

"Looking for the tape."

"I assume. And when they don't find it, they'll head for the house."

"You see any weapons?"

Morgan grunted, but the sound was drowned out by the myriad night noises, crickets, frogs, rustling tree branches. An eerie fog, visible through the darkness, drifted over the ground. Morgan wiped his forehead, his gaze still trained on the shed. "They'd be total idiots if they weren't armed."

"Jordan said you put the call in to the state police?"

"Yeah." Suddenly he pressed himself back, then glanced at Sawyer. "I don't think they're going to make it on time, though."

Sawyer curled his hands into fists, easily comprehending Morgan's meaning. He was on his haunches, and he tightened his muscles, ready to move. There was no way in hell he was letting anyone near the house, not with Honey and Casey inside.

Morgan reached past him and thrust his gun at Jordan, a silent order for Jordan to be backup. Jordan accepted the gun with a quietly muttered complaint, then braced himself.

Shadows were visible first, then the dark, indistinct forms of two men creeping quietly across the empty yard. They mumbled to each other, then the one trailing slightly behind growled, "That little bitch has been more trouble than she's worth. When I get hold of her—"

Without a word, Morgan launched himself at the first man, who caught the movement too late to turn. Sawyer was right behind him. It gave him enormous satisfaction to hear the grunt of pain from the man who'd threatened Honey as he drove him hard to the ground. His fist connected solidly with a jaw, earning a rank curse before the man shoved him aside with his legs and struggled to his feet. Sawyer faced him, taunting, anxious, confident in his abilities.

And then he heard Gabe shout, and Honey was racing across the yard, distracting Sawyer for just a moment. The man swung, but she got in the way, and his fist clipped her, knocking her to the ground.

Sawyer erupted with blind fury. He stood there heaving just long enough to insure Gabe had Honey in hand and that she was all right. He was barely aware of Morgan pounding a man into the dirt, or of Jordan standing silently in the shadows, the gun drawn. He didn't notice that his son had turned on the floodlights or that the man, knowing he was outnumbered, stood frozen before him, waiting. He'd been dealing with a clamoring swell of emotions all day, pushing him slowly over the edge. And now, seeing Honey hurt, he went into a tailspin. Sawyer felt himself exploding, and with a look of shock, the man raised his fists.

The bastard was large, but not large enough. He was strong, but not strong enough. And he fought dirty, but Sawyer had the advantage of icy rage, and after a few short minutes, Morgan wrapped his arms around Sawyer from behind and pulled him away. "Enough, Sawyer," he hissed into his ear. "The state guys are here and we don't need to put on a show."

He was still shaking with rage, his knuckles bloody, his heart pounding. Slowly, Honey approached him, and Morgan, using caution, released him.

She had a swelling bruise beneath her left eye, but it was the uncertainty in her gaze that nearly felled him. Sawyer opened his arms, and with a small sound she threw herself against him.

He hadn't wanted responsibility for another wife, but ironically, the more Honey insisted on taking care of herself, the more she agreed with his edicts, the more he wanted her. The fact she *didn't* need him, that she was strong and capable and proud, only made her more appealing and made him more determined to coddle her.

Noise surrounded them, questions, chatter. Sawyer heard Morgan giving directions for Alden to be picked up, but none of it mattered to him. He squeezed her tighter and tried not to make a fool of himself by being overly emotional. She'd been hurt so much already. He tipped her back and kissed the bruise on her cheek. "Are you okay?"

Her long hair fell forward to hide her face. "Yes. I'm sorry I got in your way. Gabe told me you'd be likely to skin me for it, after he finished fussing over me."

"What were you doing out here, sweetheart? I told you to stay safe in the basement."

"I snuck out when Gabe wasn't looking." She peered up at him, her expression earnest. "I couldn't stay down there, hiding, while you put yourself in danger for me. I couldn't." Her uncertainty melted away, replaced by a pugnacious frown. "And you shouldn't have asked me to!"

Sawyer fought a smile. "I'm sorry."

She pulled away and paced. The small cat darted out of the bushes to follow her, keeping up with Honey's agitated stride. It was only then Sawyer realized she was wearing Jordan's shirt. Her housecoat, or what he could see of it beneath the shirt, looked nearly transparent under the bright floodlights. He glanced at Jordan, who lounged against the barn wall, his arms crossed over his bare chest. Casey stood beside him, looking agog at the men being handcuffed by a bevy of uniformed officers. Morgan was in the hub of it all, a tall figure of authority.

Gabe reentered the yard with an ice pack and came

directly to Honey. "Here, sweetie, put this on your cheek."

Honey ignored him, still pacing, her bare feet now wet and her movements agitated. Sawyer took the pack from Gabe and corralled Honey and started the parade back into the house. They'd all be answering questions soon enough, but for right now, Morgan could handle things.

HOURS LATER, Honey once again found herself seated in the kitchen, the center of attention in the middle of the night. All the men were fussing around her, fretful over a silly bruise that she felt stupid for having. If she hadn't panicked, if she hadn't run into the way of a fist, she wouldn't have been hurt. And after seeing Morgan's and Sawyer's knuckles, her one small injury seemed paltry beyond compare.

She sighed. The men each jumped to her aid, taking that small sound as one of pain.

"Will you all stop hovering?" she groused. "You're making me nervous."

Gabe grinned, finally seeing the hilarity in the situation. "I kinda like doting on you, sweetie. You may as well get used to it."

Honey didn't dare look at Sawyer. She tried for a sunny smile that made her face feel ready to crack. "I don't think that'll be necessary. Thanks to you macho guys, my worries are over. There's no reason for me to keep imposing, or to hang around and get used to your domineering personalities. The police told me I could leave, that when they need me, I'll hear from them. And my sister was so anxious when I called her, I think I should be getting home."

It was as if they'd all turned to statues. Honey managed to eke out one more smile, though it cost her. "Since I don't have much to pack, I can be out of here in the morning. But in case I don't catch any of you before you leave for work, I wanted you to know…" Her throat seemed to close up, and she struggled to hold back her tears. Casey stared at her, his jaw ticking, and she wanted to grab him up and claim him as her own. She swallowed and tried again. But this time her voice was so soft, it could barely be heard. "I wanted you all to know how special you are, and how much I appreciate everything you've done for me."

Jordan and Morgan glared at Sawyer. Gabe got up to pace. Casey, still unflinching, said, "Don't go."

Honey stared down at her folded hands. "I have to, Case. It's safe now, and my family needs me."

Morgan made a rude sound. "Your sister, maybe. But your father? I can't believe you're so quick to forgive him."

"I haven't. But he is my father, and I almost lost him by marrying the wrong man. He was as shocked by it all as I was. He said his lawyers will take care of everything, but we still have a lot to talk about."

"You could stay just a little longer," Jordan suggested, and he, too, looked angry.

"I can't keep hiding here, Jordan. It isn't right."

Morgan walked past Sawyer and deliberately shouldered him, nearly knocking him over. Sawyer cursed and turned to face his brother, but Gabe laughed, diffusing the moment. "Down, Sawyer. The fight is over."

Sawyer stared at him, red-eyed and mean.

Honey didn't quite know what to think of him. He'd fought so…effectively. Yet the brothers claimed he was a pacifist. After the way he'd enjoyed punching that man, Honey had her doubts.

Gabe was still chuckling. "You know, Sawyer, it isn't Morgan's ass you're wanting to kick, but your own."

Sawyer glared a moment more, then pulled out a chair and dropped into it. The brothers seemed to find his behavior hilarious, but Honey couldn't share in their humor. She hurt from the inside out, and trying to keep that pain hidden was wearing on her.

Morgan crossed his arms over his chest. "What if she's pregnant?"

Sawyer's narrowed gaze shot to Honey. She sputtered in surprise. "I'm not pregnant!"

"How do you know?"

"Dammit, Morgan, don't you think a woman knows these things?"

"Sure, after a while, but not this early on."

There was no way she would explain with four pairs of masculine eyes watching her, just how careful Sawyer had been. Through her teeth, she growled, "Take my word on it."

Sawyer stood suddenly, nearly upsetting his chair, and he leaned toward Honey, his battered hands spread flat on the tabletop. He looked furious and anxious and determined. "Would you be opposed to getting pregnant?"

Her mouth opened twice before any words would come out. *"Now?"*

He made an impatient sound. "Eventually."

Not at all sure what Sawyer was getting at, her answer was tentative, but also honest. "No, I wouldn't mind. I want to have children." She stared at him hard. "But only if a man loves me. And only if it's forever."

Sawyer straightened, still keeping his gaze glued to hers. "Would you be opposed to sons, because that seems to be the dominate gene among us."

Honey, too, stood. She bit her lips, feeling her heart start to swell. A laugh bubbled up inside her, and she barely repressed it. "I'm getting used to men and their vagaries."

"Your father would have to change his goddamned will, because I won't take a penny from him, now or ever."

"Absolutely. I already told him that."

"Do you love me?"

There was a collective holding of breath, and she smiled. For such big, strong, confident men, they were certainly uneasy about her answer. "Yes. But...but I don't want your pushy brothers to force you into anything."

That response brought about a round of hilarity, with the brothers shouting, "Ha," and, "Yeah, right," and, "As if we ever could!"

Sawyer rounded the table with a purposeful stride and the brothers got out of his way, still laughing. Casey whooped. Sawyer stopped in front of Honey and whispered, "Damn, I love you," which made her laugh and cry, then he scooped her up in his arms and turned so she faced everyone, and announced formally, "If you'll all excuse us, it seems Honey and I have some wedding plans to make."

Morgan clapped him on the shoulder as he walked past, and then winked at Honey. Jordan gave her the thumbs-up.

Casey yelled, "Hey, Dad, just so you don't change your mind, I'm calling Grandma to tell her!"

Sawyer paused. "Now? It's not even dawn yet."

Gabe smirked. "And you know damn good and well she'd skin us all if we waited even one minute more."

Sawyer laughed. "Hell, yes. Go ahead and call her. But you can answer her hundred and one questions, because I don't want to be interrupted." He smiled down at Honey and squeezed her tight. "I plan to be busy for a long, long while."

* * * * *

COWBOY ABOVE THE LAW

Delores Fossen

For devoted reader Betty Kincaid,
who passed along her love of books to her children
and grandchildren. Betty, you'll be missed.

CHAPTER ONE

DEPUTY COURT MCCALL glanced down at the blood on his shirt. *His father's blood.* Just the sight of it sliced away at him and made him feel as if someone had put a bullet in him, too.

Court hadn't changed into clean clothes because he wanted Rayna Travers to see what she had done. He wanted to be right in her face when he told her that she'd failed.

Barely though.

His father, Warren, was still alive, hanging on by a thread, but Court refused to accept that he wouldn't make it. No, his father would not only recover, but Warren would also help Court put Rayna behind bars. This time, she wasn't going to get away with murder.

Court pulled to a stop in front of her house, a place not exactly on the beaten path. Of course, that applied to a lot of the homes in or near McCall Canyon. His ancestors had founded the town over a hundred years ago, and it had become exactly what they'd intended it to be—a ranching community.

What they almost certainly hadn't counted on was having a would-be killer in their midst.

Court looked down at his hands. Steady. That was good. Because there was nothing steady inside him. The anger was bubbling up, and he had to make sure he reined in his temper enough to arrest Rayna. He wouldn't resort to strong-arm tactics, but there was a high chance he would say something he shouldn't.

Since Rayna's car was in her driveway, it probably meant she was home. Good. He hadn't wanted to go hunting for her. Still, it was somewhat of a surprise that she hadn't gone on the run. Of course, she was probably going to say she was innocent, that she hadn't had anything to do with the shot that'd slammed into his father's chest. But simply put, she had a strong motive to kill a McCall.

And then there was the witness.

If Rayna tried to convince him she'd had no part in the shooting, then Court would let her know that someone had spotted her in the vicinity of the sheriff's office just minutes before Warren had been gunned down. Then Court would follow through on her arrest.

He got out of his truck and started toward the porch of the small stone-front house, but Court made it only a few steps because his phone rang, and his brother's name popped up on the screen.

Egan.

Egan wasn't just his big brother though. He was also Court's boss, since Egan was the sheriff of Mc-Call Canyon. By now, Egan had probably figured out where Court was heading and wanted to make sure his deputy followed the book on this one.

He would.

Not cutting corners because he wanted Rayna behind bars.

Court ignored the call, and the ding of the voice mail that followed, and went up the steps to the front door. This wasn't his first time here. Once, he'd made many trips to Rayna's door—before she'd chosen another man over him. Once, he'd had feelings for her. He had feelings now, too, but they had nothing to do with the old attraction he'd once felt.

He steeled himself and put his hand over his firearm in case Rayna wasn't finished with her shooting spree today.

"Open up," Court said, knocking on the door. Of course, he knocked a lot louder than necessary, but he wanted to make sure she heard him.

If she did hear him, she darn sure didn't answer. He knocked again, his anger rising even more, and Court finally tested the knob. Unlocked. So, he threw open the door.

And he found a gun pointed right in his face.

Rayna's finger was on the trigger.

Court cursed and automatically drew his own weapon. Obviously, it was too late because she could have fired before he'd even had a chance to do that. She didn't though. Maybe because Rayna felt she'd already fulfilled her quota of shooting McCalls today.

"Put down your gun," he snarled.

"No." Rayna shook her head, and that was when he noticed there was blood in her blond hair. Blood on the side of her face, too. Added to that, he could see bruises and cuts on her knuckles and wrists. "I'm not going to let you try to kill me again."

"Again?" Court was certain he looked very confused. Because he was. "What the devil are you talking about? I came here to arrest you for shooting my father."

If that news surprised her in the least, she didn't

show it. She didn't lower her gun, either. Rayna stood there, glaring at him.

What the hell had happened here?

Court looked behind her to see if the person who'd given her those injuries was still around. There was no sign of anyone else, but the furniture in the living room had been tossed around. There was a broken lamp on the floor. More blood, too. All indications of a struggle.

"Start talking," Court demanded, making sure he sounded like the lawman that he was.

"I will. When Egan gets here."

Court cursed again. Egan definitely wasn't going to approve of Court storming out here to see her, but his brother also couldn't ignore the evidence that Rayna had shot their father. There was definitely something else going on though.

"My father's alive," Court told her. "You didn't manage to kill him after all."

She looked down at his shirt. At the blood. And Rayna glanced away as if the sight of it sickened her. Court took advantage of her glance and knocked the gun from her hand.

At least that was what he tried to do, but Rayna held on. She pushed him, and in the same motion, she turned to run. That was when Court tackled her. Her gun went flying, skittering all the way into the living room, and both Court and she landed hard on the floor.

Rayna groaned in pain. It wasn't a soft groan, and while holding her side, she scrambled away from him. Court was about to dive at her again, but he saw yet more blood. This time on the side that she was holding.

That stopped him.

"What's wrong with you? What happened?" Court snapped.

She looked around as if considering another run for it, but then her shoulders sagged as if she was surrendering.

Rayna sat up, putting her weight, and the back of her head, against the wall. She opened her mouth as if to start with that explanation, but she had to pause when her breath shuddered. She waved that off as if embarrassed by it and then hiked up her chin. It seemed to him as if she was trying to look strong.

She failed.

"When I came in from the barn about an hour ago, there was someone in my house," Rayna said, her voice still a little unsteady. "I didn't see who it was because he immediately clubbed me on the head and grabbed me from behind." She winced again when she rubbed her left side. "I think he cracked my ribs when he hit me with something."

Well, hell. Court certainly hadn't expected any of this. And reminded himself that maybe it was all a lie, to cover up for the fact that she'd committed a crime. But those wounds weren't lies. They were the real deal. That didn't mean that they weren't self-inflicted.

"I got away from him," she continued a moment later. "After he hit me a few more times. And I pulled my gun, which I had in a slide holster in the back of my jeans. That's when he left. I'm not sure where he went."

That didn't make sense. "If someone really broke in an hour ago, why didn't you call the sheriff's office right away?"

Rayna lifted her head a little and raised her eyebrow.

For a simple gesture, it said loads. She didn't trust the cops. Didn't trust *him*.

Well, the feeling was mutual.

"I passed out for a while," she added. She shook her head as if even she was confused by that, and she lifted the side of her shirt that had the blood. There was a bruise there, too, and what appeared to be a puncture wound. One that had likely caused the bleeding. "Or maybe the guy drugged me."

"Great," he muttered. This was getting more far-fetched with each passing moment. "FYI, I'm not buying this. And as for not calling the cops when you were attacked, you called Egan when you saw me," Court pointed out.

"Because I didn't want things to escalate to this." She motioned to their positions on the floor. "Obviously, it didn't work."

He huffed. "And neither is this story you're telling." Court got to his feet and took out his phone. "Only a couple of minutes before my father was gunned down, a waitress in the diner across the street from the sheriff's office spotted you in the parking lot. There's no way you could have been here in your house during this so-called attack because you were in town."

She quit wincing so she could glare at him. "I was here." Her tone said *I don't care if you believe me or not.*

He didn't believe her. "You must have known my father had been shot because you didn't react when I told you."

"I did know. Whitney called me when I was walking back from the barn. I'd just gotten off the phone with her when that goon clubbed me."

Whitney Goble, her best friend. And it was entirely possible that Whitney had either seen his father get shot or heard about it shortly thereafter because she worked part-time as a dispatcher for the sheriff's office. It would be easy enough to check to see if Whitney had indeed called her, and using her cell phone records, they could possibly figure out Rayna's location when she'd talked to her friend. Court was betting it hadn't been on Rayna's walk back from the barn. It had been while she was escaping from the scene of the shooting.

"This waitress claims she saw me shoot your father?" Rayna asked.

He hated that he couldn't answer yes to that, but Court couldn't. "She was in the kitchen when the actual shot was fired. But the bullet came from the park directly behind the sheriff's office parking lot. The very parking lot where you were right before the attack."

Judging from her repeated flat look, Rayna was about to deny that, so Court took out his phone and opened the photo. "The waitress took that picture of you."

Court didn't go closer to her with the phone, but Rayna stood. Not easily. She continued to clutch her side and blew out some short, rough breaths. However, she shook her head the moment her attention landed on the grainy shot of the woman in a red dress. A woman with hair the same color blond as Rayna's.

"That's not me," she insisted. "I don't have a dress that color. And besides, I wasn't there."

This was a very frustrating conversation, but thankfully he had more. He tapped the car that was just up the street from the woman in the photo. "That's your car, your license plate."

With her forehead bunched up, Rayna snatched the phone from him and had a closer look. "That's not my car. I've been home all morning." Her gaze flew to his, and now there was some venom in her eyes. "You're trying to set me up." She groaned and practically threw his phone at him. "Haven't you McCalls already done enough to me without adding this?"

Court caught his phone, but he had to answer her through clenched teeth. "We haven't done anything."

She laughed, but there wasn't a trace of humor in it. "Right. Remember Bobby Joe?" she spat out. "Or did you forget about him?"

Bobby Joe Hawley. No, Court hadn't forgotten. Obviously, neither had Rayna.

"Three years ago, your father tried to pin Bobby Joe's murder on me," Rayna continued. "It didn't work. A jury acquitted me."

He couldn't deny the acquittal. "Being found not guilty isn't the same as being innocent."

Something that ate away at him. Because the evidence had been there. Bobby Joe's blood in Rayna's house. Blood that she'd tried to clean up. There'd also been the knife found in her barn. It'd had Bobby Joe's blood on it, too. What was missing were Rayna's prints. Ditto for the body. They'd never found it, but Rayna could have hidden it along with wiping her prints from the murder weapon.

The jury hadn't seen it that way though.

Possibly because they hadn't been able to look past one other piece of evidence. Bobby Joe had assaulted Rayna on several occasions, both while they'd been together and after their breakup when she'd gotten a restraining order against him. In her mind, she probably thought that was justification to kill him. And equal justification to now go after Court's father, who'd been sheriff at the time. Warren had been the one to press for Rayna's arrest and trial. After that, his father had retired. But Rayna could have been holding a serious grudge against him all this time.

She'd certainly held one against Court.

He heard the sound of a vehicle pulling up in front of Rayna's house and knew it was Egan before he glanced out the still-open door. He also knew Egan wouldn't be pleased. And he was right. His brother was sporting a scowl when he got out of the cruiser and started for the door.

Egan was only two years older than Court, but he definitely had that "big brother, I'm in charge" air about him. Egan had somehow managed to have that even when he'd still been a deputy. Folks liked to joke that he could kick your butt even before you'd known it was kicked.

"If you think Egan is going to let you walk, think again," Court warned her.

"I won't let him railroad me," she insisted, aiming another scowl at Court. "I won't let you do it, either. It doesn't matter that we have a history together. That history gives you no right to pull some stunt like this."

They had a history all right. Filled with both good and bad memories. They'd been high school sweethearts, but that "young love" was significantly overshadowed by the bad blood that was between them now.

Egan stepped into the house, putting his hands on his hips, and made a sweeping glance around the room before his attention landed on Court. "Please tell me you're not responsible for any of this."

"I'm not." At least Court hoped he wasn't, but it was possible he'd added some to the damage when he tackled her. "Rayna said someone broke in."

Court figured his brother was also going to have a hard time believing that. It did seem too much of a coincidence that his father would be shot and Rayna would have a break-in around the same time.

"You shouldn't have come," Egan said to him in a rough whisper.

Court was certain he'd hear more of that later, but he had a darn good reason for being here. "I didn't want her to escape."

"And I thought he'd come here to kill me," Rayna countered. "I pulled a gun on him." She swallowed hard. "Things didn't go well after that."

Egan huffed and grumbled something that Court didn't catch before he took out his phone and texted someone.

"Court didn't do any of the damage in this room," Rayna added. "It happened when an intruder attacked me."

That only tightened Egan's mouth even more before he shifted his gaze to Rayna. "An ambulance is on the way. How bad are you hurt?" he asked and put his phone back in his pocket.

She waved it off, wincing again while she did that. Yeah, she was hurt. But Court thought Egan was missing what was really important here.

"She shot Dad," Court reminded Egan. "We have the picture, remember?" Though he knew there was no way his brother could have forgotten that. "It's proof she was there. Proof that she shot him."

"No, it's not." Egan groaned, scrubbed his hand over his face. "I think someone tried to set Rayna up."

Court opened his mouth to say that wasn't true. But then Egan took out his own phone and showed him a picture.

"A few minutes after you stormed out of the hospital," Egan continued, "Eldon Cooper, the clerk at the hardware store, found this."

"This" was a blond-haired woman wearing a red dress. An identical dress to the one in the photo the waitress had taken. But this one had one big difference from the first picture.

In this one, the woman was dead.

CHAPTER TWO

RAYNA SLOWLY WALKED toward Egan so she could see the photograph that had caused Court to go stiff. It had caused him to mumble some profanity, too, and Rayna soon knew why.

The woman in the photograph had been shot in the head.

There was blood. Her body was limp, and her lifeless eyes were fixed in a permanent blank stare at the sky.

Rayna dropped back a step, an icy chill going through her. Because Court had been right. The woman did look like her. The one in the first picture did, anyway. The second photo was much clearer, and while it wasn't a perfect match, the dead woman looked enough like her to be a relative. But Rayna knew she didn't have any living relatives.

"Someone killed her because of me?" she whispered.

Neither Court nor Egan denied it.

She felt the tears threaten. The panic, too. But Rayna forced herself not to give in to either of them. Not in front of Court, anyway. Later, she could have a cry, tend to her wounds and try to figure out what the heck was going on.

"Who is she?" Rayna asked.

"We don't have an ID on her yet, but we will soon.

After the medical examiner's had a look at her, then we'll search for any ID. If there isn't any on her body or in the car, we'll run her prints."

It was so hard for Rayna to think with her head hurting, but she forced herself to try to figure this out. "Why would someone go to all the trouble of having a look-alike and then leave a car behind with bogus plates?"

Egan shrugged again. "It goes back to someone setting you up." He sounded a little skeptical about that though. "Unless you hired the woman in that photo to pose as you. You could have gotten spooked when something went wrong and left the car."

Even though she'd braced herself to have more accusations tossed at her, that still stung. It always did. Because this accusation went beyond just hiring an impostor. He was almost certainly implying that she had something to do with the woman's death, too.

"No. I didn't hire her," Rayna managed to say, though her throat had clamped shut. "And I didn't shoot your father. I haven't been in town in weeks, and that wasn't my car parked near the sheriff's office."

Egan nodded, glanced at Court. "She's right about the car. The plates are fake. I had one of the deputies go out and take a look at it. It's still parked up the street from the office. Someone painted over the numbers so that it matched the plates on Rayna's vehicle."

Again, Egan was making it sound as if she had something to do with that. Good grief. Why was she always having to defend herself when it came to the McCalls?

Of course, she knew the answer.

She'd made her own bed when it'd come to Bobby

Joe. She had stayed with him even after he'd hit her and called her every name in the book. She had let him rob her of her confidence. Her dignity.

And nearly her life.

But Egan and Court—and their father—hadn't seen things that way. Bobby Joe had kept the abuse hidden. A wolf in sheep's clothing, and very few people in town had been on her side when Warren McCall had arrested her for Bobby Joe's murder.

"You're barking up the wrong tree—again," Rayna added. "I didn't have anything to do with this. And why would I? If I were going to shoot anyone, why would I send in a look-alike? Why would I pick a spot like Main Street, which is practically on the doorstep of a building filled with cowboy cops?"

Egan shrugged. "Maybe to make us believe you're innocent and knew nothing about it."

"I am innocent," she practically yelled. Rayna stopped though and peered at the mess in the living room. "But maybe my intruder is behind what happened in town and what happened to that woman, as well. He could have arranged to have your father shot, killed her, and then he could have come out here to attack me. His prints could be on the lamp. It's what he used to bash me over the head."

Court looked at her, and for a split second, she thought she saw some sympathy in his intense gray eyes. It was gone as quickly as it'd come, and he stood there, waiting. Maybe for an explanation that would cause all of this to make sense. But she couldn't give him that.

Rayna huffed. "If I was going to do something to fake an assault, I wouldn't have hit myself that hard on my head or cracked my ribs. And I wouldn't have broken my grandmother's lamp."

It sickened her to see it shattered like that. In the grand scheme of things, it wasn't a huge deal, but it felt like one to her. It was one of the few things she had left of her gran. And now it was gone—much like what little peace of mind she'd managed to regain over the past year.

"Who do you think would have done something like this?" Court asked, tipping his head toward the living room.

"Bobby Joe," she answered without thinking. She knew it would get huffs and eye rolls from them, and it did. "You think he's dead, that I killed him. But I know I didn't. So, that means he could still be out there."

Court didn't repeat his huff, but she could tell he wanted to. "So, you think Bobby Joe set you up for my father's shooting and then came out here and attacked you? If he's really alive, why would he wait three years to do that?"

Rayna gave it some thought and didn't have an answer. However, she wouldn't put it past Bobby Joe. At the end of their relationship, he'd threatened to kill her. Maybe this was his way of doing that. Bobby Joe could be toying with her while also getting back at Warren McCall, who hadn't managed to get her convicted of murder.

But there was something else. A piece that didn't seem to fit.

"Tell me about the waitress," Rayna insisted. "Who was she, and why did she take the picture of the woman in the parking lot?"

"Her name is Janet Bolin," Court answered. "She

said she took the photo because she thought you…or rather the woman…was acting strange."

Egan groaned. Probably because he was agreeing with her theory of an ill-fitting puzzle piece. "I'll get a CSI team out here to process the place." He pressed a button on his phone and went onto the porch to make the call.

"You know this waitress?" Rayna asked Court.

He shook his head. "She's new, has only been working there a week or so, but I've seen her around. We'll bring her in for questioning."

Good. Because it meant Rayna was finally making some headway in convincing Court that she hadn't fired that shot or had anything to do with that woman's death.

She hesitated before asking her next question. "How's your father?" Warren was a touchy subject for both of them.

A muscle flickered in Court's jaw. "He's out of surgery but still unconscious. We don't know just how bad the damage is yet."

He might have added more, might, but a sound outside stopped him. Sirens. They were from the ambulance that was coming up the road. Since her house was the only one out here, they were here for her.

"I don't want an ambulance," she insisted. "I'll go to the hospital on my own." And it wouldn't be to the one in McCall Canyon. She would drive into nearby San Antonio.

"That's not a very smart thing to do." No pause for Court that time. "We're not sure what's going on here. Plus, your ribs could be broken. You don't need to be driving if they are."

She couldn't help it. Rayna gave him a snarky smile before she could stop herself. "Worried about me?"

That earned her another glare, but this one didn't last. And for a moment she saw something else. Not the sympathy this time, either. But the old attraction. Even now, it tugged at her. Apparently, it tugged at Court because he cursed again and looked away.

"I just wanted to make sure I didn't hurt you when we fell on the floor," Court said.

"You didn't." That was probably a lie, but Rayna was hurting in so many places that it was hard to tell who was responsible for the bruises and cuts.

Court's gaze came back to her. "Was there any-thing…sexual about the assault after you got hit on the head?"

"No." Thank God. That was something at least. "In fact, I'm not even sure he intended to kill me. I mean, he could have shot me the moment I walked into my house—"

"Maybe he didn't have a gun. He could have been robbing the place and got spooked when you came in."

True. But that didn't feel right. Neither did the spot on her ribs, and Rayna had another look. Too bad that meant pulling up her top again, and this time Court examined it, too. He leaned in, so close that she could feel his breath hitting her skin.

"It looks like a needle mark," he said. "And you mentioned something about passing out?"

She nodded. "But the man was gone by the time that happened." Of course, he could have come back. Heck, he could still come back.

That made her stomach tighten, and she gave an

uneasy glance around the front and side yards. There were plenty of places on her land for someone to hide.

"You're sure it was a man?" Court asked. He was using his lawman's tone again. Good. That was easier to deal with than the old attraction. "You said you didn't get a look at the person, so how do you know it was a man?"

"I've had a man's hands on me before, so yes, I'm sure he was male." She immediately hated that she'd blurted that out, even if it was true. But Rayna didn't like reminding anyone, especially Court, of just how wrong she'd been about Bobby Joe. After all, she'd let Court go to be with him.

"After he clubbed me with the lamp," Rayna added, "he hooked his arm around my throat. My back landed against his chest, so I know it was a man."

Court took a moment, obviously processing that, and he looked at the lock on the front door. "There's no sign of forced entry. Was it locked, and did you have on your security system?"

Everything inside her went still. With all the chaos that had gone on, it hadn't occurred to Rayna to ask herself those questions. "Yes, it would have been locked, and the security system was on. I never leave the house without doing that."

"Even if you were just going to the barn?" Court immediately asked.

"Even then." She gathered her breath, which had suddenly gone thin again. It always did when she thought of the woman she'd become. "I honestly believe Bobby Joe is alive and that he could come after me."

Court looked ready to grumble out some profanity, but Rayna wasn't sure if that was because he felt sorry for her or because he thought she was crazy for being so wary about a man he believed was dead.

"The front door was unlocked when I got here," Court continued several moments later. "Is it possible your intruder had a key?"

"No. And I don't keep a spare one lying around, either." She kept her attention on the ambulance that stopped behind the cruiser. "Plus, he would have had to disarm the security system. It's tamperproof, so he couldn't have simply cut a wire or something. He would have had to know the code."

With each word, that knot in her stomach got tighter and tighter. She had taken all the necessary precautions, and it hadn't been enough. That hurt. Because she might never feel safe here again in this house that she loved. Her gran's house. That didn't mean she would leave. No. She wouldn't give Bobby Joe the satisfaction of seeing her run, but Rayna figured there'd be a lot more sleepless nights in her future.

Egan was still on the phone when the medics got out of the ambulance and started for the porch. Rayna went out to tell them they could leave, but she spotted another vehicle. A familiar one.

Whitney's red Mustang.

"You called her?" Court asked.

Rayna shook her head, but it didn't surprise her that Whitney had heard about what happened and then had driven out to see her. They'd been friends since third grade, and even though that friendship had cooled a little after Rayna had gotten involved with Bobby Joe, Whitney had usually been there for her. Whitney was also one of the few people who'd stood by her when Rayna had been on trial.

Her friend bolted from the car and ran past the medics to get to Rayna. Whitney immediately pulled her into her arms for a hug. An uncomfortable one because Rayna felt the pain from her ribs, and she backed away.

"I came as fast as I could get someone to cover for me at work." Whitney's words rushed together. "My God, you're hurt." She reached out as if to touch the wound on Rayna's hand, but she stopped. "It must be bad if the ambulance came."

"No. They were just leaving." Rayna made sure she said that loud enough for the medics to hear.

"They're not leaving," Court snapped, and he motioned for them to wait. No doubt so he could try to talk Rayna into going with them.

Whitney volleyed puzzled looks between Court and her. "Is, uh, anything going on between you two? I mean, you're not back together, are you?"

"No," Court and Rayna answered in unison, but it did make Rayna wonder what Whitney had picked up on to make her think that.

Whitney released her breath as if relieved. Maybe because she knew Rayna wasn't ready for a relationship. Especially one with Court McCall.

"What happened here?" Whitney asked, glancing inside.

"Someone broke in," Rayna settled for saying. She planned to give Whitney more information later, but her friend filled in the blanks.

"And you think it was Bobby Joe," Whitney concluded. But she immediately shook her head after saying that. "It seems to be more than that going on. I mean, what with Warren being shot."

Court made a sound of agreement. "Do you have a

key to Rayna's house? And no, I'm not accusing her of anything," Court quickly added to Rayna. "I'm just trying to figure out how the intruder got in."

"No key," Whitney answered. "Bobby Joe wouldn't have one, either. Rayna changed all the locks after she was acquitted. She had the windows and doors wired for security, too. Did she tell you that she has guns stashed all around the house?"

Rayna gave Whitney a sharp look to get her to hush. But it was too late. After hearing that, Court was probably even more convinced that she was about to go off the deep end.

"So, are you coming with us?" one of the medics called out. He sounded, and looked, impatient.

Rayna knew him. His name was Dustin Mendoza. A friend of Bobby Joe's. Of course, pretty much every man in McCall Canyon in their midthirties fell into that particular category.

"No," Rayna repeated.

She figured Court was about to do some repeating as well and insist that she go. He didn't. "I'll drive Rayna to the hospital. I need to ask her some more questions about the break-in."

Dustin didn't wait around to see if that was okay with her. He motioned for his partner to leave, and they started back for the ambulance.

"I also think you should consider protective custody," Court said to her. "The intruder obviously knows how to get in your house, and he could come back."

That had already occurred to Rayna, but it chilled her to the bone to hear someone say it.

"You can stay with me," Whitney suggested. "In fact, I can take you to the hospital."

It was generous of Whitney, and Rayna was about to consider accepting, but Court spoke before she could say anything. "That could be dangerous. For Whitney. If this intruder is still after you, he could go to her place while looking for you."

That drained some of the color from Whitney's face. Obviously, it wasn't something she'd considered when she'd made the offer.

"It's okay," Rayna assured her. "I can make other plans."

She didn't know what exactly those plans would be, but she might have to hire a bodyguard. And put some distance between her and the McCalls. Whatever was going on seemed to be connected to them. Rayna didn't think it was a coincidence about the timing of Warren's attack, the break-in and the dead woman.

Egan finally finished his call, and the moment he turned to walk toward them, Rayna knew something was wrong.

"Is it Dad?" Court immediately asked.

Egan shook his head. "It's the waitress. Janet Bolin. She's dead. Someone murdered her."

CHAPTER THREE

ANOTHER MURDER. Two women killed only hours apart. There was no way Court could dismiss them as not being connected.

But connected to what?

Rayna. His father. Or maybe both.

He put on a clean shirt that he took from his locker and thought about that possible connection while he made his way back into the squad room, where Rayna was waiting. Or rather where she was pacing. He nearly reminded her that she should probably be sitting down. That was what the doctor had wanted anyway when he'd come to the sheriff's office to examine her. Rayna wasn't having any part of that though. And he couldn't blame her. It was hard to sit still with all this restless energy bubbling up inside him.

"Anything?" she asked the moment she saw him.

Court took a deep breath that sounded as weary as he felt. "There's no gunshot residue on your hands." He'd swabbed her hands as soon as they'd gotten to the sheriff's office but hadn't been able to run the test right away because of all the other calls.

And changing his shirt.

Court had figured he'd worn his father's blood long enough and no longer wanted it in his sight.

Rayna didn't huff, but it was close. "Tell me something I don't know. Of course there wasn't gunshot residue on my hands, because I didn't fire a gun."

He almost pointed out that she could have cleaned up afterward, but plain and simple, that probably hadn't happened. And it wouldn't explain how she'd gotten all those wounds. So, Court did as Rayna asked and gave her something she almost certainly didn't know.

"Janet was killed with a single shot to the head at point-blank range. Her body was in the alley behind the diner, and it doesn't appear as if she was moved after she was shot. No ID yet on the other woman."

But the two had something in common. There'd been no defensive wounds, which meant their killer had gotten close enough to deliver the fatal shots without alarming the women.

"No one in or around the diner heard the shot?" she pressed.

"No. But she had her purse, and Pete, the cook, said she had three more hours on her shift. She didn't have a cell phone on her, but maybe she'd made arrangements to meet someone."

And that *someone* had killed her.

That could mean Janet was in on his father's shooting. Or maybe she'd just been duped into taking the photo that had almost certainly been meant to frame Rayna.

"There aren't any surveillance cameras back there," Court added. That pretty much applied to most of the town. Simply put, there hadn't been much need for them.

Until now, that was.

There'd been only two murders in the past ten years. A drunken brawl at the local bar and Bobby Joe's. But now they had two unsolved homicides, an attempted murder, breaking and entering, and an assault. It was no wonder Egan had been tied up in the past three hours. His brother was at the first murder scene, and that was why Court had been manning the phones along with keeping an eye on Rayna.

Court hadn't mentioned it yet, but she was now a key witness, since she might be able to recall something about the man who'd attacked her. She was almost certainly in grave danger, as well.

"It doesn't make sense," Rayna mumbled.

It was something she'd said multiple times after Court had insisted that she come to the sheriff's office. Well, first he'd tried to talk her into going to the hospital, and when he'd failed at that, he'd brought her here instead. It was far better than her being at Whitney's, and both Rayna and she had finally agreed on that. Rayna had also agreed on the doctor seeing her.

"How are your ribs and your head?" Court asked.

"Fine," she answered, practically waving off his concern.

But he knew there had to be some pain. The doctor didn't think her ribs were broken, but there was a deep bruise, and a second one on her head where the intruder had hit her.

"The doctor drew blood," she added, rubbing the inside of her arm. "Whatever the thug slammed into me might still be in my system."

Yeah, but it might not give them any new info to catch him. Still, it was something they needed to know so they could make sure it didn't have any serious side effects.

He tipped his head toward Egan's office, which was

just off the squad room. "There's a semicomfortable chair in there. Some bottled water, too. You could sit and wait while I call the lab and push them to get an ID on the first woman."

Rayna stopped pacing and made eye contact with him. "You're being nice to me."

Was he? Court lifted his shoulder. "I just figured we could call a truce and try to get through this hellish day."

Rayna kept staring at him a moment before she nodded and headed for the office. Court was right behind her, but he glanced around the squad room first to make sure all was well. There was only one other deputy, Thea Morris, who was taking a statement from another waitress who worked at the diner. The other four deputies were out at their three crime scenes.

"If you want to go to the hospital to see your dad," Rayna said, "please do. I know you'd rather be with him."

He would. But his father was still unconscious, so there was nothing Court could do. Plus, his mom, Helen, and his sister, Rachel, were there. Along with a Texas Ranger, Griff Morris, who Warren had practically raised. He was like family, and he'd call Court if there were any changes in his father's condition. Or if any more trouble surfaced. Right now, Court would do his dad more good by trying to figure out who'd put that bullet in him.

"You don't have to babysit me," Rayna added.

He did indeed have to do just that, and Court didn't bother to pull any punches when he looked at her.

"Oh," she said, and Rayna looked even more unsteady when she sank into the chair across from the desk.

"It's not personal," he added because he thought

that might help. Help who exactly, Court didn't know. It certainly felt personal. And it couldn't. He couldn't let their past—either the good or the bad parts—play into this.

He made the call to the lab, promptly got put on hold, so while he was waiting, Court took a copy of her statement that he'd printed out and passed it to her.

"Look this over and try to fill in any gaps in details," he instructed. "For instance, do you remember hearing the sound of a vehicle when your attacker fled?"

"No." Rayna sounded steady enough when she said that, but when Court gave her a closer look, he saw that she was blinking back tears. Waving them off, too, when she realized he'd noticed.

"I hate this," she said. "I've spent three years rebuilding my life, and now it feels as if it's falling apart again."

Court had no idea how to respond to that, so he stayed quiet, fished out a box of tissues from the bottom drawer and passed them to her.

"I took self-defense classes," she went on. "Firearms training. I installed a security system and don't go anywhere without a gun. Except here, of course."

He would have liked to have told her there was no need for one here, that she was under the roof with two deputies, but since his father had been shot just yards from here, he doubted his words would give her much assurance. Plus, there was the part about her not trusting him.

"You did all of that because you were afraid of Bobby Joe returning?" Court tried to keep his tone neutral. They already had enough battles to fight without his adding some disbelief to that.

"Not afraid," Rayna said in a whisper. "I wanted to be able to stop him if he came after me again. I learned the hard way that I can't rely on others to help me with that."

Court couldn't help himself. It was a knee-jerk reaction, but he went on the offensive, something he usually did with Rayna. "I arrested Bobby Joe after you'd had enough of him and decided to press charges," he reminded her.

"Yes, and he spent less than an hour in jail. After that, he threatened to kill me, stormed out and then faked his death to set me up."

If that had truly happened, then Court felt bad that he hadn't been able to do more. But that was a big *if*. Most folks had liked Bobby Joe and gotten along with him just fine.

Court wasn't one of those folks.

Bobby Joe and he had always seemed to be bristling at each other. Maybe because Rayna and Court had dated through most of high school. Bobby Joe could have been jealous, and Court figured his own bristling stemmed from the fact that Rayna had crushed his heart when she'd broken up with him.

But that was water under a very old bridge.

"Are you ever going to at least consider that Bobby Joe could be alive?" Rayna asked.

He didn't have to figure out what his answer would be because Clyde Selby, the lab guy, finally came back on the line. "Sorry to keep you waiting," Clyde said. "I wanted to see what we had on the second woman before I spoke to you. Anyway, the first woman, the blonde, is Hallie Ramon. She is, *was*, a college student. She was in the system because of a drug arrest when she was eighteen. But she didn't have any gun-shot residue on her hands, so I don't think she's the one who shot your dad."

Court felt the slam of disappointment. Whoever had done this was still out there.

He immediately pulled up everything he had on her. There wasn't much. No record other than the drug possession. The woman was twenty-four and didn't even have a traffic ticket. But then something caught his eye.

"She was a drama student." Court hadn't meant to say that aloud, but it certainly caught Rayna's attention.

She moved to the edge of her seat. Court hated to disappoint her, but there likely wouldn't be anything else from the lab. Any new info now would come from working the case, and that meant talking to Hallie's friends to find out how she was connected to what had happened in McCall Canyon.

"You mentioned the second woman," Court prompted Clyde.

"Yes. Janet Bolin. Egan sent me her prints, and there's no match for her. Don't know who she is because unlike the first woman, she's not in the system. No driver's license, nothing."

Court groaned. That meant she'd lied when she'd applied for the waitress job. Had probably even used a fake ID. That was going to make it a whole lot harder. Because until they knew who she was, they wouldn't be able to figure out how she was connected to this.

"Is she here?" someone yelled. "I want to see her now!"

Court instantly recognized the voice and knew this would be trouble. It was Mitch Hawley, Bobby Joe's brother. And the *she* that he was yelling about was almost certainly Rayna.

She got right up out of the chair and whirled to face Mitch. And not just face him. She went straight out into the squad room. If she was the least bit afraid of him, she didn't show it.

But she should have.

Unlike Bobby Joe, Mitch was not well liked, and he had a nasty temper. Court had had to arrest him on several occasions for fighting. That was why Court hurried to get between them. He didn't mind arresting Mitch again, but he didn't want the man hitting Rayna. Mitch was a big guy, around six-two, and he was heavily muscled. A build that suited him because he worked with rodeo bulls, but his fists could do a lot of damage.

"Why isn't she locked up?" Mitch snarled.

"Because I haven't done anything wrong," Rayna answered.

"Right. You killed my brother, and now you shot his dad." His gaze flew to Court. "Please tell me you're not covering for her."

"No need. There's no GSR on her, and at the time of the shooting, someone was attacking her. What do you know about that?"

That put some fire in Mitch's already fiery brown eyes. "Are you accusing me of something?"

"Not at the moment. Right now, I'm asking a question. Depending on how you answer it, I'll make an accusation or not."

Rayna shook her head, maybe asking Court not to fight her battles, but he wasn't. With everything else going on, he hadn't had time to work on who'd attacked

Rayna, but because of their history, Mitch was an automatic suspect.

"No. I didn't go after her. Didn't have anything to do with this hell-storm that hit town today." Mitch snapped toward Rayna as if ready to return some verbal fire, but he stopped, smiled. "Looks like somebody worked you over good."

"Was it you who did it?" Court pressed, getting Mitch's attention back on him.

The man had to get his teeth unclenched before he could speak. "No. I wouldn't waste my time on a killer. But I can't believe you'd just let her walk. She had motive to shoot your father."

"Yeah, and so do you," Court reminded him. "In fact, I seem to remember you pressing my dad and the rest of us to put Rayna behind bars. We did, and she was acquitted. End of story."

"No, hell, no. It's not the end." He flung his index finger in her direction. "If she's capable of killing my brother, she's capable of anything."

"Apparently not," Rayna spoke up. "I'm not capable of convincing anyone that *not guilty* means I didn't do it." She spared Court a glance to let him know he fell into that category, too.

"Because you bought off the jury or something. I begged Warren to try to reopen the case against you—"

"There's no case to reopen," Court interrupted. He was getting a glimpse of what Rayna had been dealing with for the past three years. "She can't be tried again because that's double jeopardy."

"Then find something else. Conspiracy or tampering with evidence." Mitch paused only long enough to curse. "Next week is the third anniversary of my brother's murder, and no one has paid for that."

And no one might pay. Court kept that to himself though. Simply put, Rayna had been their one and only suspect.

"Why'd you go to my father with all of this?" Court asked.

Mitch huffed, clearly annoyed with that question. "I went to him because I don't get anywhere with Egan and you, that's why. I figured I could get him to sway you into doing something. Warren told me to let it go. To get a life. Can you believe that?"

Yeah, he could. Warren could be steel-hard and cold. Even though his father hated that Rayna had been acquitted, he hated even more that Mitch was blaming the McCalls for that.

Mitch rubbed his head. "I can't let it go. I keep dreaming about Bobby Joe. Nightmares. It's as if he's trying to tell me from the grave to get justice for him." He looked up, blinked, the expression of a man who felt he'd maybe said too much. Or maybe Mitch just hadn't wanted them to hear the raw emotion that was still in his voice.

"There is no new evidence to charge Rayna with anything," Court said. "Not Bobby Joe's murder and not my father's shooting."

"Then you're not looking hard enough," Mitch snarled. His face hardened. "And she's responsible for that. She's got you convinced that she's the same girl you loved back in high school. Well, she's not."

Mitch moved his hand toward Rayna as if he might take hold of her, but Court snagged his wrist.

"It's time for you to go," he warned him.

Mitch threw off Court's grip with far more force than necessary. "You should have known she'd pull something like shooting your dad. The signs were there. Even Janet said so."

Court pulled back his shoulders. "Janet?"

"Yeah, the new waitress at the diner across the street. I was in there earlier this week…" Mitch stopped. He must have realized Rayna's and Court's expressions had changed.

"What did *Janet* say about me?" Rayna demanded.

Some of that fire started to cool a bit, and Mitch got quiet for several long moments. "She knew a lot about you. About what'd happened with Bobby Joe. She asked me questions about it."

Court jumped right on that. "What kind of questions?"

Mitch volleyed some glances at both of them and shook his head. "Things like how often Rayna came into town and such."

Bingo. It meant she was spying on Rayna. "Did Janet ever say anything about hurting Rayna or getting back at her for some reason?" Court asked.

Mitch's eyes widened. "No. Of course not. She wouldn't have. I mean, what with her being a private detective and all."

Now Court was certain his own eyes widened. "What made you think she was a PI?"

"She let it slip, and I saw her ID once when it fell out of her pocket. I thought you knew."

Court glanced at Rayna to see if she had any idea about this. She didn't. She shook her head.

"I thought you knew," Mitch repeated. "After all, Janet was working for your father. Warren's the one who hired her."

CHAPTER FOUR

ANSWERS. THAT WAS what Rayna needed right now. Along with another place to stay. She only hoped she managed to get both soon.

Her place wasn't exactly safe, so that was why Court had brought her to the guesthouse on the grounds of his family's ranch. She felt as if she'd slept in the enemy's camp. With her enemy, since Court had stayed the night with her. She was betting though that there hadn't been much sleeping going on. There certainly hadn't been on her part. She hadn't been able to turn off her mind. Hadn't been able to forget that someone was trying to frame her for murder.

Again.

If Bobby Joe was truly behind this, then she prayed he'd just go ahead and show his face so she could put an end to this once and for all.

Since the cabin wasn't that large, Rayna had no trouble hearing someone moving around in the kitchen. Court, no doubt, because she also smelled coffee. While she wasn't especially anxious to face him, she did need some caffeine, and maybe he would have updates that would give her those answers. Specifically, updates on his father. She needed to know if Mitch had been right when he said that Warren had hired the now dead waitress.

If he had, then maybe this was Warren's twisted way of trying to send her to jail. This time for good.

But Rayna had to mentally shake her head at that thought. From all accounts, Warren could have been killed when he was shot. If this was a plan he'd orchestrated, he wouldn't have put his life at risk like that.

Rayna took a deep breath to steady herself and walked into the kitchen. Not a long trek at all, only a few yards. She immediately saw that she'd been right about it being Court in the kitchen. Right about the coffee, too, because he was pouring himself a cup.

"You're up and dressed," he commented, sounding relieved.

That relief was probably about the being dressed part though. It would have been too much of a trip down memory lane if she'd just been wearing her nightgown—or nothing at all—since Court had brought her here a couple of times when they'd still been dating.

"I wore my clothes to bed," she said, making a beeline for the coffee. That way, if they were attacked, she would be ready to run or fight back. "I'll need to go back to my place and check on the horses."

"I sent a couple of the ranch hands over to do that. I didn't think it was a good idea for you to be out in the open like that."

No. It wasn't a smart idea, but Rayna still wished she could at least see the horses. Just being around them usually calmed her, and she desperately needed that right now.

"Thanks," she muttered. She was surprised and glad that Court had thought to do something like that. Of course, she'd probably been on his mind most of the morning, not in a good way, either.

"In case you're still in pain." Court slid a bottle of pain meds across the counter toward her. It was the prescription stuff the doctor had called into the pharmacy for her. Apparently, someone had picked it up and brought it to the ranch.

She thanked him again but wouldn't take any. Her head was already cloudy enough without adding those to the mix. "Please tell me you have good news."

His shrug didn't give her much hope. "My dad's still not conscious, so we haven't been able to ask him about Janet or whoever the heck she is. But we did get back your results from the blood test the doctor took, and you were drugged. It was a barbiturate, definitely meant to knock you out."

Then it was mission accomplished for her attacker, and he'd likely done that so she wouldn't show up in town at the same time as Hallie Ramon, the woman in red who had been near the sheriff's office. And either the woman had been there to shoot Warren or else Hallie had been set up, just as someone had attempted to do to her.

"What about you?" he asked. "You remember anything new about the person who drugged you?"

She had a long sip of coffee and shook her head. "But last night I called the company that installed my security system. They insist no one who works for them would have given out my code to disarm the system."

"Even if they had, there's the problem with the key," Court pointed out. "There were no signs of forced entry."

"No, but getting the key would have been easier than getting the security code. I don't take my house key off the ring when I give it to the mechanic for an oil change." Though she would do that in the future. "I also don't know if the locksmith I used made a copy of the key and gave it to someone."

She knew she was sounding a little paranoid, but Rayna needed to look at all angles here. Unfortunately, there were probably other times when maybe her purse, and therefore her keys, had been out of her sight long enough for someone to make a molding of the house key.

Yes, definitely paranoid.

He paused to have some coffee, as well. "Unless you forgot to lock the door. Maybe forgot to set the system, too."

Rayna was shaking her head before he finished talking. "I don't forget those things. Not after what happened with Bobby Joe. I know you don't believe it, but he's out there."

No, Court didn't believe it. She could see the doubt in his eyes. And maybe he was right.

Rayna huffed. "If Bobby Joe's dead, I didn't kill him, and that means if he's not out there, then his killer is. That's why I lock the doors. That's why I have a security system."

He made a sound that could have meant anything. "Why did you stay if you think Bobby Joe or his killer will come back?"

She heard more of those doubts, and while Rayna didn't think she could make him understand, she tried anyway. "I wasn't born into money. And, no, that's not a dig about you and your family. It's my clumsy way of saying that I can't just pick up and leave even if that's what I wanted to do."

Which she didn't. That house was her home where

she'd been raised. Where once she'd been happy. She was hoping to reach that happy status again.

"Besides," Rayna added a moment later, "training horses is something I love doing, and I'm fortunate enough that it pays the bills." That along with the money she got from boarding horses from some folks who lived in town. The occasional riding lessons, too.

Court stared at her, and he obviously had something on his mind. "You never collected Bobby Joe's life insurance money. It was for fifty grand, and he left it all to you."

Yes, he had. Considering the big blowup Bobby Joe and she'd had just weeks before his disappearance, it surprised her that he hadn't changed his beneficiary. But then if he'd truly wanted to set her up for his murder, he would have left her name on the policy.

"I have no intentions of touching that money," she said.

Court stared at her, cursed under his breath, and he paused a long time. "I'm sorry about what happened yesterday when I tackled you like that. I was half crazy when I went out to your place."

That was true, but it was a craziness she could understand. She didn't get a chance to tell him that though because his phone rang, the sound shooting through the room. Her nerves were so frayed and raw that it caused her to gasp.

"It's Thea," he said when he glanced at the screen.

He knew the call could be important, and that was why Court answered it right away. He also put it on speaker.

"Your dad's awake," Thea stated, and with just those three words, Rayna could hear the relief in the deputy's voice. "He's still pretty groggy, but I thought you'd want to come and see him."

"I do." Court reached for his keys and his Stetson. He was already wearing his holster and weapon. But he stopped and looked at Rayna.

She could see the debate he was having. He didn't want to leave her there alone, but Court probably didn't want her near Warren, either. The debate didn't last long though.

"Rayna will be with me," he said to Thea. "What kind of security is in place at the hospital?"

"There's a guard posted outside Warren's door. Egan is there, too. And so is Griff."

Two lawmen and a security guard might not sound like a lot, but in this case, Warren was well protected.

"Good. We'll be there in fifteen minutes," Court assured Thea, and he ended the call.

Since it was normally about a twenty-minute drive from the McCall Ranch to town, Rayna guessed that they'd be hurrying. And they did. Court didn't waste any time getting her into the truck parked directly in front of the cabin, and they drove on the ranch road and then got onto the highway that led to McCall Canyon.

"It won't be a good idea for you to go into my father's room," Court said several minutes later, and he didn't give her a chance to disagree with that. "You can wait with Griff while I talk to him."

Court was right. She wanted to know if Warren had hired the dead PI, but he was far less likely to own up to anything with her in the room. Still, it wouldn't be a pleasant experiencing waiting with Griff. Yes, he would keep her safe, but he was firmly on the side of Warren when it came to anything, since Warren had practically raised Griff and his sister after their parents had been sent to jail for selling drugs.

"Keep watch," Court reminded her.

Even though she was already doing that, it caused her pulse to jump. The attack from the previous day was still way too fresh in her mind. Plus, she was having some pain, especially where the idiot had injected her with that drug. The seat belt was pulling right across the tender bruise.

"Are you okay?" Court asked.

He was frowning and glancing at her midsection. That was when Rayna realized she was holding her side. She was probably wincing, too. She nearly lied and told him everything was fine, but Rayna knew he wouldn't believe her.

"I'm hurting. I'm scared. And I'm mad. Yes, I messed up when I got involved with Bobby Joe. I should have never been with him in the first place, and I should have never stayed after the first time he hit me."

She wasn't sure how Court would react to that and expected him to dismiss it. He didn't. Even though he only glanced at her, she saw something in his eyes. Sympathy, maybe. If that was it, she didn't want it.

"I was a fool," she added. That not only applied to her relationship with Bobby Joe. She'd also been a fool to choose him over Court.

"Why exactly were you with him?" Court asked.

The burst of anger had come and gone, and now Rayna got a dose of something else that was familiar. Shame. There were plenty of emotions that came with the baggage of being in a relationship with someone like Bobby Joe.

"Because I didn't think I deserved anything better," she said. She certainly hadn't deserved Court.

He frowned. "What the heck does that mean?"

She hadn't expected him to understand. "You're a McCall from the right side of the tracks. You have a father and mother who love you." Rayna didn't have a clue who her father was, and her mother had dumped her at her grandmother's when Rayna had been in first grade.

Court's frown continued, and he added some profanity to go along with it. "You're telling you think you deserved to be with a jerk because you had some bad breaks in life?"

"I know it doesn't make sense to you." She looked at him. "It doesn't make sense to me now, either. I finally had, uh, well, an epiphany after Bobby Joe hit me the second time, and I knew if I stayed with him, the violence would only continue. Probably even get worse. That's when I ended our engagement." She paused. "And you know the rest."

Whether he believed the *rest* was anyone's guess, and there wasn't time to ask him. That was because he pulled to a stop in front of the hospital. He didn't use the parking lot. He left his truck by the curb, directly behind a cop car, and he hurried her inside.

Egan was right there to greet them.

One look at the sheriff's face, and Rayna knew something was wrong. She prayed that Warren hadn't had complications from the surgery. Or worse, that he'd died. She wasn't a fan of his, but she didn't want him dead. And that was partly because she knew how much Egan, Court and their sister, Rachel, loved him.

"What happened?" Court asked.

But Egan didn't respond. He made an uneasy glance around the waiting room, where there were several patients as well as some medical staff, and he motioned for Court and her to follow him. They did, and Egan went in the direction of the patients' ward, but he stopped in the hall. However, Rayna could see Rachel, Griff and Court's mother, Helen, just outside the door. It was no doubt Warren's room.

Egan looked at her as if trying to decide what to do with her. Clearly, he wanted to have a private conversation with his brother, but there was no way they could leave her alone.

"Dad didn't stay awake for long before he lapsed back into unconsciousness. But he did manage to say something," Egan said after he dragged in a long breath. He paused. "It's bad, Court."

And that was when Rayna heard something just up the hall. Something she didn't want to hear. Rachel and Helen were crying.

CHAPTER FIVE

COURT HAD ALREADY had a bad feeling before he saw his mother and sister crying, but that feeling went up a significant notch.

"Is Dad…" But Court couldn't even bring himself to finish the question.

"He's alive," Egan assured him.

The relief came, but the bad feeling remained. That was because of the tense look on Egan's face.

"In the few minutes that Dad was conscious," Egan went on, "he kept repeating one thing. A woman's name. *Alma.*"

Court shook his head. "You think that's maybe the real name of the dead PI he supposedly hired?"

"No." Egan took in another of those breaths. "According to Griff, it's the name of dad's longtime mistress."

That bad feeling fell like an avalanche on him. "No. Dad wouldn't cheat on Mom," he insisted.

"That's what I said, too, but Griff says it's true, that Dad's been carrying on an affair with this Alma for thirty-five years. Dad recently broke off things with her though." Egan turned back to Rayna. "And that's where you come in. It's possible this woman hired someone to kill Dad and set you up to take the fall."

"Hell," Court growled, and that was all he could manage to say.

His stomach was in knots. His heart, in his throat. And he figured Rayna wasn't feeling exactly great right now to hear confirmation that someone had set her up to take the fall for his father's attack. That part made sense—especially since they'd found Hallie dead. But none of the rest of this was sinking in.

"Alma," Court repeated. He glanced at Griff. "And he is certain it's true, that Dad cheated on Mom?"

Egan nodded, scrubbed his hand over his face. "He apparently found out a few months ago and said he told Dad to come clean. Dad obviously didn't do that, but he did break off things with this woman."

"The woman who maybe tried to set me up. I want to see her," she insisted.

Egan nodded. "You will. I'll have her brought into the sheriff's office as soon as I can arrange it." He motioned toward Rachel and their mom. "Needless to say, they're upset." He paused again. "Griff also told me that Warren had a son with Alma. I didn't say anything about that to Mom."

Court hadn't figured there'd be any other shocks, but that certainly was one. All of this was coming at him too fast. Of course, this wasn't something he could absorb with just a conversation. And he was sure there would be backlash. How the devil could his father have done this?

"The son's name is Raleigh Lawton," Egan added a moment later. "He's a year older than you."

Court belted out another "Hell." Because he knew the man. *Sheriff* Raleigh Lawton was from a small town just one county over. Warren and he had worked on a murder case about three years ago, and Raleigh had visited McCall Canyon several times. Court thought of something else that'd happened.

"Wasn't Raleigh involved with Thea?" Rayna asked.

"Yes," Egan confirmed. "But they broke things off a while ago. I'm not sure if Thea knew he was Warren's son, but Griff says that Raleigh didn't know. He thought his father died in the military before he was born."

So, the lies had extended to not only their family but to Alma's, as well. Yeah, he definitely wanted to talk to this woman. Wanted to talk to his father, too.

"Are you okay?" Rayna asked. She touched his arm and rubbed gently.

No, he wasn't okay, not by a long shot, and Court figured things were about to get worse when he glanced at Rachel again. Griff had tried to put his arm around her, but Rachel practically pushed him away. She said something to their mom, something that Court didn't catch, and then his sister started toward Egan, Rayna and him.

"Egan told you?" she asked Court. There were fresh tears in her eyes and other tears spilling down her cheeks.

He nodded, tried to hug her, but Rachel waved him off. "I just need to get out of here. Away from Dad and away from Griff," she added. Her voice was shaking now. "He knew, and he didn't tell me."

"Maybe he didn't know how," Egan said.

"Then he should have found a way," she snapped. "He definitely should have found a way before—" She stopped, waved that off, too. "I need to go. Please. I just need to leave."

"I'll drive you," Egan volunteered. "Mom, too. Just wait here for a second until I can get her."

Egan started toward their mother, and Court went with him. Rayna stayed behind with Rachel. Which was good. As upset as the woman obviously was, she might try to leave on her own. If she did, at least Rayna could alert them. It wasn't safe for his sister to be out there alone.

Court went to his mother and pulled her into his arms. Unlike Rachel, she didn't push him away. She dropped her head on his shoulder.

"Warren loves me," Helen muttered. There was some anger in her voice now. "Why would he do this?"

Court didn't know, and he wasn't sure he'd get any answers from his father, either. "I'm sorry" was all he could think to say.

Griff was clearly sorry, too. The man was shaking his head and mumbling some profanity. Neither would help. But then, there wasn't much that could help this situation right now.

Helen pulled back and looked Court in the eyes. "You think that woman could have shot him?"

"Maybe," he admitted. "But we're looking at Mitch for this, too. He hates Dad as well as the rest of us."

Still, if his father had hired that PI, then he must have believed that Alma could be some kind of threat.

"Mom, I want to take Rachel and you home," Egan insisted.

Helen didn't argue with that. She didn't look as if she had the strength to argue with anyone. In fact, she seemed broken.

"I'll stay here and help guard Warren," Griff offered. "Just tell Rachel that I'm sorry. I'm so sorry," he repeated to Helen.

But Court wasn't sure his mother heard Griff's apology. Even if she had, it wouldn't be nearly enough to help her get through this. Still, it hadn't been Griff's place to tell them.

That blame was squarely on his father's shoulders.

Egan slipped his arm around Helen to get her moving, and Court followed them. "Why don't you take Rayna to the sheriff's office?" Egan told him. "I'll meet you there after I've driven Mom and Rachel to the ranch."

Court was still feeling stunned, but he forced himself to get moving. The sooner Rayna and he got to the sheriff's office, the sooner Egan and he could get Alma in for questioning. Not that Court was especially looking forward to meeting the woman, but this might be the start of getting those answers they desperately needed.

"Did you ever meet Raleigh or Alma?" Court asked Rayna as they walked toward the exit.

"No, but I remember the talk about Hannah Neal, the woman whose murder Warren and Raleigh were investigating. She was a surrogate who'd recently given birth, and she was killed around the same time Bobby Joe went missing."

Yeah. Hannah had been murdered in McCall Canyon, but her body had been dumped in Durango Ridge, Raleigh's jurisdiction. That was why both Raleigh and his father had been investigating it. All of that had happened just a few months before his father retired.

"You don't think Alma could have been connected to Hannah's murder, do you?" Rayna pressed.

He was about to say no, but then Court remembered that Warren had been very close to Hannah. She'd been the daughter of his best friend, a single-father cop who'd been killed in the line of duty. As Warren had done with Thea and Griff, he'd taken Hannah under his wing. So, maybe Alma had gotten jealous of that. After all, if she was the one who'd hired someone to shoot Warren, then it was possible she'd killed Hannah, too.

Yeah, he definitely needed to talk to this woman.

Egan led Rachel and their mother out the exit first, and he took them straight to his cruiser, which was parked just ahead of Court's truck.

"Will your mother be okay?" Rayna asked.

Good question. But Court wasn't sure. She'd already been teetering on shaky ground with Warren's shooting, and now this. Court made a mental note to call her doctor and have him go to the ranch to check on her.

He motioned for Rayna to follow him. However, before he could even get the doors unlocked, Court saw the blur of motion from the corner of his eye. And he immediately pulled Rayna down with him.

Just as someone fired a shot at them.

RAYNA HIT THE ground hard, much as they'd done the day before in her house, and the pain from the fall sliced through her. It robbed her of her breath.

For one heart-stopping moment, she thought she'd been shot.

But no, it wasn't that. The pain had come from the bruise on her side. It hurt, but it was far better than the alternative of having a bullet in her. Or in Court.

She checked to make sure he hadn't been hit. He

didn't seem to be, but he dragged her beneath the truck and drew his gun. Ready to return fire.

Rayna took out her gun, too, from its slide holster. Not that she was in position to shoot back. She was on her stomach, and Court had positioned his body in front of hers.

Protecting her.

Something she wished he hadn't done. Rayna didn't want him to die because of her.

She waited, listening and praying. Rayna also tried to figure out what to do. If either Court or she reached up to open the truck door so they could get inside, the gunman could shoot them.

If there actually was a gunman.

There had only been the sound of that one shot, making her wonder if what they'd heard was a vehicle misfiring. That was what she wanted it to be anyway, and she hadn't actually seen a shooter.

"Call Egan and let him know what's happening," Court shouted out to someone. "But I don't want him bringing my mother and sister back into this."

Rayna caught a glimpse of a medic in the doorway before the guy took out his phone and hurried back into the hospital.

"You're sure it's a gunman?" she asked.

But it wasn't necessary for Court to answer. She got confirmation of it when there was another shot. This one slammed into the back tire of the truck just inches from where they were. That caused her heart to skip a couple of beats because the bullet could have easily hit one of them. And now they had a flat tire, which would make it harder for them to drive out of there if they did manage to get inside the truck.

"Move," Court told her. He didn't wait for her to do that though. He pushed her farther beneath the truck. He also cursed. "I should have put you in the cruiser with Egan."

She wanted to remind him that hindsight was twenty-twenty and that he hadn't known this was going to happen. But there was no way Court would believe her. No, he would feel responsible for this.

Whatever *this* was.

Was it part of the earlier attacks against Warren and her? Or maybe it was all connected to the two dead women?

They really did need to question Alma and find out if she was the one who'd hired this gunman. If she was, then it was possible that Rayna wasn't the primary target. Court could be. Because Alma could want to hurt Court to get back at Warren. That didn't mean either of them were safe though, and Court was the one taking most of the risks. He leaned out from beneath the truck, no doubt trying to see the gunman.

"Keep watch on your side," Court instructed.

Rayna was trembling, and still in pain, but she managed to get turned around so that her back was to Court's. And she immediately saw something. There were several people cowering by the sides of their vehicles.

"Stay down," she called out to them.

Another shot slammed into the truck. But the angle was different on this one than the other two. The gunman was moving. Court obviously realized that, too, because he cursed and shifted his position so that she could have a better view of the back of the truck.

"You see the gunman?" Rayna asked.

"No." But she immediately felt Court's muscles tense. "Yes," he amended. "He's directly ahead on the other side of a white car."

Rayna could see the car but not the shooter. Not at first anyway, but then he came out from cover, fired a shot, and she got a glimpse of him then.

He was wearing a ski mask, and even though she hadn't gotten a look at her attacker, Rayna sensed this was the same person. The build and height were right, anyway. But why did he want her dead now? He couldn't set her up for Warren's attack. Maybe he just thought she was a loose end, someone who could possibly ID him.

She couldn't.

But maybe he didn't know that.

The man leaned out again and fired another shot at them. This one slammed into the pavement and then ricocheted into the truck. Court rolled out from cover, too, and he sent two rounds the gunman's way.

A sound on her right caught her attention, and Rayna pivoted in that direction. Not a gunman but a car. One that she recognized because it was Whitney's. Her friend braked to a loud stop directly behind Court's truck. That meant Whitney was now in the gunman's line of fire.

"Hell, what is she doing?" Court grumbled. "She must have heard the shots."

Yes, there was no way to miss that. But maybe Whitney thought she could save them or something. If so, it wasn't a good plan because Whitney could be killed. Plus, it blocked their view of the gunman, making it impossible for them to return fire.

"Get in," Whitney called out to them.

Court and she couldn't do that, of course. It would be too risky for them to run to Whitney's car. If they were going to take that kind of chance, it would be better for them to just get in the truck, since it would take less time for them to be out in the open.

"Hear that?" Court asked her.

For a moment Rayna thought he was talking about Whitney. He wasn't. Because she heard another sound. It was a car engine. Since they were in a parking lot, it could just be someone leaving, but then there was the squeal of tires on the asphalt. Someone was driving out of there fast.

"He's getting away," Court said, and she could hear the frustration—and hesitation—in his voice.

Court no doubt wanted to go after the shooter, but it would be a huge risk. Because if it wasn't the gunman, then he could be shot. Still, he must have thought it was a chance worth taking because he rolled out from beneath the truck, his attention zooming to Rayna's right.

She lifted her head enough for her to see the car. It hadn't been the one the guy was using for cover though. This was a dark green sedan, and it was cutting across the parking lot only a few yards from them. Close enough for Rayna to catch just a glimpse of the ski-masked driver before he sped away.

"Stay put," Court warned her.

And with his gun aimed, he got to his feet and took off running.

CHAPTER SIX

COURT RAN AS fast as he could, and he kept his eyes on the green car. At best he figured he would get one shot before the shooter disappeared.

But he didn't even get that.

The car drove over the curb of the parking lot and shot out onto the road. Before Court could even stop and take aim, the gunman was already out of sight. That was not what he wanted. He needed to catch this guy so he could find out what the heck was going on.

While he ran back to Rayna, he took out his phone and texted Egan. His brother no doubt had deputies on the way, but Court wanted someone to go in pursuit of the person who'd just tried to kill them.

"Are you okay?" Rayna asked him the moment he made it back to her. She was crawling out from beneath the truck, but Court motioned for her to stay put. For a few more seconds, anyway. Just in case the shooter returned for a second round. Plus, he wanted a moment to ask Whitney one critical question.

"Why the hell did you drive into gunfire like that?" he snapped.

Whitney shook her head, her eyes widening. "I heard the gunshots and thought you needed some help."

He had. But not from a civilian. "You saw the gunman?"

Another shake of her head. "No. I only heard the shots."

Strange that most people's reaction would have been to move away from the gunshots. "You should have stayed back. Because you could have been killed." Well, she could have been if the shooter had continued to fire those shots. He hadn't. In fact, he'd stopped as soon as Whitney had driven up.

Her mouth trembled a little, and she looked as if she was about to cry. He hadn't wanted to bring her to tears—there'd already been enough of that today from his mom and sister—but he didn't want her doing anything like that again.

"You can't drive your truck on that flat tire," Whitney said. "And I don't think you want Rayna staying out here any longer than necessary. Come on, I'll give you a ride to the ranch."

Normally, Court wouldn't have given it a second thought to agree to have Whitney take them to the station, but he was having a lot of second thoughts today. Maybe because he'd nearly gotten Rayna killed along with having his world turned upside down.

Court didn't have to decline because a cruiser pulled into the parking lot and came directly toward them. Thea was behind the wheel, and she lowered the passenger-side window as she came to a stop.

"Ian and John are going after the shooter," Thea said.

Both men were deputies with plenty of years wearing a badge. Maybe their experience and some luck would help them nab the gunman.

"Is she going with us?" Thea asked, tipping her head to Whitney.

"No." Court answered so fast that it had Rayna looking at him.

He decided to soften his tone a little when he turned to Whitney and continued talking. "Go home or wherever else you're headed. You shouldn't stay around here. I'll call you about coming in to give a statement."

Whitney went stiff as if displeased with that order. Maybe because she'd already told him that she hadn't seen the gunman, but people often remembered other details when questioned.

The moment Court got Rayna into the back seat of the cruiser, Thea took off. Rayna was still trembling, of course. She probably would for a while, and he found himself slipping his arm around her before he even realized he was going to do it. Worse, Rayna moved right against him as if she belonged there.

Not good.

The last thing Court needed right now was to let down the barriers between Rayna and him. It would cause him to lose focus, and besides, he didn't have time to deal with the old baggage that existed between them.

"Griff called and told me about Warren," Thea said, pulling his attention back to her. Like Court, Thea was also keeping watch all around them as she drove to the sheriff's office.

Court figured this conversation should wait, especially since he was only minutes out of a gunfight, but it was a subject he'd planned to discuss with Thea eventually. "Did you know about my dad's affair?"

He cursed Thea's hesitation, but he had to hand it to the deputy. She didn't dodge his gaze. She made eye contact with him in the rearview mirror. "I suspected.

I accidentally overheard a conversation once between Alma and Warren. It seemed—" her gaze slid between Rayna and him "—intimate or something."

Court wanted to curse twice. Once because Thea had obviously picked up on the unwanted attraction between Rayna and him. He wanted to curse a second time because Thea should have told him about that conversation she'd overheard. Of course, she would have never done that. Thea was fiercely loyal to Warren and wouldn't have ratted him out. But that did lead Court to something else.

"You used to date Alma's son, Raleigh," Court said. And he waited.

Thea nodded. Paused. "Raleigh and Warren had a, uh, falling-out. I don't know about what. Maybe it involved the case of the dead surrogate they'd investigated together. Maybe because Raleigh learned the truth. Either way, it caused things to become tense between Raleigh and me, so we stopped seeing each other."

Court glanced at Rayna, and despite the hell they'd just been through, he could tell she wanted more info from Thea.

"Is it possible Raleigh could be behind these attacks?" Rayna asked.

"No," Thea said without hesitation. "Even if he hated Warren, he's not the sort to bend the law, much less break it."

Court would have pressed for even more, but Thea pulled to a stop in front of the sheriff's office. She didn't get out though. She turned in the seat and looked at them. "As soon as I got Griff's call, I started asking around about Alma. I'd made some friends and contacts in Durango Ridge, where she lives. Anyway, last month Alma took some firearms-training classes."

That got his attention. "She has a permit for a gun?"

Thea nodded. "A permit to carry concealed." She blew out a frustrated breath. "You asked me if Raleigh could be behind this. No. But I can't say the same for his mother."

And that was why Court had to get Alma in for questioning. For now though, he didn't want to sit outside with Rayna any longer. He threw open the cruiser door and got her inside.

"I'm pretty sure Egan took your mom and Rachel straight home," Thea said when Court glanced around the nearly empty squad room. The only other person there was a reserve deputy, Dakota Tillman, and he was on the phone. "Griff's going to get someone to fill in for him guarding Warren, and then he'll come here."

Good. Griff wasn't a deputy, but it appeared they were going to be short of manpower for a while. Still, he didn't want Egan back here, not until he had Helen and Rachel safely back at the ranch. It wasn't a good idea for them to be in town with that shooter on the loose.

Since Rayna was still looking pretty shaky, Court took her to the small break room at the back of the building, and he got her a bottle of water from the fridge. While she made her way to the sofa, he called one of the deputies, Ian, for an update on the shooter. But Ian didn't answer. Hopefully, that was because he was making an arrest.

"If you want to go out looking for the gunman," Rayna said, "I'll be fine here."

No, she wouldn't be. She was probably close to having an adrenaline crash, and what he was about to tell her wouldn't make that better. "The shooter could come to the sheriff's office."

She inhaled a quick breath, almost a gasp. Yeah, that adrenaline crash was closing in on her. Court went to her, and keeping a safe distance away, he sank onto the sofa next to her.

"He probably won't come here," he added. "But right now, we don't know which one of us is his target. Either way, he'll probably guess this is where we'd go."

Rayna groaned, pressing the back of her head against the sofa. "If he does show up, at least one of us can shoot him. But if he gets away, he'll just regroup and come after us again."

Court couldn't argue with any part of what she said. That was all the more reason to find out the person behind this. Maybe that was Alma. Or Mitch. But there was someone else on Court's radar now.

"Do you think it's odd that Whitney showed up at the hospital when she did?" he asked.

That brought her head off the sofa, and she stared at him. "You think she could have put together an attack?" Her tone made it seem as if that would be impossible, but then she huffed. "What would be her motive?"

Court had to shrug. "You tell me. Are things solid between you two?"

"Yes." But Rayna hesitated. "No. They haven't been the same since Bobby Joe disappeared."

Court had picked up on that vibe, but he'd wanted to hear Rayna confirm it. "Is that because Whitney believes you killed Bobby Joe?"

"Possibly," she admitted. "Whitney really liked

Bobby Joe. She used to tell me how lucky I was to have him. Of course, that was before he hit me. After that, she didn't seem to be so much in his corner."

He gave that some thought. "Is it possible that Whitney had feelings for Bobby Joe, that maybe she could have been jealous of you?"

Rayna opened her mouth as if to deny that. She didn't. "Possibly," she repeated. "But it's a stretch to go from jealousy to attempted murder."

True, but jealousy could be a motive. "Bobby Joe's blood was in your house." Of course, she knew that, but Court wanted to look at this in a different light. "Blood that had been cleaned up."

"Yes, and the prosecution said I'd done that after I killed Bobby Joe. Since I didn't kill him, I'm guessing he put his own blood there and did the shoddy cleanup so that I would be arrested. But now you're suggesting that Whitney could have done that?"

"No. Just wondering if it's possible. Whitney would have had access to your house."

"At the time, so did Mitch." Rayna groaned softly. "Besides, what's happening now might not even be connected to Bobby Joe. It could be happening because of Warren. If so, then Whitney couldn't be a suspect."

Maybe. But Court was going to keep her on the list just in case. Whitney not only had access to Rayna's place three years ago, she had access to it now. She could have possibly even gotten the code for the security system.

"I know this isn't comfortable for you." Rayna's voice was a rough whisper now. "It's okay if you put me in someone else's protective custody."

No. It wasn't okay. He refused to let their past play

into this. "I'll do my job," he said, but he hated that it came out rough and edged with too much emotion. "Or rather I'll do my job better than I have so far. I nearly let you get killed."

"You nearly got yourself killed protecting me," she corrected. "I don't want anything happening to you because of me." That certainly wasn't a whisper, and she looked him in the eyes when she said it.

That riled him. And gave him an unwanted jolt of memories. Memories of what used to be between them. Memories of Rayna. She'd always been a little fragile. Probably because of her troubled childhood. And while she was trying her hardest not to look fragile now, she still was.

She continued to look at him as if she expected him to say that he would be pawning her off on someone else. But then her expression changed, and he saw something more than the feigned strength in her eyes.

Hell.

Rayna had almost certainly gotten a jolt of those memories, too.

Court didn't move. Neither did she. That wasn't good. Because he was thinking about doing something, like kissing her. Thankfully, his phone rang, and it was the reminder he needed that kissing should be the last thing on his mind. Especially when he saw Rachel's name on the screen.

"Are Rayna and you okay?" Rachel asked the moment he answered.

"Yes." That was probably a lie, but his sister had already had too much bad news. "How about Egan, Mom and you?"

Rachel gave a heavy sigh. "We're at the ranch, and

the shooter didn't come after us. But Mom is, well, hysterical. Egan is with her now, but I had to call her doctor to come out here."

Court's stomach tightened. He wanted to be there. No way though could he risk taking Rayna out into the open. "Tell Egan to stay there with her," Court instructed. "The other deputies are out looking for the shooter, and I have Rayna here at the station. Griff should be here soon."

Silence. Except it wasn't an ordinary silence. Rachel was obviously angry that Griff had known the truth about their father and hadn't told them. Court wasn't too happy about it, either, but he was going to cut the guy some slack on this. Yes, Griff should have told them, but the person who was at fault here was Warren. And now Helen might be falling apart because of what he'd done.

"I don't want to see Griff," Rachel added a moment later. "Please let him know he's not welcome at the ranch."

Court wanted to refuse to do that. After all, the Mc-Call Ranch was Griff's second home, but he'd go with Rachel's wishes on this. Still, there seemed to be more going on that his sister wasn't saying.

"Is there something else you want to tell me?" Court came out and asked.

He got another round of silence from Rachel. "No. I just made a mistake with Griff, that's all. A big mistake."

Court definitely didn't like the sound of that. Griff and Rachel had been skirting around an attraction for years. Mainly because Warren hadn't thought they'd be a good match. But maybe something had happened.

If they had indeed landed in bed without Griff telling Rachel the truth, then, yeah, it would have been a big mistake.

"Let me know if there's anything I can do," Court settled for saying. "And call me after the doctor has examined Mom. I'll be here if you need me."

He ended the call, and he glanced at Rayna. A reminder that Griff and Rachel weren't the only ones who'd been skirting attractions. Rather than sit there and continue to let the heat build, Court stood, ready to find out if there was any news on the search for the gunman. However, before he could do that, the break room door opened, and Thea stuck in her head.

"I just got off the phone with Alma Lawton," the deputy said. "She's on her way here now."

Good. That was a start. Now Court only hoped he could keep his emotions in check around the woman.

"Alma's not coming alone," Thea added a moment later. "Her son and lawyer will be with her."

Court amended his earlier thought of "good." He figured he'd have enough on his plate just dealing with his father's mistress, but apparently that dealing was also going to include his half brother.

"If she's bringing her lawyer, Alma must realize she's a suspect in the attacks," Court pointed out.

Thea nodded. "She says she's innocent."

"Of course," Court grumbled, and he didn't take out the sarcasm. "Did she say anything else?"

Thea nodded again. "Alma says she has proof of who shot your father." Then Thea hesitated. "She says it was your mother."

CHAPTER SEVEN

Rayna had no trouble hearing what Thea had just said. And she supposed it wouldn't be much of a surprise that Warren's mistress was accusing his wife of attempted murder. Helen might be making the same accusations against Alma.

But Alma had to be wrong about this.

Judging from the way Court cursed, he felt the same way. "My mother didn't know about the affair until today, a day after my father was shot."

Thea held up her hands in a "you don't have to convince me" gesture. "Alma wouldn't say what kind of proof she had, but they should be here any minute." She stared at Court a moment. "You want me to be the one to interview her?"

It was a reasonable request, since it was obvious that Court wouldn't be objective about this, but Court shook his head.

"We need to keep everything by the book," Thea reminded him. "Remember, she'll have her sheriff son and her lawyer with her."

Yes, and they might be looking for anything they could use to have any possible charges dismissed against Alma. Court cursed again and then nodded. "I'll watch from the observation room."

Thea headed back toward the squad room, no doubt

so she'd be there to "greet" Alma and her entourage. Court started there, too, but then he stopped and turned to Rayna. "You can watch the interview with me."

Rayna wasn't sure why Court was including her, but then if Alma was guilty of trying to kill Warren, then that meant Alma had also been the one to try to set Rayna up. She definitely had a vested interest in hearing what the woman had to say.

She thanked him and followed Court into the squad room just as the front door opened, and someone walked in. But it wasn't Alma.

It was Mitch.

Rayna groaned. She so didn't have the energy to deal with this hothead today. She braced herself for Mitch to start throwing insults and accusations their way, but he stopped in front of them, sliding his hands into his pockets. Court noticed what Mitch had done because he stepped protectively in front of her.

"I'm not armed," Mitch grumbled, but his comment didn't have his usually venomous tone to it. "I just wanted to find out if you'd learned anything new about Janet."

"No." Court huffed. "Rayna and I have been busy dodging bullets."

"I heard. And no, I don't know who it was doing the shooting." He also didn't sound the least bit concerned, either. "Like I said, I'm here about Janet."

Court stared at him a moment. "You seem awfully interested in this woman that you hardly knew. Is there something you didn't tell us about her?"

Now Rayna saw the familiar fire in Mitch's eyes. "I'm interested because someone murdered her. Just the way someone murdered my brother." He shifted his attention to Rayna. "I just want justice."

Court drew in a long breath before he answered. "I want justice, as well. But for that to happen, I need more information. And right now, you're the only person in town who seems to have known her."

"Your father did," Mitch quickly pointed out.

Court lifted his shoulder. "I haven't been able to confirm that. Right now, I'm more concerned about what you know about her. Were Janet and you *together* or something? And I'm not talking about chatting over coffee at the diner. Oh, and before you say no, I'll remind you that you said you saw her ID when it fell out of her pocket. I doubt she had that in her waitress uniform."

Mitch's eyes were already dark, and they stayed that way. "So? We were *together*. That doesn't mean anything."

"It means plenty," Court argued. "Since Janet was possibly the one who help set Rayna up, then she could have been working for her lover. *You*. Not my father. You could have been counting on Warren never waking up so that your secret would stay safe."

"There is no secret," Mitch said through clenched teeth. "This is just another case of the McCalls putting themselves above the law."

With that, Mitch turned to leave, but he practically stopped in his tracks when he saw the three people who were approaching the building. A dark-haired woman with a slender build flanked by two men. One was in a suit, and the other was dressed like a cowboy. A cowboy with a badge pinned to his chest.

This was no doubt Alma, her son, Raleigh, and her lawyer.

The corner of Mitch's mouth lifted, and he looked back at Court. "Things are about to get fun around here. Don't guess you'd let me stay for the show?"

"How do you know those people?" Court snapped.

Mitch blinked as if he'd said too much. "I don't. They just looked like the fun-causing sort." He strolled out, heading up the street away from their visitors.

"Mitch is lying," Court muttered. "I'll get him back in here after Alma's interview."

Rayna completely agreed with the lying part, and she watched to see if Alma or the men would have a re-action to Mitch. However, if they saw him, there didn't seem to be any signs of recognition. Of course, Alma wasn't exactly looking at Mitch. She had her attention zoomed right in on Court.

Raleigh opened the door, and Alma stepped in. She never broke eye contact with Court, but she swallowed hard. "I didn't expect you to look so much like War-ren," she said, her voice a delicate whisper.

Actually, the rest of her looked delicate, too, with her pixie haircut and pale skin, and she was wearing a gauzy light pink dress. Rayna's first impression was that Alma looked much too young to have a son who was in his thirties.

Court ignored her observation and instead turned to Raleigh. Neither man said anything, but they seemed to be sizing each other up. Rayna did that as well, and she could see the strong resemblance. Both of them favored Warren.

She silently cursed. For Court's sake and the sake of his mother and sister, Rayna had been hoping this affair was all some kind of misunderstanding. Judging from his scowl, Raleigh had hoped the same.

"Sheriff," Court greeted.

"Deputy," Raleigh greeted back. "Who'll be interviewing my mother?"

"It won't be you," the guy in the suit said before Court could answer. "I'm Alma's lawyer, Simon Lindley."

Thea came forward and shook her head. "I'm Deputy Thea Morris, and I'll be doing the interview."

Raleigh and she exchanged a long look. The kind of look former lovers gave each other. Rayna was certain she'd given Court that same look a time or two.

"I would have thought your brother, the sheriff, would have wanted to be here for this," Simon remarked.

"He's busy." Court's tone was as icy as his expression. "My mother isn't doing well, and my father is unconscious in the hospital. You might have heard someone murdered two women and tried to kill him." His gaze shifted to Alma when he added that last part.

Alma nodded. "Yes, I heard about Warren." She didn't offer any opinion about that and didn't ask how he was doing. The woman walked to Thea. "Perhaps we can go ahead and start?"

Simon looked as if he might stay and sling a barb or two at Court. He didn't. He hurried after Thea and Alma as they went up the hall to the interview room. Raleigh, however, stayed put.

"I'd like to listen," Raleigh said. "I suspect you'll want to do the same."

Court nodded and started for the observation room. Raleigh lagged behind and fell in step with Rayna. "You're a person of interest in Warren's shooting."

"Not anymore," Court answered before she could say

anything. "Rayna was being attacked and drugged at the time of the shooting, and she was miles away at her house. No. I'm looking more at your mother for doing this." Now there was some anger lacing his words.

"And my mother is accusing yours of doing the same." No anger in Raleigh's voice, but he did take in a weary-sounding breath.

"My mom didn't do this," Court insisted. "I don't care what Alma says because my mother had no idea my dad was cheating on her."

Raleigh made a sound that could have meant anything, and the three of them went into the observation room. In the interview room, Alma and Simon were having a whispered conversation. Thea was already at the table, waiting for them.

"Did you know about the affair?" Rayna came out and asked Raleigh. She wished she hadn't said anything though because Raleigh gave her a sharp look. Maybe because he thought she had no right to be here. But Rayna stayed put.

"No," Raleigh finally answered. His jaw clenched. "We raise horses, and apparently Mom was meeting Warren on her so-called business trips."

"And you didn't suspect?" Court pressed.

"No. Did you?" Raleigh fired back.

Even though they both had practically growled those responses, it seemed to bring them to some kind of truce. No, they didn't like what had been going on, maybe didn't even like each other, but they hadn't known this train wreck was about to happen. By now though, they probably knew plenty about each other. Rayna figured they'd both used their law-enforcement channels for some background checks.

"You're not going in the interview room with your mother?" Court added to Raleigh a few seconds later.

"No." He paused, and she could have sworn his jaw got even tighter. "I'm guessing you were upset when you learned about the affair." Raleigh didn't wait for Court to answer. "Now imagine if you found out you were born on the wrong side of the sheets to a man who hasn't acknowledged you or the affair for thirty-five years."

Court didn't actually jump to offer an opinion on that, but Rayna figured he could understand that Raleigh wasn't in a good place right now. He'd been lied to his whole life about his father, and now his mother was a murder suspect.

Yes, definitely not a good place.

The three of them turned their attention back to Thea once she began the interview. The deputy started with simple questions, asking Alma to state her full name and address. Rayna had been through enough interrogations to know what Thea was doing. She was establishing baseline responses of a potential suspect. Like many people, Alma's eyes went to the right when she answered truthfully. Now Thea had created a body-cue lie detector she could use for the harder questions.

And Thea jumped right into that.

"Tell me about your relationship with Warren Mc-Call," Thea said.

"There is no relationship. Not any longer," Alma insisted. "We ended things two months ago."

"We?" Thea questioned. "Did you end it or did Warren?"

Alma glanced at Simon before she answered. "Warren. But it was time. All that sneaking around is fine when you're as young as you are, but I was tired of it.

I wanted something more out of life. Something that Warren couldn't give me."

Thea jumped right on that. "So, you weren't upset when the breakup happened?"

Alma made another glance at her lawyer. "I suppose I was. At first. But then I got over it. I certainly wasn't so enraged that I would plot to kill Warren."

"And it's ridiculous that you'd bring my client in for questioning about something like that," Simon added.

Thea ignored him, and she opened a folder she'd brought into the interview room. She extracted a photo of Hallie. Obviously, the woman was dead, and it caused Alma to gasp. Raleigh didn't have a verbal reaction to that, but Rayna could feel the tension practically flying right off him.

"Do you recognize her?" Thea asked.

"No." Alma closed her eyes and shook her head. She also dropped her head on Simon's shoulder.

"Showing her that wasn't necessary," Simon growled. "You could have just asked Alma if she knew the woman."

Thea ignored that, too, and she took out a second photo. This one was of Janet. "How about her?"

Simon slipped his arm around Alma as if to turn her away from the grisly picture, but Alma not only opened her eyes, she leaned in to have a closer look. "I know her. That's the woman who's been following me." Alma shifted her attention to Thea. "Who is she?"

"We're trying to confirm that now. When did she follow you?"

Alma huffed. "She's been doing it for the past couple of weeks. I got so worried that I took some firearms training."

Court turned to Raleigh to see if he would verify that, and Raleigh nodded. "She told me about someone following her, but I never saw the woman. You really don't know her identity?"

"Janet Bolin," Court answered after a long pause. "She was a PI."

Raleigh moved closer to the glass, staring at the picture. "Cause of death was a gunshot wound to the head." It wasn't really a question, but Court made a sound of agreement.

Even though Court didn't add anything about Warren possibly hiring the PI, it might make sense if Warren was concerned about how Alma might take the breakup.

Alma tapped Janet's picture. "She was carrying a gun the last time I saw her. I guess she thought it was concealed, but I could see the outline of it in the back waist of her jeans."

"Where and when did that happen?" Thea asked.

Alma's brow furrowed. "About a week ago, maybe less than that. She was at the coffee shop in Durango Ridge." She paused a heartbeat. "Helen McCall was with her."

Court cursed and moved as if he might charge into the room, but Rayna took hold of his arm. She didn't remind him that Thea would get the info they needed, but Court must have remembered that he wouldn't be doing his mother or him any favors if he went in there and accused his father's mistress of lying.

Alma tapped the photo again. "This woman and Helen were talking. I know it was Helen because I've seen a photo of her in Warren's wallet. That's why I got so worried. I mean, my ex-lover's wife was chatting with an armed woman who'd been following me.

And when I heard Warren had been shot, I figured these two had something to do with it. Specifically, I thought Helen had hired this woman to kill Warren."

Court cursed again. Obviously, this was hard to hear, and it wasn't making sense.

"I saw Helen minutes after she'd learned of the affair," Rayna said, "and she was genuinely upset. If she'd known for a week, those emotions wouldn't have been so raw."

Thankfully, Raleigh didn't argue with that, but he probably wasn't as convinced of Helen's innocence as Rayna and Court were.

"Any idea why Helen McCall was in your hometown?" Thea asked the woman.

"I just assumed Warren had confessed all to her and that she was there to confront me or something. She didn't. And I never saw her again."

"You knew Helen was there?" Court asked Raleigh.

"No," he answered without hesitation. "But then if my mother had told me about Helen, she would have had to spill everything about Warren. It's my guess she wasn't ready to do that."

No, and Raleigh didn't seem happy about that, either. Alma's secret affair was also his secret paternity.

"Did Helen or Janet see you when you spotted them at the coffee shop?" Thea asked Alma.

Alma quickly shook her head. "But I went in through the side entrance and sat at a table on the other side of the wall from them. I couldn't hear much because it was noisy that day, but I did catch a word or two. They both mentioned Warren, of course. Oh, and a woman named Rayna."

That put a heavy feeling in her stomach, and she

exchanged glances with Court. Uneasy glances. Because why would his mother and a dead PI have been talking about her?

"What did the two women say about Rayna?" Thea pressed when she continued with the questioning.

"I didn't hear that part," Alma insisted, "only the mention of her name."

Rayna wanted to believe they were talking about someone else. Or maybe that Alma had just misheard. Heck, all of this could be a lie.

But it didn't feel like a lie.

Mercy, had Court's mother been the one responsible for all this violence?

"I'll call the ranch and talk to my mom," Court insisted. He took out his phone and stepped into the hall. However, it rang before he could press the number.

Rayna was close enough to see Griff's name on the screen, and that put some fresh alarm in Court's eyes. He answered it on the first ring.

"Is something wrong?" Court immediately asked.

"Yeah," Griff answered. "Someone just tried to kill Warren."

CHAPTER EIGHT

COURT'S FIRST REACTION was to jump into a cruiser and head straight to the hospital. Someone was trying to kill his father—again.

His dad was in danger.

But Court forced himself to stop and think. This could be some kind of trap. Not for his father but for Rayna and him.

"Is Dad okay, and who tried to kill him?" Court asked Griff.

"Warren's fine. As for the intruder, I'm not sure who he is, yet, but we did stop him before he could actually get into the hospital room. I just cuffed him. But I can't take him anywhere because I don't want to leave Warren with only the security guard."

Neither did Court. He glanced around to see if he could come up with a solution. There were only two deputies in the sheriff's office, and Thea was still questioning Alma. The other deputies were out chasing down the shooter.

"We should go to the hospital," Rayna insisted.

Considering they'd just been attacked there, it surprised him that she would be so accommodating, but maybe Rayna didn't like the idea of staying behind with Alma. Court didn't like that, either.

"I'll be there in a few minutes," Court told Griff, and he ended the call.

Court turned to Raleigh, not sure of what he should say to the sheriff. Not sure what Raleigh would say, either. He'd likely heard what Griff had said and now knew that there'd been another attempt on Warren's life. However, if Raleigh had any reaction to that, he didn't show it.

"If you don't question your mother about what you've just heard in the interview," Raleigh said, "then I'll request the Texas Rangers do it. Helen McCall needs to explain why she was talking with a now dead person of interest in this case."

It bothered Court that Raleigh was dictating to him how to do his job, but at this point anything the man said or did would probably bother him. There wasn't much about this situation that Court liked.

"I'll question my mother," Court assured him. Though it probably would be smart to have a Ranger do it. Not Griff, either. But someone who could be objective about all of this. Of course, his mother might not be in any shape to hold up to a full-blown interrogation.

Raleigh nodded, tipped his head to Alma. "I'm sure Thea will call you if there are any problems with the rest of the interview," he added.

It was pretty much a blanket invitation for Court to leave, so that was what he did. He took Rayna by the hand, hurried her to a cruiser that was just outside the door, and he prayed they wouldn't be shot at along the way.

Court's phone rang again, and this time he saw Rachel's name on the screen. He took the call on speaker, tossing his phone on the seat so his hand would be free.

Court also kept watch around them, something that Rayna was doing, as well.

"Egan just told me about Dad," Rachel said the moment she was on the line.

"Yeah. I don't know anything yet, but I'll be at the hospital soon." Court debated if he should even bring this up now, but it was a conversation that needed to be started. "Once I'm sure Dad is okay, I'll need to talk to Mom. Alma Lawton said some things about her during her interview."

Rachel groaned. "I hope you don't believe anything Dad's mistress would have to say."

In this case, he did believe her. Either that or it was a stupid lie on Alma's part, since his mother's meeting with Janet was something that could be easily verified. Well, easily if his mother wasn't coming unglued.

"I just need to talk to Mom," Court settled for saying. "I'll call you when I have info on the intruder. All I know right now is that Griff was able to stop him, and he's still with Dad right now."

"Griff," Rachel repeated like profanity. "Call me the minute you know anything."

Court assured his sister that he would, ended the call and pulled to a stop in front of the hospital entrance. As close as he could, anyway. The CSIs were there, and so were several Texas Rangers. Obviously, that was Griff's doing, and Court made a mental note to thank him.

He threaded Rayna through the crime scene tape and got her into the building as fast as possible. There was another Ranger posted just inside, and the waiting room had been cleared. Good. The fewer people, the better.

"No way would your mother have done something to put you in danger," Rayna said as they walked.

Court believed that, too, but there might be another side to this. If Helen had found out about the affair sooner than she had let on, she could have wanted to harm Warren. Court hated to even consider it, but it was something he had to do. It sickened him though to think his mother might have had any part in this.

The moment they were in the patients' hall, Court spotted Griff and the security guard, David Welker, someone who Court knew and trusted. He also saw the man they had on the floor. The guy was on his stomach, his hands cuffed behind his back.

"How's Dad?" Court asked Griff first off the bat.

"Still unconscious."

That was better than the alternative or his father being bedridden and aware that someone had come back to finish him off.

Court looked down at the intruder. So did Rayna, but she shook her head, indicating that she didn't know him. Neither did Court, but he pulled the man to his feet so he could have a face-to-face talk with him. Except it wasn't really a man. The guy looked to be a teenager, but he was also dressed like an orderly.

"Did he have any ID on him?" Court asked Griff.

"No. The only thing in his pocket was this." He took out a small Smith & Wesson handgun. "He doesn't work here. The badge he's wearing is a fake."

The badge looked real enough, but something must have alerted Griff. "What made you stop him from going into Dad's room?"

"A bad gut feeling. That, and he looked too young to be an orderly."

He did, and Court thanked Griff before he turned back to the kid. "Who are you?" Court demanded.

The kid lifted his head, making eye contact with Court, and the deputy cursed. "He's high on drugs or something."

"That was my guess, too," Griff agreed.

The corner of the kid's mouth lifted. "I only had a pill or two." His words were slurred, as well.

"Who are you?" Court repeated, and this time he got right in the guy's face. His scowl must have been mean-looking enough because it caused the kid's smile to vanish.

The kid shook his head. "You don't know me. My name won't mean anything to you." He glanced over Court's shoulder at Rayna. "Might mean something to her though."

Rayna went stiff. "I have no idea who he is."

The kid shrugged. "Figured you would, since you're the one who hired me to come here and all."

"I didn't," Rayna snapped, and she repeated it, her gaze volleying between Court and Griff.

Court grabbed on to the guy's shirt, and the last scowl was a drop in the bucket compared to the one he gave him now. "I want to know your name."

"Bo Peterson," he finally answered.

That meant nothing to Court, and judging from Rayna's reaction, it meant nothing to her, either.

"When did I supposedly hire you?" Rayna demanded.

"Yesterday morning. You were wearing a red dress then."

Rayna groaned. "Hallie hired him."

"She said her name was Rayna." Bo leaned in,

blinking and trying to focus on her face. "But you don't talk the way she did. And you don't look the same."

"Because she's not that woman," Court fired back. "In fact, that woman is dead. Someone murdered her and a second woman. Since you just tried to kill my father, you're my number one suspect in those killings and several attacks. That means you could get the death penalty."

Bo's eyes widened, and he suddenly looked a lot more alert than he had just a few minutes ago. "I didn't kill anyone. And I wasn't supposed to kill the person in that room. I was to put the gun behind the toilet."

Court's stomach tightened. That meant someone planned to retrieve the gun later and use it. Probably on Warren. Of course, that would have happened only if Bo was telling the truth. Court wasn't anywhere near convinced of that yet.

"I didn't kill anyone," Bo said when Court, Rayna, David and Griff just stared at him.

"Even if you didn't, you're still an accessory to murder and attempted murder. That carries the same penalties."

"No," Bo practically shouted. "I didn't know anyone was going to get killed." He snapped back toward Rayna. "That other woman is really dead?"

She nodded. "And that's why you have to tell us everything you know about her."

"I don't know anything." He shook his head and tears watered his eyes. "Several times she told me her name was Rayna."

She'd done that no doubt so Bo would remember it. "What else did she say, and how did she pay you?"

"She paid me in drugs. Oxy and Ecstasy. But I

screwed up. I was supposed to put the gun in the room yesterday, but I took some of the pills and got a little messed up."

"What time yesterday?" Court pressed.

Bo's forehead bunched up, and he groaned. "Around nine or so. She didn't know what room number. She said I was to find out what room number Warren Mc-Call was in and plant it there."

So, maybe Hallie had met with Bo shortly after the shooting. That would have meant he was perhaps the last person to see her alive. Of course, Bo could have also been the one to kill her.

"Who was going to use the gun you were supposed to hide behind the toilet?" Court continued.

"She didn't say, and I didn't ask."

That last part didn't surprise Court. Bo had likely been in a hurry to down those drugs he'd been given as payment.

"Can I go now?" Bo asked.

Court didn't even bother to laugh and he looked at Griff. "Any chance one of your Ranger friends can drive this clown to the sheriff's office so he can be locked up?"

"Locked up?" Bo howled. "But I didn't do anything. I didn't even make it into the old man's room."

Yeah, thanks to Griff and David. That was why Court had to continue to make sure whoever had hired Hallie and Bo wouldn't send someone else to try to finish off Warren.

"I'll wait in your dad's room," David said when Griff led Bo away.

Court thanked him and took out his phone to call Rachel and Egan, but first he looked at Rayna to make sure she was okay. She wasn't. She was looking shaky again, so he had her lean against the wall.

"Who's trying to set me up?" she muttered, but it didn't seem as if she expected him to answer. Good thing, too, because Court still didn't know.

Court pulled her into his arms, intending for it to be just a quick hug, but it didn't stay that way. That was because Court realized Rayna wasn't the only one who'd just felt as if the rug had been pulled out from beneath them.

"Bobby Joe," she said. "He's the only one who hates me enough to do this."

Maybe. But this might not be about Rayna. "Or you're the perfect scapegoat because of the bad blood between you and the McCalls."

Of course, at the moment that bad blood didn't look so bad. After all, Rayna was in his arms, and when she lifted her head and looked up at him, it put their mouths much too close together. The memories came. The good ones. Of other times when he'd kissed her and she'd responded.

Much like she was responding now.

Her breath kicked up a notch, and he could see her pulse fluttering in her throat. And he caught her scent. Something warm and silky. Definitely nothing that had come from a bottle, and it stirred him in a very bad way. That was why Court stepped back before he made a mistake both Rayna and he would regret.

Well, they'd regret it afterward anyway.

He was certain there wouldn't be much of anything but pleasure during the actual kissing.

"We keep doing that," she said.

He didn't ask her to clarify. Because he knew. They

kept moving much too close to giving in to this heat. That reminder caused him to take yet another step away from her, and before he could go back and play with fire, he made that call to Rachel. But it wasn't his sister who answered.

It was his mother.

"Rachel left her phone by my bed when she went to make me some tea," his mother said. "She won't be long though. Is everything okay? Egan and she are whispering."

Court wanted to assure her that everything was okay. But it wasn't. Far from it. "Dad is still asleep," he said.

"I guess that's good. He probably needs to rest and heal. If Warren really did do this to me, then I can't forgive him."

"Just give it some time," he said, because Court didn't know what else to say.

"Time won't fix this. I'm sorry," she added. "They gave me some pills, and they've made me a little woozy. Did you want me to get Rachel for you?"

"No, I need to talk to you." And because he had no choice, Court had to pause and take a deep breath. "We brought Alma Lawton into the sheriff's office for questioning."

"I see." His mother paused, too. "Did she know about me?"

Court went with the truth on this. "Yes. She also admitted to the affair."

Another sob. "Oh, God. It's true."

"According to Alma. But you still need to talk to Dad about it." In fact, Court definitely wanted to hear a confession from his father's own mouth, and part of him wouldn't fully believe it until he heard it.

"No, I can't talk to him. If Warren did have an affair with that Alma, then he had a child with her. A son."

Court was a little surprised that his mother could put all of that together—especially considering she'd been given those sedatives. It also made him wonder who'd told Helen about Raleigh. Maybe she'd overheard it in one of those whispered conversations she'd mentioned.

"Yes, they possibly had a son," Court admitted, but he didn't give her a chance to ask him any more about that. He jumped right into his question. "Alma said you had coffee with a woman named Janet in Durango Ridge. Did you?"

"No. I don't know a Janet." She didn't pause that time.

Court felt the relief. He could see that relief in Rayna's eyes, too, since she was still close enough to hear the phone conversation. But the relief didn't last because Court knew that Janet might not even be the PI's real name.

"Did you meet with a woman in Durango Ridge?" Court pressed.

"Yes."

There went the rest of his relief. At least his mother hadn't denied it, and that meant he might be able to get the truth from her. He only hoped the truth didn't lead to her arrest.

"I met with a reporter named Milly Anderson," Helen added a moment later. "She said she was working on the old Hannah Neal murder case. You know, the one that's troubled your father for the past three years."

There was no need for his mother to add that last

sentence. Because Court definitely knew about Hannah's case. Her murder was still unsolved. "Why did Milly want to talk to you about Hannah?" Court asked.

"Because she's an investigative reporter. You know, one of those journalists who digs through cold cases. She didn't really have anything new. I guess she thought maybe I would remember something that would help her."

Court doubted that. No, Janet or whatever her name was had probably had a different agenda in mind. Court just didn't know what that was.

"Did you tell Dad about this chat with Milly?" Court continued.

"I mentioned it to him. He said I shouldn't talk to any other reporters, that Hannah's murder was a police matter. He seemed really angry or something. God," she quickly added, "you don't think Milly had anything to do with Alma, do you?"

Court intended to find out. That meant digging more into Alma's background and talking to Raleigh. He might have run into Milly, as well.

"Oh, here's Egan," his mother said. "He's motioning to talk to you."

"I just got off the phone with Thea," Egan explained the moment he came on the line. "She told me what Alma said. You asked Mom if it was true?"

"Yes, she met with Janet in Durango Ridge."

Egan cursed, causing their mother to scold him, and Court heard footsteps, letting him know that Egan was taking this conversation out of Helen's earshot.

"Janet told Mom she was a reporter," Court added when he could no longer hear his brother moving around. "How is Mom, by the way?"

"Upset. Dr. Winters wants her to have a psych eval, and he's set her up an appointment."

That caused his chest to tighten. "You think she needs that?"

"Yeah."

Court wished he'd heard some doubt in Egan's voice. He didn't.

"I'll keep you posted on that," Egan went on. "In the meantime, the CSIs tested the guns at Rayna's house, and none had been fired recently. That's good news. For her, anyway."

Yes, it was, and while Court figured that pleased her, it also wasn't a surprise. Rayna had been adamant from the start that she hadn't fired a weapon. Especially one aimed at Warren.

"Thea said other than Mom's meeting with Janet, she didn't get much else from Alma," Egan continued. "Alma did agree to have her hands tested for gunshot residue. There wasn't any. And she also said the CSIs could test the weapons she owned."

Court was betting those wouldn't be a match, either. If Alma had been behind the attacks, she wouldn't have used her own gun. And she would have taken precautions to make sure there was no residue.

"What's going on between Rayna and you?" Egan came out and asked.

The question threw Court. It threw Rayna, too, because her eyes widened in surprise. "What do you mean?" Court grumbled.

"You know what I mean. Are you two involved again? And no, it's not just me being nosy. I don't care who you take to your bed. I just want to make sure you're not sleeping with a woman who's neck deep in a murder investigation."

"I'm not sleeping with her." Though Court had thought about it. Those thoughts had come shortly after their near kiss. Heck, they were still coming now.

"Good. I just wanted to make sure you hadn't lost your mind." Egan paused. "I'm guessing Rayna thinks Bobby Joe is responsible for the attacks."

"Yes," she answered.

Egan didn't seem surprised that Rayna had been close enough to Court to hear what they were saying. "I figured as much. Of course, I don't believe it, but I'll take a harder look at Mitch. Once this situation with Mom is settled." And with that, Egan ended the call.

"I'm sorry," Rayna said. "I probably shouldn't have let Egan know I was listening."

"He already knew." Court wished that weren't true, but Egan was definitely aware of the attraction between Rayna and him. Aware, too, of the problems that it could cause.

"Let me check on my dad, and we can go back to the station," Court told her. "I want to question Bo."

He opened the door to his father's room and came face-to-face with David. "I was just coming to get you." The guard stepped back. "Your father's awake."

CHAPTER NINE

RAYNA STOPPED IN her tracks after hearing what the guard said to Court. *Your father's awake.* That meant Court was finally going to get to question Warren about the affair and the attack, and he almost certainly wouldn't want her there to hear it.

Or so she thought.

Court motioned for her to follow him. "It'll be safer in here. Bo might not have been working alone."

That caused her throat to snap shut, and she wondered why that hadn't already occurred to her. It was because there was a tornado of emotions going on in her head right now. In her heart, too. But Rayna tried to push all of that aside for the possible firestorm they were about to face.

"I'll let the nurses know he's conscious," David said, heading out into the hall.

"Dad," Court greeted. "You know why you're here in the hospital?"

Warren nodded. "Someone shot me."

Rayna stayed back against the wall as Court walked to his father's bed. She'd hoped that Warren wouldn't even noticed her.

He did.

Warren looked past Court and directly at her. Court

followed his father's gaze and shook his head. "Rayna's not the one who tried to kill you."

"No. But it looks as if someone tried to kill her." He'd no doubt seen the injury on her head before Warren's attention shifted to Court. "I know you'll ask, but I didn't see the person who shot me."

Too bad. Rayna was hoping they could have cleared all of this up right now.

"I felt the bullet go into my chest." Warren touched that part of his body. "I fell, and the only thing I remember after that is bits and pieces of conversations I've heard from the nurses and guards."

"What did you hear?" Court pressed.

Warren groaned softly and closed his eyes for a moment. "That there was another attack. Are you two okay?"

"Fine." Court sounded disappointed. And probably was. If that was all his father could recall, then there was going to be a lot more information they'd need to gather. "What about you? Are you in much pain?"

Warren shook his head, but that was probably a lie, since the head shake caused him to wince a little. That was the only reaction he managed to have, because the door flew open and one of the nurses came in. Rayna knew the woman, Ellen Carter, and she made a beeline to Warren, immediately checking one of the monitors.

"I'll let the doctor know you're awake." Ellen glanced at both Rayna and Court. "I know you'll want to question him about the shooting, but don't overdo it."

Court nodded but didn't say anything. Neither did Warren until the nurse was out of the room. "How's your mother? Is she here?"

"Not at the moment." Court didn't pause too long

before he said that. "She's at the ranch with Rachel and Egan."

"Egan," Warren repeated. "Yes, he should be with her. Rachel, too." He looked up at Court again. "Do you have the person who shot me in custody?"

"No." Court took a deep breath. "But we have two dead bodies. Both women. One was an actress that we believe was posing as Rayna to set her up to take the blame for your shooting. The second one was perhaps a PI who was linked to you. She was using the name Janet Bolin."

For a man who'd just again regained consciousness after surgery, Warren suddenly seemed very alert. And frustrated. Because he groaned. "That's not her real name. It's Jennifer Reeves."

She couldn't see Court's face, but he did pull back his shoulders. If Warren knew the woman's real name, then he was indeed linked to her.

"You said she's dead?" Warren questioned.

"Murdered," Court clarified.

Warren grimaced and then cursed. "How? Did the person who shot me also kill her?"

"We're still trying to sort that out." Court dragged up a chair and sat next to his father's bed. "After surgery, you kept saying someone's name. Alma."

And the silence began. However, Warren did have a response. The shock, followed by a mumbled "Ah, hell."

That probably wasn't what Court wanted to hear. Maybe he had still held out hope that the affair was some kind of misunderstanding.

Warren looked Court straight in the eyes. "Your mother knows?"

Court nodded. "We all know. Griff filled in a few blanks for us."

Warren's mouth tightened. "He had no right. If I'd wanted all of you to know, it should have come from me."

"But it didn't," Court quickly pointed out. There was anger in his voice. Understandably so. That "if" probably didn't set well with him, and it meant that Warren hadn't planned on confessing to the affair any-time soon.

"That's why your mother's not here," Warren added. He also added some more profanity. "Call her now. Tell her I want to see her."

"That's not a good idea." Court didn't break eye contact with Warren when he said that, either. "The doctor sedated her, and she needs some rest."

Warren threw back the covers as if to get up, but Court quickly stopped him. "You need your rest, too. And I need answers. You really had an affair with Alma Lawton for thirty-five years?"

Warren stared at him almost defiantly. Obviously, he wasn't a man accustomed to being challenged, but Rayna saw the exact moment he mentally backed down. Warren stared at his hands. "What else do you know about her?"

Rayna wanted to groan. Even now after he'd been caught, Warren wasn't ready to spill everything.

"I know Alma gave birth to your son Raleigh," Court readily answered. "And that you and Alma only ended things a couple of months ago. I believe you were concerned Alma might go to Mom, and that's why you hired the PI." He paused. "How am I doing so far?"

Warren's mouth tightened even more. "Alma and I

didn't end things. I did. I stopped seeing her, and she was upset about that. So, yes, I thought she might go to your mother."

"Why would Jennifer aka Janet meet with Mom in Durango Ridge?" Court pressed.

Warren lifted his head. "She wouldn't have."

"She did. Or rather according to Alma, they did. She said she saw them at a coffee shop there."

"You've already talked to Alma?" Warren snapped.

"Thea interviewed her. You have to know that she's a suspect. You really think she could have been the one to shoot you though?"

"No." But Warren immediately shook his head. "Alma's never done anything violent before."

That didn't mean she hadn't done this. It depended just how riled Alma was. Warren's scorned lover could have shot him, set up Rayna to take the fall, and when that didn't work, she could have hired someone to shoot at Court and her.

But that still didn't explain why the PI that Warren had hired would meet with Helen.

The door opened, and the doctor came into the room. He no doubt noticed the agitation on his patient's face because he huffed and turned to Court. "I need to examine Warren now. You two can wait out in the hall."

That definitely had a "get out of here" tone to it, and Rayna couldn't blame him. Yes, Warren had messed up big-time, but he was still in serious condition. Just a day earlier, he'd been at death's door, and the doctor probably wanted to give Warren some time to mend.

Court and she went out of the room, and he immediately took out his phone. He pulled up Egan's number, but he didn't press it. Court just mumbled some profanity and looked at her.

"I'll get you out of here soon," he said.

She got the feeling that he'd wanted to say something else. Maybe an apology or something. She didn't want one. Because none of this was his fault, and it was obvious that what his father had done was tearing him apart.

Court stared at her a moment longer before he finally pressed Egan's number, and this time he put the call on speaker. Court opened his mouth, probably to tell Egan that Warren was awake, but Egan spoke before he could speak.

"Mom swallowed a bunch of pills," Egan blurted out. "I've already called an ambulance, but she's unconscious."

Oh, mercy. Not this. Court and his family already had enough on their plates.

"When did this happen?" Court snapped.

"I'm not sure. Rachel's the one who found her. Are you still at the hospital?"

"Yeah. Dad is finally awake. I'll talk to you about it when you get here. You are coming in the ambulance with Mom, aren't you?"

"I am, but I'm not sure they'll keep her there. Once they've pumped her stomach or whatever the hell it is they'll do, she'll probably have to go to a place that has a psych ward."

Court groaned, scrubbed his hand over his face. "I'll meet you at the ER. How soon before you get here?"

"Soon. The ambulance is already on the way out here."

Still, that could be a good thirty minutes by the time

the medics picked up Helen at the ranch and brought her in.

Court got them moving when he ended his call with Egan. Maybe because he needed to put some breathing room between his father and him. Also, he might not want to have to tell Warren about this.

He stopped just short of the ER waiting room, and they peered around the corner. The Rangers were still there, so hopefully that meant a gunman wouldn't be stupid enough to show up there.

"I'm sorry," Court said.

Since she was about to tell him the same thing, Rayna lifted her eyebrow. "For what?"

"Everything. You could be in the middle of this danger because of my father's affair." He didn't say the word *father* with too much affection. However, there was plenty of anger. "I can't believe he did something like this."

After everything Warren had put her through with the trial, Rayna wanted to say that she had indeed thought he was capable. But yes, even she was surprised. Warren could be a bulldog when it came to seeking justice, but he'd seemed to genuinely love his wife and family. And now he was tearing them apart.

"If my mom dies…" Court started.

But Rayna didn't let him finish that. She stopped him by brushing her mouth over his. In hindsight, kissing him hadn't been the right thing to do. But it certainly caused the heat to slide right through her.

She leaned back, their gazes connecting, and this time she saw more than the worry and fatigue. There was some confusion. And a little fire.

"Have only good thoughts about your mother," she warned him. "Or I'll kiss you again."

Despite everything going on, the corner of his mouth lifted. "Not much of a threat." But then he huffed, and she understood what he meant.

In some ways, kissing was the greatest threat of all.

And that was why she stepped back. Just like that, the moment was lost, taking the fire right along with it. Unfortunately, Rayna knew it would return.

His phone rang, and since he still had it in his hand, she had no trouble seeing the screen. Not Egan this time but rather Thea. He put this one on speaker, too.

"How's Warren?" Thea immediately asked.

"Awake. He confirmed the affair with Alma."

"I see." Thea sounded very disappointed about that. "Griff is here with the prisoner. I'll send the gun he had on him for testing. Anything specific you want me to look for?"

"Fingerprints or some DNA," Court answered. "It's possible this gun was going to be used to set someone up."

He looked at Rayna then, and she knew the someone might be her. She didn't remember touching a gun that wasn't hers, but it was possible someone had gotten a sample of her DNA.

"I finished the interview with Alma," Thea added a moment later.

"Yeah, Egan told me."

"Figured he had. Alma will be back tomorrow though to go over her statement. If you or Egan wanted to question her, you could do it then."

Court made a sound of agreement. "We don't have any grounds to arrest her. Not yet. But I need to look into her possible connection to the dead PI. According to my dad, her real name is Jennifer Reeves. And yes, he did hire her. Can you see what you can pull up on her?"

"Sure." And Rayna could hear the clicking of the computer keys. "Alma said Jennifer met with your mother. Do you know why?"

"No idea, and it might be a while before I can ask her." Judging from the sudden tightness in his jaw, that was all he wanted to say about that right now.

"Jennifer Reeves," Thea repeated a moment later. "Yes, she was a PI. Thirty-four. No record. She owns… *owned* an agency in San Antonio but didn't have any other employees. Let me check her social media and see if I find any connection to Helen."

"And check connections to Alma, too," Court insisted.

"You think Alma could have been lying?"

"I don't know, but if Alma is on some kind of vendetta, then she might have used Jennifer to do it. Alma could have found out my father hired Jennifer and then paid her more money to set him up."

Yes, because after all, it'd been Jennifer who'd taken the photo of the woman who resembled Rayna. But then Rayna thought of something else.

"Maybe you'll find a connection between Jennifer and Mitch," Rayna threw out there.

Thea made an immediate sound of agreement. "There did seem to be something going on between those two, and Mitch is definitely someone who'd want to get back at Warren and you." She paused. "I'm not seeing anything on her social media, but I'll see about getting her case files. It's possible… Oh."

Rayna definitely didn't like the sound of that "oh." Thea wasn't exactly the sort to be easily surprised.

"What is it?" Court asked when Thea didn't continue.

"I think we should be looking into someone else," Thea finally said. "I'm sending you a photo that I found on Jennifer's page. You want me to bring her in for questioning?"

It took a few seconds for the photo to load on Court's phone. It was a shot of two women, and they appeared to be at some kind of party. When Rayna looked at their faces, it felt as if someone had drained all the air from the room.

The woman on the left was definitely Jennifer. But Rayna recognized the other woman, too.

Because it was Whitney.

CHAPTER TEN

COURT DEFINITELY DIDN'T like this latest turn of events. Why the heck had Whitney not mentioned that she knew Jennifer?

From all accounts Jennifer had been working at the diner for a couple of weeks, and Whitney lived in town. As small as McCall Canyon was, she would have likely run into her, seen her friend and then been very concerned that her *friend* had turned up dead. The very friend that from all appearances had tried to set up Rayna for a crime she didn't commit.

Court drove away from the hospital while Rayna tried to call Whitney. They were alone in the cruiser but not alone on the road. He hadn't wanted to risk that. Deputy Dakota Tillman and a Texas Ranger were in a second cruiser behind them, and Court hoped that three lawmen would be enough to deter another attack.

"Whitney's still not answering her phone," Rayna said. It was her fifth attempt to get in touch with the woman, but each of the calls had gone straight to voice mail.

Court figured that wasn't a good thing no matter which way they looked at this.

"You think it's possible Whitney got wind that you learned she was connected to the dead PI?" Rayna asked.

"Yeah," he admitted. Since Whitney was a dispatcher for the sheriff's office, she could have heard and might now be avoiding them.

Or…

There was another possibility. One that he didn't want to mention to Rayna just yet. If Whitney had gotten involved in some kind of scheme to kill Warren, a scheme that involved Jennifer and Hallie, then she could be dead, too.

"I keep going back to what Whitney did earlier in the hospital parking lot," Rayna said. "She pulled her vehicle between us and the shooter."

Whitney had indeed done that, and while that alone wasn't an indication of guilt, she was starting to look very suspicious. "I'll question Whitney as soon as she checks in with us." And the woman had better do that soon. She'd also better have the right answers.

Rayna glanced at the sheriff's office as they drove past. "You can leave me there if you want, and go back to the hospital and be with your mother."

"Rachel and Egan are there, and the doctor said he didn't want her to have visitors for a while. Even if she were allowed, I'm not sure I should be answering questions she'll have about my dad's affair. It would only upset her even more."

It had certainly upset Court. And worse, he didn't know what to do about it. Part of him hated his father for this, but hating wasn't going to fix the danger. Or his mother. No. He had to focus on getting the person responsible for the attacks and then make sure his mom had the kind of help she needed to get better.

His phone dinged with a text message, and Court handed it to Rayna so she could read it to him.

"It's from Thea," she relayed. "No signs of the shooter. Also, Bo is only seventeen, and he lawyered up."

The first wasn't a surprise, since the shooter was probably long gone by now. But seventeen! That meant Bo was a juvenile and might not be charged as an adult. That could be especially true if Bo didn't have a record. Of course, he had tried to slip a gun into a hospital room, and that was a serious enough charge that he might end up with some actual jail time.

"Text her back," Court instructed, "and ask her to question Bo as soon as his lawyer arrives. I want to find out if he knows who hired Hallie to give him the gun and the drugs."

Bo probably didn't know the answer to that, but they had to try. Right now, Bo was the only living link they had to the dead woman.

Rayna was about to hand him back his phone, but it rang before she could do that. This time it wasn't a number he recognized, and he motioned for Rayna to answer it. She did and put it on speaker. Court braced himself in case this was the shooter, but it wasn't.

It was Raleigh.

"I've got something that I'm sure you'll want to see," Raleigh immediately said. "The coffee shop here doesn't have a security camera, but there's one at the bank across the street. I'm emailing the footage to you now."

That was a pleasant surprise. "Is my mother's meeting with the PI on the footage?" Court asked.

"Yeah. It's grainy because of the glass window that's between them and the camera, but you can see their faces well enough. At first, your mother doesn't appear to be agitated, but that changes at about the five-minute mark. She appears to start crying."

Hell. That could mean that Jennifer had told Helen about the affair. But why would the PI have done that?

"I don't see any exchange of money or anything," Raleigh went on. "And your mother didn't stay long in the coffee shop after that."

So, a short meeting. One that had upset his mother. Coupled with the fact that Helen hadn't mentioned the meeting until he'd asked her about it, it wasn't looking good.

"You'll let me know what your mother has to say about this after you've viewed the footage?" Raleigh asked.

"That might be a while." Court debated how much he should say and then went with the truth. After all, Raleigh would be hearing it soon enough, anyway. "My mother tried to kill herself. Pills. I won't be able to question her until I get the all clear from her doctor."

"Sorry about that." And even though Raleigh had muttered it, he sounded genuine. "We're in a bad place right now with our mothers. Alma hasn't tried to end her life, but she's not as strong as she looks."

"Is she strong enough to have hired a killer?" Court blurted out. He wished though that he'd toned it down a little, since Raleigh actually seemed to want to get to the bottom of this.

"As her son, I'll say no. As a cop, I'll say anyone is capable of pretty much anything. But ask yourself this—if my mother was so upset at Warren, then why would she have waited two months to go after him?"

"Maybe because it took her that long to put a plan

together." But Court had to shake his head. "How long ago did my mom meet with the PI?"

"Four days," Raleigh readily answered.

That meant Helen had had that meeting three days before Warren had been shot. If his mother had learned of the affair at the meeting, it was possible she'd somehow gotten Jennifer to help her with a plan. It sickened Court to think that might be true because the plan had included setting up Rayna. Plus, both Rayna and his father could have been killed along with the two women who'd been murdered.

"I'm not saying either of our mothers killed anyone," Raleigh went on, "but we have to consider they could have hired someone who went rogue. Someone they can no longer control."

Yes, and that someone had maybe fired shots at Rayna and him.

Court's phone beeped with an incoming call, and when he saw John Clary's name on the screen, he knew he'd need to talk to his fellow deputy. "I'll review the footage and get back to you," he told Raleigh and switched over the call.

"Please tell me you found the shooter," Court immediately said.

"No. But we do have a problem. Someone tripped the security alarm at Rayna's house. And since it's still taped off as a crime scene, I came here to check it out. There's someone here all right, but he or she ran into the barn when they spotted the cruiser. I just wanted to make sure it wasn't Rayna or someone she sent out here."

"It's not me," Rayna assured him. "But this morning Court had some of his hands go over and tend my horses. Maybe it was one of them."

"Seems funny though that the person would take off running like that," John commented.

It did, and it put an uneasy feeling in Court's stomach. Besides, those hands would have been long finished by now and back at the McCall Ranch.

"Every now and then some kids will come out to my place," Rayna added. "I think I'm the local bogeyman, since many people believe I killed Bobby Joe."

She glanced away from Court when she added that. It was a reminder that her life probably hadn't been so great in the past three years.

"So, you think it might be just a prank or something?" John pressed.

"I don't know," Rayna said after a long pause. "The kids don't usually go in my barn."

None of this was giving Court assurances that all was well. "Are you alone?" he asked John.

"Yeah. I was headed back to the office when I got the call. You think I should get some backup?"

It wasn't an easy question to answer. The sheriff's office was maxed out, and Rayna and he were only a couple of miles from her place. Court turned in that direction, but he definitely wasn't sure it was the right thing to do. He also motioned for the other deputy and Ranger to follow them.

"Just stay put," Court told John. "I'll be there in a few minutes." He ended the call and immediately looked at Rayna. "You won't be getting out of this cruiser. Understand?"

She didn't argue with that, but she huffed. "You really think the shooter would be stupid enough to go to my house?"

"He might if he thought he'd left something when he attacked you."

That put some new fear back in her eyes, and Court nearly turned around to get Rayna out of there. Then he saw a familiar car on the road just ahead of them.

Whitney.

Rayna immediately took out her phone and tried to call the woman again. Again, it went straight to voice mail.

Court had another decision to make. He wanted to talk to Whitney, but he wasn't sure it was worth putting Rayna at risk this way. That decision was taken out of his hands though when Whitney pulled off onto the shoulder of the road. She got out of her car, and she'd obviously seen them because she started flagging them down.

"Stay inside the cruiser," Court repeated to Rayna. He drew his gun and pulled up behind Whitney. However, he didn't get out, and he only lowered his window a couple of inches. Dakota stopped his vehicle behind them and did the same thing.

"What are you doing out here?" Court snapped when Whitney ran up to the car.

She practically stopped in her tracks, and she pulled back her shoulders. "What's wrong? What's going on?" She looked at Rayna when she asked that second question.

"You tell us. Why are you here?" he repeated.

She opened her mouth, her attention volleying between Rayna and him. "Mitch. Did he call you, too?"

Mitch? Court certainly hadn't expected her to say that.

"No," Rayna answered, "but I've been trying to call you for the past half hour."

"I know. I'm sorry, but the battery died, and—"

"You didn't tell me you knew one of the dead women," Rayna interrupted.

Whitney shook her head. "I don't."

"You do," Rayna argued. "I saw a picture of you with her. Her name was Jennifer Reeves."

It took several moments for Whitney to process that. Or maybe she was pretending to process it. "The dead woman is Jennifer? I thought her name was Janet."

"She was using an alias," Court explained. "So, you did know her?"

"Of course." Whitney's voice was barely a whisper now, and if she was faking it, she was doing a darn good job. "Jennifer's dead?"

Court verified that with a nod. "When's the last time you saw her?" And that was the first of many questions he had for her.

She shook her head again, pushed her hair from her face. "Months. Maybe longer. We met on a cruise about ten years ago and have stayed in touch." She uttered a hoarse sob. "I can't believe she's dead."

Again, her shock seemed genuine, and later he intended to question her more about her friendship with Jennifer. For now though, there was something more pressing. "What does Mitch have to do with you being out here?"

Whitney paused again as if trying to gather her thoughts. "He called me, and he sounded frantic. Maybe scared. It was a really bad connection with a lot of static, but I thought he said there was something in Rayna's house that he had to get."

"Something?" Court questioned.

Whitney glanced away. "He didn't say exactly what, but I think he maybe meant a gun. He could be looking for the gun that he thinks killed Bobby Joe."

Both Court and Rayna groaned. "And why did Mitch think the gun would be there after all this time?"

"I don't know. That's about the time my phone battery completely died, and I started driving out here. I was afraid the Rangers would still be here, would see him and think maybe he was the person who'd shot at Rayna and you."

They might have indeed thought that, but it was still no reason for Mitch to run.

"Get in your car and go to the sheriff's office," Court told Whitney.

"But what about Mitch?"

"I'll take care of him."

Whitney didn't look at all comfortable with that. *Well, welcome to the club.* Court wasn't comfortable with it, either, but he didn't want Mitch trespassing on a crime scene, especially with another of their suspects around.

And Whitney was indeed still a suspect.

She'd had explanations as to why she hadn't told them about Jennifer or answered her phone, but Court wanted to do some more digging into her story.

"You want me to take Rayna back to the station with me?" Whitney asked.

"No." Court couldn't answer that fast enough. He raised his window and drove off, leaving Whitney there to gape at them. Probably to curse them, too, since she didn't look very happy with Court's obvious mistrust of her.

Court considered calling John to let him know that Mitch was likely the intruder, but he decided against that, since they were nearly at Rayna's house. Plus, it might not be Mitch at all, and he didn't want John walking into the barn and finding a gunman waiting for him.

"Keep watch around us," Court reminded Rayna, though he was certain she was already doing that. They were both on edge.

When her house finally came into view, he had no trouble seeing that the front door was wide-open. He also spotted John. The deputy had taken cover behind his cruiser and had his gun drawn. And Court soon realized why.

Mitch had his hands raised in the air, and he was coming out of the barn. "Don't shoot," Mitch called out to them.

Court parked next to John so that the deputy's cruiser would also be between Rayna and Mitch, and he took aim. Behind him, Dakota and the Texas Ranger did the same thing.

"Mitch, are you armed?" Court asked.

Mitch tipped his head to the barn. "I was, but I left it in there. Didn't want either of you getting trigger-happy when you saw me trying to do your jobs."

Court didn't like the sound of that, but then he rarely liked anything Mitch said. "And doing our job includes trespassing on private property and breaking and entering?" Court fired back.

"Yes, in this case. I didn't get a chance to try the security code or the key. The door was busted open when I got here."

That didn't make sense, and Court was about to demand more, but Mitch looked past John and Court and into the cruiser where Rayna was sitting.

"You might not have actually murdered my brother, but you're not off the hook," Mitch said to her, and he smiled.

That brought Rayna out of the cruiser. "What are you talking about?" It was the exact question Court had been about to ask.

"Are you admitting Rayna didn't kill Bobby Joe?" Court demanded.

Mitch nodded.

That nod might have been a simple gesture, but Court could hear the sound it caused Rayna to make. She gasped. "He's alive," she muttered.

Mitch nodded again, and he stopped when he was about ten feet from them. "I need to get my phone from my pocket, and I don't want you to shoot me when I do that." He waited until Court nodded before Mitch took out his cell. "Bobby Joe left me a message. That's why I called Whitney and told her to come. She'll want to hear this, too."

"She can hear it later," Court snapped.

Mitch nodded, pressed the play button, and he held the cell up in the air for them to hear. It didn't take long before Court heard the voice.

"It's Bobby Joe. Meet me at Rayna's."

There was a lot of static, and the message was choppy as if he'd been thinking about each word before he said it.

"The security code is seven-six-two-one," the message continued, "and there's a spare key in the birdhouse on the end of the porch." The static got even worse. "I want to show you where she hid the gun. The gun she used to try to kill me."

CHAPTER ELEVEN

THE MESSAGE KEPT repeating through Rayna's head, and she couldn't make it stop. Bobby Joe was alive.

But now he was accusing her of attempted murder.

She'd denied it the moment she'd heard the message, and she thought Court believed her. Not Mitch though. But then, he'd always thought the worst of her. And would continue to think it, too, now that Mitch had heard the accusation from his own brother.

"There is no smoking gun," she said to Court. "So why would Bobby Joe tell Mitch to meet me at his house?"

"Maybe to plant something to incriminate you," Court said without hesitating. Which meant that message was likely replaying in his head, as well.

Not necessarily a good thing, since they were both trying to focus on the drive back to the sheriff's office. Dakota hadn't followed them for this part of the trip. That was because Court had wanted the Ranger to go ahead and take Mitch to the sheriff's office so that Dakota could stay behind and search for Bobby Joe. Rayna had wanted to do that, too, but it wouldn't have been very smart, since Bobby Joe could have just gunned her down. Of course, maybe he wanted to torment her first, to punish her for breaking off things with him.

"Everyone knows now that you didn't kill him," Court said. "I'm sorry for not believing you in the first place."

"There was a lot of circumstantial evidence," she reminded him. Evidence that Bobby Joe had planted. "He must have stockpiled some of his own blood that he put in my kitchen."

Court made a sound of agreement. "And he made sure he cleaned it up in such a way to make us believe you'd tried to cover up the crime scene." He stopped, cursed. "It could have worked, too. You could be in jail right now."

Since it was obvious he was beating himself up about that, Rayna touched his arm. "It's okay. Right now, I'm more concerned about what Bobby Joe's going to do next."

"He'll try to kill you," Court quickly answered. "That's why you'll need to stay in protective custody. That's why we have to find him. We might get lucky and be able to trace his call to Mitch."

Yes, and that brought her back to the message Bobby Joe had left on Mitch's phone. Why risk bringing in anyone else, even his brother? Why not just plant the gun and then arrange for someone to find it? And why do the whole gun-planting thing if Bobby Joe was the one behind the attacks? Why not just continue the attacks until he was successful?

A thought that twisted her stomach into a knot.

But there was something else about this that didn't fit.

"The security code," Rayna said. "The one Bobby Joe gave Mitch. It was the old code. That's why he tripped the security alarm when he tried to get in."

"Did you know about the key in the birdhouse?" Court asked.

"No, but if he was telling the truth about that, it would have been the old one, too. I changed the locks after the trial."

And Court obviously picked up on where she was leading with this because he cursed. "It means Bobby Joe wasn't the person who broke into your house and drugged you."

No, because whoever had done that had the correct key and code. With everything else going on, she hadn't followed up on finding who could have gotten those things, but she had to move that to the front burner.

Well, as soon as she dealt with the news of Bobby Joe's return.

Even though she'd known he was alive, it was another thing to deal with the proof of it. Plus, he was out there, probably trying to figure out his next move. He probably hadn't counted on that move including Mitch ratting him out.

They pulled to a stop in front of the sheriff's office, and Rayna immediately saw the cruiser the Ranger had used to bring back Mitch. What was missing was Whitney's car, but Rayna held out hope that her friend had parked elsewhere and walked to the station. She didn't want to accept just yet that Whitney could be avoiding her because she'd had something to do with those attacks.

"The Ranger had to leave and go back to the hospital to guard your dad, but Ian just went in the interview room with Mitch to take his statement," Thea said the moment Court and Rayna walked in. "Is it true? Is Bobby Joe really alive?"

"It's true," Court verified.

But he didn't stop to add more. With his arm hooked around Rayna's waist, he kept her moving to Egan's office, where he had her sit in a chair next to the desk. He also shut the door.

He stared at her as if waiting for something, and that was when Rayna realized he was looking at her hands. They were shaking. Heck, she was shaking. And before she even knew it was going to happen, the tears came.

The emotions hit her all at once. For three years she'd been battling the stigma of being branded a killer, and that wasn't just going away despite the fact of Bobby Joe's return. She'd hated him for a long time now but never so much as in this moment. Bobby Joe had taken her life and torn it into little pieces, and he was still tearing it, still trying to break her.

"I don't want to cry," she insisted. But that didn't stop the tears.

Court grabbed her some tissues, but instead of just handing them to her, he wiped her face. Their eyes met. And she saw more of that frustration and guilt in his expression. Yes, she could see that even through the tears.

He muttered some profanity, pulled her to her feet and eased her into his arms. "You can yell at me if it'll make you feel better."

She didn't want to yell at anyone. Especially Court. Right now, he was the only sane thing in her life.

That stopped her.

And Rayna felt herself go stiff. Court obviously felt it, too, because he looked down at her. Again, he seemed to be waiting for something, but she didn't know what exactly.

Not until he kissed her, that was.

Even though she figured he was doing this to comfort her, Rayna instantly got a jolt of other emotions. Familiar ones. Because the kiss spurred the old fires between them. And it kept on stirring it because he continued to kiss her. This went well past the comforting stage, especially when he pulled her against him.

Court made a sound, a grumble from deep within his chest. It seemed like some kind of protest, maybe a plea for him to stop. But he didn't. He continued the kiss until the taste of him was sliding right through her.

Yes, this was a cure for tears, but it soon gave her a new problem. The touch of his chest against her breasts, the way he took her mouth…that only made her want him even more.

Rayna found herself slipping her arms around his neck to bring him even closer. Not that she could actually do that. Not while they were clothed anyway, and there was little chance of them stripping down in Egan's office. However, there was still a chance of things escalating.

Court backed her against the door, and the kiss raged on. Until they were out of breath. Until Rayna was certain she could take no more. Only then did he pull back from her, and she braced herself. Court would almost certainly curse and remind her that kissing her had been a huge mistake.

He didn't.

But she saw something else in his eyes that she hadn't wanted to see. Sympathy. He was feeling sorry for her, maybe because he and his father hadn't believed her about Bobby Joe. Maybe because he knew she was probably very close to losing it. Either way, she didn't want that from him, and that was why she moved to the side.

"We should review the security footage Raleigh emailed to you," she managed to say. Not easily. It was hard to talk with her breath thin and her head light. "And talk to Mitch. Plus, Whitney will be here soon."

She would have gone back into the squad room to his desk if Court hadn't caught her hand. He looked at her as if trying to figure out what was going on in her head. Then he cursed.

"That wasn't a pity kiss," he snarled. "Trust me, when I kiss, it's for just one reason, and it doesn't have anything to do with pity."

That pretty much took care of what little breath she had, but he didn't give her a chance to respond. He threw open the door and went to his desk.

Thea glanced up from her computer screen but then quickly looked away. She could no doubt see what was going on between them and had wisely decided to stay out of it.

"Any updates on my father?" Court asked Thea. He sat at his desk and started downloading the email from Raleigh.

"Nothing, but I'm hoping in this case that no news is good news."

Rayna agreed. "What about Whitney? Have you seen her? She was supposed to come in."

That was definitely a surprise to Thea. "No sign of her. Should I call her?"

"No," Court answered. "I'll deal with Whitney, but I am going to need you to run that trace on the phone call he got from his brother. Did Mitch ask for a lawyer before Ian went in to take his statement?"

"No. I suspect he will though if he really did break into Rayna's house."

"He claims someone else did the actual breaking in," Court said. "What about Bo's lawyer?"

"Not here yet, either. He called and said he was stuck in San Antonio, so it might be a couple more hours."

Rayna wished they could get the answers from the teenager now, but it was possible that Bo was going to be a dead end when it came to helping them with this investigation.

While Thea got to work on the phone trace, Court loaded the security footage. "Raleigh said my mom's demeanor changed at the five-minute mark, but I want to watch it from the start."

He pulled up a chair for her, their gazes connecting again when she sat. "For the record, I didn't let you kiss me out of pity," she whispered.

The corner of his mouth lifted for just a second, but that seemed to indicate they'd declared some kind of truce. Rayna was okay with that, especially since the images loaded on the screen, and she knew that had to push kissing, and thoughts of kissing, to the side. That didn't mean this heat was going away though.

Rayna leaned in closer to the monitor when she spotted Helen making her way to the coffee shop. She certainly didn't look upset.

As Raleigh had warned them, the images weren't so clear when Helen went inside, but they could still see when she greeted Jennifer with a handshake. After that, the women sat at a table so that only the sides of their bodies were facing the camera.

"Too bad this doesn't have sound," Court mumbled as they reached the five-minute mark.

Rayna agreed because there was definitely a difference in Helen's body language. "Maybe your mom was just upset about reliving the details of Hannah's murder."

"Maybe." But he didn't sound especially hopeful about that.

They watched as Alma came in through the other entrance, and as the woman had said, she stayed back behind a half wall that would have hidden her from view of Helen and Jennifer. Alma hadn't been in the shop very long when Helen stood. She took something that Jennifer handed her, perhaps a business card, and slipped it into her purse before she hurried out.

Once Helen was outside, it was easier to see her face. She wiped at her eyes as if wiping away tears and then disappeared out of camera range. Court reached to turn off the footage but then stopped.

They both zoomed in on the man who was outside of the coffee shop. He was in position to have watched the meeting between Helen and Jennifer, and now he was watching Helen as she left. And the man was someone they both recognized.

Mitch.

"Mitch sure as hell didn't mention any of this," Court grumbled, and he got to his feet. "I think it's time to question him."

"So do I, but why would he have been spying on them? You think Jennifer told him about the meeting?"

"That's my guess. I'm betting Mitch knows a lot

more about Jennifer than he's letting on." He started for the door but then stopped when Rayna's phone rang. "If that's Whitney, tell her to get her butt in here right now."

But it wasn't Whitney's name on the screen.

It was Unknown Caller.

She hadn't thought her stomach could tighten even more, but it did. Rayna showed the screen to Court and waited until he got out his own phone to record the conversation before she answered the call and put it on speaker.

Nothing. Not for several long moments.

"Hey, Rayna. It's me," the caller said.

Bobby Joe.

Like the message he'd left for Mitch, this one was filled with static, too.

"Can't wait to see you," Bobby Joe added.

Rayna could have sworn her heart went to her knees, and she fired glances outside the window. There was a trickle of people on the sidewalks, but there was no sign of Bobby Joe.

"Where are you?" Court snapped.

There was a long pause. "Rayna's gonna pay for what she did."

Rayna hated that he could still get to her like this, and she mustered up as much steel as she could manage. "Is that a threat?"

Bobby Joe didn't confirm that, but after another hesitation, he just laughed.

It did indeed feel like a threat. And there was nothing she could do about it. Not unless they caught Bobby

Joe, that was. Then he could be charged with fraud for trying to frame her for his murder.

"Bye, Rayna," Bobby Joe added. "See you soon." And the call ended.

CHAPTER TWELVE

COURT COULD FEEL the dangerous energy bubbling up inside him, and he hated what this was doing to Rayna. All those feelings and energy were so strong that they almost overshadowed his lawman's instincts.

"Something's not right," he said.

That caused Rayna to fire glances all around them again.

"No, I don't think Bobby Joe is nearby," Court added. "In fact, I'm not sure that call was actually from him. I think it was a recording of old conversations that have been spliced together."

She opened her mouth as if she might dispute that, but then Rayna frowned. She was obviously going back through what she'd heard. "Maybe."

"That would account for the static and the long pauses in between some of the words."

Rayna shook her head. "But who would do that? Why would someone want to make us believe it was Bobby Joe?"

"Maybe to rattle us." And if so, that had worked. But Court got the feeling there was much more to it than that.

He handed his phone to Thea. "I recorded a call that Bobby Joe supposedly just made. I need the voice analyzed on it. Also the voice on the message left for Mitch."

Thea nodded. "I've already started working on tracing that call to Mitch. It came from a burner, so no luck."

That was too bad. A burner was a prepaid cell phone that couldn't be traced.

"But I did find something strange," Thea added a moment later. "Using that same burner, someone called Mitch three times before leaving that message. It appears Mitch answered the other three calls, but Bobby Joe or whoever it was didn't talk to him. Or if he did, they were very short conversations. It appears the only time the caller actually communicated was through the message he left on the fourth call that Mitch didn't answer."

Yeah, that was strange, and it was right in line with Court's theory about Bobby Joe's conversation being spliced together. Maybe someone had taken old recordings and used them.

But again. Court didn't know why.

"I'm done with his phone," Thea added. "I've gotten everything I can from it—including copying the message from Bobby Joe. Now I'm just waiting on the phone company to email a complete record of all the calls and texts he's made in the past couple of months."

It might take a while to get that, especially since Mitch wasn't being charged with a serious crime.

"I can give Mitch back his phone when I talk to him," Court said, taking it from her.

Thea nodded again. "It can't wait until Ian is done taking his statement?" she asked. Her concern wasn't because she had doubts about his interrogation skills.

It was because Mitch was a hothead who could set off Court's own temper.

"No. I'm not going to interview him right now. I just want to ask him about that message."

Thea still looked a little skeptical. So did Rayna, and she followed him to the interview room. Ian was typing something on a laptop. It was no doubt Mitch's statement.

Mitch immediately got to his feet when Court opened the door. "Did they find Bobby Joe?"

Court shook his head and quietly apologized to Ian for interrupting the interview.

"You're sure your brother is actually alive?" Court asked Mitch. He put the man's phone on the table next to him.

The surprise went through Mitch's eyes. "Of course he is. You heard the message."

"I heard what could have been something recorded years ago. Something that was put together to make you believe it was actually from Bobby Joe."

"It was from him," Mitch practically shouted. But then he stopped and slid glances at both of them. "Is this some kind of trick?"

"You tell me," Court argued.

"If you're accusing me of…whatever the hell this is, then I want a lawyer." Mitch's voice got even louder, and his hands went to his hips. "And I want bail. You can't lock me up for trespassing."

Well, he could put him in jail, but Court couldn't hold him for long, since right now the only charge he could make against Mitch was a misdemeanor. But maybe there was another way of going about this.

"Can you think of a reason why someone would want you to fake that message?" Court asked.

"No! My brother wanted to meet me. He wanted to show me the gun that Rayna has hidden somewhere."

Not likely. There'd been plenty of searches of Rayna's place that should have already revealed a gun if there was one. Of course, Bobby Joe could have hidden it as he'd maybe done when he'd put the key in the birdhouse.

And that led Court to an idea.

Bobby Joe might not try to see Mitch as long as he was here, but if he was indeed alive, he might contact Mitch as soon as no cops were around.

"You'll be able to leave as soon as you're done with the interview," Court told Mitch.

Ian made eye contact with Court and seemed to know what Court was thinking. "We're done. Well, unless you're going to press charges against him for trespassing," Ian said to Rayna.

She glanced at all of them. Paused. Then shook her head. "No charges unless we prove Mitch actually broke down the door."

"I didn't," Mitch insisted.

Maybe he was telling the truth, but it didn't matter. "Just stop by Thea's desk," Court told Mitch. "She'll print out a copy of what Ian just typed up so you can read through it and sign it. Will you need a ride?"

"Thanks, but no, thanks. I left my truck on a trail near Rayna's, but I'll find a way to get home." Mitch grabbed his phone and hurried out of the room.

"I know it's a risk, letting him walk," Court said to Rayna.

"But it might help us catch Bobby Joe," she finished for him. "If he's really alive, that is."

Yes, that was the million-dollar question, but Mitch might be able to give them the answer to that.

"You want me to follow him?" Ian asked the moment that Mitch was out of earshot.

Court nodded. "But I don't want you to go alone. And we don't have another available deputy." He didn't like this much, but it was a temporary solution until he could get some Rangers in place to pick up the tail on Mitch. "Rayna and I will go with you."

Ian didn't look so certain about that. Neither was Court, but he had no intentions of leaving her at the sheriff's office, where Thea already had her hands full.

"It'll be okay," he told Rayna. Without thinking, he brushed a kiss on her cheek.

He immediately cursed himself for doing that. Yeah, that other kiss had definitely broken down some barriers that should have stayed in place. At least until this investigation was over.

Court texted Thea to let her know what was going on, and Ian, Rayna and he went out the back to one of the two unmarked cars they kept there. It was reinforced just like a cruiser, but maybe Mitch wouldn't recognize it was a cop car. Ian got behind the wheel, and after Court got in the back seat with Rayna, Ian pulled to the side of the building so they'd be able to see when Mitch left.

Court was so caught up in keeping watch that it gave him a jolt when the sound of his phone ringing shot through the car. Not Unknown Caller this time. It was Rachel.

"How's Mom?" he asked the moment he answered.

"Not great. They're transferring her to the hospital in San Antonio." Rachel was crying. No doubt about that. Court could hear her sobs. "They'll commit her there until she can have some evals done."

"You need me there?" Though he wasn't sure how he would manage it. Still, he would if necessary.

"No need. We won't be here much longer, and Mom won't be allowed visitors for a while at the other hospital."

That meant Court wouldn't be able to question his mother anytime soon about what he'd seen on the surveillance footage. However, there might be a way around that. "By any chance did Mom bring her purse to the hospital?"

He could tell from Rachel's slight huff that the question had surprised her. "No. It's at the house. Why?"

Court hoped he didn't alarm Rachel unnecessarily with this, but it was something they had to know. "I believe she might have gotten a business card or something from the murdered PI, Jennifer Reeves. That was a couple of days ago. I know it's a long shot, but I need to see if she still has it."

Rachel's slight gasp let him know that he'd alarmed her after all. "I'll be going back to the ranch when Mom is transferred. I want to get some things and go to the hospital in San Antonio. I can check her purse as soon as I'm back at the house."

"Thanks. But I don't want you driving alone."

"Egan's already told me that. He'll take me back, and then we'll drive to San Antonio together. He's arranging to have some local cops guard me."

Good. He thanked her again and ended the call when he saw Mitch finally come out of the building. The man didn't even look their way. He immediately took out his phone, made a call and started walking on the sidewalk away from them. Ian eased out of the parking lot so they could follow him.

Mitch had made it only about a block when Court's phone rang again. For a moment he thought it was Mitch calling him, but it was Whitney's name on the screen. Court pressed the answer button, ready to blast her for not coming directly to the sheriff's office as he'd ordered her to do. However, Whitney spoke before Court could say anything.

"Oh, God. You've got to help me!" Whitney blurted out. "Oh, God. There's a fire."

And then Court heard something on the other end of the line that he definitely didn't want to hear.

The sound of a gunshot.

RAYNA HAD NO trouble hearing the sound. Or Whitney's bone-chilling scream that quickly followed the blast from what had to be a gunshot.

"Whitney?" Court yelled into the phone. "Where are you? What's going on?"

"You have to help me," Whitney begged. "I'm just up the street by the hardware store."

That was the direction Mitch was walking. The direction that Ian went as well, and both Court and he drew their guns.

The hardware store was about two blocks away, but the moment Ian pulled out of the parking lot, Rayna saw the smoke. It was thick and black, billowing in the air, and the wind was blowing it right toward them.

Mitch obviously noticed it, too, because he turned and started running back to the sheriff's office. Maybe he would stay there instead of trying to get to Bobby Joe. That way, someone could still follow him after they took care of this situation.

"I'm calling the fire department," Ian said, and he did that while he continued to drive closer to the smoke. It wouldn't take the fire department long to get there at all. Well, it wouldn't take long if there wasn't any other gunfire.

"Get down on the seat," Court told her, and he handed her his phone. "Try to find out exactly where Whitney is and who fired that shot."

Rayna did get down, and she tried to level her voice. Whitney had sounded terrified, and it wouldn't do the woman any good if she heard the panic in Rayna's tone, too.

"Where are you?" Rayna asked.

Whitney started coughing, which meant she was probably very close to the smoke. Maybe in the middle of it. "I think I saw Bobby Joe."

So, not just a message or phone call this time but a possible sighting. Of course, Hallie had posed as Rayna, so someone could be doing the same when it came to Bobby Joe. "Where did you see him?"

"In the alley by the hardware store." Whitney coughed some more. "I'm not sure he saw me, so I went running after him. I saw a car parked back there, but that's when the fire started. The flames just popped up right in front of me, and I couldn't get to him."

Which meant someone had almost certainly set it. Before Rayna could ask her who'd fired the shot, there was another one. Then another. They sounded much too close, which was probably why Ian pulled off the street and into a parking place outside the bookstore.

"Everyone, take cover now!" Court shouted when he lowered his window.

Rayna could hear people running and shouting. She prayed that none of them would be hurt.

"Where are you?" Whitney said on another of those sobs. "I need to find you. And we need to find Bobby Joe so he can clear your name once and for all."

"No. You need to go inside the nearest building and stay put," Rayna assured her. "You could be shot."

Whitney said something that she didn't catch, and the line went dead. Rayna didn't try to call her back because she didn't want the sound of a ringing phone to cause a gunman to home in on Whitney. Maybe she had done as Rayna told her and had taken cover.

Behind them, she heard the wail of the sirens from the fire engine. But she also heard a fourth shot. It was even closer than the others had been.

The fifth one slammed into the front windshield.

Both deputies cursed, and Court pushed her even farther down on the seat. "You see the shooter?" Ian asked.

"No." But Court was glancing all around them. "Tell the fire department not to approach. It's too dangerous."

Another shot cracked through the air, and this one hit just a few inches from the previous one. The glass held, but it was cracked enough that other bullets might be able to get through.

"Get us out of here," Court told Ian.

The deputy did. The moment he finished with radioing the fire department, Ian threw the car into Reverse and hit the gas. He didn't get far though, probably because of other vehicles.

"Hold on," Ian told them.

His warning came only a few seconds before he made a sharp turn, causing Court and Rayna to slam against each other. She lifted her head enough to see that Ian had turned around in the middle of the street and was now heading back in the direction of the sheriff's office.

The shooter fired a flurry of shots at the car, all slamming into the back windshield.

"I see the guy," Court said.

She followed his gaze to the left side of the street. The same side as the fire. But she was too far down on the seat to see what had captured his attention.

"It's a man wearing a mask," Court added.

It was probably the same person who'd shot at them at the hospital. But had he also been the one to set the fire? And if so, why? Maybe he thought it would conceal him, and if so, it'd worked. The guy had managed to get off at least ten shots before Court had spotted him.

"You want me to go back?" Ian asked.

She saw the quick debate in Court's eyes. He wanted to catch this guy and would have almost certainly gone after him if she hadn't been in the car. "No. Let's take Rayna to the sheriff's office. We'll regroup and go after him."

Which meant Court was going to put himself in the line of fire. Of course, that was his job, but it sickened her to think that he could be hurt or worse because some goon was after her.

Ian screeched to a stop in front of the sheriff's office, but none of them got out. They sat there, no doubt waiting to see if the shooter would continue. If he did, it wasn't safe for them to run inside. Even though they would be out in the open only a couple of seconds, that would be enough time for them to be gunned down.

Rayna lifted her head again. Thea was in the doorway of the sheriff's office, and she had her gun drawn. There was no sign of Mitch, but Court's phone rang again, and she saw Whitney's name on the screen. Rayna answered it as fast as she could.

"Please tell me you took cover," Rayna told her.

"I couldn't. For your sake, I had to find Bobby Joe."

Rayna groaned. "No, you don't. There's a gunman out there."

"Yes. I saw him. Are you sure it was a man? I thought maybe it was a woman wearing a ski mask."

That gave Rayna a jolt of adrenaline. It wouldn't be Court's mom, since she was on her way to a hospital in San Antonio, but it could be Alma. Still, that seemed like a stretch. If Alma wanted them dead, she could have just hired someone. That included a female assassin.

Whitney gasped, the sound coming through loud and clear. "Rayna, tell Court he needs to get here. He needs to see this."

That didn't help with the adrenaline, either. "See what?" Rayna pressed.

"Oh, God. There's a body in that fire."

CHAPTER THIRTEEN

COURT DIDN'T LIKE anything about this, but there wasn't much else he could do but stand and watch as the fire department finished up with what was now a crime scene.

One with a body.

Once they were done, the medical examiner and CSIs could get in the alley and maybe figure out what had gone on here. He could question not only the fire chief, Delbert Monroe, but also help track down possible witnesses. Until that happened, Court could only speculate. And worry about Rayna.

He'd left her at the sheriff's office with Thea and Ian, and Egan was on the way now that he'd put the ranch on lockdown. Three lawmen would hopefully be enough to keep her safe, but she was in the building with not only Bo but Whitney, as well. At least Bo was still locked up, but he couldn't do the same to Whitney because there were no charges against her. Still, that didn't mean Court trusted her.

Ditto for Mitch.

But Court hadn't heard a peep from the man since he'd left shortly before the fire. He wasn't answering his phone, and no one had seen him. That meant Mitch could have been the person who'd worn a ski mask and shot at them. He would have had time to duck into the alley and do that.

Whitney had said though that she thought the shooter was a woman. So far, no other witness had managed to corroborate that, but it didn't mean she was mistaken or lying. That was because their other suspect—Alma—wasn't answering her phone, either.

No, there wasn't any part of this he liked.

Plus, there was the whole problem of an unidentified shooter. There hadn't been any shots fired in over an hour, so that probably meant the gunman was long gone. That didn't mean he wouldn't be back though.

Court took out his phone to call and check on Rayna, but he finally saw Delbert making his way toward him. He was sporting a weary expression, along with soot and ashes on his clothes.

"Our DB is male," Delbert said right off the bat. "We didn't touch the body, of course, but it's badly burned. Too burned to make a visual ID."

That didn't surprise Court because the vehicle that had contained the body was a charred mess. "I smell gasoline," Court pointed out.

Delbert nodded. "An accelerant was used. I suspect it was poured over the car and then lit. Most of his clothes burned off, but there's some tissue remaining. Plus, his teeth are in good shape. We can compare them to dental records."

Good. Because the person's identity might lead Court to finding out why he was dead. "Any signs that the guy struggled to get out of the burning car?"

"No. He was lying on the back seat."

That possibly meant he was unconscious or even already dead before the fire. Often criminals tried to use fire to cover up any DNA or trace evidence they might have left behind. Of course, it would be bold for a criminal to do that in broad daylight.

Or maybe not bold after all.

Court motioned to the blackened strip on the concrete between the dead guy's car and them. It was where a second fire had been set, and it was a good fifteen feet from the other deadly one. "Can you think of any good reason why someone would do that?"

Delbert immediately shook his head. "No, but I can think of a bad one. A strip fire like that would conceal whatever was going on in the car."

Yeah, that'd been Court's theory, too. If the person who'd set it had been behind the first set of flames, it would have made it very hard for someone on the street to see him or her. Then the person could have escaped through the back alley.

There were no cameras back there, either.

"I went ahead and called in the CSIs," Delbert went on. "They'll be here soon." He hitched his thumb back to the alley. "Just thought you should know there's a cell phone on the ground. It's not a fancy smart one. Just one of the cheap ones you can buy just about anywhere. Again, we didn't touch it, and it might not even belong to the vic."

Court would definitely have it collected and tested. If it was the vic's though, he wasn't sure why it was out of the car when the body was inside.

Delbert glanced around the street, which was empty now. But Delbert wasn't looking at the sidewalks. He was studying the buildings and the streetlight that was to their right.

"There aren't any cameras," Court told him.

Of course, Court would check to see if anyone had recently added one, but this area of Main Street was essentially a dead zone when it came to surveillance. Alma might not have known that, but Whitney and Mitch likely would have.

Ditto for his mother.

That was because it'd come up in a discussion when there'd been a robbery at the hardware store a couple of years ago. Many people then had lobbied to get security cameras for all of Main Street, but it hadn't been in the budget.

Court wanted to exclude his mother as a suspect, but he kept going back to the point that Raleigh had made. Whoever had hired the shooter might no longer have a leash on him or her. If that proved to be true, then his mom was still a possible person of interest.

When Court saw the CSI van pull up, he figured it was time for him to go back to the station. He could do a lot more good there—including keep watch on Rayna—while the CSIs processed the crime scene. However, he did remind both the CSIs and Delbert to call him the moment they had anything on the body or the phone. Too bad Court couldn't just take it now, but he couldn't touch it until the CSIs had gotten pictures.

Court drove his cruiser back to the sheriff's office, parking behind the shot-up unmarked car. Just seeing it made him feel sick and riled him to the core. Once again, Rayna had come close to being killed, and they still didn't know why.

"Anything?" Rayna asked the moment he stepped inside. She was in the doorway of Egan's office, her hands bracketed on the jamb. Her knuckles were white.

"We'll know something soon," he assured her and hoped that wasn't a lie.

Rayna wasn't alone. Both Thea and Ian were in the squad room, but there was no sign of Whitney.

"Egan got here about fifteen minutes ago, and Whitney's in the interview room with him," Rayna said. "She seemed really upset." Court didn't miss the *seemed*, and he wondered if that meant Rayna was having doubts about her friend.

Because he thought they could both use it, he went to Rayna and pulled her into his arms for a hug. Yeah, he needed it all right, and that was why Court lingered a moment before he eased back from her—along with easing her deeper into Egan's office. Not so he could kiss her, though that was something he suddenly wanted to do. No, it was because the shooter was still at large and could try to fire through the windows of the sheriff's office.

"Did Whitney say anything to you before Egan got here?" Court asked her.

"Not really. She was crying a lot. I asked her why she didn't come straight to the sheriff's office after you told her to, and she said she had to pick up some meds first. She'd felt a migraine coming on."

Since Whitney did indeed suffer from migraines, it wasn't much of a stretch that she'd need meds for the headaches. Still, the timing was suspicious.

"Come on." Court took Rayna by the hand. "We'll go to the observation room and listen to what she's saying to Egan." That was better than standing there with all this energy still zinging between them. "I'll also try again to track down Mitch."

He took out his phone, but it rang before he could

make the call. However, this one could be important, since it was from one of the CSIs, Larry Hanson. Court put the call on speaker and hoped it wasn't bad news. They'd already had enough of that for the day.

"I went ahead and photographed the phone," Larry said right off. "I was about to bag it when I saw there was a missed call on the screen. I don't have the password to see if there's a voice mail, but I got the name of the caller."

"Who?" Court immediately asked.

"Alma Lawton. You know her?"

Hell. "Yeah. I know her." And he was going to get her right back in here for questioning. "I don't suppose you can tell whose phone that is?"

"Nope. Not without the password. I'll get it to the lab though to see if they can come up with something. We might have something on the body soon, too."

That got Court's attention. "Dental records?"

"We'll try those, sure, but it seems as if the back of the body might still be intact. The ME thinks he can see a wallet in the back of the guy's jeans. We won't know though until we can lift it, but that shouldn't be much longer."

If there was a wallet, there might be an ID. Of course, it didn't mean the ID or, for that matter, the wallet belonged to the dead guy. However, it could be a good break if it did.

Court thanked Larry and went back into the squad room so he could get Alma's number from the computer.

"It must not be Alma's phone they found, since she was the caller," Rayna said. "But I don't think she knows any of our other suspects. Not personally, anyway," she added.

Rayna was no doubt referring to his mother. Alma had definitely heard of her, but neither Alma nor Helen had mentioned being in contact with each other.

The moment he had Alma's number, he tried to call her. It went straight to voice mail, so Court left a message for her to get to the sheriff's office ASAP for questioning. He tried Raleigh next, but the deputy who answered said the sheriff was in the process of arresting a burglary suspect. Since Court had struck out with both Alma and Raleigh, he made another call to his sister. Unlike the other two, Rachel answered on the first ring.

"Are you okay?" Rachel asked before he could even say anything.

"We're fine. You?"

"I'm as well as can be expected. Egan said there was a body, that that's why he had to go in."

"There is. The CSIs are working on the ID right now." He gathered his breath for the next question. "By any chance, did Mom have a new phone? Not the one we got her for Christmas but a cheaper one?"

"I don't think so. But I can look in her purse. I was going to do that anyway because you said you wanted me to check for a business card."

"Yes. Could you do that now?"

Since Rachel was the daughter and sister of lawmen, she knew that wasn't a casual question and that it likely had something to do with the investigation. "What's this all about?"

"Just checking to see if she called anyone."

It was a pretty sorry explanation, and Rachel made a sound to indicate she wasn't buying it. Still, she was obviously looking because several moments later she added, "Her phone's not on her nightstand." Court could hear her moving around. "I'm looking through her purse now. No phone. You think she lost it?"

He hoped not, and he hoped even more that she hadn't bought another phone and used it to call Alma. Of course, even if she had, that wouldn't have explained why it would be in that alley.

"There's a card," Rachel added. "Yes, it's for Stigler Investigations. You think Jennifer Reeves works for this PI agency?"

No, that hadn't come up at any point, so he sandwiched his phone between his shoulder and ear, went to his desk and typed in the name on his computer. It was another agency all right.

One that specialized in getting proof of cheating spouses.

That felt like a punch to the gut. Because it meant that his mother had likely known about Warren's affair days ago. That would have been plenty enough time to hire someone to fire that shot that'd gone into his father's chest.

"Do you have access to Mom and Dad's bank account?" Court asked.

"No," Rachel answered, hesitation in her voice. "But I'm sure I can get it. Why?"

Court didn't go with the full truth on this. "I just want to see if maybe Mom hired a PI, too. It might have gone on her credit card if she hired someone over the phone. Also, look for a check."

"Now, are you going to tell me what this is all about?" Rachel demanded.

"Just making sure there's not another PI out there to interfere with this investigation." But what he really wanted to know was if there was enough money missing for his mother to have hired a gunman. "Call me if you find anything." With more of that skepticism in her tone, Rachel assured him that she would.

Since it might take a while for Rachel to do that, Court led Rayna to the observation room. Egan and Whitney were there, and Whitney was still crying. He wanted to give her the benefit of the doubt, not only because she was Rayna's friend but also because she worked at the sheriff's office. He hated the possibility that he'd been working with a would-be killer after all these years.

Rayna stared at her friend through the glass. "Whitney hasn't been the same person since my trial. She's been, well, distant."

Maybe because Whitney had thought Rayna was really a killer. But there was another angle on this. "You think Whitney could have had feelings for Bobby Joe?"

"It's possible." Since Rayna hadn't hesitated, it meant she'd given that some thought. Then she shrugged. "But there were times when I felt as if Whitney wanted me to ditch him. Whenever we'd have a girls' night out, she was always trying to fix me up with other guys."

Again, that was maybe because Whitney wanted Bobby Joe for herself. She did seem to be genuinely upset, and maybe that was because of the possible Bobby Joe sighting.

"Who do you think set the fire?" Egan asked her.

Whitney's head whipped up. "You're not accusing me of doing that, are you?" There was some bitterness in her voice.

"Just asking," Egan calmly clarified.

"Well, I don't know. I told you the flames just shot up right in front of me. I would have caught up with Bobby Joe if it hadn't been for that."

If she was telling the truth, it meant someone had put that line of gasoline there before Whitney had even gone into the alley, and it was possible someone had triggered it with a remote device.

But why?

That was the question Court was asking himself when his phone rang, and he saw Larry's name on the screen.

"We got the wallet from our dead guy," Larry immediately said. "And there was a driver's license. The name on it is Dustin Clark, but the photo is one I'm sure you'll recognize. I'm texting it to you now."

Court knew Larry was right the moment he loaded the photo and saw the man's face.

Bobby Joe.

HE WAS FINALLY DEAD.

For the first time in three years, Rayna actually believed that was true—that Bobby Joe was no longer a threat to her. Of course, they'd have to wait for more proof of the dental records, but she didn't need anything else.

"You should sit down," she heard Court say.

He didn't wait for her to do that though. He practically put her in the chair in the observation room. That was when Rayna realized she was wobbling some and wasn't feeling very steady. Court probably thought she was about to collapse. She was, but it was from relief.

That relief didn't last long though.

"Will people once again think I killed Bobby Joe?" she asked.

Court shook his head, sighed and brushed a kiss on the top of her head. All of those gestures eased some of the gut-wrenching tension inside her. "You were with Ian and me when that fire started."

True, but since many people in McCall Canyon thought she was a killer, they might think she'd set this up in some way.

"Who would have killed him?" Rayna pressed.

Court shrugged. "For us to know that, we'll have to figure out what he's been doing all this time. I doubt this was suicide, so that means either someone killed him in the car and set fire to it or they put him in the vehicle after he was already dead. Either way, it's murder."

Yes, and she couldn't rule out the rogue gunman who was running around shooting at them. The person wearing that ski mask would have had time to set the fire before launching this latest attack against them. For that matter though, so would Mitch, Whitney and maybe even Alma.

"Wait here," Court instructed.

Since she didn't trust her legs, Rayna didn't have a choice about that. She watched as Court went into the interview room to whisper something to Egan. He was no doubt telling his brother about Bobby Joe, but Court didn't wait around for Egan's or Whitney's response. He left and went back to the squad room. A few seconds later, he returned with a bottle of water and a laptop.

In the interview room, Egan was breaking the news to Whitney, and Rayna watched the shock wash over the woman's face. More tears followed, but Rayna didn't focus on that. She turned her attention to Court, who was running a computer check on Bobby Joe's alias, Dustin Clark.

"That's all there is on him," Court said, pulling up the driver's license. "No record. Not even a parking ticket."

Probably because Bobby Joe had been living under the radar, waiting for his chance to come after her again. Of course, she still didn't know why he'd waited all this time.

"I'll check the address he gave the DMV," Court added, but he stopped when they heard the sound of voices in the squad room.

Alma.

"Why would Deputy McCall leave a message like that for me?" Alma snapped. She sounded angry. Looked it, too, when Rayna saw the woman after Court and she stepped out into the hall.

"Because I need to talk to you about a possible murder," Court answered. He sounded angry as well, but Rayna knew there was also plenty of frustration. Each thing they found only seemed to lead them to more questions.

Alma gave him a flat look. "Murder? Really? Did Warren die?"

Court matched her look with a scowl. "Not Warren, but a man you called shortly before he was murdered."

Alma started shaking her head before he'd even finished. "The only person I've called today was one of my former hands, Dustin Clark."

Bingo. Well, at least she hadn't claimed it was a setup.

Court motioned for Alma to follow him to Egan's office, and once the three of them were inside, he shut the door. Bobby Joe's picture was still on the laptop, so Court turned it in Alma's direction.

"Is that the Dustin Clark you called?" he pressed.

Alma had a closer look at the screen. "Yes. Did something happen to him?" If she was concerned about that, she didn't show it. She could have been discussing the weather.

"He's dead. Now, tell me how you know him and why you called him. Then you can explain how you got here so fast. You didn't have enough time to drive from Durango Ridge."

"I was already here in McCall Canyon," Alma admitted. "I was coming to pay Dustin what I owed him. He's been working for me out at my ranch."

It didn't sound like a coincidence that Bobby Joe would be working for someone with ties to the Mc-Calls.

"There's no record of his employment with you," Court pointed out.

"Because I paid him in cash. That's the way he wanted it, and I was happy to oblige. He was good with the horses." She glanced at the screen again. "You're sure he's dead?"

"We have a body that we believe is his. When's the last time you saw him?" Court continued without even pausing.

Alma huffed, and she frowned. "Maybe about a week ago. He was at my ranch and told one of the other hands that he had to leave to take care of some personal things. He didn't come back. That's why I called him to make arrangements to meet him so I could pay him."

"And he answered that call?" Rayna wanted to know.

"Yes. Like I said, that's why I'm here in town." Alma's attention shifted back to Court. "Is this about your father?"

Court pulled back his shoulders. "Why do you ask that?"

"Because Dustin hated Warren, that's why. He never did tell me why, but a few months ago Dustin saw Warren picking me up at the ranch, and he pulled me aside later and said Warren couldn't be trusted, that he'd been a dirty cop when he was still sheriff here. I got the feeling there was some bad blood between them, but when I mentioned it to Warren, he said he didn't know anyone by that name."

And he wouldn't have, since Bobby Joe was using an alias. Still, it made Rayna wonder why Warren hadn't followed up on that. Or maybe he had so many people who disliked him that it wasn't anything that concerned him.

"Dustin's real name was Bobby Joe Hawley," Court provided. "Ever hear him mention that?"

She quickly shook her head. "I only knew him as Dustin." She stopped, looked at Rayna. "That's the man you were accused of murdering. The one that Warren was certain you'd killed," she added. "Since you were acquitted, that means you couldn't be tried for his death now."

"I didn't kill him," Rayna insisted. She kept her stare on Alma.

"Well, neither did I." Alma huffed again. "What possible motive could I have for wanting him dead?"

"Maybe you hired him to shoot my father," Court answered. "Or maybe Bobby Joe found out you'd hired someone to do that and he was trying to extort money from you. This is a long way to come to pay a ranch hand some wages. You could have just mailed him the money."

Alma's mouth tightened. "I always pay my debts." And since she'd said it through clenched teeth, it sounded like some kind of threat. But she glanced away, her expression softening a little. "Dustin... Bobby Joe or whatever his name is...said he didn't have an address here. Nor a car. He asked me to meet him."

Court and Rayna exchanged another glance, and Rayna could almost see the thought going through his head. He was wondering if Bobby Joe had been planning to set up Alma in some way. Though that still didn't explain who'd killed him.

"Bobby Joe hated my father and Rayna," Court said to Alma. "It's possible he hated them even more because she wasn't convicted of his murder. Now, think back to your dealings with Bobby Joe. Did he ever ask you any questions about Warren or Rayna?"

"Not Rayna," she answered right off. "But like I said, we did discuss Warren after he'd come to the ranch. Bobby Joe was upset, but after what I've just learned about him, maybe he was just trying to make sure Warren didn't come back. If he was supposed to be dead, he wouldn't have wanted Warren to recognize him."

True. In fact, it'd probably given Bobby Joe a jolt, or maybe a secret thrill, when he'd seen Warren.

"But Bobby Joe did mention Helen," Alma added a moment later.

Rayna saw Court's muscles go stiff, and he motioned for Alma to continue.

She did not until she'd taken a deep breath first. "It was after Warren's visit. Bobby Joe told me that Warren was married, and that his wife, Helen, was the darling of McCall Canyon. *Darling*, that's the word he used. Bobby Joe didn't come out and say it, but I could tell he suspected an affair between Warren and me." She paused. "I lied and said Warren was there on ranching business and that there was absolutely nothing going on between us."

If Bobby Joe had truly been suspicious of the affair, Rayna wondered why he hadn't exposed it. He couldn't have personally done that, but he could have sent Helen or someone else an anonymous note or maybe even pictures of Warren's visit to the Lawton ranch.

"Anyway, I told Warren it wasn't a good idea for him to visit me at my house again," Alma continued. "Warren and I ended things shortly after that."

Court stayed quiet a moment, obviously processing that. "And you didn't mention *Dustin* or what he'd said to you about my dad?"

"No." She paused again. "I didn't want to know anyone was suspicious. I mean, I could feel Warren already pulling away from me, and I didn't want to give him a reason to break things off."

That was the first time Alma had admitted that she'd wanted to stay in the relationship.

And, of course, it was also her motive for Warren's attempted murder.

It was hard for Rayna to stand there so close to the woman who might have tried to kill Court and her, but if Alma had indeed done that, then things hadn't gone according to plan. After all, Court, Warren and she were all still alive.

"Am I free to go now?" Alma asked. "Or should I call my lawyer?"

Court gave that some thought. "I don't have a reason to hold you, yet. But I'll be checking your phone records. Now would be a good time to tell me if there's something else you want to add about Bobby Joe, or anything else for that matter."

Alma's mouth tightened again. "I haven't done anything wrong, and the next time you want to speak to me, call Simon." With that, she walked out.

"You believe her?" Rayna said the moment the woman was out of the sheriff's office.

Court shrugged. "I'd love to pin this on her, but I don't think I'm objective when it comes to Alma."

No, neither was she. The woman had basically been living a lie for over thirty years, and she could be lying now.

"I meant it when I said I'll be checking out her story," Court said, "but I can do that at the ranch. I doubt you want to stay around here much longer."

She didn't. Rayna was exhausted and was now dealing with the aftereffects of the spent adrenaline. "But what about the gunman? And what with the fire and attack, I doubt Egan can spare a deputy to go with us."

"I can have a couple of the hands come here and then drive back with us. The ranch is already being guarded."

Yes, but that didn't mean it was safe. Of course, the sheriff's office wasn't exactly safe, either. Someone could easily fire shots into the building.

"Let me talk to Egan before I call the hands," Court added. But his phone rang before he could do that. "It's Larry."

Since this was the CSI, Rayna definitely wanted to hear what he had to say, and thankfully Court put the call on speaker.

"We found something," Larry said as soon as he was on the line. "Court, it's another dead body."

CHAPTER FOURTEEN

COURT STARED OUT the window of his house. It was something he did often as the sun was setting, something that usually relaxed him. But it was going to take more than familiar scenery to take this raw edge off him.

Four murders. Probably all connected, and yet they still didn't make sense. Now he could add the latest body to the "not making sense" category.

Mitch.

One of their top suspects was dead, shot at point-blank range, two bullets to the head. Since the PI and Hallie had been killed in a similar way, it was possible it'd been the same shooter. But if it was, Court didn't have any proof. All he had were those damn questions that just wouldn't stop going through his mind.

Who'd killed those people? And why? Of course, one of the biggest questions of all—was his mother involved?

So far, Rachel hadn't found any unaccounted-for funds in Helen's checking account. No missing cash, either, from the safe at the family home. But there were other ways people could get cash. His mom could have sold some jewelry or had money stashed away that no one else had known about. The fact she'd known about the affair and had even gotten that business card from Jennifer were red flags that he couldn't ignore. The problem was it was going to be days, maybe even weeks, before he could question his mother.

"You're going to drive yourself crazy, you know that?" Rayna asked.

Her voice cut through some of his mind-clutter. So did the sound of her footsteps as she walked toward him. She'd showered and looked less tense than she had when they'd arrived back at his place. But then, if she'd looked more tense, he would have had to call the doctor because she'd been right on that edge. With reason.

She was probably the killer's next target.

Judging from the other attacks, so was he.

She came closer, and he caught the scent of the soap and shampoo she'd used. *His* soap and shampoo, but it smelled better on her than it ever had on him. She'd dressed in the jeans and blue top they'd gotten from her house. And she was holding the gun he'd given her.

The gun had been a compromise. Court hadn't wanted to give her one because he hadn't wanted her to do anything to put herself in even more danger. If there was another attack, he wanted her to get out of harm's way rather than returning fire.

But that wasn't practical.

The truth was someone could get on the ranch. Yes, the hands were watching the road, but someone could get to his house using the back trails. Heck, a gunman could climb over the fence. Rayna knew that. And that was why she now had the gun.

"Any updates?" she asked. She tucked the gun in the waistband of her jeans at the small of her back, poured herself a cup of coffee and joined him at the window.

This wasn't exactly a topic to keep her nerves steady,

but Rayna needed to know. "We don't have a dental match ID on the dead guy in the car, but the other body they found is definitely Mitch. No one heard gunshots, but there was a lot of commotion what with the fire."

"Yes," she said as if giving that some thought. "The unidentified gunman could have killed him. He could have set the fire, too."

"Or Alma or Whitney could have done it," Court quickly pointed out.

Rayna flinched, probably because it was hard for her to hear that her former friend could be a cold-blooded killer. It was especially hard since they weren't sure what Whitney's motive would have been for that.

Alma was a different story though.

"I've gone through Alma's phone records," he explained, "and she did call Bobby Joe aka Dustin three times." That wasn't a large number, and the calls could have been legit if Bobby Joe had actually been working for her.

"What about her financial records?"

He shook his head. "I haven't gotten those yet, but even when I do, I'm not expecting much. If Alma has been putting this plan together for months, then she probably would have been smart enough not to use funds that would create a money trail leading right back to her."

"True."

Court didn't think it was his imagination that she was waiting for more. "Nothing on my mother, either," he added. "Warren also hasn't been much help. He says he didn't know about Mom meeting with the PI."

"You think he could be covering for your mom? He

might feel so bad about the affair that he doesn't want her punished."

That was possible, of course, but Court just couldn't buy it. "If the attacks had only been limited to Dad, he might have covered for her. *Might*. But no way would he sit back and not spill something that involved four murders. Plus, there were the attacks on us. My dad might not have valued his marriage vows, but he'd do anything to protect his kids."

She had a sip of her coffee. "You're right."

That caused him to breathe a little easier. It was already hard enough to accept his mother might have had a part in this without believing the same of his father.

"What about Bo and Whitney?" she asked. "Did Egan get anything from them when he questioned them?"

"No. Whitney stuck to her story about not having a clue what was going on. And Bo didn't say anything that he hadn't already told us. The DA plans to charge him as an adult. That might spur him to spill something new." If there was anything new to spill, that was. Bo did seem like a pawn in all of this.

Like Hallie. Maybe Jennifer, too. And since they were both dead, it meant Bo needed to be in protective custody.

The sun finally dipped below the horizon, so Court went to the foyer, turned off the interior light and turned on the ones outside. There were about a dozen of them, and they went all around the house and grounds. When he'd had them installed though, it hadn't been with the idea of seeing an intruder. It had been to try to keep the coyotes and other wildlife away. Now it might keep that gunman from trying to sneak up on them. Just in case he did, Court made sure the security system was armed and ready. It was.

"Rachel is at the hospital with my mom," Court continued. "Egan's at the main house. Or at least he will be when he finishes up at the office."

Whenever that would be. Court figured it'd be a late night for his brother, and he was feeling guilty about that. Still, someone needed to stay with Rayna at his house, and it might as well be him.

That thought stopped him for a moment.

He *wanted* to be the one to stay with her.

Hell, that wasn't a good sign. Coupled with those kisses he'd been doling out to her, it meant he'd had a big-time loss of focus. He looked at her, to warn her about that, but one look in her eyes, and he realized no warning was necessary. Rayna knew exactly what was going on.

"Sometimes, it feels like we're back in high school," she murmured. Rayna set her coffee cup back on the counter. "Well, with the exception of someone trying to kill us, that is."

She managed to make that sound, well, light, and it caused Court to smile. She smiled, too, but then she quickly looked away as if trying to remind herself neither smiling nor looking at him that way was a good idea.

It wasn't.

Court stayed in the foyer on purpose. Best to keep some distance between them. But Rayna didn't go along with that. She went to him, her steps and body language hesitant. There was nothing hesitant about the feelings going on inside him.

He wanted her.

And no distance between them was going to remedy that. Silently cursing himself and cursing Rayna, Court strode forward to meet her and pulled her into his arms.

RAYNA HAD KNOWN the kiss was coming even before Court's mouth landed on hers. Still, she hadn't been prepared for the shock of the sensations that went through her. Yes, in some ways it did feel as if they were back in high school, but she also hadn't remembered anything this intense when they'd been teenagers.

"You know this is a big mistake, right?" Court asked when he broke away from her for air.

She did know that. So did he.

But apparently knowing wasn't going to make a difference here because he went right back for a second kiss. Rayna had been hesitant about that first one, since it'd thrown her off guard a little, but with this one, she just gave in to the moment and kissed him right back.

Rayna slid her hands around the back of his neck, pulling him closer until they were body to body. Along with the new slam of heat that gave her, it also tapped into some old memories. Of other times when Court had kissed her.

And made love to her.

He'd been her first, something she wouldn't have been able to forget even if he hadn't been doling out some mind-blowing kisses.

Court stopped again, easing back so they could make eye contact. It seemed to be his way of giving her an out. He was giving her time to put a stop to this. But Rayna had no intentions of stopping it. That was why she pulled him right back to her.

He deepened the kiss, stoking the fire between them. And he stoked it even more when he took those kisses to her neck. It didn't take her body long to realize it wanted a lot more of what Court was giving her.

Years ago, Court and she had kissed like this for hours, driving each other crazy, until they'd finally become lovers. All of that came back now and upped the urgency even more.

She reached for the buttons on his shirt, but his hands got in the way. That was because he pulled off her top, tossing it onto the floor. In the same motion, he kissed her breasts. First, the tops, and then he shoved down her bra to kiss her the way Rayna wanted. He'd remembered those were sensitive spots for her, and he made sure he gave her as much pleasure as possible.

But soon, it wasn't enough.

Rayna went after his shirt again and managed to get enough buttons undone so she could kiss his chest. Apparently, that upped the urgency for him, too, because Court pulled her to the floor.

There were no lights on inside, but the exterior lights were enough for Rayna to see his face. Mercy, he was hot. Always had been, and that hadn't changed. If anything, the years had made him even better, and she regretted the time she'd lost with him.

Regretted, too, that she might never have him again like that.

That tugged at her heart, but Rayna didn't have time to dwell on it. That was because the kisses continued. The touches, too, but it was obvious that foreplay wasn't going to last much longer. That was okay with Rayna. For now, she just needed Court to soothe the fierce ache inside her. She needed him to make her forget all the bad things that had been happening.

Of course, she wouldn't forget for long, but that didn't matter.

All that mattered right now was having him.

Court did his part to speed things along. He took out her gun, placing it on the floor next to them, and he shimmied her out of her jeans. Since he'd already taken off her bra and top, it made her aware of just how naked she was. He wasn't. So, she rid him of his shirt and tackled ridding him of the rest of his clothes.

It wasn't pretty, but she was about to get him unzipped and shove off his jeans when he stopped her by sliding his hand over hers.

"Condom," he managed to say. He rummaged through his back pocket to get his wallet and took out a condom from it.

She groaned because she hadn't even remembered safe sex. Then she groaned again, this time in pleasure, when Court started kissing her again.

Those wildfire kisses didn't make it easier for her to move around, but Rayna managed to get him unzipped, and Court broke the kiss long enough to put on the condom.

He looked at her again, and Rayna thought maybe she saw some hesitation in his eyes. But no. There was no hesitation whatsoever when he pushed into her.

She got another huge jolt of pleasure, and it just kept coming when Court started to move inside her. This was familiar but also new. He'd obviously learned more about how to please a woman since their make-out sessions in high school. He seemed to know just how to touch her. Just how to move. Just how to make her crazy with need.

The need couldn't last, of course. That meant the pleasure couldn't, either.

When the pace became harder and faster, it pushed Rayna right over the edge. There was nothing she could do but hold on to Court and make sure he went over the edge with her.

CHAPTER FIFTEEN

"I'M GETTING TOO old for floor sex," Court grumbled.

Though it really wasn't much of a complaint. His body was slack and practically humming, but if Rayna and he stayed on the hardwood floor much longer, that slackness was going to be replaced with some back aches. That was why he got up, scooped her up in his arms and carried her to the bedroom.

Rayna made a sleepy moan of pleasure and kissed him before he headed to the bathroom. Once he was done, he fully intended to slide right into bed with Rayna and maybe make another mistake tonight.

And it had been a mistake.

Still, he wasn't seeing how he was going to stop himself from making another one. He wanted her, and Court doubted anyone would be able to talk him out of that. Maybe Rayna would get a sudden dose of common sense and tell him to go back to keeping watch.

Or not.

When he went into the bedroom, she patted the spot next to her, motioning for him to join her. She also had a sly smile on her face. Couple with the fact that she was naked, and it erased any chance of him putting a stop to this.

He got on the bed, automatically pulling her into his arms and kissing her. The kiss would have gone on a lot longer if he hadn't heard the ringing sound. It wasn't in his head, either. It was coming from his phone, which he'd left in the foyer. Since it could be a critical call, he bolted from the bed and ran to get it.

Rachel's name was on the screen.

"Is everything okay?" Court immediately asked.

"Fine. Well, you know that's a lie. What I should say is that Mom and I are safe. What about Rayna and you?"

"We're safe, too," he settled for saying.

He really wanted to enjoy seeing Rayna naked a while longer, but when she came into the foyer to gather up her clothes and start dressing, Court did the same. He also put the call on speaker for her.

"Good." Rachel hesitated, and Court wondered if his sister had sensed what'd just gone on. If she did though, she didn't mention it. "Mom is all settled in her room here. It looks like a regular hospital room, but it's, well, noisy. Lots of people coming and going, and every now and then I can hear someone shout. Apparently, they have patients in here who get agitated easily."

His sister wasn't painting a good picture of the place, but maybe his mom wouldn't have to be there for long. "What about security?"

"There's a Texas Ranger in the hall and another out front. I've come to the cafeteria for a while so we can talk about that business card she had. Mom's been sedated since we got here, but I asked her if she hired someone." Rachel paused. "She did. His name is Abraham Stigler. But she insists he didn't really do much for her."

Court replayed that last bit word for word. "But he did do something?"

He could hear more chatter along with Rachel's frustrated breath. "Stigler apparently wanted to try to lure Dad into a compromising position with Alma so he could get photographs. Of course, Stigler wanted her to use those pictures to launch into a divorce where Mom could get a better settlement than she otherwise would have gotten. Mom refused. Stigler got mad and stormed off."

He definitely didn't like the sound of that. "Is it possible this Stigler is unhinged? Because that doesn't sound like the behavior of a professional PI. If so, he could be the triggerman in these attacks."

"I asked Mom about that in a roundabout way, but she didn't think he would do anything violent. She said he was just frustrated that she was going to let herself be treated like that. Apparently, his dad cheated on his mom, so it's a sore spot for him. Anyway, I've got my laptop here, so I did some checking and didn't find anything on him, either."

That didn't mean there wasn't something to find. "Thanks, sis. I'll let you know if I come up with anything. Try to get some rest," he added.

Since checking on the PI could take a while, Court gave Rayna another kiss. One that he hoped would let her know that…except he didn't know what he wanted her to know. That was because he didn't have a clue where this was going. Worse, he really didn't have time to figure it out.

"Work on the PI," Rayna prompted. "I'll make a fresh pot of coffee."

Coffee wasn't much of a substitute for kissing, sex or even a "where is this going?" discussion, but she was right. It could wait.

Court called the sheriff's office to get someone to access the computer, and Ian answered. However, Ian spoke before Court could say anything.

"I was about to call you. The dead guy in the car had a receipt in his wallet. One for the Lone Star Inn here in town. The CSIs found out that a person matching Bobby Joe's description had a room there, and they're going through it now. Court, they found something."

Judging from Ian's tone, that *something* wasn't good. He tried to steel himself, and he waited for Ian to continue. He didn't have to wait long.

"The dead guy has to be Bobby Joe because he has some recordings saved on a laptop, and I'm emailing them to you now so you can see for yourself," Ian explained. "Uh, is Rayna with you?"

"Yes."

"Okay. Well, the recordings will probably upset her. Just thought you should know that up front."

Hell. Court wished there was a way to keep this from her, but he couldn't. After everything Bobby Joe had put her through, she deserved to know the truth.

Since it sounded as if Ian had his hands full, Court decided to wait on having the deputy check on the PI. Instead, he ended the call, and with Rayna right there next to him, he went to his laptop and accessed the file. It didn't take long for the images to appear on the screen.

Bobby Joe.

Yeah, it was him all right. Court could tell that even though Bobby Joe wasn't looking directly into the camera. He had also grown a beard. Court checked the date on the recording, and it'd been made just three days ago. Or rather that was when it'd been uploaded.

"It's time to make Rayna pay," Bobby Joe said. He was resting against the headboard of a bed and drinking a beer. "Revenge is best served up cold, you know."

Someone else in the room said something that Court couldn't hear. It was a mumble, and whoever had said it wasn't on the screen.

"Because she made a promise to love me forever, that's why," Bobby Joe snapped in response to whatever the other person had said. There was pure venom in his tone. "That's what you promise when you accept a marriage proposal. It's like a lie when you break a promise, and no one's gonna get away with lying to me."

Rayna's breathing became faster, and she inched closer to the screen. "I'm not sure he knows he's being recorded."

Neither was Court, but he was surprised that Rayna could pick up on that, considering the hatred in Bobby Joe's voice.

The other person mumbled something else, something that caused Bobby Joe to bolt up from the headboard. "It matters," he snarled. "It was fun, watching her always looking over her shoulder. Living like a monk because she was too scared I'd come jumping out at her."

Rayna shuddered, and Court knew why. This meant Bobby Joe had indeed been watching her all this time.

"Rayna's gonna have to pay," Bobby Joe grumbled after downing some more beer. "I'm gonna burn that bitch alive."

That was obviously a little more than Rayna could take because she dropped back a step. Court slipped his arm around her. It wasn't much, but then there wasn't much they could do except finish listening to what this snake had to say.

"That'll teach her to file charges against me," Bobby Joe went on with his rant. "That'll teach her what happens when she breaks a promise."

The recording ended, but it was more than enough to let Court know that Bobby Joe had indeed been out to kill Rayna.

"Someone intentionally left this recording for us to find," Court said.

"Yes." She agreed so quickly that it meant she'd come to the same conclusion. "Is there any chance there can be a voice analysis done on the other person in the room with him?"

"Maybe." And considering this had been recorded three days ago, it could have been any of their suspects. "Ian's probably already sent it to the Ranger Crime Lab, but I'll make sure." He paused. "Whoever was in that room, Bobby Joe felt comfortable enough with him or her to admit to conspiracy to commit murder."

She nodded. "Plus, the recording might not even be recent." Rayna motioned toward the background of the shot Court had frozen on the screen. "I've never been to the inn, but I'm not even sure that's where this was recorded."

No, and if it hadn't been, maybe someone had planted the laptop with the recording in the room. For that matter, the person could have planted the receipt, as well.

Court's phone rang, and with all the things that'd been going on, he expected it to be Ian calling with more bad news of something they'd found at the inn. But it wasn't. It was Rachel.

Since his sister could have her own version of bad news, something else she'd perhaps learned from their mother, Court took a deep breath before he answered.

"You have to come right away," Rachel said, her voice filled with panic. "Mom's missing. I just got back to her room, and she's not here. God, Court, I think someone kidnapped her."

RAYNA KNEW THIS could be some kind of setup. A ruse to get Court and her out of his house. But the problem was, it was going to work.

Because there was no chance Court was going to stay put if his mother was in some kind of danger. That was why they'd practically run to his cruiser when they'd heard what Rachel said, and Court had started driving the moment they were inside. He'd also had Rayna use her phone to call Ian and tell the deputy to meet them on the road that led from the ranch to San Antonio. That way, they would at least have some backup.

"Rachel, tell me exactly what happened," Court insisted. He still had her on the line, and he'd put the call on speaker.

His sister didn't answer right away though, something she'd been doing since her bombshell of Helen being gone. That was because Rachel was also answering frantic questions from people who most likely were the staff and the Texas Ranger.

"Rachel?" Court said in a much louder voice.

He wasn't panicking like his sister, but he wasn't exactly cool and calm, either. That lack of calmness wasn't just limited to his mom though. His gaze fired all around them, keeping watch, and he motioned for

Rayna to do the same. She did, and she also kept a firm grip on the gun he'd given her.

She prayed she didn't have to use it, but it was nearly an hour's drive to San Antonio, and plenty could go wrong between here and there. Maybe it wouldn't take Ian long to join them. Of course, someone could attack them while Ian was with them, but at least they'd have an extra gun if things went wrong.

"No, I don't know where she went," she heard Rachel say. "I've already told you that a dozen times. Now find her." Rachel made a hoarse sound before she came back on the phone. "Court, I don't know where she is. They think I helped her escape, but I wouldn't do that."

"I believe you. Now, tell me what happened."

"I'm not sure." Rachel made another of those sobbing sounds. "I was in the cafeteria making some other calls, and when I came back to her room, Mom wasn't there."

"But you said you thought someone kidnapped her," Court pointed out.

"Someone did. I should have never left her alone."

"You thought she was safe. You didn't do anything wrong," Court said, and he somehow managed to speak calmly. "What about the Ranger? Who is he and how did someone get past him?" His voice got a little harder on those two questions.

It took Rachel a moment to answer. "The Ranger's name is Marcus Owen, and he said someone dressed like a janitor walked past him and hit him with a stun gun. After he was down, the guy used pepper spray on him."

That tightened Rayna's chest. The memories of her own attack came flooding back, and the man who'd gone after her had used a stun gun, too. No pepper spray, but Helen McCall hadn't gotten a syringe of drugs pumped into her. "Mom's room is a mess, like there was some kind of a struggle," Rachel said. "Items had been knocked off the stand next to her bed. Her things are still here, so I don't think robbery was the motive."

Neither did Rayna. "What about the Ranger? Did he see the face of the man who used the stun gun on him?"

"I don't think so. Ranger Owen's still coughing from the pepper spray, so he might remember more once his head is clearer."

Court cursed. "What about security cameras? They should be all over that place."

"They are, and someone's trying to get the surveillance footage from them now. The ones in the parking lot, too."

That was a start, but even if they could identify the guy, it didn't mean they could stop him. By now, he could have already taken Helen out of the hospital. Plus, since the woman had been sedated, it was possible she wouldn't be able to figure out a way to escape. Even if she did fight off the sedation, her attacker could obviously use the stun gun or pepper spray on her.

"Mom must have screamed or something," Court added. "No way would she just let a stranger take her."

"She wouldn't have. I think that's why the room looks as if it's been trashed. Oh, God. Court, you don't think he would hurt her, do you?"

"No, I don't," Court quickly answered, but judging from his suddenly tight jaw muscles and the death grip that he had on the steering wheel, he was considering the same thing.

"Whoever took her probably wants to use her for leverage," Rayna suggested. "That means he won't hurt her."

"Leverage for what?" Rachel asked.

"I'm not sure," Rayna lied. But she had a strong inkling this was either tied to Warren or Court and her. "Did you let your dad know what's going on?"

"I called his guard," Rachel said. "I wanted to make sure he hadn't been taken, too, but he's okay. I told the guards to make sure it stayed that way."

"Thanks for doing that," Court told her. "Are the local cops out looking for this guy who took Mom?"

"I think so. If not, Egan will make sure they are when he gets here. How long before you can come?"

"I'm on the way now. Whatever you do, don't leave the hospital, and don't go looking for Mom. Just stay put until Egan and I get there, and we can figure out what to do. Don't worry, we'll get Mom back."

Rayna knew that Court would do anything in his power to make that happen, but this might be beyond what he could do. She hadn't wanted to mention it with Rachel on the phone, but the moment Court ended the call, she knew she had to say something.

"This could turn into some kind of ransom demand," Rayna told him.

Court nodded. "For either us or Dad." He cursed again and continued to keep watch. "There's another thing to consider. We're not sure that burned body is actually Bobby Joe. He could be the one behind this."

"Yes," she admitted, "but that doesn't explain the recording on the laptop." Rayna hated to even consider that Bobby Joe might be innocent in this, but she had to force herself to at least consider it. "The recording on the laptop could have been made years ago, and now someone could be using it to set up Bobby Joe."

"I agree," Court answered several moments later. "Since someone used Hallie to try to set you up and then murdered her, the person could have done the same to Bobby Joe."

She hated Bobby Joe for what he'd done to her, but he didn't deserve to be murdered. If that was what had happened. It was entirely possible that the body in the car wasn't his. Maybe it belonged to someone else that this unidentified killer had eliminated to tie up some loose ends.

"Call Ian so we can find out his location," Court instructed.

Rayna did, putting the call on speaker and holding the phone so that Court would be able to speak to his fellow deputy. Ian answered on the first ring.

"We're about five miles from the exit to the highway," Court said abruptly.

"I'm on my way there now, too. I should arrive in just a couple of minutes. If I make it ahead of you, I'll wait."

"Good." Court opened his mouth to say more, but he stopped. "What the hell?" he grumbled, and he hit his brakes.

It took Rayna a moment to realize why he'd done that. It was because someone had stretched a spike strip across the road. It was the kind of thing that cops used to stop bad guys from getting away. They ran right over it, the spikes tearing through the tires.

The cruiser jolted from the impact, and Rayna immediately felt something she didn't want to feel.

The tires were quickly going flat.

And that made Court and her sitting ducks.

COURT DIDN'T TAKE the time to curse, but that was what he'd do later. For now though, he got the cruiser to the side of the road so he could stop and draw his gun. Rayna had hers ready, and like him, she was looking all around, trying to find out who'd just set this trap for them.

"What happened?" Ian said from the other end of the line.

"Spike strip. Head this way, but approach with caution. I'm betting the person who put it there is still around."

Rayna pulled in a hard breath. Of course, she'd already known that, but it was probably unsettling to hear it said aloud.

"I'll get there as fast as I can," Ian assured him.

Court ended the call and put his phone back in his pocket. That way, he'd be ready when Ian arrived. He didn't want anything slowing him down when he moved Rayna from his cruiser to Ian's.

"Do you see anything?" she asked. Her voice was shaky, but he had to hand it to her, she was looking and sounding stronger than he'd expected. He hoped that she wasn't actually getting used to being put in danger like this.

"No," Court answered.

But it was hard to see much of anything. There was only a sliver of a moon, and even though the headlights were cutting through the darkness, that allowed them to see only directly ahead. It was pitch-dark behind them. It also didn't help that there were ditches and plenty of trees in the pastures on both sides of them. It'd be easy for someone to hide out there and wait to attack.

"No way could the person who took Mom have made it out here already," Court said.

He was talking more to himself than Rayna. But it could mean that the man who'd previously attacked them wasn't behind this. Well, he wasn't if he'd been the one to take Helen.

"It could be another hired gun," Rayna muttered.

Yeah. A hired gun who was enjoying watching them squirm. Now that their car was disabled, why hadn't the person come after them? Why wait when he or she would know that backup had to be on the way?

His phone rang again, and Court glanced at the screen to see Rachel's name there. He was debating whether or not he should answer when he saw something. A blur of motion to their right, on the passenger's side of the cruiser.

Someone was in the pasture.

"Get down on the seat," he told Rayna.

"You need me to keep watch," she argued.

He hated that she was right. Hated even more that he might need her help to get out of this.

Rayna already followed his gaze to the pasture, but Court could no longer see anyone moving out there. He kept watch. Not just there, but he looked around them, too, in case there was more than one person involved in this.

"There," Rayna said. She motioned toward the road just ahead. "I think someone just got in that ditch."

Court hadn't seen it, but it was possible, especially since the headlights weren't focused on the ditch. He put the cruiser into Drive, knowing he wouldn't get far, but he wanted to move the vehicle only enough to shine some light in that specific area.

And it worked.

He saw the person then. Whoever it was, he or she was definitely in the ditch.

"I could lower my window enough to try to get off a shot," Rayna suggested.

But he was already shaking his head before she even finished speaking. "Not a chance. Just keep watch to the side and behind us." That way, he could deal with this snake.

The windows were bullet resistant. That was both the good and the bad news. It meant the guy in the ditch wouldn't be able to execute an immediate kill shot. He'd have to fire enough to tear through the glass. But it also meant Court wouldn't have an easy shot, either.

Even though it was a risk, he lowered his window a couple of inches and aimed his gun out the narrow space. He put his finger on the trigger.

And he waited, his attention nailed to the spot where he'd last seen the person. He doubted this was some hunter or innocent bystander out for an evening stroll. No, this was the person who'd put out the spike strip. The person who probably wanted them dead.

The seconds crawled by, but it didn't take him long to get a whiff of something in the air.

Gasoline.

Rayna obviously smelled it, too, because she practically snapped her head in his direction.

"It could be coming from the cruiser," he told her.

Though there was a slim to none chance of that being the case. Still, Court held out hope that maybe the spike strip had somehow flipped up when he'd driven over it and punctured the gas line.

His phone rang, and again it was Rachel. It was a

bad time to be talking on the phone, but Court hit the speaker button anyway.

"We got a call," Rachel blurted out the moment he answered. "God, Court. It's really bad."

His chest went so tight that it was hard for him to breathe. "Is Mom okay?"

"I don't know. The caller said he'll exchange her for Rayna."

That definitely didn't help with the tightness. "I want that call traced."

"Ranger Owen's trying to do that now." His sister sounded even more desperate now than she had earlier. "The kidnapper said he'd kill Mom if we didn't hand over Rayna in thirty minutes."

"I can't get there that soon," Rayna said, and Court knew then that she was indeed planning on surrendering to the kidnapper to save his mother.

"There's no guarantee the kidnapper will let either you or my mother live," Court pointed out.

"We have to try. Someone disabled Court's cruiser," Rayna said in a louder voice to Rachel. "But as soon as Ian is here, I can get to San Antonio. Tell the kidnapper when he calls back."

Rayna looked at Court. "We have to try to save your mother."

Court was certain he would have come up with an argument for that, but he saw the headlights ahead. Then his phone dinged with a message from Ian.

"Rachel, I have to call you back," Court insisted, and he switched his screen to the text.

Is it safe to approach? Ian texted.

No, it wasn't. Someone's in the ditch to your left, Court answered back.

He waited for Ian's response, and since Ian was a lot closer to that particular section of the ditch, he might be able to see the person. The moment that thought crossed his mind, there was another blur of motion.

Then Court heard the swooshing sound.

As a wall of fire shot up right in front of them.

CHAPTER SIXTEEN

FROM THE MOMENT the cruiser had hit the spike strip, Rayna had known they were in trouble. Now that trouble had just escalated.

"I can't drive off because of the flat tires," Court grumbled under his breath, and he cursed.

No, and that meant if the fire started to come toward them, they would have no choice but to get out of the cruiser and run. That would no doubt make it much easier for them to be gunned down.

If the smoke and fire didn't get to them first, that was.

Because of the direction of the wind, the smoke started to come right at them. Using the cruiser's AC would help, but not for long. Worse, the smoke was making it very hard to see anything.

Court's phone rang. It was Ian, and he answered it without taking his eyes off their surroundings.

"I'm going to try to drive through the fire to get to you," Ian said. "Maybe the flames will conceal you enough so you can jump in."

He didn't sound very hopeful about that, and neither was Rayna. Any hope whatsoever vanished when there was a gunshot. It was a loud blast, and judging from the sound, it went in the direction of Ian's cruiser. A few seconds later, another sound followed the gunfire.

The hiss from the new flames that flared up between Ian and them.

Also on the side of them, too.

The ditch across from the driver's side of the cruiser burst on fire, too.

Now there were two new walls of flames and smoke, these latest ones even higher than the first. That would make it too dangerous for Ian to drive through it because if he got stuck, it could cause his gas tank to explode.

Court cursed again, and he started coughing. "Whoever's behind this had to have put more than just accelerant on the road. There has to be incendiary devices."

Yes, ones that were probably operated by remote control, since Rayna didn't see anyone close enough to set the fire by hand. However, the person had to be nearby, waiting for them.

And Rayna didn't have to guess the location.

There was only one path—to her right—that wasn't on fire, and that was almost certainly where their attacker wanted them to go. It meant that was where an ambush had to be waiting for them.

The smoke started to smother her and burn her eyes. Again, it was exactly what their attacker wanted. They couldn't sit there much longer.

"I called the fire department," Ian said. His voice was laced with frustration and fear, and he was also coughing from the smoke. "When they get here, they might be able to get close enough to put out the flames."

Not likely, since they wouldn't be able to approach if there was gunfire.

And that meant Court, Ian and she had to figure out a way to find the fire starter and take him or her out of commission. If the fire jumped the road and ditch, it could start burning the pastures and the nearby ranches. Of course, that didn't seem so urgent as the danger that was right on top of them.

"Can you go in reverse?" Court asked Ian.

"I can, but I'd rather get closer to Rayna and you. I can maybe help you."

"That's too risky," Court warned him. "Put some distance between the fire and you."

"I'll try… Wait, I've got another call coming in," Ian said.

So did Court. It was Rachel again, and Rayna could see that he was hesitant about answering it. She knew why, too. He probably didn't want to tell his sister about their situation. Rachel was already frantic enough about their mother, and hearing this wasn't going to help. Still, Court hit the answer button, and as he'd done with Ian, he put it on speaker and continued to keep watch.

"Where are you?" Rachel blurted out.

Court hesitated, obviously trying to figure out how to say this. "Rayna, Ian and I are trapped on the road. Someone set fires, and that means I'm not going to be able to get to you right away."

A sob caught in Rachel's throat. "Are you okay?"

He didn't even attempt a lie. "No. If the kidnapper calls back, negotiate for more time for Mom. I'll call you when I can."

Court ended the call just as another wave of smoke came at them. Now it was impossible to see anything, and even though the flames weren't advancing on them, the cruiser was getting hotter with each passing second.

"We can't stay here." Court looked Rayna straight in the eyes when he said that, and she saw the apology that she hoped he wouldn't say.

Because this wasn't his fault.

It was the fault of that snake out there who'd put all of this together. Rayna only hoped she learned the reason for all of this. While she was hoping, she also wanted to catch the person and put an end to this danger once and for all.

"What do you need me to do?" Rayna asked before Court could add that *I'm sorry*.

"Put your phone in your pocket so you don't lose it and then switch places with me," he said through the coughs. He tipped his head to the ditch on the passenger's side of the cruiser. "I'll go out first. You'll be right behind me. We'll take cover and try to shoot this guy before he shoots us."

It was a simple enough plan, and they might get lucky. *Might*. But there were plenty of things that could go wrong. As thick as the smoke was, their attacker could be already waiting right outside the door, and Court and she wouldn't know it until it was too late.

Court sent a text to Ian, no doubt to tell him what they were about to do. Maybe Ian would be able to help in some way, but at this point, the deputy just needed to figure out a way to get out of that fire and be safe.

Rayna pushed back the seat as far as it would go to give Court space to maneuver. It wasn't easy now that they were coughing nonstop. Plus, Rayna felt on the verge of panicking. It was hard to breathe with the rising heat and the adrenaline. Even harder to catch her breath when Court brushed a quick kiss on her mouth.

"Stay safe," he said.

She repeated that to him and prayed that both of them and Ian could manage to do just that.

Court threw open the cruiser door, and they immediately caught another wave of the smoke. No bullets though, so maybe the visibility wasn't so good for the shooter, either.

Using the door for cover, Court got out, and while staying in a crouched position, he inched closer to the ditch. He glanced around, but she could tell from the way he was blinking that the smoke was doing a number on his eyes.

"Let's move now," he whispered.

He took hold of her wrist, pulled Rayna out of the cruiser. In the same motion, he hurried toward the ditch. They didn't make it far.

Before the shot came right at them.

COURT SHOVED RAYNA into the ditch as fast as he could, but it hadn't been quite fast enough.

The shot slammed into the ground, kicking up the dirt and sending some of it into his eyes. Not good. He was already having a hard enough time seeing as it was. And now his heart was beating so fast that it felt as if his ribs might crack. That was because he wasn't sure if the bullet had ricocheted and hit Rayna.

She could be hurt.

Rayna made a sharp sound of pain, and Court caught her in his arms, dropping down as far as they could go. The ditch was soft from the recent rain, and it helped break their fall a little. Still, it was a hard landing.

"I'm okay," Rayna said. Though she certainly didn't sound okay. "I just hit my head."

That wasn't good, since she already had an injury there, but it was better than the alternative. They could have been shot. Hell. How had he allowed it to come to this?

Because he was stupid, that was why.

He'd let the news of his mother's disappearance cloud his mind, and now Rayna might pay for that mistake.

Since he didn't know where the shooter was, Court adjusted his position so that Rayna's back was against the side of the ditch and he was in front of her and facing the pasture. The lower ground helped with the smoke, too, and thankfully the wind seemed to be blowing some of it away. That was a good thing because he needed to be able to catch his breath in case they had to run.

Court tried to pick through the smoke and darkness to spot their attacker. Nothing. Nor did the person fire any other shots. Normally, that would have been a good thing, but it could mean the person was moving closer—maybe trying to get in place for a kill shot.

His phone buzzed with a text message. It was Ian, again. But Court didn't answer it. He didn't want to be distracted even for a second, so he passed it to Rayna so she could read it to him.

"Ian says he's going to try to go back up the road and find a way to get into the pasture where we are," she whispered.

That was beyond risky, but at this point, everything they did fell into that category. If Court had been alone, he would have told Ian to get to safety, but since Rayna was involved, Court was willing to take all the help he could get.

Behind them, the fire snapped and hissed, but it didn't seem to be burning itself out. Not good. Because the flames could still reach the gas tank on the cruiser. If it exploded, Rayna and he were plenty close enough to be hurt or killed.

"We have to move," he said, keeping his voice as soft as he could manage. And there was only one direction in which to do that. Too bad it would mean moving away from Ian, but he had to get Rayna away from the fire. "Stay behind me and try to keep watch," he added.

She nodded, and he could feel the tightness in her body. Her too-fast breath on his neck. As a lawman, he'd faced danger, but Rayna shouldn't have to be going through this. Unfortunately, they didn't have a choice about that right now.

With him still in front of her, they started moving to their right. Inch by inch. It was very slow going because they had to stay crouched down. They made it about two feet before Court saw something.

A person darted behind a tree directly in front of them.

Because of the smoke, he couldn't tell if the person was a man or a woman, but he definitely saw the gun. A rifle. If it had a scope, which it probably did, it was going to make it much easier to target Rayna and him. Court instantly got proof that he'd been right.

The next bullet tore into the ditch, and if Rayna and he hadn't ducked down, it would have hit them. That was way too close for comfort.

It didn't stay just one shot, either. A second one came. Then a third. All of them were ripping into the dirt just above them. Court had no choice but to pull

Rayna back down to the ground. That meant he no longer had a visual on the shooter.

Behind them, he heard another hissing sound, and almost immediately new flames shot into the air. This fire was even bigger than the others and jumped up right next to the ditch. If the ground caved in any more from the shots, it would send that fire spilling down on them.

"How much ammo do you have?" Rayna asked.

That wasn't a question he especially wanted to hear. Because it sounded as if she was thinking about doing something he wouldn't like.

"I have two extra magazines plus what's in my gun," Court answered. "Why?"

"Because we can't stay here. If we can pin down this guy, then we can get farther down the ditch and away from the smoke and heat."

She was right about the "staying here" part, but there was no way he wanted her high enough out of the ditch to return fire. But he did have an idea.

A risky one.

It might work though if there was only one shooter. If there were more than that, well, things were going to go from bad to worse.

Still, it wasn't as if they had many options here, and those options decreased when their attacker started sending more shots their way. Each bullet was slamming into the very dirt that could bury them in that fire.

Court tipped his head to their right. "Stay low but move as fast as you can," he told Rayna.

He couldn't see her expression, but he felt her tense even more—something that he hadn't thought was possible. "What about you?" Her voice was shaking now, too.

"I'll be right behind you."

Or at least he would be once he was certain he'd pinned down the shooter enough for him to do that. For now, his goal was just to get Rayna as far away from that fire as he could manage.

He doubted she believed that "right behind you" part, but she moved out from behind him. "Just be careful," she whispered.

Court nodded, told her to do the same. "Go now," he instructed.

He came out from cover, lifting his head and gun high enough so he could send a shot in the general direction where he'd pinpointed the shooter.

The gunman fired back.

Court dropped down, and from the corner of his eye he saw Rayna doing exactly what he wanted her to do. She was practically on all fours and was scrambling down the ditch away from him. She wasn't nearly far enough though, so he came out from cover and fired another shot.

That was when Court finally got a glimpse of the shooter. The person immediately darted behind a tree that was about twenty yards from them. Unfortunately, there were plenty of trees and underbrush on each side of their attacker, so Court had no way of knowing which way he would go.

There was a slash of bright lights to his left, and Court whipped his gun in that direction. But he didn't think it was a gunman. It was hard to tell with the smoke, but he thought it might be Ian, and that he might be seeing the headlights from the cruiser.

Court glanced at Rayna again. She was still moving. Still staying down. And so the shooter would stay pinned down, too, Court fired another shot where he'd last spotted him.

Nothing.

He doubted that meant the guy had just left, though it was possible the headlights had given him second thoughts about leaning out to shoot.

The lights came closer. Yeah, it was Ian all right. Maybe the deputy would get in position to help them. But that hope barely had time to register in Court's mind when there was another hissing sound.

Much, much louder than the others. The flames came. Not just on the road this time, either.

But into the ditch.

The line of fire flared between Rayna and him. And the flames came right at Court.

CHAPTER SEVENTEEN

"WATCH OUT!" RAYNA called out to Court.

But it was too late.

She'd seen the new flash of fire, but she hadn't been able to warn Court in time for him to get out of the way. Rayna turned to hurry back to him, and that was when she realized she couldn't.

Because the line of fire was coming in her direction, too.

Whoever had set this latest fire had obviously meant to burn Court and her alive in the ditch. Well, Rayna had no plans to die, and she wanted to make sure Court didn't, either.

Since she couldn't move very fast on all fours, she got to her feet and started running. She hated putting more distance between Court and her, but maybe she'd be able to get into the pasture and then double back for him. Something that he was hopefully doing as well, since Rayna didn't want him staying near that fire. Of course, being in the pasture wouldn't exactly be safe, either.

The line of fire finally stopped moving behind her. Probably because there was no more accelerant to fuel the flames. She stopped and ducked back down in the ditch. Low enough for cover but high enough so she could try to spot the shooter.

Nothing.

The smoke and darkness were acting like a thick, smothering curtain all around her. Worse, the sound of fire might be able to mask the footsteps of anyone trying to sneak up on her. That was why she stayed facing the pasture. If the attacker came at her, that was the direction he'd likely come from.

Rayna could see the headlights from Ian's cruiser to her left, but she had no idea where the deputy was. Maybe Court would be able to get to him, and they could use the cruiser to come after her. At least then they'd be protected from gunfire.

Her phone buzzed with a text, and even though it meant taking her eyes off the pasture, she glanced down at the screen, since it could be important.

It was.

Get as far away from the fire as you can, Court texted her. I'll come for you soon.

Despite their god-awful situation, relief flooded through her. Court was okay. For now, anyway. Rayna prayed that it stayed that way. But it didn't last.

A shot blasted through the air.

The bullet wasn't fired in her direction though but rather had gone near Court. She doubted either Court or Ian had fired it, since it'd seemed to come from the area by the trees.

There was another shot.

Then another.

Rayna ducked down even farther into the ditch, but with the fourth shot, she was better able to pinpoint the location of the shooter. The person was moving away from Court and in her direction. Since the line of trees continued almost to the ditch, she had to keep watch not just in front of her but also to the side.

In the distance she heard sirens. Probably from the fire department. They wouldn't be able to help, but at least they'd be close enough to put out the fires once the shooter was no longer a threat. Whenever that would be.

Her phone dinged again. It wasn't from Court this time but rather from Ian. And the message he sent her had her stomach going straight to her knees.

Court was hit, Ian texted.

Rayna forced herself not to scream and bolt from the ditch to hurry to him. That was exactly what the shooter wanted her to do, and he would almost certainly gun her down. But while she could make herself stay put, she couldn't stop the strangled groan that made its way through her throat.

No. This couldn't be happening.

Somehow, she had to get to him, had to help him, but she couldn't just go running into the pasture. Rayna forced herself to stop, and breathe, so she could try to think this through. It was hard to think though with the worst-case scenarios going through her head. And that was when she realized something.

She was in love with Court.

That was why she was reacting this way. That was why losing him suddenly seemed unbearable.

Maybe part of her always had been in love with him, but it had taken something like this to make her see it. Now she might not even get the chance to tell him how she felt.

How bad is he hurt? Rayna texted back. No way

could she ask if Court was dead. She refused to believe that could happen.

The seconds crawled by, turning into what felt an eternity. Because her legs suddenly felt as if they couldn't support her weight, Rayna leaned her back against the wall of the ditch. And waited. Even though she was expecting it, the jolt of surprise still went through her when her phone dinged.

Court says it's not bad, that it's just a flesh wound, Ian finally answered. He'll be okay.

Rayna had no idea if that was true or if Court was merely trying to prevent her from panicking. If so, it wasn't working.

Can you get Court into the cruiser? she texted Ian.

She didn't have to wait nearly as long for a response. No. We tried to get to it, and that's how he got shot. But Court wants me to try to get to you.

Of course he did. But Rayna had to nix that with a semi-lie of her own. I'm safe where I am, she answered.

She definitely didn't want Ian leaving Court alone, especially since Court might not be able to defend himself.

Thea and John will be here soon, Ian added a moment later.

Good. Two more deputies might help them put an end to this. Again though, they might not be able to get close because of the fire.

Rayna slipped her phone back in her pocket so she could free up her hands, and she looked around the pasture again. There was no more gunfire, no glimpse of anyone in the trees. That didn't mean someone wasn't out there, but for now they were staying hidden.

That surprised her.

She would have thought the shooter would have wanted to go ahead and put an end to this, since he had to know that backup was on the way. Maybe it meant the guy had pulled the plug on this attack and had fled. Even though she wanted to catch this snake, right now her priority was helping Court.

When the next minute crawled by without any other gunfire, Rayna figured it was now or never for her to get to Court. Since she couldn't risk the pasture in front of her, that meant taking an alternate route. She could hurry into the pasture on the other side of the road, skirting along the edges of the fire until she could get to a clearing to cross back over.

She got her gun ready and looked over her shoulder at the road behind her. The only thing she could see was thick smoke, and Rayna knew the moment she stepped into it, she'd start coughing, something that would slow her down. That was why she took a deep breath and turned to scramble out of the ditch.

But turning was as far as she got.

Someone wearing a gas mask reached out from that smoke, and that someone had a stun gun. Before Rayna could move or make a sound, the person rammed the gun against her neck.

The jolt went through her. So did the pain, and even though she heard her phone buzzing with a text, there was nothing she could do about that, either.

Rayna had no choice but to fall back into the ditch.

"Rayna didn't answer," Ian relayed to Court.

Court knew that wasn't good. Especially since Rayna had answered the other texts from Ian. And this one had been important because it had been an order for her to stay put.

Where the heck was she? And why hadn't she answered?

Court grimaced and bit back some profanity. He could feel the blood on his arm. Could feel the pain, too, where the bullet had sliced across it. It wasn't a deep cut, but he would need stitches. Eventually. But for now, he just needed to get to Rayna.

Everything inside Court was yelling for him to get to her. Because he knew something was wrong.

Ian had sent that first text before Court could stop him, and Rayna now knew that he'd been shot. Despite Ian's assurance that it wasn't serious, she probably thought he was dying and would try to help him. That would almost certainly put her in danger, and unlike him, she didn't even have any backup. Heck, he wasn't even sure she knew how to defend herself if it came down to it.

"You know you shouldn't be doing this," Ian warned him when Court climbed out of the ditch.

Yeah, he did, but that wasn't stopping him. Nothing would.

"You should wait here," Court told Ian, but he knew that wasn't going to fly. This was a stupid idea, but Ian wasn't going to let him go out there alone.

Something that Court had allowed to happen to Rayna.

He cursed the fire that had shot up between them. He cursed their attacker, too, for putting them in this situation. Now he only prayed he could get to her in time to stop whatever was happening.

Somehow, Court made it out of the deep ditch onto

the pasture grass. And he immediately got slammed with a wave of smoke. He had no choice but to cough, which only made his arm hurt even more. He ignored both the pain and the coughing and started moving. He also kept as low as he could while keeping watch of that treed area where he'd spotted the shooter.

No sign of the person now.

That didn't make Court feel better. Because it could mean their attacker had gotten to Rayna.

That caused him to hurry. Well, hurry as much as he could, anyway. Everything seemed to be working against him, and it didn't help that he didn't know how far she'd managed to go. Hopefully, though, she had stayed in the ditch where he could find her. But even if she was close by, it wouldn't be easy to spot her with the smoke and darkness.

The fire was dying some, but there were still some flames in spots being fanned by the wind. There was still enough of a threat from the shooter, too, that he couldn't give the fire department the green light to enter the area. But when Thea and John arrived, they would almost certainly get as close as they could. In some ways that would make this situation even more dangerous.

Because Court didn't want the deputies hit with friendly fire. Ditto for the deputies shooting toward Ian and him.

Court and Ian were both on edge and braced for a fight. Not the best conditions for having other lawmen arrive on the scene. Especially since Ian and he were having to keep watch all around them.

Court stopped when he heard a sound. It was like a gasp, and it had come from just ahead of them. He stopped for a second to see if he could pinpoint it. And he did hear something else. A thud. As if some-one had fallen.

That got him moving even faster, but Court was well aware he could be walking into an ambush. At least there were some trees to his left that he could maybe dive behind if the shooter was lying in wait for them.

He got a break from a gust of wind that cleared a section of the smoke, and he saw some movement in the ditch. He heard another moan, too.

Hell, it sounded as if Rayna had been hurt.

Nothing could have stopped him at that point. He readied his gun and ran toward that sound. The wind stopped cooperating though, and the smoke slid right back in front of him, stinging his eyes and blocking his view.

The moment he made it past the fire, Court climbed back down into the ditch. It was clearer there, and he finally saw more than just movement.

He saw Rayna.

She was on her feet, and at first he thought she was okay. Then Court saw someone standing behind her. And that someone had a gun pointed at her head.

Before Court could even react, that someone pulled the trigger.

He watched in horror as Rayna fell, and for several heart-stopping moments he thought she'd been shot.

But she hadn't.

She had dropped down just as the shot had been fired. She was moving, trying to get away, but it was as if she was dazed or something. Her attacker had no trouble latching on to Rayna and dragging her in front of him.

Except it wasn't a *him*.

With the gun back at Rayna's head, the shooter yanked off the gas mask she was wearing, and Court got a good look at her face.

Whitney.

Rayna glanced back at her, too, shock and then anger going through her. But Court got only a split-second glance of both Whitney and Rayna before Whitney turned the gun on him.

And she fired.

RAYNA TRIED TO shout a warning to Court, but her mouth still wasn't working well just yet. That stun gun hit had caused her muscles to spasm, and if Whitney hadn't dragged her to her feet, she'd probably still be on the ground.

On the ground and fighting to save Court.

Thankfully, Court and Ian climbed out of the ditch and scrambled behind some nearby trees, but before they could make it to cover, Whitney shot at them again. Since the gun was right against Rayna's ear, the sound was deafening, and she groaned in pain. She prayed that groan didn't send Court racing toward her though. Because Whitney would almost certainly shoot him.

But why?

Rayna didn't know why a woman she'd once considered her friend would now want Court and her dead. One thing she did know was that Whitney was trapped—something she probably hadn't planned on happening. No. By now, she'd likely thought she would have been able to kill Court and her and then escape.

"Backup's on the way," Court shouted out. "Let Rayna go, and we can talk."

"Talk," Whitney repeated like profanity. "It's a little late for that. Rayna should already be dead, but if I shoot her now, then you'll shoot me."

Rayna hadn't thought for a second that the shot Whitney had aimed at her had been some kind of bluff. No. It was meant to kill her. Except Rayna had managed to fall just in time. She might not get that lucky again.

She wiggled her fingers and toes, trying to get back the feeling in her body so she could fight off Whitney if she tried to pull the trigger again.

"Why are you doing this?" Rayna had to ask. But as soon as the question left her mouth, she thought she had the answer. "Bobby Joe. You're the one who helped him hide all this time."

Whitney didn't jump to deny that. "I was in love with him," she told her "And he threw it all back in my face. He was coming back to town to confess everything."

That didn't make sense. "You mean confess that he'd tried to frame me for his murder?"

"No. To confess that *I* had tried to frame you for his murder."

Oh, mercy.

She couldn't imagine that being true. Until she remembered how Whitney had changed after Bobby Joe's disappearance. And that'd happened because Whitney had fallen in love with him.

"Bobby Joe helped with the framing, at first," Whitney added a moment later, "because he had to collect some of his own blood. But then he had *a change of heart*. That's what the SOB called it. A change of heart, and he was coming here to try to win you back."

Rayna felt the sickening feeling wash over her. "It wouldn't have worked. I would have never gotten back together with Bobby Joe because I've always been in love with Court."

A burst of air left Whitney's mouth. A laugh, but definitely not from humor. "Too bad Bobby Joe didn't know that before he died."

"You mean before you killed him," Rayna snapped.

Whitney didn't deny that, either.

All the missing pieces suddenly fell into place. Well, many of them, anyway. Whitney would have had the chance to get both a spare key to Rayna's house along with the code for her security system. That would have made it easy for Whitney to send a hired thug to break in, drug her and then set her up for Warren's shooting. That same hired thug had probably been the one who'd fired shots at them at the hospital.

The same one maybe who'd taken Court's mother.

Unless the guy was out here somewhere. But Whitney didn't seem to be waiting for her own version of backup. No. Her jerking motions and gusting breath told Rayna that Whitney had been backed into a corner and was now looking for a way out.

"You thought if I was in jail for Warren's murder that Bobby Joe wouldn't try to get back together with me," Rayna concluded.

Still, no denial, and every bit of that silence cut Rayna to the core. She'd been a fool to trust this woman.

"Whitney?" Court called out again. "This is the last warning you'll get. Put down that gun."

Rayna couldn't be sure because she was still light-headed, but she thought maybe Court had moved farther to the right. Whitney must have thought so, too, because the woman shifted their positions, putting her back to the ditch while keeping Rayna in front of her.

"If you try anything, Rayna dies," Whitney shouted back. "Since she just confessed to me that she's in love with you, I doubt you want her dead."

That caused Rayna's chest to tighten even more than it already was. Whitney's outburst wasn't something she wanted Court to hear. Not like that. And not now. He didn't need any more distractions.

"I didn't want my father shot. Or Jennifer and Hallie dead, either," Court responded. "But you killed them. Killed Mitch and Bobby Joe, too. You know what that makes you, Whitney? A serial killer. And people aren't going to go easy on you just because you work for the sheriff's office."

Whitney made a loud sob, and Rayna didn't think it was fake. No, that was real emotion, and Whitney was probably just now realizing the horrible things she'd done. A string of murders that had all started because she wanted to keep Bobby Joe away from Rayna.

There was some more movement, and even though Whitney was crying now, she still pointed the gun in those trees. Which meant she was probably pointing it at Court or Ian. No way was Rayna going to let her claim another life.

Rayna knew she still wasn't steady, but that didn't stop her. She could tell from the way that Whitney tensed her arm that she was about to pull the trigger. That was why Rayna gathered all the strength she could and rammed her elbow into Whitney's stomach.

Whitney howled in pain, cursed.

And she turned the gun on Rayna.

Even in the darkness Rayna could see the hatred in the woman's eyes. Could see that Whitney was going to kill her.

The shot came. Blasting through the air. And Rayna braced herself for the pain. It didn't come though. But there was pain on Whitney's face. Along with some shock. That was when Rayna saw the blood spreading across the front of Whitney's top.

Court stepped out from the trees. He had his gun in his hand, and it was aimed at Whitney.

The woman looked down at the blood, then at Court before she laughed again. Like the other one, there was no humor in it.

But there was *something*. Something evil.

"You might have put a bullet in me," Whitney said, "but you'll never see your mother again. By the time you get to her, she'll be dead."

Whitney dropped to the ground, gasping on the last breath she would ever take.

CHAPTER EIGHTEEN

COURT'S MIND WAS shouting for him to do a dozen things at once. He needed to get to his mother, to save her, but he had to make sure Rayna was safe, too. Whitney appeared to be dead.

Appeared.

But since the woman had already murdered at least four people, Court didn't want to take any chances. He scrambled into the ditch so he could get Rayna out of there.

"Your mom," Rayna said. "We have to find her."

Yes, they did, but first they had to confirm that Whitney was indeed dead. Court kicked the woman's gun away from her hand and touched his fingers to her neck to see if he could feel a pulse.

Yes, she was dead all right.

"She hit me with a stun gun," Rayna muttered.

So, that was why she was so wobbly, but it could have been worse. Whitney could have used a real gun, and the only reason she hadn't was because she'd intended to use Rayna as a human shield to try to make an escape. And now even though Whitney was no longer a threat, she still could claim another victim.

His mother.

Ian hurried out from the trees, his gun pointed at Whitney. He didn't get in the ditch with them. He stayed in the pasture keeping watch. He also gave the all clear for backup and the fire department to come closer.

Because they could possibly use it to track the person who'd kidnapped Helen, Court went through Whitney's jeans pockets and located her phone. Actually, there were two of them. One was probably the one she regularly used, and the other was likely a burner cell that couldn't be traced. He put them both in his pockets.

"You're bleeding," Rayna added when he scooped her up and lifted her out of the ditch. Not easily. His arm was still throbbing, but he had to take her to the cruiser so that she wouldn't be out in the open.

The night was suddenly filled with flashing lights from the approaching deputies and the fire engine. With Rayna still in his arms, Court started moving with Ian right behind them.

"You shouldn't be carrying me," Rayna protested. "You've been shot."

That was true, but Rayna wasn't in any shape to run and probably wouldn't be for at least another couple of minutes. Those were minutes he didn't want to risk her being in the pasture.

The moment Court reached Ian's cruiser, he got her in the back seat, and Ian took the wheel. The deputy radioed backup to let them know they were about to drive out of there. Good move, since Court didn't want the other deputies thinking they were perps trying to make an escape.

Despite Rayna still being shaky, that didn't stop her from checking his arm. It was still bleeding, which was probably why she made a slight gasping sound.

"Here's a first-aid kit," Ian said, passing it to her

when he took it from the glove compartment. Rayna immediately got to work applying a bandage to Court's arm to slow the bleeding. "Should I take you directly to the hospital—"

"No. To San Antonio. I need to help Egan look for our mother."

Neither Rayna nor Ian argued with him about that. Probably because they figured it wouldn't do any good.

Because he needed it, Court brushed a quick kiss on Rayna's mouth. She looked up at him, their gazes connecting for just a second before he took out his phone and the two he'd taken from Whitney.

"Glance through those and see who Whitney called," Court told Rayna.

He'd put his own phone on vibrate when he'd gone into cover by the trees and had three missed calls. Two from Rachel and another from Egan. He pressed in Egan's number. And his heart sank when his brother didn't answer. He tried his sister next, and unlike Egan, she answered on the first ring.

"Court," Rachel said on a rise of breath. "Are Rayna and you okay?"

He'd expected her to blurt out some bad news about their mother, so the question was somewhat of a relief. "We're fine. Ian, too." He paused a heartbeat. "Whitney's the one who had Mom kidnapped."

"Whitney?" Rachel repeated, and her tone said it all. She was as shocked as Court and Rayna had been. "Why would she do that, and where does she have her?"

He didn't want to get into the "why," but he had also been hoping that Rachel would know the "where." Hell.

"God, Court. Why did Whitney do this?" she repeated.

"To get back at Rayna. Maybe to get back at me, too, for helping Rayna." Or Whitney could have been hoping to set up Helen some way and pin the murders on her. "When's the last time you heard from Egan, because he's not answering his phone?"

"About fifteen minutes ago. He said he was getting ready to meet with the kidnapper."

Now it was Court's turn to be shocked. "Meeting with him? How'd Egan find out where he was?"

"The guy made a ransom call to Egan. It was a man, and he sounded frantic, like maybe things weren't going as planned."

Maybe because he'd realized that the woman who'd hired him was dead or about to be dead.

Rayna held out Whitney's phone for Court to see. "Is that the kidnapper's number?" she asked.

Court read off the number to Rachel. "Yes, that's it," Rachel verified.

Whitney had called the man multiple times in the past two hours. And not just during that time frame, either. When Court scrolled through the history, he saw that Whitney had been calling the man often for the past two days. That was the link they needed to prove that Whitney had hired him. And it was the reason the woman had no doubt used the second phone. It almost certainly wasn't a number assigned to her actual name.

"The kidnapper's using a burner cell so Egan couldn't trace it," Rachel went on, "but the guy wants Egan to meet him and give him some money."

That was good news and bad. Good because the kidnapper would almost certainly keep his mother alive if he wanted to ransom her. But it was bad, too, because it meant Egan could be hurt or killed in an exchange like that.

Court debated if he should call the kidnapper's number, but he decided to wait a few more minutes. Until he'd heard from Egan. If he called now, he might distract his brother at a critical time. It could make things even more dangerous than it already was.

"Please tell me Egan didn't go alone," Court said.

"No. Griff and another Texas Ranger are with him. Egan said I was to wait here, but I'm going crazy. I have to do something to help Mom. I have to do something to stop this."

"You can help her by staying put." Court made sure he sounded like a lawman giving an order and not just like a big brother. "Rayna and I are on the way there to the hospital. I'll drop Rayna off with you and go out and help Egan. Do you know his location?"

"No. He wouldn't tell me."

Probably because Egan hadn't wanted Rachel to try to follow him. But Court could track Egan through his cell phone, since it wasn't a burner.

"Court was shot," Rayna blurted out. "He should see a doctor."

"It can wait," Court said at the same moment Rachel said, "Shot? You said you were fine."

"I will be," Court assured his sister. "Or at least I will be once Mom and Egan are safe." And after he'd made sure that Rayna was okay. Then there'd be time for stitches. "We're about thirty minutes out."

"Forty," Ian corrected.

"Light up the sirens and get us there in thirty," Court told him.

"Stay put," he repeated to Rachel, and he ended the call so he could try Egan again.

Still no answer.

Rayna gave his bandage another adjustment, and when he looked at her, Court saw the tears in her eyes.

"I'm okay, really," he assured her.

She shook her head and blinked back more of those tears. "This is all my fault."

Court had known she was going to say that before the words had even come out of her mouth. Since it wasn't her fault, and he didn't want to hear her continue with an apology, he kissed her.

All in all, it was an effective way to put an end to it. An effective way to make him feel instantly better, too. He was still in pain, but he no longer cared. After several moments, he didn't think Rayna cared, either, because she moved right into the kiss, and she only broke it when she took in a huge gulp of breath.

"You're trying to distract me," she said with her mouth still very close to his. Close enough for him to kiss her again, so that was what he did.

"Yeah," he admitted. "But I need distracting, too." After all, his mother was a hostage, and his brother was out there trying to rescue her. Something that Court wanted to be doing.

Rayna nodded, eased back even more, and he saw the look in her eyes. She was about to apologize again. This time it would no doubt be for his mother.

"None of this was your fault," he said. "Put the blame right on Whitney where it belongs."

She nodded again, but the agreement didn't seem very believable. "I shouldn't have trusted her. I mean, I always knew she had feelings for Bobby Joe, but I thought it was just a crush. I had no idea she was in love with him."

"That seems to be going around," Court muttered.

Her eyes widened. Because she knew they weren't talking about Whitney now. They were talking about her.

"You told Whitney you were in love with me," Court reminded her, though he was certain it wasn't a reminder she needed.

Those words were no doubt as fresh in her mind as they were in his. But it might not be true. The fear and the adrenaline might have caused her to blurt that out.

"Yes," Rayna answered.

She glanced in the front at Ian, but the deputy was on the phone with Thea. Besides, Ian had almost certainly heard what Rayna had said to Whitney.

"It's true. I am in love with you." Rayna's voice was barely a whisper, but Court still heard it loud and clear.

"You're in love with me?" he said just to make sure. Though he didn't want her to take it back.

She nodded but didn't add more because a ringing sound cut through the silence. It wasn't his phone though but rather one of Whitney's. And it was the kidnapper's number that appeared on the screen.

Court steeled himself as much as he could. Even though he wanted to rip this guy limb from limb, he reined in his temper and hit the answer button.

"Whitney?" someone said. But it wasn't the kidnapper. It was a voice Court recognized.

"It's Court," Court answered. "I have Whitney's phone. She's dead."

"Good. Because I just found out from this piece of slime that Whitney's the one who hired him."

Court hoped that meant Egan had not only the kidnapper but their mother, too. "Is Mom okay?"

"She's shaken up but fine. Not a scratch on her even though she did try to fight off the kidnapper. Griff is taking her back to the hospital right now."

"She's alive," Rayna said, her breath rushing out.

"Yeah," Egan verified. "And it's good to hear that Court and you are, too. What happened?"

Rayna shook her head, obviously not trusting her voice and motioned for Court to give the explanation. He would, but since he didn't want to repeat a lot of the details in front of Rayna, he just kept it simple.

"Whitney killed Jennifer, Hallie, Bobby Joe and Mitch. Then she tried to kill Rayna and me." The woman had almost succeeded, too.

"That's what I got from her hired thug. By the way, his name is Burris Hargrove, and he's talking even after I read him his rights."

"Good." Because Court was sure they would need some details filled in, and Hargrove was the only one who might be able to do that. "How'd you catch him?"

Egan took a deep breath first. "I met Hargrove at the drop site he arranged. It was a gas station about two miles from the hospital. We'd agreed that I would bring thirty grand in cash."

Not much, considering the McCalls were worth millions, but then maybe Hargrove had asked for such a small amount because he'd figured Egan would be able to get it together quickly. Then he could have used it for a fast getaway.

"When I got to the gas station," Egan went on, "I had Griff and Ranger Jameson Beckett come up behind Hargrove. He had Mom gagged and tied up in his car, so Griff got her out of there before Hargrove even knew what was happening. Jameson moved in behind Hargrove so we could trap him. I offered him a choice. He could put down his gun or I'd kill him." There was plenty of anger in Egan's voice. "He put down his gun."

So, Egan had managed to rescue Helen without any shots being taken around her. That was something at least. But he was certain these nightmarish memories would stay with his mother for a long time. They'd certainly stay with him, and he could add nearly losing Rayna to those memories.

"Did Mom say anything?" Court asked.

"Plenty. She was mad Hargrove took her, and she tried to punch him. I let her get off a swing before I pulled her back."

Even though he hated that his mother had been through that ordeal, this was a normal reaction, and he much preferred it to her breaking down again. Maybe that meant this situation wouldn't interfere with her treatments and healing while she was trying to get her mind back in a good place.

"What about Dad?" Court pressed. "Was it Hargrove who shot him?"

"He says no. He claims the only thing he did was fire shots at Rayna and you, but that he didn't intend to kill you. Yeah," Egan snarled when Court huffed, "I'm not buying that, either. I think Whitney got riled because her plan to set Rayna up wasn't working, and she gave Hargrove the order to kill her. That order probably included you if you got in the way. Which you would have done."

Definitely. No way would Court have just stood by while some snake attacked Rayna.

Rayna's forehead bunched up. "But why did Whitney stop the attack at the hospital?" she asked. "Hargrove had us pinned down. He could have carried through on her orders to kill us."

Court figured he knew the answer to this. "We had backup moving in fast. It wouldn't have been but another few minutes before the deputies would have gotten to him. Whitney wouldn't have wanted us to catch—and interrogate—her hired thug because he might have implicated her."

Rayna made a sound of agreement. "That way Hargrove could regroup and come after us again. Which he did."

Yes, he had. Well, maybe the man had done that. They might never know if it was Whitney or Hargrove who'd fired at them near the sheriff's office. Or set that fire in the alley. And it really didn't matter. Whitney was dead, and whether Hargrove realized it or not, he'd be charged with accessory to murder, which would carry the same penalties as murder itself. The man would probably get the death penalty.

Court was going to make sure that happened.

"The CSIs are still going through Bobby Joe's room at the inn," Egan explained. "But I'll get a team out to Whitney's place, too. I'm betting we'll find some other pieces to this puzzle there."

Probably. And one of those pieces might explain the recording they'd found on Bobby Joe's laptop. Court was betting that Whitney made the recording so that it would look as if Bobby Joe still wanted to go after Rayna.

He hadn't.

Though it did sicken him to think that Bobby Joe

had come to town in an attempt to win Rayna back. There'd been no chance of that happening, but Bobby Joe might have turned violent again when Rayna turned him down. No way would Court have allowed the man to get away with something like that.

"I need to get Hargrove to jail," Egan went on a moment later. "Ranger Beckett will help me with that. You're on your way to the hospital now, right, so you can check on Mom?"

"We are. We'll be there in about twenty minutes, maybe less. And before Rayna says anything, I probably need a stitch or two. I got grazed by one of the bullets Whitney shot at us."

"The cut is deep, and he's bleeding," Rayna corrected.

Egan cursed. "Make sure my knot-headed brother sees a doctor as soon as he gets to the hospital."

"Don't worry, I will," she answered right before Egan ended the call.

Since she sounded adamant about doing that, Court figured he wouldn't be able to delay getting those stitches. That meant he needed to finish up whatever he was going to say to Rayna now, because once they arrived at the hospital, things could get hectic fast.

"I'm glad you told Whitney you were in love with me," he said. "And I'm especially glad you meant it. It saved me from asking you how you felt about me."

She stared at him, obviously waiting for something, and he was pretty sure what that *something* was.

"I've cared about you for a long time," he added and would have said more if she hadn't interrupted him.

"Yes, but that stopped when you thought I got away with murder."

"No, it never stopped." He was certain of that. "So, this isn't exactly love at first sight. It's me finally coming to my senses and admitting something I should have admitted to you ages ago—that I'm in love with you, too."

He'd been so sure she had expected him to say that. Judging from her shocked expression, she hadn't.

"Uh, should I pretend I'm not hearing this?" Ian asked.

"Yes," Rayna and Court answered in unison.

Rayna continued to stare at him, and despite everything they'd just been through, she smiled. Then she kissed him. The kiss was a lot hotter and went on a lot longer than it should have, considering that Ian was only a few feet away from them.

When she pulled back from the kiss, the smile was still on her mouth. "You're in love with me," she said as if that were some kind of miracle.

"Oh, yeah," he assured her.

It wasn't a miracle, either. She was a very easy person to love. Not just for this moment. But forever.

And that was why Court pulled her right back to him for another kiss.

* * * * *

We hope you enjoyed reading

Sawyer

by *New York Times* bestselling author
LORI FOSTER
and

Cowboy Above the Law

by *USA TODAY* bestselling author
DELORES FOSSEN.

Both were originally Harlequin® series stories!

From passionate, suspenseful and dramatic
love stories to inspirational or historical,
Harlequin offers different lines to
satisfy every romance reader.

New books in each line are available every month.

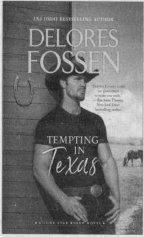

SPECIAL EXCERPT FROM

HQN

*Deputy Cait Jameson is shocked to see Hayes Dalton
back in Lone Star Ridge. What's even more surprising
is that her teen crush turned Hollywood heartthrob
has secrets he feels comfortable sharing only with her.
As they grow closer, Cait wonders just how long their
budding relationship can last before fame calls him back
and he breaks her heart all over again...*

Read on for a sneak peek at
Tempting in Texas,
the final book in the Lone Star Ridge series
from USA TODAY *bestselling author Delores Fossen.*

"I need to ask you for one more favor," he said. "A big
one."

"No, I'm not going to have relations with you," she
joked.

Even though he smiled a little, Cait could tell that
whatever he was about to ask would indeed be big.

"Maybe in a day or two, then." His smile faded, and
he opened his eyes, his gaze zeroing in on her. "I have
an appointment in San Antonio next week, and I was
wondering if you could take me if I'm not in any shape to
drive yet? I don't want my family to know, so that's why
I can't ask one of them," Hayes added.

She nodded cautiously. "I can take you. Are you sure you're up to a ride like that?"

"I have to be." He stared at her. "Since I know you can keep secrets, I'll tell you that it's an appointment with a psychiatrist."

Well, that got her attention.

"Okay," she said, waiting for him to tell her more.

But he didn't follow through on her suspected more. Hayes just muttered a thank-you and closed his eyes again.

Cait stood there several more moments. Still nothing from him. But she saw the rhythmic rise and fall of his chest that let her know he'd gone to sleep. Or else he was pretending to sleep so she would just leave. So that's what she did. Cait turned and left, understanding that he was putting a lot of faith in her. Then again, she was indeed good at keeping secrets.

After all, Hayes had no idea just how much she cared about him.

And if she had any say in the matter, he never would.

Don't miss
Tempting in Texas *by Delores Fossen,*
available February 2021,
wherever HQN books and ebooks are sold.

HQNBooks.com

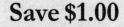

HARLEQUIN
INTRIGUE

SEEK THRILLS. SOLVE CRIMES. JUSTICE SERVED.

Save $1.00

on the purchase of

ANY Harlequin Intrigue book.

Available wherever books are sold, including most bookstores, supermarkets, drugstores and discount stores.

- ✂ - - -

Save $1.00

on the purchase of ANY Harlequin Intrigue book.

Coupon valid until March 31, 2021.
Redeemable at participating outlets in the U.S. and Canada only.
Not redeemable at Barnes & Noble stores. Limit one coupon per customer.

52616958

5 65373 00076 2 (8100)0 12487

Introducing the
McKenzies of Ridge Trail,
an all-new sexy contemporary
romance series from
New York Times **bestselling author**

LORI FOSTER

"Storytelling at its best! Lori Foster should be on
everyone's auto-buy list."
—#1 *New York Times* bestselling author
Sherrilyn Kenyon on *No Limits*

Order your copy today!

HQN
HQNBooks.com